S0-DSO-951

Gustafson

Joseph E. Sandford

Out of Print
800
(SBS)

Folded Hills

IN this story of Andy Burnett, the Yankee hidalgo,
and his fiery young son Djo who hated the
Americanos, Stewart Edward White
tells the dramatic history of the
winning of California.

BOOKS BY
Stewart Edward White

FICTION
THE GLORY HOLE

Of the Far West: THE CLAIM JUMPERS
BLAZED TRAIL STORIES—THE WESTERNERS—THE KILLER
ARIZONA NIGHTS
THE LONG RIFLE

Of the Far North: CONJUROR'S HOUSE—THE SILENT
PLACES—SKOOKUM CHUCK—SECRET HARBOUR

Of the Lumber Woods: THE BLAZED TRAIL
THE RIVERMAN—BLAZED TRAIL STORIES
THE RULES OF THE GAME

Of California: THE RULES OF THE GAME—THE GRAY
DAWN—GOLD—THE ROSE DAWN—ON TIPTOE
RANCHERO—FOLDED HILLS

Of Mystery: THE MYSTERY (With Samuel Hopkins Adams)
THE SIGN AT SIX

Of Africa: THE LEOPARD WOMAN—SIMBA—BACK OF BEYOND

ADVENTURE

THE OUT OF DOORS—EXPLORATION
THE FOREST—CAMP AND TRAIL—THE MOUNTAINS
THE LAND OF FOOTPRINTS—THE CABIN
AFRICAN CAMPFIRES—THE PASS—THE REDISCOVERED
COUNTRY—LIONS IN THE PATH

HISTORICAL AND PHILOSOPHICAL
THE 'FORTY-NINERS
DANIEL BOONE: WILDERNESS SCOUT
CREDO—WHY BE A MUD TURTLE?
DOG DAYS

JUVENILE
THE MAGIC FOREST
THE ADVENTURES OF BOBBY ORDE

Folded Hills

By STEWART EDWARD WHITE

Doubleday, Doran & Company, Inc.
GARDEN CITY   NEW YORK

PRINTED AT THE *Country Life Press*, GARDEN CITY, N. Y., U. S. A.

COPYRIGHT, 1932, 1934
BY STEWART EDWARD WHITE
ALL RIGHTS RESERVED

Contents

PART I

Folded Hills

CHAPTER I

DON ANDRÉS sat in a Boston rocker beneath the spreading live-oak tree before his ranch house. His long form looked relaxed and idle; but he was busily engaged in a number of things at once. They were of the utmost diversity, but they did not intermingle or interfere one with the other. They worked in different layers, as it were.

The top of his mind was remembering, with a trace of vexation, that as yet, though they had lived there now for nearly eight months, neither he, nor his young wife Carmel, had been able to think of a good name for the ranch. They had tried dozens, but none seemed to fit with the click of decision that indicates the wholly appropriate. Ramón Rivera, who rode over occasionally to visit his friend and his sister, could suggest nothing better than recourse to the saints' calendar. But most ranches were San or Santa Something. So up to now the place had been known simply as Don Largo's place, in reference to its owner's nickname.

But that was a mere cockle burr, a faint vexation of incompletion; and not, at this moment, the active ingredient of Don Andrés's mood which was rather of content. If it had a truly active ingredient. The moment was sunset. A drowsing powder of gold was momently deepening in precipitation through all the lower air, draining the zenith sky to the thin green lucence of freed space. Overhead an unseen wild dove uttered its soft notes, a mourning not so much of sadness as of some mysterious farewell. These, and the sleepy distant clucking of Vicenta's fowls, were almost the only animate sounds. The world seemed to have hushed its voices for the high ceremony of the day's passing.

3

So Don Andrés's mind wandered comfortably among many contemplations and satisfactions. Shortly Panchito would ride in with his *vaqueros* to tell the state of the cattle and the range. Benito too, with his kindly moon face, and his exquisite manners, hat in hand, would carry the tale of the growing things in the *milpas* and the grain fields into the high ceremony of consequence. The cattle throve: the *milpas* and the grain fields flourished. This Don Andrés already knew. It was one of the satisfactions, soothing and warm and quiet and golden, like the light on the hills. It enveloped and supported the freedom of his reverie which floated on it idly, directed by mysterious currents; so that shortly Don Andrés was remembering when he was not Don Largo, but Andy Burnett. And for the first time he looked back on the old fierce life of hardship and warfare and danger and tragedy detachedly, as though they had happened to someone else; or, if to himself, in a different state of being. And this was another of the satisfactions. But the deepest of them lay beneath all the others; it permeated the others as part of their very essence, the very warmth of their life. He did not contemplate it consciously: it had become too much part of himself; though always it waited ready for summoning. It would evoke, smiling, soft, mysterious, with eyes of love. Before he had known Carmel, Andy had fought the world for his foothold in it. Now the fact that she was in that world made Andy part of it. It was very mysterious: a holy miracle, Father Viador would say.

Andy's gaze wandered over the prospect before him, his eyes unfocused for the details. Nevertheless the impressions came to him and found their welcome in his soul. What he saw was his own; the wide green fields of the *milpas* and the grain fields, with the wandering dark line of the *barranca* in which flowed the gift of a living stream; the nun-gray sage of the low rise that bordered it; the smooth hills beyond; the dark high mountains above,

veiled now in rose and purple. Tiny specks moved slowly on those hills; his cattle. How suave the blended shadows in the hollows; how soft the surface of their rounded flanks as of folded green——

Andy struck the arm of the old Boston rocker a mighty slap with the palm of his hand.

"Carmel! Carmel!" he cried.

"*Querido!*" she responded instantly from within; and fluttered through the door to his side. "*Querido,*" she repeated anxiously, "what is it?"

"Look!" cried Andy. "The hills!"

"The hills? What of the hills?" She laughed a little breathlessly. "But you frightened me, *alma de mi alma,* you sounded so excited."

Andy too laughed and drew her to his knee.

"I did not mean to frighten you, *querida,*" said he, "but look at the hills with the light falling across them and the shadows."

"Yes, they are very beautiful," agreed Carmel, nestling into his arms.

"But what do they look like to you?"

"Look like?"

"Yes; how do they seem to you?" The tall young frontiersman was boyishly eager.

Carmel contemplated them doubtfully.

"They are very beautiful," she repeated. "Yes, and soft—soft like velvet; and they lie there like velvet, folded there——"

The *ranchero* caught her to him in an ecstatic hug.

"That is it!" he cried triumphantly. "That is what we shall call the *rancho!*"

"What?"

"Folded Hills."

"Fol-ded Heels," she repeated carefully. "But that is a beautiful sound. What means it?"

"*Collados plegados,*" translated Andy.

"Rancho de los Collados Plegados," she pronounced experimentally. "Folded Heels—yes, I like better Rancho de los Fol-ded Heels."

"Folded Hills Ranch," corrected Andy. "That is how it is said in English. This is a good day."

"Yes," assented Carmel. "The Day of Naming." She dropped her head to his shoulder, "*El día del Nombre,*" she repeated softly. "Let us then decide on the names for our son."

Andy thrust her upright until he could see her face.

"It is true then?" he cried excitedly. "Are you sure?"

She broke through to his shoulder again.

"*Hijo nuestro,*" she repeated: then in painstaking English, each vowel stressed, "Ou-er esson."

"*Querida; querida!*" murmured Andy. He gathered her close, as one holds a child, rocking slowly back and forth. "Why have you not told me?" he asked after a little.

"Onlee today do I myself know for essure." Suddenly she sat bolt upright on his knees, her mood changing to one of sparkling and mocking vivacity.

"But is it esstrange that we who have much love should have a son?" she demanded.

"How do you know it will be a son?" challenged Andy. "Perhaps it will be a little girl. I think I would like a tiny one, like you."

"Ah no! no-no!" she cried vehemently. "He shall be a esson, tall and esstrong like hees papá, and you shall titch him to be brave and so beeg of the heart, like the you; and when you do ride together to the *fiesta* the hearts of the *doncellitas* shall jump up——" She broke off, her head to one side in sudden admiration of herself. "But leesten how I do talk the English! Do I not learn queek? Do I not speak heem perfect?"

"Oh, quite perfect," agreed Andy gravely. "But when——"

"Oh, not for long long time," she answered his unspoken question. "Not until the esspring come."

"That is a long time to wait," sighed Andy.

"I think yet he is still in heaven with the blessed saints," said Carmel.

A strongly built broad-headed black dog wandering idly around the corner of the ranch house in abysmal boredom stopped short. Dogs are creatures of routine. The spectacle of his master at this time of day was foreign to his conception of the universe, and was not to be accepted until tested for hallucination by a more trustworthy sense than sight. He raised his nose; sniffed delicately. Convinced, he was suffused with a rapture too intense for ordinary expression. He wrinkled his nose; he ducked his head to sneeze ingratiatingly; he advanced in a series of complicated contortions that attested the wagging incompetency to the occasion of a mere tail.

Carmel clapped her hands joyfully together and uttered her trilling laugh.

"But see!" she cried, "Cazador, he know it is the beeg day! See! He is all smiling behind!"

CHAPTER II

ANDY was not yet *californio* in all things. His Anglo-Saxon mind required a little room to turn from its old ideas as to such matters. It was with a distinct effort that he learned to accept the fact that his wife's condition, so far from being a matter of secrecy, was to be made known at once to family, friends, and neighbors. The *padrinos*, the godparents, must be chosen without delay, that they might offer their candles and their prayers. So Ramón came from the hacienda, together with Don Sylvestre and Doña Engracia and a host of *parientes;* and Conchita de la Questa, who was to marry Ramón in the spring, and another host of her *parientes;* and good old *padre* Seria made the journey from Nuestra Señora de la Soledad for the ceremony. Andy was, for the moment, a trifle appalled as to what was to be done with so many people. But he need have had no fear. The women of the visiting parties took over the whole place, and each immediately went about the various tasks and duties as though this household had been her own. Indeed many of the less pretentious of the *parientes* brought with them accumulations of their own laundry, and after the ceremony of the *padrinos*, they had a grand sociable wash-up in the creek bottoms, followed by a feast and an informal dance, and so departed, both their linen and their social consciences clean.

The *rancho* wore a smiling face. Even grim Panchito's saturnine countenance, incapable of alteration from its carved and wooden lines, nevertheless glowed with an inner illumination. Riding in from his long day in the hills, he

8

would pluck from his hatband a handful of mariposa lilies, or flaming poppies—somewhat wilted, to be sure, by the heat of the sun—and thrust them into Carmel's hands.

"For the little *patrón*," he would say gruffly and turn away on his spurred heel.

"The little one thanks you, Panchito," Carmel would answer graciously, without embarrassment.

As for Benito, he was always making excuse to toil up the sun-soaked hill from the *milpas* in the valley, bearing especial vegetables or fruits. He stood respectfully, his hat in his two hands, and small beads of perspiration glistened on his round kindly face. He liked to linger and chat, and had theories of his own as to diet, which he expounded directly and earnestly.

"These things I have found to be true," said he, "for, as you know, the good Lord has blessed me with many, as, I doubt not He will bless you, too, *señora*, for we Riveras are good soil for the planting. But later, when one must think of the milk. . . ."

He went on calmly in discussion of intimate detail, often stoutly maintaining his point against the scorn of Vicenta, the too fat one, who considered such matters her own province. She stormed and browbeat Benito, who remained placidly unmoved in face of her contention that he was a mere man.

"But I have had many," he repeated, "and we Riveras . . ." Which latter exasperated Vicenta almost, but not quite, beyond words; for Benito was undoubtedly a Rivera—which Vicenta was not—though over the left shoulder, a fact that did not trouble him in the least. Sometimes their contentions caused Andy, if he happened to be present, to beat a hasty retreat. Carmel was unmoved, smiling faintly into mysterious distance. And in time Andy himself warmed to open and joyous acceptance of the shining blessing.

2

The baby was born in March, and proved indeed to be a son. All the Riveras moved up for the occasion. This was as well, but rather on Andy's account than for the comfort of the girl. In spite of Vicenta's common-sense assurances, and the faint derision of Carmel herself, Andy could not prevent himself from feeling increasingly nervous. He was glad to have Ramón and his brothers, and Don Sylvestre himself. The Californians developed enormous interest, most of it genuine, in the state of the *rancho*, so that Andy must ride with them over the hills and to distant valleys, even up to the highest *tinajas* under the dark peaks. He could not in courtesy refuse these excursions; though he would have much preferred to remain at home and near Carmel. However, he had been assured, her hour was not yet come.

Because of this assurance his first emotion was a flash of indignation at being fooled when, on their return from the third of these excursions, they were met at the foot of the hill by a clamorous mob that with three exceptions included every person attached to the *rancho*. The exceptions were Carmel herself, Vicenta, and Cazador, the black, wide-headed dog. Andy's horse leaped under his spur. His first flash of resentment had been instantly succeeded by a more poignant stab of alarm, though, if he had stopped to think, there was nothing but joy in the shouting confusion of the reception committee. He flung himself from the saddle and rushed to the door where he all but collided with Vicenta, and only just saved himself from falling over Cazador, the dog. Vicenta's comfortable bulk filled the doorway. Cazador had stationed himself squarely before her. Andy perforce must stop.

"The *señora!*" he gasped.

"The *señora* sleeps. All is well," said Vicenta.

"I must see her." Andy moved as though to push by, but Vicenta did not move.

"Presently, presently!" said Vicenta soothingly. "But would you not look upon your son?"

And only then did Andy observe that across her arm she held a blanketed bundle. His surprise was evident. Vicenta snorted, but refrained from expression of her scorn. She drew back a fold of the blanket. Andy bent over eagerly. For ten seconds he struggled to master his dismay, the crash of high hopes and anticipations, to grasp a control he must find to face this cruel visitation of fate.

"Is—is it also deformed?" he managed at last.

"Deformed!" cried Vicenta, indignantly, "deformed! But what are you saying, *señor*? It is a beautiful baby, the most beautiful baby I have ever seen! Why do you say such a thing, *señor*?" Her fine black eyes snapped, and she drew the infant to her ample bosom. "How dare you say such a thing of your own son?"

"He—well, isn't he just a little—well, *queer*-looking?" Andy stammered. "He is so red—and wrinkled."

Vicenta's eyes flashed sparks.

"He is a most beautiful baby," she repeated. "Red and wrinkled indeed!" She surveyed Andy for a moment, then softened. "But all new-born babies are so," she said more gently, "like petals of the rose. Wait, *señor*, you shall see." She withdrew again the blanket from the infant's face. Andy looked once more. He was not entirely reassured, but his panic had passed. The rose-petal analogy still seemed to him a trifle far-fetched. Something leaned against his leg. He looked down. It was Cazador. The dog was looking up with liquid adoring eyes, not at his master, but at the bundle in Vicenta's arms. A whimsical irrelevance cut across Andy's distractions. He grinned in appreciation, for the dog had beat him to it. And with this lightening of his mood, the queer strangeness began to pass. He looked again at the child. It opened its eyes. They were blue-gray, like Andy's own. And suddenly, with a rush, as though of waters released, his soul was filled.

Vicenta slowly drew aside.

"Go to the *señora, señor*," said she.

Andy tiptoed across the *sala* to the *patio*, and so to the door of the bedroom. He peeped within. Carmel's eyes were closed. She looked very small and white. Her abundant hair was spread wide over the pillows. As he looked, her eyelids fluttered, then opened. For a moment she seemed to be looking at him from a vast distance; then she smiled faintly.

"*Querido*," she murmured.

Instantly Andy was kneeling at her side. He was almost afraid to touch her, for she seemed to him fragile and remote. She laid her hand in his. A great awe and wonder filled his soul. His capacity could not contain it, this evocation of a new human being that yesterday had not existed in the world.

"You have seen him?" breathed Carmel. "Is he not wonderful? Is he not beautiful?"

"Beautiful," said Andy from his heart.

3

The custom among the Spanish-Californians was—and is—to erect a name of significance, like a totem pole. The thing was built up from the firm foundation of the family name. This new infant was a Burnett by plain right of birth. But also, on its mother's side, it was a Rivera; and the Riveras were a noble family, and should be somehow recorded. So, although he would be known as Burnett officially and commonly, on especial dress occasions the most punctilious might call him Señor Burnett y Rivera. Then there was his saint's name, which must of course depend on the day of his birth. Next in order was a string of complimentary or memorial names, limited in number only by memory or good taste; and finally, in front of the whole procession, the familiar name by which informally he was to be known.

So it happened that this particular infant was rather remarkably labeled, even for California. In his veins flowed the blood of two races; but in his name marched the syllables of three.

Carmel, naturally, wished to call him Andrés. Andy shook his head.

"Don't you think one is enough?" he asked. "Does it matter much to you, *querida?*"

"You have a name you would like," said Carmel keenly. "What is it?"

"I think I would like to call him Joe."

She stumbled a bit in repeating it, for the letter "j" is difficult to the Spanish.

"D-jo," she stumbled thoughtfully. "It is a word of the teeth." Then, catching his expression, "Who was D-jo, Andreo *mío?*"

"He was my best friend in life—over there, beyond the mountains," said Andy soberly.

"You loved him much; that I see," said Carmel

"Much," said Andy.

She watched the somber aloofness of his face for a moment, then placed her hands behind his head and drew him toward her.

"Come back to me, *amado,*" she said softly. "This friend of your heart—now—he is dead?"

"He was killed," said Andy.

"Ah," breathed Carmel. Then after a moment, "Sometime you must tell me."

"Sometime; not now."

"D-jo." She repeated the name again softly. "And now, for the rest?"

"The rest?" echoed Andy blankly. It seemed to him that the infant was already sufficiently labeled for identification at least.

"But yes: are there no others you would honor?"

"Ramón."

"That is good: I hoped you would say Ramón. And?"

"That is surely enough of names!" protested Andy.

"It is enough of names," agreed Carmel, "but is it enough of honor? Are there no others so dear to your heart that you would have your son to remember?"

"There was one," said Andy after a moment's hesitation, "but he was an Indian."

"An Indian!" exclaimed Carmel in a dismay she could not conceal.

"Not like these Indians you know," cried Andy, flaming to defense. "He was not like anyone you have ever seen. He was an *hidalgo*, a great warrior, a true friend. He belonged to a great people." Andy was of the reticent type of frontiersman. He rarely spoke of his past: it would never have occurred to him to do so unless stirred by especial occasion. But this was such an occasion. The simplicity of his desire to make Carmel understand freed his spirit to vividness. She listened breathless lest she break the spell. It was a living picture—the wide plains, the buffalo, the gathering peaks, the icy winds of hardship and of danger and of great deeds simply done, and through it moving figures heroic in the magnitudes of stark simplicity, the plumed Indians and the mountain men. Andy was trying, as best he might, and without thought of himself, to bring to the girl a realization of the things he had known. He succeeded; but this he did not realize or intend: that to her the great significance was himself. She gazed at him with parted lips, for if these things were splendid, by so much more was he glorious who had been of them a part. So lost was she in the vivid reality of those past days that she came to herself with a little gasp.

"Why have you not talked to me of these things before?" she demanded.

"Why—I do not know——"

"But you must tell me all, all, *all!*" she cried passionately. "Do you not see? If I shall love you, all of you, so must I know all about you so I may go with you in my soul through all that has been, just as we shall go together, forever, through all that shall be. No! No-no! Nothing you must not tell me, nothing; even when you were a little, little boy. Promise you shall tell me all!"

She shook him so fiercely that Andy laughed.

"Why, of course I will tell you anything you wish to know," he agreed. "It did not occur to me you would be interested."

"I shall make it 'occur to you,'" she promised.

So it was agreed that the name of Kiasax should be added to the already imposing list. Andy wrote it all down to see how it would look: he had to laugh at the result.

Joe Ramón Kiasax —— Burnett y Rivera.

The blank stood for the missing saint's name, which must depend on the day of the birth.

Carmel was enlightened.

"Oh!" she cried. "I did not understand! This name is the same as José, not-so? Ho, now I see heem."

"No, not Ho; *Joe!*" corrected Andy.

"Then you cannot spell him so. Every *californio* call that Ho." She took the quill, and in the unformed script she had learned from Father Seria she wrote:

"Djoe."

Then, after consideration, elided the final "e":

"Djo."

"Thus you write, 'Joe'," said she with satisfaction; and so it was written, so that many people wondered but few ever knew the origin of the quaint syllable.

But the climax to the cognominal joke on the poor infant came from the fact that he was born on the day of the blessed San José, so that the blank was filled with the name José, and that neither Andy nor Carmel knew that José in Spanish is Joseph in English.

When the child was twenty days old came its *padrinos*, its godparents, Ramón Rivera and his fiancée, Conchita de la Questa. They rode gayly, playing guitars; and they were met at the door of the house by Andy, Carmel, and the baby; and the lot of them proceeded to Soledad, where Father Seria baptized Djo Ramón Kiasax José Burnett y Rivera in the presence of the assembled family kneeling in the blue dimness of the church. But after the ceremony, outside, they were greeted by a great acclaim of people from all the countryside, with a delirious clanging of bells, and music, and the flare of rockets. And all returned to Folded Hills, where they dutifully ate *panecito*, as custom required; and afterward a more satisfactory feast, and there was a great ball, and sports and *meriendas* such as the Californians loved.

CHAPTER III

THE two years required by Djo to become a dependable personality were contented years for Andy Burnett. The life and interests of the ranch satisfied him completely. He had a wife whom he loved increasingly; a fine young son; a grant of beautiful land; an increasing stock of cattle and horses; a comfortable house of the kind that obviously absorbs tradition quickly; a whole community of almost feudal retainers; friendly and congenial, though somewhat distant, neighbors; a dependable and beloved man friend not too far away. In addition to these things he possessed what the *californios* did not, an experimental nature. He was not content with things as they had always been, no matter how comfortable or how adequate to this simple and charming life these things were. His grain fields in the bottomlands, guarded by wide ditches in lieu of fences, proved astonishingly productive. He grubbed the sagebrush from a side hill, and on it planted grapes which he procured from Father Duran at the mission of San José. The vineyard interested him. Hearing from Father Duran of one Luis Vighnes who had come to Los Angeles in '31, and who had there planted a great vineyard with the purpose of making wine, he sent to him a courier with a letter; and received a reply; and so began a lively correspondence the perusal of which, even today, delights the historian by its mixture of shrewd practicality as to technical details and its quaintness of magniloquent phraseology; for Andy was American, and Luis Vighnes was French, and they met in Spanish. The fact that each exchange required a ride by someone of sixty leagues each way was not permitted to interfere with the correspondence. Some day, Andy resolved, he would himself go south to visit Luis Vighnes; but just now he was too busy.

Andy had dozens of irons in the fire whose fashioning had never occurred to the easy-going, simple-living *californios*. There was the matter of the wheat, for example. It had always been the custom to supply personal needs by crushing the grain—procured, generally, from the nearest mission—by hand, in stone *metates*, with a pestle of the same material. After that it was cleaned by tossing in a basket, and sifted through a coarse sieve. The process was laborious and the resultant flour coarse and full of grit. Andy tried to evoke from his boyhood recollections how millstones had been rigged. He experimented for some months, with very moderate success. The flour produced by his rude contraptions was even coarser and grittier than that made in the *metates*. Vicenta, as a privileged character, openly mocked his efforts to invade what she considered a distinctly feminine field.

"Leave the priest to say Mass," she advised him.

But Andy was obstinate. And one afternoon he was recalled from his absorbed contemplation of his latest effort by a deep-throated chuckle, and looked up to see a thickset bearded man, his sturdy legs apart, his head to one side, his hands behind his back, eyeing him sardonically.

The man was of a type familiar enough in that day. For one reason or another, ranging from ill treatment to the fascination of the country, sailors were always deserting from their ships. Until the vessel had sailed they were hunted by the *vaqueros* for the offered reward; but thereafter they were safe enough. Some of them, of initiative and independence, became accepted in time as citizens, over the left shoulder, as it were, for rarely was their status legalized. Of such was John Gilroy, who already was a *ranchero*. Others, the majority, skulked from *rancho* to *rancho*, or gravitated to the gangs of such men as Isaac

Graham, who made whiskey at Natividad; a sort of outlaw tolerated until they became a nuisance.

"What do you know about this?" Andy demanded.

"Everything," replied the man, without surprise, for everybody knew of the *hidalgo-americano*. "I used to be a miller before I took to the sea."

"Take hold," said Andy.

The result was a six-mule-power mill that turned out from ten to twenty barrels of passable flour per day. Andy's grain fields were justified; for he sent the product to Monterey, where he found a market in the visiting ships, and occasionally to the north when a vessel called on the Russians. Abel Means, the sailor, became a fixture at Folded Hills: and after Andy lost the first keenness of his interest, as he did in every problem solved, gradually took supervision of the business. He ground flour for the *ranchos* and the *haciendas*, even for some of the missions, on the basis of equal division; half the flour for him who brought the grain, half for the mill. It is significant that up to that time Andy had not thought of making a charge for this service, but performed it as a matter-of-course neighborly convenience.

The dairy was the result of Vicenta's demand one day for milk to supplement Djo's natural diet. She got the milk; but four men were required to do the milking, three of them mounted. One held the distracted cow by a *reata* about the head; the second stretched her by means of a *reata* about both hind legs; the third's job was to keep off the calf. The man afoot milked with one hand into a cup held in the other. Everybody else connected with the *rancho* was present as spectator. Andy could see no sense in all that fuss over so simple a matter; nor, when he stopped to think of it, did he see why a place that supported fifteen or more thousands of head of cattle should not also have butter and cheese and cream. To be sure, nobody else had these luxuries habitually; and Panchito assured him

it was no great trouble to the *vaqueros* to milk as many wild
cows as might be necessary; but Andy insisted. The *lacti-
feras* were held apart, and fed, and gradually gentled, and
at length placed in charge of Benito's eldest, who proved
to have a flair for dairy matters. This set Benito up
enormously. In the old order, at the *hacienda*, the gardener,
the keeper of the *milpas*, was no great shakes in the hier-
archy of esteem. His function was humble and subsidiary.
But here, what with the expansion of the grain and milling,
and the vineyards on the side hill, and now this dairy
business, Benito began to perk up. However, he would
never have dreamed of openly arrogating to himself any
importance. His disposition was much too kindly and easy-
going. But he adored Andy, and so became the *ranchero's*
head man when it was a question of innovation; just as
Panchito, the *vaquero*, was his head man when the old order
was to do.

As a matter of fact, barring minor improvements of
method here and there, the flour business and the dairy
business and the wineries yet in the making were the only
really important departures from the traditional pastoral
life. Unless one counts the flower garden. On second
thought, that should be counted; for in time it became of
equal importance with the others in deflecting travelers
toward Folded Hills. To be sure, most houses of the better
class had the customary *patio* fountain with its surrounding of vines and shrubs and flowers. But the outsides had
invariably been left blank and bare in almost fortress-
like simplicity, so that the dust of the dry season powdered
the doorsteps, and the ground squirrels burrowed and
chirked to the very walls, and the bones of the cattle
slaughtered for domestic use lay in the wide white ring of
a semicircle. Andy had, when the *casa* had been built, over-
thrown all tradition by preserving the great live-oaks.
Every other ranch house in California stood stark and
bare and naked on its hill. The custom had had its use of

defense in the earlier days, but the necessity had passed. Now he was impelled further by the nostalgic recollection of a ruined garden before the prim old Pennsylvania farmhouse of his boyhood, his only link with a mother who had died so young that all memory of her had gone.

So, though he knew nothing of gardens and the gentle growing things, he had made for himself a dooryard with flowers, and led water cunningly through conduits of stone for its refreshment. Far and wide he sent for new plants and shrubs and vines. It was a curious hodge-podge at first, for Andy's instinctive desire far outran his feeling for detail. He was a mountain man at heart; a runner of the wilderness; and in such matters his spiritual fingers were awkward and fumbling. But Carmel had the quick Latin eye for beauty, and Benito the growing hand. So Andy had his garden, vivid and glowing in its seasons; and so this happy time of his life was linked back across the years to his origins, and some mysterious reaching of his soul was contented. In the cool of the evening, after the long riding in the hills, he loved to stroll with his pipe, absorbing some instinctive satisfaction from the garden. He knew nothing of the detail of plant or shrub; their variety had passed beyond his recognitions. It was the blended gentle harmony of the whole that entered his spirit. Benito and Carmel talked earnestly together of this or that. He was told names, and promptly forgot them. He liked the bright colors, and the perfumes, and the soft wet freshnesses. Linnets built nests in the vines; humming birds shot like bullets or poised like brilliant jewels; busy swarms of chickadees and kinglets searched with intent singleness of purpose the under sides of leaves; hordes of robins and varied thrushes raided the red *toyon* berries and departed, leaving bare the bushes, to the disgust of the fat towhee who had looked upon them as his winter's supply; great flickers sat on the shingles surveying the world, occasionally drumming against the reverberating hollowness of the rooftree an absent-minded ratatat of contemplation. Andy recognized these and many others; but rather as people than as species. His classifying observation was for the practical; all other things stole into his heart by the door of feeling.

2

All these things were a matter of great interest. Travelers went out of their way to stop at Folded Hills, where they were welcome and abundantly entertained. They praised and enjoyed; but it is curious and significant that they did not imitate. Nevertheless Andy was considered of remarkable energy and enterprise and ingenuity, and a valuable citizen of the commonwealth. It was he, and a number of others like him, who established a favorable reputation for Americans that persisted even after the first immigrations, and into the very gold-rush days. Though the Boone rifle hung on the wall, and though to himself Andy seemed to have settled down to peaceful content, nevertheless his destiny bore him on.

The frame of his routine seemed established. It was a frame capacious to contain many varieties.

He was a true *ranchero* and followed the customs of his kind. Each morning he was awakened at dawn. He drank chocolate in bed, at the same time naming, to the servant who attended, the horse he would ride. Attended by Panchito he rode the range until about nine o'clock when he returned to the *casa* for breakfast. After four hours of riding this was justified as a hearty meal. When he had finished this, and had dawdled a little with the fascinating Djo, he mounted another horse until near one o'clock. An hour and a half later, after a light meal and a short siesta, yet a third horse was brought, on the back of which he remained until dusk. All his business, practically, was conducted from horseback. The saddle was his movable throne, or council seat, as it were. He went to bed early.

That was the ordinary pattern of his days. It was simple, almost monotonous when viewed from a far perspective. Leaving aside the spiritual content of love of wife and child, of social contact with visitor and resident, the merely material problems and exactions were sufficient to keep the frontiersman's active interest fully occupied; at least for the present. When Andy rode on the *palomino*, Ramón's gift, or one of the other "mannered" horses—the *generosos* —of his favoring, he did more than take horse exercise. The handling, to the best advantage, of fifteen thousand or more head of cattle is a highly technical matter. Panchito and the *vaqueros* knew their business, none better. Andy was a frontiersman trained through years of dangerous necessity to keen observation. But in this one matter of cattle—and horses—he never quite equaled his men. They seemed not only to know the individual animals by sight, but to be able to recognize them almost as far as they could see them. This ability was a continual astonishment to Andy. Panchito would rein his horse, and stand in his stirrups, puckering his dark eyes in focus upon a distant hillside.

"It is as I thought, *señor*," he would say presently. "Last week those ones were at Boca Estrecha. Juan, ride you to Boca Estrecha and find out why those ones have come away."

And Juan would ride, and later would report his findings —the water was low; there had been a fire; a plague of locusts had swept clean the grass; a grizzly had come down from the hills; or possibly it was merely a case of drift, a sudden aimless seizure of the wandering foot. One must know these things and be guided by them, must carry in one's mind a bird's-eye picture of the entire *rancho* and its shifting distributions and conditions. And of course there were the small daily jobs that were never ending; a creature caught in a bog hole to be extricated; the injured or sick

to be roped and thrown and treated; the increase to be
noted, sometimes to be branded and marked in the field.
At least once a fortnight there must be a rough and informal *rodeo*, with every man asaddle driving the cattle to
established rendezvous, where they were held for an hour
and then permitted to disperse. This maneuver was essential and could not be omitted or postponed. Its object was
to accustom the animals to handling. Otherwise they would
soon scatter in the brushlands and become true wild
beasts, elusive as the deer themselves. In spite of all vigilance a certain number did thus revert. They inhabited
the chaparral and were a total loss, except for the few that
could be hunted down and roped and brought in by means
of the especially tamed cattle, the *cabestros*, to which they
were lashed by the horn.

In the spring of the year was held the great *rodeo* when
the calves were branded, the excess of bulls castrated, and
the cattle that had drifted in from contiguous *ranchos*
separated out and driven home. This was also a festival;
or rather a sequence of festivals, for each *rancho* in turn
had its *rodeo*. These were great gatherings. Every owner
of stock was supposed to attend, bringing all his grown
sons and all his male servants and dependents. The obligation was rigorous. The only permitted exceptions were the
"unmounted"— that is, the mechanical workers—the
sick, and those above sixty years of age, and the "non-
owners." A non-owner was defined as one who had less
than a hundred and fifty cattle. Each brought not only his
remuda of horses—from six to ten per man—but his own
little herd of *cabestros* by means of which to hold and handle such of his cattle as might be found. One of the older
men of position and influence was appointed *juez-de-campo*
to settle disputes, should any arise.

The gathering was notable. Ordinarily the women of the
ranchos and *haciendas* came along for the fun of the thing.
Though not a formal fiesta, there were feasting and music

and dancing and love-making. The dances had not the stately formality of the *baile*. They were made up impromptu by those nearest at hand; *valecitos casaros* they were called. They ended early. The women were indefatigable and would have continued all night. They poked fun at their escorts for not holding out better. But the latter were tired business men after their hard day's riding, which had begun at dawn.

When the round of *rodeos* had been finished came the *matanza*, when the selected cattle were slaughtered, their hides prepared, and the tallow tried out and packed in skin containers, ready for transportation to the seacoast to be sold or traded to the Boston ships. Only a small proportion of the meat could be utilized. Andy was always troubled at this waste, but he could not see any way out of it, though he saved more than did his neighbors, drying quantities of jerky, which he found to be moderately acceptable to some of the poorer people near the sea. Panchito shrugged his shoulder.

"There is no waste, *señor*," he expostulated. "This is the fat season for some. And are they not also the creatures of God who must be fed?"

And indeed the California of that day was aswarm with vultures and coyotes bred to this abundance. The night hills were vocal with the diabolic ululations of the little wolves. The sky was never vacant of the slow-circling birds. With the passing of the great cattle ranches the vultures disappeared, where or why no man knows. Certainly not through the efforts of man, as in the case of the coyote. Nature withdrew them, their need fulfilled.

Andy was not entirely convinced.

"And how about the rest of the year, when there is no *matanza*?" he inquired. "How then are they fed?"

"That," said Panchito, "is the affair of God."

At the time the *rodeo* was held at Folded Hills, appeared a dignified and courtly gentleman, who traveled in some

state. He introduced himself as named Castañares, adding
that he was *alcalde* of the *pueblo* of Monterey. He apologized further for what he called his "slight delay." Andy
had difficulty in making out what it was all about. When
finally he understood, he was dismayed. He had thought
the governor's grant had given him legal ownership of his
land. It seemed not. The title amounted to nothing until
the land's boundaries had been properly measured and
marked by the proper official, who was Judge Castañares.
All the labor and improvements meant nothing, less than
nothing, if a governor should change his mind, or someone
of influence should come along covetous of the land. He
had been nothing better than a squatter. He shivered a
little at the thought; but no one else seemed disturbed.
The day following the *alcalde's* arrival he, two mounted
assistants, Ramón and Estevan Rivera as witnesses, together with Andy himself, rode to the southwest corner
of the grant. This corner was supposed to start upon El
Rancho Soledad, but the monuments of the latter holding
had disappeared, or could not be found, at least without
a more diligent search than the *alcalde* was inclined to
undertake. He perused his copy of the Soledad grant, and
peered about him, and finally gave it up.

"It is undoubtedly somewhere in this valley, *señor*," said
he to Andy, "and I do not imagine you and Señor Linares
will quarrel over a few tufts of sagebrush."

So he caused to be piled a heap of rounded stones from
the wash, and on it planted a wooden cross. This was the
official starting point and was called the *mojonera*. Its existence was solemnly witnessed by Ramón and Esteban.
The *alcalde* then began the business of marking the boundaries of the seven leagues comprised in the grant. This
was a leisurely process and must consume several days.
Andy's business at the *rodeo* did not permit him to assist;
though he rode with the party for an hour or so. The process was very simple and not at all laborious. Señor Cas-

tañares rode ahead, following the proposed boundary line, sometimes in consultation with a small pocket compass, sometimes with an eye on the sun, but frequently following merely his sense of fitness as to where a proper *rancho* should end. He was followed by a man on horseback dragging a fifty-foot *reata*. This was the measure of length. The horseman noted in a lazy sort of fashion how often he thought this fifty feet spanned the course of the party, and announced each five units in a somnolent voice; whereupon the clerk, who rode another horse, made a mark in his little book. As long as Señor Castañares held his mount to a foot pace this rough measurement was not as inaccurate as it sounds; but when, as occasionally, he indulged himself in a canter, the measurement entered the realms of fantasy. Nevertheless the *reata* man continued to announce results in all confidence.

The *alcalde* said nothing, save when the little procession came directly against some natural object in the line of its course. Then he would fling over his shoulder to his clerk, "A large live-oak tree," "A white oak riven by the wind," "A curious rock," or the like.

After the latest of the little tallies in his book the clerk would note down the observation, which constituted it duly an official landmark. Later, when Andy received the parchment that represented his grant, all these things were imposingly set forth. It read well: south three hundred and fifty *estradas* ro a large live-oak tree, thence a hundred and twenty-five *estradas* to a white oak riven by the wind; thence two hundred and ten *estradas* to a curious rock; and so on. The document had a beautiful seal, and ribbons. Andy was quite satisfied with it. A degree or so of compass bearing; the perishability or surprising similarity of trees, or the abundance of rocks that might be called curious was not to be called to his attention for many years to come, and certainly not by his present neighbors.

CHAPTER IV

THE *rodeo* at Folded Hills was the last of the spring
gatherings. At its conclusion Andy rode to Monterey.
He had there certain business to accomplish concerning
hides and flour. Carmel accompanied him. It was their
first excursion to the capital since their marriage. They
had a good time and were much dined and fêted. Andy
renewed his few old acquaintances and made many new
ones. But Figueroa he saw only briefly and formally, for
by now the governor's health had much declined; Alvarado
was away; and Thomas Larkin was so busy with new
commercial ventures that for some days he did not come
to any extended discussion with his astute countryman.
Thus he missed at first the significances of a piece of news
that much interested the society of the capital.

This was the arrival of a body of colonists from Mexico
organized and conducted by José María Padres and José
María Hijar. The astonishing thing was that these were
people of good quality. Past attempts at colonization had
been mainly recruited from convicts. Nobody in Monterey
had seen many of the newcomers. They had, most of them,
proceeded to the Sonoma country, where they were establishing themselves more or less under the protection or
surveillance of Guadalupe Vallejo. But they were obviously
gente de razón. There were various rumors about. The first
that gained currency was that Hijar, with Padres under
him as second, had secretly been appointed as civil governor, and had subsidized his colonists to assure his rights,
but that Figueroa had refused to recognize his authority;
that was why the newcomers had retired, almost in a body,

to Sonoma, to consolidate their strength by alliance with the wild tribes. A fillip of reality was given this yarn by the arrival of Rafael Amador. He had come on horseback, alone, from Mexico City, over the Anza Trail in just forty days, a phenomenal, nay, a miraculous journey. Don Rafael brought dispatches for the governor, which he delivered, and then slept two days. Before retiring, however, he was said to have remarked to someone that the Mexican government had changed; whereupon the wise ones placed finger by nose and deduced that Figueroa was not to be supplanted after all. Certainly the governor was more complacent after receiving the dispatches.

There were other rumors, differently directed. One theory, reputed to be held by Vallejo, Osio, Alvarado, and others of their group was that the true object was the spoiling of the missions. For a number of years the process of secularization had been under way. Andy's ignorance of the subject was complete, but his interest was aroused by the garbled and conflicting but lazily indifferent arguments he heard. To his astonishment he learned that general opinion was that the power of the missions was crumbling. His few personal experiences—at Soledad, at San Juan, and especially at Santa Clara where the spell of Viador had drawn him into the Church—had given him an impression of enduring solidity and strength. He cast about for someone who could talk with authority, and bethought him of Thomas Larkin, his compatriot, whose good sense and keenness of observation had so impressed him. So one afternoon, at the hour of siesta for all the California-born, he plowed through the powdery dust of the plaza to the long low adobe Larkin had built for himself and his Santa Barbara bride on the side hill overlooking the bay.

As he had surmised, the American was awake and alone, sitting in the cool of his library, reading a book, which he laid aside as Andy entered.

"I heard you were in town, and intended to pay my respects to the *señora*," he said, a smile of genuine welcome illuminating his dark thin face, "but I awaited the subsidence of the first exuberance of welcome. Sit there. Will you drink something? No?" as Andy shook his head, "Well, I think myself it is not the time of day. I am glad you have come. It is always a pleasure to see a fellow countryman. It is long since we met. Almost two years, isn't it? Tell me of yourself."

"Why, there isn't much to tell," said Andy.

"No?" Larkin smiled amusedly. "But it seems to me there is. You have a son, haven't you?"

Andy nodded.

"That's fine!" said Larkin heartily. "And how about all those other wonderful things I hear of—a flour mill and grain fields and so on?"

Andy merely nodded again. His eyes were roving about the room. He had never seen so many books, and said so. Larkin was pleased.

"Why, yes," he acknowledged, as though to a compliment. He arose and walked across the room to lay his hand on a row of fat volumes. "Here is a complete set of Scott. You like to read?"

"Why, sir," confessed Andy, "I've never had a chance to read—not since I was a boy," he amended. "There wa'n't many books in the Indian country," he added, with his engaging grin.

Larkin selected two of the fat volumes and placed them in Andy's hands.

"You take these with you," he commanded. "No, I insist. You can bring them back, or send them."

"I'm scared something will happen to them," said Andy. He turned them over in his strong hands, spelling out their titles letter by letter with visible movements of his lips. "*Ivanhoe* and *The Talisman*," he then pronounced aloud. "And what might they be about?"

"They are stories about people who lived a good many hundreds of years ago. You'll like them."

"Yes, sir," agreed Andy submissively, but without conviction. He laid them on his knees.

"You read them," insisted Larkin.

"Yes, sir, I will."

"Now what's on your mind? I can see there's something. Anything I can do for you?"

2

"Why, yes," said Larkin a little later. "What you hear is more or less true. Things are in a good deal of a mess. But it is inevitable. At least that is how it seems to me. The theory on which the missions were established was bound, sooner or later, to bring this state of things about."

"I know nothing of these things," said Andy. "I wish you'd tell me."

"It is interesting," agreed Larkin, settling back more comfortably. "Why, you see when the Spanish first came to this country the general idea was that the *padres* were to convert the Indians, and while they were doing that they were to be protected by the soldiers. The missions were built for that purpose. The theory I spoke of was this: that the land really belonged to the Indians, and they were to have it eventually, but only after they had been converted and civilized and taught so that they would be capable of running it. Until then the friars were to run it. The missions, really, owned only the land they were built on. Practically, of course, they owned it all. Now they were to control it all for ten years. That was supposed to be long enough to educate the Indians to take care of it for themselves. After that the missions were legally to become *pueblos*, towns, and the friars were merely to conduct the churches."

"How long ago was this?"

"Exactly," Larkin approved the shrewdness of Andy's comment. "It was a long time ago, a lot longer than ten years. The friars, and every inhabitant of California, soon realized perfectly that ten years—or twenty, or thirty, for that matter—was too short a time to educate these Indians to take care of anything. But the ruling powers in Spain, and later in Mexico, were too far away. What did they know about it? Or care, for that matter? But there was always someone, for one reason or another, who wanted the letter of the law enforced."

"That would be a sweet mess," said Andy.

Larkin nodded agreement.

"So obvious a mess that nobody even considered it—in California. They passed a law, in Spain, in 1813 I think it was, that all missions that had been established ten years or over should turn over all their lands and all their wealth. Some of them by then had a lot of it, too. It was so silly that it was not even published in California until eight years later, and then it was not enforced. Nobody paid any attention to it. Then there was the revolution, and Spain was defeated, and Mexico took over the government. By this time the missions were very rich indeed. The Mexicans began to press matters."

"What were they so interested in the Indians for?" asked Andy.

Larkin laughed shortly.

"Come now, Burnett, you're not as simple as that!"

"You tell me," said Andy, unruffled.

"The friars were all Spanish,"—Larkin was curt—"and Mexico had just gained independence and was fanatically distrustful of everything Spanish. The wealth of the missions was now enormous. Isn't that enough?"

"The last will do," said Andy dryly. "Go on. It's interesting."

"They kept sending governors up here with instructions.

When they got here, the governors, if they had any sense at all, saw it wouldn't do. So they did as little as they could. But they had to do something. They appointed committees to report on conditions—your friend Alvarado was on one of them; they gave a certain few picked Indians permission to leave the missions and hold land under certain conditions—if they had been Christians for fifteen years, and could prove they could support themselves, and I don't know what all. In that way a few small *pueblos* were established. They were very small, and very few, and they did not amount to much, and they did no great immediate harm; but in another way they did a lot of harm."

"How was that?"

"You know Indians. If you were to turn over to an Indian a certain amount of land and a certain number of cows and implements and so on, what would you expect to happen?"

"I'd expect him to sell the whole caboodle and get drunk," said Andy.

Larkin popped out of his chair, hit Andy's shoulder a resounding whack, and sat down again.

"By God!" he cried. "It's like a breath of fresh air to talk with a man who can use his head!"

"Surely anybody can see that!" expostulated Andy.

"Most do not think of it one way or another," said Larkin. "Of the few who do, only a small proportion care. *Mañana, mañana!* They are beginning to take notice lately, however," Larkin presently went on after a short pause, "—and to take sides," he added. He fell again into a brown study. Andy waited in Indian patience.

"This governor we have now, Figueroa," Larkin resumed, "he really takes an interest. He was instructed to 'proceed with secularization.' He took the trouble to make a tour of the missions in person. You've stopped at a mission?"

"Yes," said Andy, "at Santa Clara and San Juan Bautista."

"Then I don't need to tell you anything about their wealth and prosperity and their hospitality to the traveler. But Figueroa is shrewd enough to see below the surface. He talked to me about it. His opinion was that mischief beyond repair had already been done. By what we were talking about, I mean—the turning over some property to a few; the small *pueblos*. Except in a very few cases the Indians had done just what you said—sold everything and got drunk, and were back on the missions in no time at all. All the other Indians had become restless, and they wanted their 'freedom' too. Freedom to their simple minds meant no more work, no more punishment, and food from the *padres* just the same. It was becoming increasingly difficult to get anything out of them. Discipline had all gone to pot. So Figueroa tried a plan of his own, a sort of compromise. It was," said Larkin, "a good idea; but it didn't work."

"What was it?" asked Andy.

"To give such Indians as seemed fitted for it their share of land and implements and seed and so on; but the Indians to remain under the authority of the Church."

"Yes," agreed Andy after a moment's consideration, "that seems like a good plan; the *padres* could keep them from selling out. Why wouldn't it work?"

"Because the Indians wouldn't do it. They were offered the chance. At San Diego there were just two applicants. I think the most they got anywhere was ten. That was at San Luis Rey."

"Those Injuns didn't want land and hard work: they wanted a drunk," observed Andy with a laugh.

"Exactly. It looked like a complete demonstration. The *padres* had known it, of course, all along. So had any of the Californians who had bothered to think about it at all. Figueroa saw it. He wrote to Mexico opposing all

further steps in the matter; and he advised passing a law
that in no case were any of the mission lands ever to come
legally into the hands of white men—if any Indian got
rid of them it must be to some other Indian. He got an
immediate answer."

"Yes?"

"Yes," echoed Larkin dryly. "It was an order to
complete secularization within four months. No ifs and
ands about it."

Andy whistled.

"So there you are!" said Larkin. "And that's where this
Hijar and Padres colony outfit comes in."

"Anon?" queried Andy.

"Why, a good many people think—that is, the few who
do think," amended Larkin with a trace of bitterness—
"that they have been collected with the sole idea of getting
in on the loot. Some people claim to know positively
that Hijar has with him twenty-one men to be appointed
as civil administrators of mission property."

"Is that so?"

"I don't know," confessed Larkin. "It looks reasonable.
This Padres is a great talker. He is very active among the
younger men. He doesn't say much about missions direct;
but he theorizes a lot about the rights of man, and the
wrongs of the neophytes, and the tyranny of the friars.
Right out of Rousseau. Ever read Rousseau?"

"I never read much of anything," Andy reminded him.

Larkin nodded.

"I'm sorry for Figueroa," he submitted. "He has his
orders; and he has to obey them. If he does not, he will be
recalled and someone else sent who will do as he is told.
I think only the change of government in Mexico saved
him as it is. He's moving as slowly as he dares. If the
Californians would only wake up to the situation—they
like their *padres* well enough. But only a few of them—your

friend, Alvarado"—he shrugged his shoulders—"most of the friars know the situation. Some of them are clear-sighted enough. Your friend Father Viador has given up in despair and gone back to Spain. He has been here for forty years."

"Father Viador!" cried Andy. "But I'm sorry to hear that."

"Yes; he, and others—Father Peyri at Santa Barbara; it is reported that, when he left, his people, weeping, waded out into the sea after his boat. At San Gabriel they say Father Sanchez is having all the mission cattle slaughtered. Father Duran—he is the head of the order, you know—is fighting desperately against the change."

"Why, I had no idea——" exclaimed Andy

Larkin lighted a cigarette.

"It is interesting," said he, "but, I think, inevitable. The conduct of human affairs—what we call history—is always interesting: and inevitable." He suddenly threw away the cigarette and sat forward in his chair. "It's the most interesting thing there is! Why, Burnett, the very air is full of change. You and I will live to see it; your son will see more of it." He waved his hand through the open window through which could be seen the somnolent plaza and the blue waters of the bay. "I'm going to tell you something, Burnett," said he impressively. "That looks quiet and peaceful enough, doesn't it? Looks as though it had been that way forever; as if it would stay that way forever. It won't."

Andy's eyes followed his.

"What do you mean? What are you expecting to happen, sir?" he asked.

"I'm waiting to see," said Larkin.

Andy arose to go. He was strangely stirred; stirred as he had not been since a day long past when, in another library of books, in another little city far away, he had listened to the words of another man, Benton of Missouri,

groping as this man groped into a dim and troubled future.
He drew a deep breath.

"Well, sir," he said. "I thank you. This has been for me
most interesting."

Larkin aroused himself.

"Good-bye," said he, "I am glad you came. It has been
good to talk. Do not concern yourself too much with these
matters. Who are we to meddle with destiny? But we can
at least stand prepared—prepared to fall in step when
she moves forward on her appointed way." His mood fell
from him almost visibly. "After all," he said whimsically,
"it is not our affair. You have your *rancho* and your son
to make into a man. I am a merchant. It does not greatly
matter whether the Mexicans or the friars win."

"I like the *padres*," said Andy.

"Some of them," corrected Larkin. "There's more than
one kind. I could tell you things—I won't: there are always
two sides. I don't know."

3

For the moment Andy was much aroused by his talk
with Thomas Larkin. But the feeling lost its power very
shortly. It had no fuel on which to feed. Most of his Californian friends and acquaintances merely laughed good-
naturedly at his earnestness. A few were willing to discuss
things; but they could see no reason for personal agitation.

"Undoubtedly it is as you say, Don Largo," said they,
"and it is to be regretted that these things should be thus.
But such has always been the law, as is well known from
early days. And," they added reasonably enough, "undoubtedly the situation is satisfactory to the good Lord
and the blessed saints; for, if it were not, would they not
protect their own holy *padres* who burn so many candles
and offer up so many prayers?"

There was really no refutation of this argument of the

pious. As for those not so religiously inclined, it was difficult to stir up much interest in the question of who owned what lands. There was plenty of land. When Andy argued that possibly the whole business was to result in sequestration of the land, not only from the missions but from the Indians as well, they shrugged their shoulders. Nobody even spared a thought to the Indians. The only point that elicited the smallest interest was the rumor that Hijar had brought with him twenty-one men who were to be appointed civil administrators of the mission properties. That was of a piece with all the rest of Mexican impudence. If civil administrators were necessary, were there not plenty of Californians? Their facile emotions flared up. They became indignant over the outrage. They would demand . . .

But Andy knew they would not demand. They were momentarily stirred by the traditional and persistent discrimination, that was all. It is fair to say that no envy of possible loot influenced their indignation. Andy's own first interest cooled. After all, it was none of his affair. He had his family, and his wide acres, and his friends. Life was very full. They laughed at him gently.

"*Guárdese*, Don Largo!" they warned him. "If you do not look out you will become *político*, like Alvarado."

4

Nevertheless Monterey was abuzz with one aspect of the Hijar-Padres incursion, the women perhaps more than the men, but men and women both. This aspect interested Andy not at all; nor could he see that it was of the slightest importance. For all that, it did have importance, for in essential it was a genuine revolution.

The Spanish had now been in California for sixty-odd years. These had been years of isolation from influences of the outside world, the changes in which had passed them by. They lived by a tradition that extended even to the little things of life. In all that time the costumes of both men and women had remained unchanged. Hijar had brought in new fashions! *Calzoneras*—the long trousers slit down the sides to expose white linen—took the place of the breeches of ceremonial wear; on horseback, it seemed, men were to wear *botas* that extended to the middle of the thigh, but which could be doubled over a garter below the knee when the rider dismounted. These *botas* could be made of particolored leather. They had a sole of rawhide, pointed, and led up and over the toes to protect the foot in the stirrup. A waistcoat should be worn under the jacket. High combs for the women's hair were definitely endorsed. The hair itself must be differently dressed; the old square-cut bang and the cheek curls were out. Now it must be drawn smoothly to the back and twisted into a single braid, and tied above by a ribbon and below by a rosette or a bow. It was very ill-bred to expose the ears. The old narrower skirts—*de medio paso*—became flowing. There were a number of other things.

Andy was amused, and a little disdainful, at the interest in all this foofaraw. Just at first he did not think the girls looked nearly so well; but soon, after his eye had become accustomed, he began to change his opinion, so that it was not long before the few who had not changed to the new costumes looked somehow old-fashioned and queer. The Boston ships did a thriving trade in dress goods.

Left to himself he would never have dreamed of following the new fashion in his own case. This would have been sheer indifference, and no matter of stiff conservatism, as in the case of Don Sylvestre and a number of the older grandees, who clung to the old style for several years to come. But Carmel would have none of it, and Andy good-naturedly submitted to a fresh rigout, in which she admired him more than he admired himself. He thought the *calzoneras* a floppy nuisance with their easily soiled

ruffles; though he acknowledged there was something to
be said for the *botas* from a practical point of view. But
as long as he was in the renovation business he added a
touch of his own. He had his hair cut short. He had never
liked the queue, either as foofaraw or as a matter of comfort. So much hair was hot, and it rubbed his collar, and
every day Carmel had to braid and arrange it, which annoyed him. Nobody but the wife should have that privilege, she insisted. Carmel was at first sight horrified and
almost inclined to weep. But Andy pointed out that Alvarado and Guadalupe Vallejo and Guerra and others of
the leaders were already wearing their hair short. She
looked at him with new eyes and ended by finding him
distinguished-looking. When they returned to Folded
Hills, nothing must do but that they must give a *fiesta*,
ostensibly to celebrate the wine-pressing of the new vineyard's first product; but actually, as Andy himself was
shrewd enough to surmise, to furnish an opportunity to
put it all over the neighbors with the latest from the great
metropolis. Ramón, whose wedding was near at hand, was
immensely tickled.

"She is one devil, that Carmelita," he told Andy. "Now
what must happen? Conchita must go to Monterey! And
I? Zip!"—he slashed the flat of his hand sidewise—"I cut
heem the hair! When I am young, a man who is in dis-
grace, they cut heem the hair and everybody point the
finger at heem and say 'See the bad man.' Now!"—he
shrugged his shoulders—"now, I think pretty soon we are
all bad mens!"

It was a good *fiesta*. They built a platform and covered
it with cleaned hides, and on it piled high the grapes.
Then several thoroughly washed Indians clad only in loin-
cloths were hoisted aloft to tread out the wine. The
juices were caught in leather bags called *coras*, which
were emptied into wooden tubs, and the liquid strewn
with grape skins, thoroughly emptied so they would float,

under cover of which the fermentation would take place.
Everybody stood about with bared and bowed head
while Father Seria, who had come from Soledad for the
purpose, blessed the vintage.

Andy tried for a little serious conversation with Father
Seria on the subject of the state of the missions; but he
did not get far. Father Seria was an old man, a beautiful
character compound of goodness, charity, and meekness,
a profound scholar. He walked in humility and did not
presume to raise his eyes. Doubtless these greater matters
were astir, but they were not for him. They were in God's
hands—and in the hands of the august princes of the
Church; and in due time their purposes would become apparent. Father Seria lived in profound faith and trust
and acceptance. So they feasted and played music and
rode afield to *meriendas*, and danced *la zorrita*, singing the
tune very sweetly of:

> *"The little fox, she went up into the hills,*
> *And because naughtily she went there for a lark*
> *She came back shorn."*

Since at this *fiesta* the men were doing no hard work
at *rodeo* or *matanza*, they took part in it fresh and joyous
and were as ready as the girls to dance the night through.
But in the women's enjoyment was just a trace of the
divided mind. They wanted to get home and set about
the new fashions. And that, in California at large, became
really the significance of Hijar.

ANDY began to take Djo horseback-riding before the latter could walk. Most of the time he held the infant before him in the saddle; but occasionally, when he had other occupation for his hands, he attached the child to the crupper behind him by means of a snap and ring. It might dangle; but it could not fall. As a matter of fact, it did very little dangling. In some instinctive monkey fashion it learned almost at once to cling like a limpet to a rock, with its legs stretched wide across the barrel of the horse. Carmel, and Vicenta even more vehemently protested at first. But Andy was unexpectedly firm.

"No," said he, "Djo is not too young; and the bouncing is not going to hurt him."

"What does a man know of young children?" demanded Vicenta vigorously.

Andy turned and looked at her gravely in silence. Vicenta knew this look and subsided.

"I know a great deal," he said after a time. "I have watched the children of the Blackfeet, and I know that what I am saying is so."

"*Los indios!*" snorted Vicenta. "Do you consider your son as an Indian?"

"I should like to think that he will be as good a man— in many ways," said Andy gravely. "But I should hate to think a son of mine could not do what an Indian child can do," he stated the case the other way around.

Andy was surprising that way. He brought over several bits of Blackfoot lore as to babies, which he calmly applied to Djo. Djo was never known to cry after his third

42

or fourth week, even when hurt or disappointed or en-
raged. Andy had trained him by the simple expedient of
placing the flat of his hand across the infant's mouth
whenever the latter began to cry, and holding it thus
until all symptoms had subsided. Even the embryonic
mind early recognizes absolute futility. That was the very
beginning of Djo's education: and it worked so well and
so promptly that Andy's imagination kindled. He looked
ahead through the years. He took out and examined with
renewed interest his old-time mountain skills and knowl-
edges, and dusted them off, for soon Djo would be old
enough to learn. Andy began to look forward eagerly to
the time when he and Djo could slip off together in the
hills—with the old Boone gun. Suddenly Andy was appalled at the thought of how much there was to learn, for-
getting the child's gift of perceptive access to race wisdom
which we call instinct. Later when that gift was in full
play he was to be proud and delighted.

"He takes to it like a duck to water!" he bragged to
anyone who would listen.

Exactly like a duck to water, or a bird untaught to the
intricate weaving of its first nest. But he found no one
on the *rancho* to deny that this was the most remarkable
child that ever existed.

One thing this arousing of Andy's imagination did effect.
It shook him out of a certain easy routine into which he
was unconsciously falling, in spite of his experimental
gropings toward innovation. He took the Boone gun from
its pegs on the wall and climbed with it to the bare high
peaks where the fat bucks were hardening their horns.
He began again to exercise his faculties, noting the small
matters of the open—the tracks and signs and little indications and from them reading the history of the day.
He discovered, to his chagrin, that he had to a certain
extent lost the fine edge of skill in matters for which he
had been famous in the past. He brushed up on them; he

practised. They had fallen below the level of his interest
for the simple reason that in this new life he was living
he had had no practical use for them. Now again he had a
vital use for them: he must teach them to Djo: and therefore they became interesting again. He even hunted up
the old balanced knife of his trapping days and regained
the deadly accuracy of its cast. He gave no thought to the
practical application of many of these things. It would
seem unlikely that Djo would ever find occasion to use
them. That was not the question. Djo was to be as good
a man as his father. Better. Andy turned from a survey
of his own attainments to his deficiencies. He read the
two books that Larkin had lent him, and which he had
from day to day postponed. He enjoyed the romances
amazingly; but their final effect was disconcerting in
that they opened to him glimpses of a world whose existence he had never even suspected. Andy's education
was slight. He sent a man on horseback to Monterey, returning the books, and bearing a letter to Larkin, asking
the loan of others.

"If you got any that tells about things," he wrote in
his sprawling unformed hand, "pleese send me those. I
will take good care of them. I mean books that are not
made up, but tells about things that really happened."

Larkin sent him three volumes of Gibbon's *Decline and
Fall*, whose first effect on Andy was merely to appall him
for a time with a sense of the vastness of the unknown in
human knowledge.

2

About midwinter one of the *vaqueros* came pounding in
to report a raid by the Tulare Indians. The greater part
of two *manadas* had been driven off. Andy immediately
rode to investigate. The tracks were already over a day
old. The Indians had craftily selected the place and the
moment; in all probability they had been hanging around

in the hills for some days. They had come afoot; and were after horses only. They had little use for cattle and none at all for trouble, if they could possibly avoid it.

Andy returned to the ranch house, collected his men, took down the Boone gun, and started at once in pursuit. He alone was calm in a great and clamorous excitement. He grinned cheerfully at Carmel, too elated and eager even to notice her fears. For the moment he was like a boy let out of school.

Through the hills and the low mountains the trail was plain enough to follow; for the several hundred horses had been held together in a compact band. The pursuers could push on at top speed of their mounts. But Panchito shook his head.

"It is always thus, *señor*," he told Andy, as they raced along. "I have been on many like pursuits. As soon as we reach the Valley, you shall see. These *indios* are clever. The trail will be lost."

Until they had emerged from the hills Andy rode carelessly, with only sufficient attention to keep to the trail. These were Tulare Indians, and they would get out of the coast ranges as fast as possible, without lingering even to scout their back trails for pursuit. But when the little party had reached the Valley, Andy slowed its pace. He rode twenty yards ahead of the *vaqueros* spying keenly for every indication, no matter now small, stowing each away in the corner of his mind for later synthesis. Every half-mile or so he halted his companions and circled wide to right and left of the trail. He was enjoying himself zestfully. This old familiar matching of his wits against the peoples of the wilds was to his lungs like a cold breeze from the mountains. It brought back to him the fierce old times. Especially did he breathe again the spirit of a long past day when he and Fitzpatrick—good old Bad Hand!—and the others followed the Shoshone horse thieves and stole past the village at night to the restless

herd, and leaped almost blindly in the dark, and stampeded away, the horses bareback and uncontrolled,
through the very lodges. He remembered the lad he was
then, and the stickiness in his mouth. But that was deadly
earnest, when a slip meant a life. Somehow now Andy
could not rid himself of a feeling of play-acting. This was
a soft and gentle land. These were a debased and primitive savage. They had little in common with the proud
fierce warriors of the plains. But he knew better than ever
to hold any antagonist too lightly. He was carefully approaching an estimate of the intelligence of those with
whom he had to deal.

. Andy could not have told you, much less himself, the
steps of his processes; and he would not have known what
you were talking about if you named them to him as
psychological. The thing had become instinctive to him:
so instinctive that for some time it never occurred to him
that Panchito, and the other *vaqueros*, had no idea of what
he was about or why he did certain things. Any mountain
man would have understood, and no word spoken. For
the moment Andy was reliving the mountain man's life.

So, while he was keenly reading the signs of the trail,
and determining by his wide circles to right and left that
as yet no scouts had been detached to spy the back track,
his mind was busy trying to form an estimate of the
marauders' intelligence and craft. Andy knew Indians,
none better; and how, in general, Indians would act.
But he could not predict in detail how these particular
Indians would act until he had to some extent got himself
into their skulls. And after he had done that he must re-
verse the process and try to get the Indians' point of view
on their pursuers, and what the savages probably thought
the white man would do. Had he to deal with Blackfoot
or Crow or Shoshone his course of action would have been
clear to him. These were a strange people.

They had not thrown out flankers or scouts. Andy had

not expected this in the hills. They would want to get out of the hills as rapidly and directly as possible. But out here in the open country, with a long ride ahead to the Sierra, it seemed elementary common sense. Did these people lack that common sense? Or were they contemptuous of their pursuers?

That was Andy's unrecognized psychological problem which underlay all the keen zestfulness of his observation. The thing, to now, was too open and shut. He knew perfectly, before Panchito had told him, that shortly the stolen horses would be divided and divided, again and again, until the herd, as a herd, had been melted and scattered to the four winds. That was routine strategy. But sooner or later they must come together again. How promptly? Where? With what intervening precautions?

He stopped his horse and interrogated Panchito. Had that been thought of? Had the pursuing parties of the past tried the expedient of tracking one of the little bands, no matter how small, in the thought it might lead them to the rendezvous?

"But surely, *señor*," replied Panchito in rather an injured tone. "One would have to be a fool not to have thought of that. But you shall see, *señor*. After a time the tracks will vanish; as though the *caballos* had taken wings and flown. No man living can follow beyond the river they call the Joaquin. There is nothing to follow. *Nada! Nada!*" He caught the skeptical gleam in Andy's eye and became earnest in defense. "The *señor* knows that I am not unskillful in following the tracks of animals. But I speak not of myself. Old Cochuco—he is an Indian of the missions, *señor*, and an honest man. I think, *señor*, he can follow the track of a lizard on the bare rock or a humming bird in the air. But he cannot follow *los indios* beyond the Joaquin. Never but once," Panchito corrected himself.

Andy nodded. These Indians, then, could blind a trail after all. Andy doubted whether they could do so against his own eye and training. He had been a Blackfoot himself. He knew how they did it; and therefore what to look for. But that was unimportant. He had one more bit to fit into his psychological mosaic. Belatedly Panchito's last remark came to him.

"Never but once?" he repeated it. "And then? Did you come up with them?"

"We rode hard and came up with them, *señor*, but——"

"Nay," Andy stopped him, "I shall tell you. The horses had all been killed and the Indians had gone."

"Why, how know you that, *señor!*" cried Panchito, astounded.

Andy did not reply. He was again happily in pursuit of the inner trail, like a hound on the slot. Here was another bit to the mosaic. It was evident to him that when the Indians began to blind the trail, they also began to watch the back track for pursuit. If they discovered that, in spite of their precautions, they were still followed, they most certainly turned aside, luring their pursuers from the agreed meeting place. If, again, they found they could not shake them off, it was a simple matter to kill the horses, and then eventually, by devious ways through the brush-clad foothills, to rejoin their people in enjoyment of the bulk of the spoils. Andy's spirits rose. These foemen were like to prove worthy of his metal after all. And, tentatively, he was beginning to think with their minds.

He rode forward again, now at a walk. Panchito and his men followed, but without enthusiasm.

A short distance from a shallow stream bed in which grew several magnificent specimens of sycamores, the *álamos pintados* of the Spanish, Andy drew rein with an exclamation of pleasure. In the dry and stony wash his quick eye had noted indications that had escaped even Panchito. With a gesture he halted the men and alone rode aside to investigate. A stone had been freshly overturned. That might mean nothing, of course—a deer or an elk, perhaps. But there was no question that the stone had been recently displaced. Only after an ever widening search of a half-hour did Andy discover what he sought, and knew positively that two horses had turned aside. It was unlikely that these were strays; for surely the riders would have turned them back, but Andy spent five minutes more eliminating that possibility. He followed the tracks until they led over difficulties that an unguided wandering animal would have avoided. He continued until, after a wide circle, their definite turn eastward proved them not to have been made by scouts sent out to watch the back tracks. Then he returned.

"We shall find the horses," he told Panchito. Then he grinned, relaxing for the moment from the intense concentration in which until now he had held himself. "Your Indians are not such fools," he said. "But they do not know mountain men; only *californios*,"—then instantly repented. "Your people have not had time to learn these things." He explained a little. "Two men have ridden away alone. Perhaps the chief and another. Perhaps only messengers. At any rate alone. We shall follow them. It will not occur to them that they may be followed, for they will think that we will surely follow the horses."

Panchito caught the idea with a sudden enthusiasm in almost ludicrous contrast to his previous glum endurance.

3

"*Viva!*" he cried; then as an afterthought, "But they will see us, *señor!* On these wide plains——"

"We shall camp tonight here, at the *álamos*," said Andy, "and perhaps half the day tomorrow. By that time they will have reached where they are going. There is no rain; their trail will not grow old."

They bivouacked without fire under the spreading *álamo pintado*, hobbling the horses to graze until dark,

munching their emergency rations of jerked meat and
panoche—ground corn and sugar. The *vaqueros* sat apart,
respecting the obvious withdrawal of Andy's mood. They
had plucked up some interest, and more curiosity, in this
expedition; though, when it came to Andy's hypothesis,
they were not so certain.

But Andy was certain. He knew Indians. He dismissed
all further theorizing from his mind and basked happily
in contentment. His first, long-continued revulsion, succeeding the murder of Joe Kelly and the massacre of his
Indian friends at Pierre's Hole, had been soothed, finally
healed. He could contemplate the old life without recoil.
This little campaign warmed his heart with the wine of
old times. To be sure, it was only an approximation. A
number of elements were lacking. By no stretch of the
imagination could Andy imagine himself in any danger:
in this soft and lovely climate, in this soft and lovely
land was—could be—no hardship as Andy knew hardship. Certain faculties must therefore remain unemployed.
But to follow, and to come up unobserved, and to recover
against what must undoubtedly prove to be great odds
of numbers, that would call for something of mountain-
man skill. Thank the saints these Indians were proving
not to be as dumb as at first they had appeared. Andy anticipated the morrow with relish; as one anticipates contest in any game one enjoys and plays well.

And that, perhaps, was just the difference. This was a
game. One welcomes, sometimes sets up, artificial difficulties in a game. One does not do so when it is a matter of life.

Nevertheless it proved to be a good game, not easy,
and moderately exciting. The two lone riders went straight
enough and carelessly enough, but at times their pursuers
were baffled for a space. Eventually, however, they always
managed to pick up the trail again. The changes of soil
or terrain did not bother them much, though at times the
going would have been blind to any but these trained

trackers. Their chief difficulties were caused by the over-lying spoor of game and especially of wild horses. In that day game swarmed in the plains of the great Valley, as it does on the veldt of Tanganyika today. Sometimes the trail was lost completely. Then one of the *vaqueros* stood landmark at the last clearly recognized sign, while the others rode slowly in ever widening circles until unmistakably they cut it again. By this time each and every one of them was as familiar with the individual hoofprints of those two horses as they were with one another's face.

Progress was necessarily slow. The Indians ahead of them had traveled without pause, evidently with the intention of crossing the Valley in a single day. This suited Andy. The plains were flat, and there was no concealing cover. He wanted them to get as soon as possible into the foothills.

If he had not been so wholly intent, he must have enjoyed the excursion for its own sake. North and south the plains spread wide and flat to the horizon's fall. Their surface was brown with the high grasses that rippled in the wind like the waves of the sea. In all directions were the herds of game animals; elk, antelope like shimmering ghosts, deer near the occasional bottomlands of the sloughs, even once in a while a bear or so lumbering about, lost in the deliberate somnolence of bears. Wild horses, at once inquisitive and shy, paralleled them, raced across ahead of them, wheeled to snort and stamp at them. The latter were rather a nuisance in their persistent curiosity, for their movements might indicate disturbance to an alert watcher. But then they were equally obstreperous in the presence of the bears; and Andy was satisfied that the men he followed felt quite secure, for their spoor continued undeviating and unhurried. A wind from the distant cool sea drove the dancing heat waves down the breadth of the valley. The sky was a deep and polished blue. The grasses were full of birds.

Behind them the Coast Range dropped steadily lower, lost the definition of its folds and cañons, blued with distance. Ahead they began to make out the Sierra. At first a half-guessed haze belting the azure of the sky; then a suggestion as of piled clouds on the horizon; at length, as though reluctantly, they were dropping their veils of remoteness to stand forth in their still and distant beauty. And below them the thin dark lines of the foothills began to rouse themselves to visibility.

Andy watched their slow defining with appraising eye. When he began to make out the details of their foldings he turned abruptly south, abandoning the trail they had been so painfully following. He straightened in his saddle and began to look about him in enjoyment of the pleasant day. He had the appearance of a man relaxed from concentration. He laughed at Panchito's dismay and poked a little fun at him before he condescended to explain.

"No wonder you *californios* catch no Indians!" said he. "What have I heard you say so many times? 'He that would enter a low door must stoop.' Well, to catch Indians you must enter a very low door."

"I do not understand, *señor*," submitted Panchito.

"Why," said Andy, "unless these Indians are very complete fools—and they do not appear to be quite that, though I think any of my old people in the mountain country would call them so—when they get to the hills someone will watch from a hilltop, and if we were to follow the trail so would we surely be seen, for the plains are flat and there is no cover, and one can see a grasshopper moving. These men have ridden straight as the flight of a crow, so it seems to me they will so continue and thus will enter the broken country where yonder dark line marks a cañon."

"And?" urged Panchito, as Andy showed no disposition to go on.

"We will not oblige them," said Andy.

"What shall we do, *señor?*"

"We will go south, and then we will go east, and so we will enter the hills, and then we will go north under their cover, and then we shall get behind these robbers, and so after a time, if we are careful and lucky, we shall come upon them or their tracks."

"The *señor* is *sabio!*" exclaimed Panchito in unaffected admiration.

"Not very," said Andy, laughing good-naturedly. "It is truly very simple."

"Would that Don Ramón were here," cried the *vaquero*, "for this he would enjoy!"

The Californians followed Andy now with kindled enthusiasm. They too were beginning to enjoy the game as its possibilities developed.

4

By the afternoon of the third day they had completed the circle, had advanced north through the low wide Sierra foothills, and had reached the transverse cañon which Andy had made out from afar. Panchito and the other *vaqueros* learned a great deal about travel in a hostile country. Andy recalled the time of his own initiation as a youth, and how patiently Joe Crane had elucidated things that must have seemed to him obvious. He stopped every once in a while to explain, then, to the Californians, the reasons for what he did. They crowded their horses about him, bending forward to catch his lowered voice, their teeth flashing in their dark faces with pleasure of comprehension. The things he told them were, to him, so elementary that they should need no telling. But again he remembered Joe Crane.

They rode the slopes just below the ridges of the hills where the footing was difficult, what with chaparral and rock formations, and the route was tortuous and long

rather than in the valleys where the going was good and
the distances were shorter. Thus one gained cover; one
could see abroad; one followed the unexpected way. Below every new summit, short of each new shoulder of hill
or twist of valley, Andy left his horse with his men and
went forward afoot. If there were no cover behind which
he could crawl to skyline or angle of bend, he thrust forward a bit of cut brush, moving it into place by inappre-
ciable degrees. After which he lay on his belly and scru-
tinized the new prospect into which next they must
venture. His patience was exhaustless. Long after a man
of ordinary pertinacity might have seemed justified in
concluding the valley, or the pocket, or the hill vacant
of human life, Andy continued to lie flat against the sun-
baked earth, his keen eyes sweeping back and forth, back
and forth tirelessly, never for a moment losing their focused concentration, though there appeared to be nothing
to see. That there were no chance wayfarers he had determined in the first ten seconds; and as to lookouts or
scouts, he knew better than to look for them, for they
would be hidden. But he knew also that a man watching,
unless in immediate expectation, will, within his concealment, move about more or less, stretch and yawn in mo-
notony, shift his position for comfort or a better view; and
that these movements must be remarked in vigilance or
in curiosity by the animals and birds. So until he had
taken account of every living thing, and had satisfied himself that its conduct was undisturbed, he continued his
scrutiny. Any deviation from the normal must explain to
him its cause. This made a long job, for wild creatures
are wary, and a passing cat or coyote, a lolling bear, even
the swift gliding shadow of a hawk creates its flutter of
resentment or of fear. Sometimes Andy was quickly reassured, at least as to certain localities. Whenever, for
instance, he could make out the blue of a jay whose mind
was tranquil; for he knew well that jays are prone to

violent indignations over the slightest intrusions and feel called upon to tell the world, and to continue to tell the world. In the body politic of the wilds the jay was always, on the slightest excuse, viewing with alarm.

At times it seemed to his companions that their master would never finish his inspection. That was when the larger and more trustworthy indications, like jays or jack rabbits or deer, were entirely lacking, and he had to depend on the reports of littler and more indifferent people. But when at last he arose to his feet and motioned them up, he did so with complete confidence.

Early in the afternoon of the third day, then, Andy slipped back after his first searching glance over the hill crest. He returned to the waiting men, his eyes shining with satisfaction.

"The luck is with us," he told them in a low voice. "They are there, in the bottomland. Come with me, Panchito; you others remain here. And keep quiet."

5

Below them the cañon-like valley widened to an oval flat through which flowed a stream. On the hither bank a fire burned. Around the fire, close-gathered, milled perhaps a score of Indians. Others sat apart gnawing at bones and chunks of meat. Still others were stretched out here and there, asleep or torpid with gorging. The two men lay side by side taking in every detail, but each according to his interest and knowledge.

"There are no women: they are not yet home," said Andy.

"The horses are up the cañon, *señor*," said Panchito. "I see where they have been driven."

"They imagine they have not been pursued," continued the American. "They have been here already since yesterday at least. See, there are the ashes of another fire and the bones of another feast."

"True, *señor*. *Diablo*, to think they care nothing for a good horse but to eat him! What now, *señor?*"

Andy considered. Except for an old smooth-bore pistol, which Panchito carried, his own rifle was the only long-range offensive weapon. The *vaqueros* carried merely light lances and their *reatas* and knives. The white men were nine against fully four times that number of savages. The latter were armed with short strong bows and stone-tipped arrows. The sensible thing was to wait until after dark and then to drive away the stolen horses by a sudden swift rush. That would certainly have been the procedure in like situation east of the Rockies. But, unexpectedly, Panchito objected.

"These *bárbaros* must be taught a lesson, *señor*," he interposed firmly, "so that all the Valley shall know it is not well to steal from Fol-ded Heels."

"What do you suggest, Panchito?" asked Andy, interested.

"Why, *señor*, it is very simple. We shall ride yonder until we are behind the horses. Then we shall drive them very fast down the Valley right over these *indios*. If we do so secretly enough and quickly enough, perhaps we may kill some of them before they get away into the hills."

Andy considered.

"If you and the others had only *cueros* against the arrows," he half assented at last.

Panchito brushed this aside.

"The *señor* does not know these *bárbaros*," he said contemptuously, "They will not fight. You shall see; they will run like quail. Until they reach the brush they will not shoot their arrows."

His black eyes were glittering with eagerness, watching Andy's face. Andy gave way. According to all his training in such matters it was a fool thing to do. He was in an exalted boy mood for doing fool things.

"But this is what we shall do," he rapidly outlined to

Panchito. "I shall remain here where I can watch. Bring my horse as near to me as you can without his being seen. Do you and your men ride above the horses. Do not start until you hear a shot. Then drive the horses as fast as you can. As soon as I shoot I shall charge straight down the hill to join you as you come past."

They departed to execute this order. Andy relaxed in the hot sunlight, waiting for sufficient time to elapse. The sun made him sleepy. He yawned. The excitement and interest of the game were about over. In the stalking, not in the kill, is the true ardor of the chase. Panchito was correct: there would be no fight worth the name.

He blew through the nipple of the Boone rifle, for it had not been fired since the start of the expedition, casting his eye appraisingly at the distance and seeking among the sprawling savages his target. Andy was relying on the effect of his shot so to astonish and demoralize the Indians as to permit a safe passage for the stampeded horses and the *vaqueros*. The savages were acquainted with the Californians and their methods and might conceivably put up some resistance to them; but they had no experience with American riflemen. Andy did not want any of his men hurt, even by accident, if he could avoid it. Besides, as Panchito had said, it would be wise to teach them a lesson. At length he made out the chief by his characteristic headdress. Experimentally he leveled the long rifle, testing his estimate of the range by the apparent size of the bead on the man's chest. It was going to be pretty shooting at that distance. He loaded the piece, gauging the powder with meticulous exactitude, selecting from the several chargers that hung to his horn belt the one appropriate to the range.* Next he wriggled about under

*Some readers of this story in a magazine have objected that Andy would not have waited until now to load his rifle. As a matter of fact such was the habit of experienced old-timers, who varied the powder charge according to the range.

cover until he found a place, sufficiently concealed, where he could sit comfortably. Here he sat down and kicked places for his heels and, resting his elbows inside his bent knees, again leveled the long rifle and squinted over the sights. Satisfied, he glanced at the shadows and settled himself to wait a few minutes more. By these things one qualified to judge would have known him for what he was, an expert rifleman, for your real expert, on business bent, never shoots offhand when he can sit down to it, and much prefers a dead rest when he can get it. After a little, judging the time had come he cocked and capped the piece and once more took his position.

The shot was indeed a pretty one. Its problems engrossed all his technical interest. It was downhill; a moderately stiff breeze was sucking from the plains up the cañon; the heat of the sun rose from the earth in shimmering waves. All Andy's faculties were concentrated on these different elements of the problem. The palm of his left hand was flat beneath the wooden forearm of the long barrel, the elbow inside of and steadied by the left knee; the butt of the rifle was high on the round muscle of his shoulder; his right elbow he braced against the inside of his right knee. Thus the extended rifle was held in the support of two isosceles triangles braced one against the other. But Andy knew—though he had long since ceased thinking of it—that it must there rest lightly and easily, without tension from knee or shoulder or hand, for the smallest undue pressure by the smallest of the muscles concerned would be sufficient to destroy the nice coordination of accuracy. One muscle alone, of all his body, must function, that of the trigger finger. So at the moment when the point of the front sight swept to its mark, Andy's whole body sank to complete relaxation. This necessary physical passivity, Andy had found, must always be deliberately attained. This, in his 'prentice days, had been the most difficult thing of all to acquire. The human mind can take in and direct only about so many things at a time. Did he find the muscles of his knees contracting and so turn his attention to loosening them, at once he discovered his left hand tightening its clasp, or his right hand contracting so that his trigger finger was bound. But after a time, being of an analytical habit, he had happened upon a discovery. At first Joe Crane, whose skills and mental processes were mainly subliminal, hooted at him; but after he had examined himself in action his derision was changed to admiration.

"Doggone if you ain't right, Andy!" he cried. "And I been doin' it all the time and never knowed it!"

Joe had taken great joy in spreading the gospel. He would stand for a time watching the despairful inaccuracies of some tenderfoot, and then would spit sidewise and remark:

"Yo' stand good enough, pardner, and yore hand is stiddy, but when she goes off she jerks."

"I know it," the greenhorn would confess, "but somehow I kaint seem to help it."

"Next time," Joe then would observe with an air of owlish wisdom, "when yo' go to pull trigger, yo' sag yore belly."

That was Andy's discovery: that the muscle of the abdomen was a master muscle that must tighten first before any other part of the body can become tense; so that if it is relaxed, all others must be relaxed.

Long habitude had by now sunk all other elements of marksmanship below the necessity of Andy's conscious direction. Even his alignment of the sights had become instinctive, "grooved" as the golf players say. But this one thing he always accomplished by a single mental impulse. It was the one thing he thought to do.

These things all flooded into his spirit as his cheek

cuddled the velvety warm wood of the rifle's stock, like
friends returning from afar, the old joys in the exercise
of familiar skill. The sights aligned themselves on the
breast of the unsuspecting Indian chief, settled to meticulous nicety on the exact spot of paint that was to be
the mark for the ball. Andy's concentration was centered
on that one little spot. He was too experienced a hand to
"shoot at the whole thing." For the moment he had no
other thought in mind than sheer marksmanship. He relaxed his abdominal muscles, and his forefinger pressed
back softly and smoothly against the trigger.

And at the last instant, seemingly without reason and
certainly without his reasoned volition, he swung the
sights to the left. The rifle cracked. The Indian whirled
to the impact of the bullet, fell, was up again, dashed for
the brush, his right arm dangling. Andy leaped to his
saddle and set his horse at full speed down the steep slope.
He reloaded in full career; but he neither measured the
powder nor patched the ball. The charge he poured in
direct from the horn, stopping the flow with his thumb.
The bullet he spat into the barrel from his mouth. He did
not bother with the ramrod, but struck the butt of the
piece smartly atop the saddle horn to drop the missile
home where the saliva would hold it well enough for the
needs of close-range battle. Andy thenceforward carried
the rifle muzzle up until he should use it. He could an-
ticipate no fine accuracy from this rough-and-ready method; but in a mêlée fine accuracy is not important.

He reached the bottom of the hill just as the *manada*
swept into view urged on by the whirling *reatas* of the
vaqueros. Andy drew back, lest he head the horses; then,
as they passed, joined his men in the rear. Had not the
Indians, to a man, taken to the brush, they must have
been trampled or brushed aside. Andy had not really ap-
preciated until this moment what an overpowering weapon
is such a band of half-wild horses driven through a con-

fined space by native Californians. The *vaqueros* had a faculty, when they chose, of setting horses wild, partly by their activity with the *reata*, but principally by weird and peculiar half-cries. Andy rather regretted his shot: this overwhelming rush might have taught a better lesson had it burst upon the Indians unaware.

He reined back, with Panchito, as they overpassed the site of the feast, to spy about him curiously. There was not much to see. Evidently three horses had been killed and eaten. Of loot or trophy there seemed nothing, save a few of the short bows trampled and broken by the horses. But Andy's eye caught a gleam of white behind a protecting boulder; and he stooped from his saddle to pick up the feather headdress that had fallen from the head of the wounded chief. At the same moment Panchito's keen eyes detected blood on the stones.

"They carried him away, *señor?*" he asked.

Andy shook his head.

"I hit him here," said he, placing his hand on his shoulder.

"You did not wish to kill him?" Panchito's mind was incapable of entertaining the idea that Andy could not hit anything he wished, anywhere, at any distance.

"No," replied Andy.

Panchito considered this a moment; then nodded with satisfaction.

"Why, yes," he agreed, "it is better so: that way they will be more afraid, for they shall see him always with his shoulder broken. The *señor* is *sabio;* as always."

For an instant Andy accepted this explanation with a certain comfort; but he was basically too honest. That had not been his reason. He did not know his reason. Deep down he wondered a little uneasily whether he was getting soft.

"It would be well if we rode on, *señor,*" suggested Panchito. "These ones have not gone far. They know we cannot follow, and they are there in the chaparral; and it might be that some will pluck up courage and creep near enough to shoot at us the arrow."

Andy nodded. He leveled the long rifle to discharge it; for it was necessary to empty the piece of its makeshift battle-loading.

At the last moment his eye fell on a vulture perched obscenely half spread in the top of a digger pine part way up the hill. Without thinking he swerved the muzzle in its general direction and pulled trigger. The bird struggled for a moment to retain its hold, then flopped down with a beating of broad wings.

Andy laughed aloud. The result of the shot was pure fluke. The range was far beyond accuracy for the careless, unpatched loading of the rifle; and he had not even troubled to raise the rifle to his shoulder, let alone align the sights. The half-dozen or so of possible errors had compensated one against another. Every rifleman can remember in his own experience such accidents. But to Panchito this was only another demonstration to be expected of his master's skill. A low wail or keening of astonishment or dismay arose from the bushes.

"That also is a lesson those ones will remember!" the *vaquero* exclaimed with satisfaction.

And indeed never again was Folded Hills raided.

6

They camped overnight far out on the plains of the Valley. Andy shot a fat buck and they feasted. Next day they returned to the *rancho*, which greeted them with an emotion that first surprised and then amused him. Carmel clung to him almost convulsively, sobbing in an excess of relief. Until that moment it had not occurred to him that she had been awaiting news with any anxiety. He learned from Vicenta that she had ridden the long journey to

Soledad to burn candles and to command Masses for his safe return. There were actually dark circles of sleeplessness under her eyes. For a time she would not let him out of her sight. She insisted on his kneeling with her while she clasped her hands with streaming eyes in gratitude before the still, faintly smiling effigy of the Madonna on the wall of their bedroom. He was uncomfortable as at a disproportion. This was a lot of fuss about nothing. But at the same time he was touched.

"But there was no danger, *querida*," he expostulated again and again. "None! Not as much as when one rides the wild cattle in the hills!"

His mind flashed back to the old days, and he tried to tell her of times when danger had been real—the wild night dash of the mountain men on horses, bareback, unbridled, and uncontrolled, through the wild Shoshones. But he had to desist. The recital failed of its intended effect. Instead of minimizing the situation just past, it seemed to heighten for her its terrors. He ended by holding her silently in his arms; which was what was needed after all. He was very tender; and he was filled with emotion that he had been so stupid; and he would never be so thoughtless again. But underneath, nevertheless, persisted a half-guilty unregenerate satisfaction. It was good to his tongue, this little taste of the old wild freedom. He was repentant: he wondered again if he was getting soft.

TIME, for the next few years, passed swiftly and pleasantly. Djo grew to the responsive age and absorbed more and more of his father's delighted attention. He was a great freshener. Things that had grown stale from constant accustomedness took on a new interest to Andy when he thought of them in relation to Djo. The fact that Djo had somehow acquired a sister broke the feminine concentration on himself; freed him fully to his father's companionship. By his fourth year he was riding, and conducting, a horse of his own under the careful supervision of Andy or Panchito or some one of the trusted *vaqueros*. Not long thereafter he began to accompany them on their shorter excursions afield. Soon he was known to the whole valley as Don Largo's shadow. He was amusingly like a shadow, made small by noon, in his similarity as well as in his invariable presence. He had Andy's straight thick eyebrows; his figure gave promise of the same long supple strength. There were other similarities; but analyzed they proved not to be physical, but rather replicas of small mannerisms, for Djo adored his father. He had even the same steady, intent, unwinking way of looking at anyone or anything, a habit in Andy derived from the wilderness, but now reproduced in Djo as a "family trait." Though his eyes were Andy's, also, their furnishings were Carmel's, long curling lashes, a bit of nature's foofaraw more appropriate to a girl. Djo was a grave child when with Andy, and he was with Andy most of the time. At first this bothered his Uncle Ramón.

"He is like you, *valedor*," he told Andy, "and that I

like, all but one thing. He is *serio*, like you when I first
see you, before you learn to be *californio*."

"I am still *serio*, as you call it," said Andy. "My face
gets tired grinning all the time. It ain't trained to it—like
yours," he added with a disarming smile. "I have to rest
it."

"The face!" Ramón shrugged aside the face. "That is
as God has willed it, and some, like yours and Panchito's,
He cut from the oak so never they change at all. But it is
here,"—he thumped his chest—"inside. There you are
not *serio* any more as when I first saw you. You do not
deceive me, *valedor*, with the face. Is it not so? Is there
not something there inside that is warm, that sings?"

"I am happy, Ramón," said Andy soberly. "And why
not?" He looked about him slowly. "When first you saw
me, *amigo*, I had nothing, and I had had much. Yes,"
he insisted, "much." Abruptly he shifted to Spanish.
Strangely enough, when it came to the expression of sentiment he felt more at home in that language than in his
mother tongue. Possibly in it he was less self-conscious.
"I know what you would say. But over there—in the wild
country of the mountains—I had friends, true, and dear
to me as you are dear, Ramón *mío*. I was not then *serio*,
I think, in the way you mean. The Blackfeet named me
I-tam-api, and in their language that means Happiness.
I lost them all, everyone. I lost even my name."

"I know," said Ramón.

"But the Above People led me to you, *valedor*."

"The Above People?" repeated Ramón.

"That is what my Blackfeet called them, the——"

"The blessed saints," cut in Ramón.

"So why should I not be happy? What more can a man
need for happiness? A wife like Carmel, children, all this"
—he swept his hand abroad—"friends. A friend." He laid
the hand briefly on Ramón's arm.

"What I tell you!" cried Ramón. "That you do not

fool me with the face! But this Djo. It is danger. So small
a one to walk so grave and make no smile. If he is like
that when he is so young! The young thing always he
skip. If he is so *serio* when he is young, then when he
grow up, what? You don't want him come to be monk,
eh?"

"If he's as good a man as Father Seria," said Andy.

Ramón searched his face anxiously for a moment.

"You fooling with me," he decided with relief. "Just
the same, he's too *serio*."

He worried over the matter off and on. Andy, accustomed to the contained taciturnity of the mountain men,
forgot all about it. But before the conclusion of Ramón's
visit the young *californio's* anxiety was lifted. He had had
opportunity, unobserved, to inspect the conduct of Djo
off duty, as it were, down at the *milpas* in free commerce
with Benito's numerous progeny. At once he sought out
Andy in laughing relief.

"It is I who have been the fool and blind," he confessed. "Djo is not *serio*, like I did think. No, no-no!"
He slapped his thigh. "Ah, that one! No, I shall not tell
you what I see. Djo is my *amigo* also. I mus' not—what
you call?—give him away! But he is not *serio*. No, no-
no! But I tell you this, what I think. He try to make hisself all like you, all, all! And I think, *amigo mío*, you—
what you call?—watch yourself, because everything you
be like, he's goin' to be like that also!"

Ramón and Conchita departed the next day, after ar-
ranging for a jovial celebration by all of the festival of
Santos Inocentes. Andy and Carmel stood together before the *casa* to see them off. By Andy's side was Djo,
very solemn, holding himself as tall and straight as he
could. Ramón looked from one to the other and burst out
laughing.

"Remember what I say, *valedor!*" he cried. "Watch
yourself!"

2

They rode, Andy, Carmel, and the small Djo, to the
Rivera *hacienda* for the feast of Santos Inocentes, leaving the baby, Amata. Ramón's marriage to Conchita de
la Cuesta was supposed to have steadied him to the point
of responsibility; so that he was now in full charge of the
activities of the *hacienda*, while Don Sylvestre took the
ease he had earned, and surveyed with satisfaction the
increase of his descendants. Ramón proved a vigorous
and energetic executive, conducting affairs with a dash
and enthusiasm and attention to detail astounding to
all those who had known him. All were in exclamation
over his zealous wisdom and piety. But Don Sylvestre
smiled quietly to himself and took with him in his pleasure
rides Ygnacio, the younger brother, whom he instructed.
Andy was shrewd enough to notice this.

"Ramón has a wild hawk in his heart," said Don Sylvestre. "The pot that boils fast is the soonest emptied."
He glanced from beneath his thick brows at his tall son-
in-law. "The time will come for you also, *hijo mío*, for
you, too, have the wild strain. When it flutters in your
breast, go where it calls you. Do not resist. You will the
sooner return."

Andy laughed.

"I have plenty to keep me home," said he comfortably.

"The hawk's wings are folded and he sleeps," said Don
Sylvestre.

Andy laughed again. He could not conceive of com-
pleter satisfaction than his present life and responsibilities
afforded him. He was busy from dawn until dark with his
growing concerns, which never became routine. He grew
closer and closer into the heart of his adopted people.
Half those on the *rancho* were *parientes* in some sort of
fashion which he never quite understood. The other half
were devoted retainers of the sort that at last become iden-

tified by the family name. No one even remembered Panchito's own name. If one wished to distinguish him from
other Panchitos, one referred to him as the Riveras'
Panchito; or, later, as Don Largo's Panchito. Andy gradually learned to move gracefully, in the spacious and leisurely courtesy that distinguished all intercourse even between the highest and lowest. But a few years ago he
would have looked on it as foofaraw, and his ruthless
directness would have squirmed uncomfortably in its presence. Now he was not even conscious of it. It had become
his natural element. In outside manner and appearance he
was at this time more Spanish than American, a strange
contrast to the Andy of old mountain days.

There were many visitors to Folded Hills. Some of them
were Americans, new-come to the region, and some of
these Americans were stragglers from the fur country.
Andy was always especially glad to see them, and kept
them at the *rancho* as long as they would stay. Most of
them did not stay very long. The foofaraw of which Andy
had become unconscious made them just a little uneasy.
It did not quite forfeit their respect, for the reputation of
I-tam-api was still strong in the Indian country, but it
did interpose a barrier and made them uncomfortable. So
they escaped and drifted over to Natividad where Isaac
Graham ran a still and clung sturdily to his rough and
uncompromising Americanism, in which was the deliberate contempt of racial provincialism. There they were
more at ease. They could chaw and drink, and the complaisant señoritas—who would not have rated that title
to anyone else—did not skeer a man for fear he'd step a
hole through somethin'. The majority did not stay even
there very long. After a few months, or a season, they
became restless and drifted back over the mountains or
by way of Santa Fe to the growing excitements of the fur
country. Most of them made these visits with at least a
gesture of deference to authority. They applied for and

received *cartas de seguridad* for a limited stay, a sort of passport, which they carried for protection in deerskin pouches inside of bladders thoroughly greased against the wet. These they were rarely called upon to show, for it was known that many neglected the formality, and at that time the easy-going authorities made no determined issue against the obviously transient.

Occasionally, however, someone of the genuine old-timers came along, men who had personal acquaintance with Andy on the plains or in the mountains. These men knew him too well to be influenced by mere surface foofaraw. They rode with him. He took them hunting in the mountains, where they sought the California grizzly—the "white bear"—then abundant. The deer did not interest them much. The country was all right; but it was, in their concealed opinion, not much of a country for a white man. No buffalo. Some day they'd be comin' back, they veered abruptly and illogically.

In the evening they squatted with Andy beneath the big oak before the house and talked things over. Carmel tactfully left them alone together. Djo listened wide-eared as long as he was permitted to remain.

These sessions sat late. A little fire flickered beneath the tree. There were things to drink and meat to roast before the fire and chaw on. As the evening progressed, all constraint thawed. They talked in brief spurts, punctuated by ruminative silences.

The trade was shifting, changing in character. The old free trappers were about gone. The American Fur Company had things pretty much its own way: Sublette's outfit had quit in '34. But they were not alone in the field. Rivals constantly sprang up, like mushrooms; men who were of particularly adventurous or defiant spirit. They did not last long. The company bought them out, if they proved too annoying; or ran them out. If the new enterprise looked particularly promising, the company would sometimes buy it off before it even started. Everybody used liquor freely in the trade. It was now illegal even to take it into the Indian country. In this the little fellow distinctly had it over the company; for the company operated under government license which could be revoked. So they had to watch their step. The trading was all done from forts now. There were no more old-fashioned rendezvous. Why? The Injuns were bad. Why, Andy, you got no idee. It's partly the likker; and partly they're gittin' skeered they're agoin' to lose their kentry, white men's gittin' so thick!

"Yas," drawled Bill Cummings, "and part that the pickin's gittin' better and better in the way of stealin'."

For the wagons were moving, crawling over South Pass along the Oregon Trail following the tracks of Marcus Whitman; winding over the wastes of the Cimarron to Santa Fe. The pioneers to Oregon were as yet few; but along the southern route the commerce of the prairies had developed to a highly specialized affair, so that with the caravans dashing blades and their furbelowed ladies tooled blooded horses attached to stylish vehicles, the first genuine tourists to the Southwest. The caravans were splendid affairs, well organized and well equipped. They traveled in parallel columns.

"Thar's the job that pays, eff'n you don't mind herdin' fools," struck in John Dawson. "It pays you big—guidin', I mean. A passel of the boys has gone in fer it, some of them stiddy on the rolls, and some, like Kit Carson, just now and agin. I tuk an outfit onct myself."

"Tell Andy about the preacher, Jack," suggested Cummings.

Dawson grinned.

"'T want nothin'," he disclaimed. "You see, Andy, these yere wagon trains is different. You kain't jist project out 'cross kentry the way we used to. Got to stick to wheel tracks—or where you kin make 'em—and you don't know what real genuwine grief is until you go snakin' bull-drawn wagons through a river or boggy kentry—or over rocks—or," he concluded derisively, "anywhar else. The critters moves 'bout as fast as a foundered horny toad and just about as jerky. They's always gittin' sore feet or bellyache or somethin'. These dang wagons is always bustin' a wheel or smashin' a tongue or losin' a tire or somethin'. And then the whole outfit has to squat till they fix things up. And they's women; and squallin' children. And——"

"How about the preacher?" Andy reminded.

"That's right. Well, what I was aimin' to git to you is that to git whar you're goin' afore winter ketches you, you got to start as soon as the ground hardens in the spring, and *keep pushin'!* And then mebbe you don't git thar. This outfit I tuk had a preacher with it, and when it come Sunday and the boss yelled to 'catch up,' this feller just squatted and allowed it was sinful to travel on the Sabbath and he wasn't a-goin' to do it. We was right in the middle of a dry scrape and the critters hadn't had a drap of water since yisterday, and wouldn't git none till night—eff'n we was lucky. To stop whar we was—wall!" Dawson shrugged his shoulders.

"They argyed with this preacher, and they cussed at him, and they got mad with him. Mout as well argy with a mule. Some talked big about tyin' him up and takin' him along anyhow; and some talked bigger about leavin' him, but the talk didn't amount to much. We was right in the middle of Comanche kentry, and ye mout as well shoot him and be done with it as leave him. And somehow, him bein' a preacher, everybody seemed to balk off from layin' hands on him. When they all give it up, I tuk a hand. I fetched him."

"How?" asked Andy, as he was expected to do.

"Oh, I tuk him off one side from the mad bunch, and I talked to him reasonable. I told him about how we'd all finish thar eff'n he didn't shift his mind. Seems like he knew all that: but he stuck to it that he couldn't travel on Sunday nohow.

"'She's a bad fix we're in, dominie,' sez I.

"'The Lord has put us in this fix to test our obedience to His commands, to test our piety,' sez he. He was a funny cuss. He talked at me loud, and free wide and handsome, like I was a whole camp meeting.

"'Dominie,' sez I, 'mebbe it ain't that. Mebbe He put us in this fix *to test our common sense.*' And do you know, that got him. He come off'n the boil, and hitched up his bulls, and come along meek as a squaw. Funny critters. It's like that all the time. Some folks don't mind. Some of the boys is dry-nussin' these outfits as a reg'lar business. It's all right for them that likes it. Onct was enough fer me. But thar's good pay in it, and a heap of fun eff'n you like Injun-fightin'. Andy, when it comes to bull trains the Injuns is *bad.* Why not?" concluded the trapper philosophically. "Lots of sculps, and bull meat, and vally-ables, and the wagons makes 'em a grand fire, and eff'n the guide ain't *sabe* every minute, that's what happens."

Still, Cummings put in, more and more of the mountain men were taking it up. The fur trade was no longer rightly such. Beaver had become secondary. The forts were bartering for wolf skins, and small stuff like mink and marten, and even buffalo and deer hides. The trade could be no longer an affair of individuals, unless one followed Jim Bridger's example and built him a fort of his own. Andy inquired at last of the Blackfeet. Yes, they'd managed to open the trade there. A man named James Kip had started it. Pretty good trade. But some of the tribes, after holding aloof so long, had gone abruptly to the other extreme. They had become drunkards.

"Yo' kin trade a man's squaw away from him eff'n he wants likker," said Bill.

These men had never had much use for the Blackfeet,

but it was evident that they entertained a sentimental regret. It was only part and parcel of the old-timer's nostalgia for the "good old days"; possibly a lingering respect for foemen who had been worthy of their metal. They and their kind alone retained the remnants of human friendly feeling for the Indian. The present type of plainsman looked upon the red man as completely alien. They used him, made their profit from him, despised him, fought him wherever they found him and whenever no reason of self-interest softened temporarily their policy. Indians were not people; they were a type of wild beast. Nobody made any serious effort to understand them.

"Now you take old Standin' Hoss. You remember that Crow, Standin' Hoss? I allus got on fine with him. One time when I was trappin' over on the Little Fork I got stole blind of my hosses, only had two left. It made me kinda mad, but I was keerless like, and got what was comin' to me. A'ter about two months I moseyed over to make a visit at Standin' Hoss's village, and dang if thar warn't my hosses, big as life! I rubbed my eyes and took another look, fer me and the Crows had allus been good friends. I tackled Standin' Hoss *pronto*.

"'Ain't them my hosses I see over thar?' I asks him. He didn't make no bones about it.

"'Yes,' sez he, 'they're yores. We stole them.'

"'Why in blazes did you do that to me?' sez I.

"'We had been walking a long time,' sez he. 'We were tired of walking. If we had gone to your camp you would have given me tobacco, for I am your friend. But tobacco would not carry me. So I had to steal them. When I stole them they were very thin. Now they are fat. I have now plenty of horses. Take yours and as many more as you want.'

"Kin you beat that—excep' from an Injun? He thought he was all right and friendly. So did I, becuz I knowed Injuns. But these new men on the plains would have been hostile, and probably started shootin' or actin' up or somethin'. It *was* aggravatin'. I had to *cache* my fur and go back a'ter it. But I knowed Injuns, so I let it go; and old Standin' Hoss and I are still friends. But these fellers don't know Injuns. And it's gittin' wuss fast."

"They got a smoke boat comin' up the Missouri now," put in Dawson, "two-decker, name the *Yallerstone.* I don't know how fur up she goes, but I've seen her as fur as Fort Union. She helped a lot to make the Injuns think Americans is better than Britishers. They ain't got no steamboat!"

The old rivalry between the Hudson's Bay Company and the Americans was still alive. Andy heard some familiar names, but some that were new to him. Jim Bridger had halfway joined up with the American Fur Company after the old Rocky Mountain disbanded; at least he was, in company with Vasquez, acting as professional hunter for some of the forts. Old Fitzpatrick—Bad Hand—was guiding: they say he sure makes the greenhorns toe a mark! Kit Carson had growed into quite a feller. He had become a great Injun man: spent a lot of time in Taos. Mackenzie? Mackenzie was out. Dawson and Cummings looked at one another and laughed.

"What's the joke?" asked Andy. "I never cared much for Mackenzie; but he was a good company man."

"I expect so," admitted Bill reluctantly, "but I got no use for him. Too much foofaraw."

"Wore a uniform all the time," interpolated Jack.

"Hear what he said when somebody came in to report an Injun attack on one of his companies? 'Any losses?' he asks. The scout sez no, no men killed; but they had run off the hosses! 'Damn the men!' sez Mackenzie. 'Eff'n the hosses had been saved, that would have amounted to somethin'!'"

"Funny thing, though," submitted Jack, "a lot of his men swore by him."

"Well, anyways," Bill resumed, "he was an enterprising cuss. Bill Sublette and Bob Campbell was gittin' likker by and up in the Injun kentry. It was easier fur them than fur the big company becuz they was movable and hadn't no forts and such for the gov'ment to keep track of. Then Mackenzie had a bright idee. The law reads that you kain't *bring* no likker into the Injun kentry: but, Mac thought, it didn't say nothin' against makin' it thar. So he starts him a distillery at Fort Union. He was as tickled with it as a dog with two tails. Actually showed it to Wyeth and Cerré when they stopped thar on their way down river. Cerré was head man for this yere Captain Bonneville that sent Joe Walker out yere a few years ago. He tuk 'em around and showed 'em everything. You wouldn't know Fort Union now, Andy."

"I never did know it," said Andy.

"Wall, she's quite a place. Mackenzie started cornfields, and has milk and cheese, and makes wine. Then when Wyeth got down river he told about the distillery, and the gov'ment pounced on the company, and the company had to let Mackenzie out."

"Why did Wyeth do that?"

"Don'no," said Bill carelessly. "Some says becuz he was a blue nose—he come from New England, you know. Some sez he tried to buy some supplies and Mackenzie charged him four prices. Somethin' like that."

It occurred to none of the three that mere trade rivalry could be a sufficient motive. They shook their heads and dismissed Mackenzie from their minds.

But the mention of Fort Union set them off on another track. A curious new type of people came occasionally into the country and stopped generally at one of the company's forts. They were queer people, having, as far as the mountain men could see, no sane excuse for existence, harmless enough, sometimes likable enough, but either childish or *loco*.

"They was two on 'em that put in their whole time shootin' dicky birds with leety-bit fine shot. They wouldn't even look up for a buffalo or an ellick or a deer or ary other thing worth while. A'ter the fust, they didn't even bother with the good-size birds, but chased around lookin' fer leetle ones."

"What did they want of them; did they say?" asked Andy.

"They take their skins. And," admitted Bill, "they shore were good at that; even hummin' birds."

"Foofaraw, for the women to wear on their hats?" suggested Andy.

Bill shook his head.

"No, they said they was jist collectin'. And they used to lie on their stummick and watch 'em by the hour."

Bill and Jack, both, evidently looked upon these antics with contempt. Andy's slightly wider contacts gave him a little better understanding; but not much better. Only when, in after years, he accidentally happened upon the works of Townsend and Nuttall did he fully appreciate what it was all about.

But the ornithologists were not the whole of it by any means. Others with strange and specialized interests came up river on the *Yellowstone;* men who drew pictures or grubbed around among rocks or—more understandably— came simply to shoot game. One year appeared a formidable expedition that combined everything. It had a man who drew pictures, mostly of Indians; it collected every bit of Indian junk it could lay its hands on; it snooped around in the most incomprehensible fashion; and it was mostly "Dutch," with a feller who was some kind of a big bug bossing the show. So came to Andy the first rumors of the famous visit of Maximilian of Wied to the western plains, though he never did happen across the sumptuous illustrated volumes in which the prince recorded his experience. All these people lived in the company's forts, and were well guarded, and taken out on a leash, as it were. They'd git gobbled and sculped in no time at all if they were to be allowed fifty miles from shelter.

"I tell you the Injuns is *bad*," Cummings repeated, "and an outfit like that is easy pickin's. Much as even a good mountain man kin do to git around hisself, let alone trail a lot of greenhorns with him."

Wagon trains—that was a little different. At least they were numerous and armed; and a good man, who knew how to impose discipline, could get them through.

"At that there's a many burned and massacreed," remarked Bill. "Bad part is, they's the women and the children."

Nevertheless more and more were heading over through South Pass. The Oregon Trail was widening as the ruts grew deeper and had to be abandoned. What did the White Eagle—McLaughlin, the Hudson's Bay factor up there in Oregon—think of this tide of immigration? The mountain men shook their heads: they did not know. There was some kind of a row on about it.

These bull-pushers were a dumb enough lot at taking care of themselves; but, the mountain men admitted, they could perform the impossible when it came to getting wheeled vehicles across country. Each had his experience to relate of ingenuity and dogged persistence in this respect. Rivers to cross; wagons let down steep banks by ropes; teams doubled or quadrupled; trees and brush cut and carried from great distances to assure footing, or to construct rafts; the wagons dismantled, their bodies caulked, covered with hides, and floated as boats, while the animals swam; three hours to pass an insignificant stream, two days or more a sizable river. And in the hills nothing stopped them finally. There was always a way. Sometimes the wagons were dismantled, carried piecemeal, reassembled. The animals were lowered by ropes.

Sometimes they had to lighten up a lot. The Trail was slowly becoming landmarked by wagons that must be abandoned so that the remainder could be brought through. And superfluities brought by inexperience.

"I seen a pile of bacon and flour higher'n my head," said Cummings. "Had a sign on her. 'This is clean; help yourself.' Injuns hadn't touched her. Skeered of poison."

Difficulties of water; difficulties with the cattle; unexpected and dismaying difficulties that a man would not naturally foresee. The arid heat shrunk the wagons so that the tires came off, the very spokes of the wheels dropped out.

"They fixed 'em," said Cummings briefly. "Only thing was, it all made 'em jumpy. Git up a fight over nothin' at all. They kain't stand grief that way like a mountain man. If yo're guidin' 'em you got to watch every minute. They're always wantin' to split up. Sometimes they do. Then, ginerally, it's all over. And when it comes to an Injun raid! 'My gun's got wet!' 'I done broke my ramrod!' 'I've spilled my caps all out!' 'Jehosaphat! I done got the ball in afore the powder!' 'Charge 'em boys!' 'Fire on 'em!' 'Reserve yore fire!' 'Yere, you take my gun; you can run her better'n I can!' Sounds like a flock of geese. And run around, from one place to another whereever anybody thinks he sees an Injun. Eff'n it warn't for a few cool old hands you kin pick out, the Injuns would run right over them. But Injuns is *sabe* that way, and know when somebody's in charge." He spat into the fire and filled his pipe. "Ary wagons got to Californy yet?" he queried.

"No; nor won't unless they come from Oregon or Santa Fe," said Andy.

"No? Why not?"

"No wheels will cross the Sierra," said Andy.

"I bet you they do," said Bill.

They fell silent, staring into the last embers of the fire.

They glowed dull orange. Occasionaly little flames leaped singly from the coals, as though to take a look, and dropped back again, satisfied. Overhead, in the branches of the oak trees, a bird muttered a sleepy twitter of protest against such late hours.

"Jim Bridger got that arrowhead dug out of the gristle of his back," Bill remarked after a while. And then, after another long interval, "Preacher done it, name o' Whitman."

3

Andy saw his guests bestowed, then returned, as a good Californian, to extinguish the last coals of the fire. For a moment, after he had finished his little task, he stood enjoying the quiet of the night. It seemed to him that never had he known such complete suspension, such absolute stillness, such profound repose. He stood looking east. Already the hilltops had more sharply defined themselves against the coming of the new day. His imagination had been stirred by the talk of the evening, roused to the immense turmoil and vitality of the plains. Standing here, he felt himself a part of a remote world, of a settled order of things which had long endured and must so continue as it had always been, quiet, charming, peaceful, friendly, constituted of the grace of life. Like the sheltered bay at Monterey, where the lazy, slow-pulsing wavelets crept up the sands and receded with a sigh of contentment. He saw it vividly in his mind's eye, and the slow-sailing pelicans, and the warm quieting gold of the sunlight like an infusion in the blue sky. And in his mind's ear the stern thunder of the distant surf beyond the barrier. He raised his head, startled. For the flash of a moment the analogy completed itself. He seemed to catch the faint far menace of another tide rising against the age-old barrier to the east. As he listened it died. The night resumed the serenity of its peace.

CHAPTER VII

CUMMINGS and Dawson finished their visit and disappeared. The impression faded in the resumption of the busy, charming, carefree life of the *rancho*. No uneasiness of change could long persist against the settled and immemorial quality of tradition. Spanish-American civilization on the Pacific Coast was actually less than a hundred years old, but its impression was of a ripe permanence derived from many centuries. That illusion, if illusion it be, is even today peculiar to the country. California's time ratio differs from that of the rest of the world. It is a cross section of history, passing in a single century, without haste, without abridgments, without omissions, through the phases of a social evolution that in other countries has taken a thousand years. Today the buildings of the missions stand monument to a venerable antiquity comparable to that which invests the great cathedrals of the Middle Ages. Yet many an unremarked New England farmhouse had been standing for generations before their first stone was laid.

It was, in a way, a curious double-consciousness of time. For though each era—that of discovery, of conquest, of the nomadic, of pioneering, of the pastoral, and so on into the agricultural and finally the modern—was destined to develop and flower and pass within the memory of two long-lived generations, each possessed in its own consciousness that due sense of space and dignity of permanence necessary to its ripening. So now this pastoral interlude seemed, to those carrying it forward, borne in the current of uncounted years. If change it must, that

change was destined in a future so remote that its outlines
were obscure.

Nevertheless, in the paradox of time ratio, the years
sped fast. And pleasantly. Andy's property increased.
Sometimes he remembered with a smile one of the old
daydreams of his early years, a projection of his boy's
imagination stirred by his first approach, after the terrible
crossing of the Cimarron, to the unknown romance of
old Santa Fe. The details arose vividly from his subconscious. For a brief interval, under the spell of that
little devil Estrellita, he had in fancy shamelessly abandoned his companions, the mountain men. He had seen
himself in velvet and linen and silver lace riding gravely
a coal-black steed, and people bowing to him and respectfully greeting him as Don Americano, the wealthy *hidalgo*; and an adobe mansion with roses; and *peónes* running to hold his stirrup; and an interior, polished, simple,
and richly dim, where a girl waited; and an atmosphere of
grave, worshipful, very Spanish dignity of which Don
Andrew, the *americano*, was the center, with, he remembered, clipped side whiskers down the cheek. Andy grinned
at the picture. It had not lasted long. It had faded in the
wild years. Now it returned. And it was not so far off after
all. The details had pretty well fulfilled themselves—except for the side whiskers which he had sacrificed at the
time he had cut his hair.

Life was varied enough, in spite of its basic simplicity.
The cattle, the flour mill, the wine-making, a hundred
small activities. The routine plentifully and pleasantly
broken. Visits to the *hacienda* that lasted a week or more.
Anniversaries and *fiestas* of all kinds. Excursions to Monterey on business that were made to include many pleasures. He and Carmel, and Ramón and Conchita, enjoyed
themselves thoroughly. They celebrated Holy Week with
a grand mixture of churchgoing and merrymaking, ending
with a solemn procession from the *cuartel* to the plaza

escorting a cart in which was a ridiculous effigy of Judas bound. Soldiers escorted him. The bystanders hooted him and pelted him with pebbles and handfuls of dry adobe. He was propped up below a gibbet and lectured at by sundry *magníficos* who accused him of all sorts of things, including the robbing of hen roosts, stealing old clothes, and cheating at cards. At the close of the lecture he was solemnly asked if he had anything to say in his defense. The populace waited, breathless; but as, naturally, Judas remained silent, judgment was delivered against him. He was hanged on the gibbet. The soldiers delivered one disciplined volley into his body at command; after which they fired at will. There was for this purpose never lack of powder and ball. They popped away, to their own huge delight and that of the bystanders. Soon there was no more Judas. The concourse attended Mass and then scattered to its pleasure. The *gente de razón* danced, and the men and women sought opportunities undetected to break *cascarones*—eggshells filled with gilt confetti or cologne—over one another's heads. The maneuvers to this end were very spirited. Andy created a laughing furore by seizing and soundly kissing his assailants, which was decidedly a rather scandalous innovation. Andy was no longer *serio*.

Christmas was a more decorous festival, with a good deal of church in it, and the giving of presents, and feasts at which one partook of an especial delicacy made at no other time, a round cake something like a doughnut, called a *buenuelero*. These two festivals, and Santos Inocentes, were the big events of the year. The latter was great fun, a sort of combined April fool and game of forfeits. Anyone who could be beguiled into lending anyone anything must redeem the article on the borrower's terms. The more unlikely or difficult the object borrowed, the greater the triumph. Conchita and Carmel carried off the honors, the one by borrowing money of a broker, the other his own rosary from a priest. There were innumerable more personal gatherings, weddings, christenings, or the like. Carmel's sister, Faquita, revised her announced determination to become a nun and was married to Carlos Lugo. Andy was astonished to realize she had grown up. Ramón and Conchita moved to a *rancho* of their own on the Jolón plateau. There were always new babies.

They returned to the *rancho* and its work and its simple pleasures very much refreshed.

Djo learned to shoot. This was considered a quaint and useless accomplishment by everybody but Andy. He began with the old Boone gun rested over a stump. But shortly one of the Boston ships brought a little rifle ordered long before by Andy from Ike Hawkens in St. Louis, an exact replica in miniature of the weapons then in use on the great plains. It was a beautiful piece of work and may still be seen in a private collection of arms. Djo became a very good rifle shot and did considerable execution among the ground squirrels and jack rabbits. These were available at all months of the year, for they were pests; but Andy taught Djo that serious game, except in necessity, should be sought only in the hunting moons. Djo was still too small to go afield alone; but when autumn came he and his father did considerable sneaking about after the band-tail pigeons that swarmed to the ripened acorns. These were good to eat, and a triumph to bring down. Some day, Andy promised, he would take Djo to the higher country to shoot a buck. That time, Andy determined, should be when Djo was big enough to handle the Boone gun. His own little rifle was too light for heavy game, except in the hands of an expert. The balls ran some hundred and twenty to the pound. Andy had a strong aversion to wounding animals, which was a curious sentiment in that day and age.

hanow the one by burrowing money of a broker, the other
his own roster, from a prince. There were innumerable

2

Andy had become a pretty good *californio*. His attitude
toward the internal politics of the time was that of his
neighbors. A few, like Alvarado and Vallejo, took things
seriously; and occasionally these managed to get the
country stirred up to some kind of half-action. But the
ranchos and *haciendas* were remote and withdrawn from
such things. They could not scare up any real interest.
Indeed half the time they did not learn the news until
weeks or months after the event, and then probably in
garbled form. A lot of things happened; but somehow
they seemed to have no intimate, no vital concern, though
they were interesting to talk about and sometimes gratifying to learn.

Thus Andy's Monterey friend, Alvarado, had fulfilled
Don Sylvestre's joking prediction and become governor.
Mexico had at last gone a little too far; made the mistake
that gave Alvarado his excuse. After Figueroa's death
she sent as his successor a most peculiar individual named
Mariano Chico. He was a queer little man, wore goggles,
spent a lot of his time grubbing among flowers, from which
he invented remedies for what he supposed were his ailments. He had strong political views as to Mexico's
powers; was a martinet; and extremely punctilious of his
personal dignity. These things need not have mattered;
California had seen much worse. But Chico's contempt
—or indifference—to California society finally permitted
him to appear at a formal Monterey dance with his
mistress, Doña Cruz. Now nobody cared that Chico had
brought with him a mistress, though mistresses were
against the California idea; and nobody did more than
shrug the shoulder when the fair lady proved complaisant
to many. But to attempt to force her on formal society
was too much. Doña Cruz was a vivid and vulgar creature.
She brought with her to the ball as companion a local

light o' love. The assembly promptly dissolved. There
were indignation meetings that became more indignant
the more they talked about it. Even Chico's pig-headed
arrogance became alarmed. He sent messengers to the
military commanders, Vallejo and Portilla, summoning
the troops. Both sent back polite messages to the effect
that they were fighting Indians and could not come,
though the students of documents can find none recording any such troubles at that time. Matters became more
threatening. The *caballeros* of Monterey were highly in-
censed over this insult to their ladies. Alvarado smiled
sardonically at this sudden ebullition over a social error
succeeding the bland indifference to crying injustice; but
he seized the occasion. He managed to scare Chico into
what amounted to abdication. The governor took ship
—with Doña Cruz—with the announced intention of
seeking reinforcements in Mexico. His departure was as
peculiar as his administration. On the beach, before the
grim and silent assemblage of *caballeros*, he embraced
Alvadaro and presented him with a recipe for a cure-all;
but as he set foot in the small boat he turned a contorted
face on the *político*.

"May crows peck your eyes out!" he yelled.

He bowed ceremonially to the *caballeros;* then rushed
forward to kiss a wrinkled old Indian squaw, shouting:

"I thus take leave of the best man in California!"

"May I never set eyes upon this accursed land again!"
he snarled at them; and yet, after he had gone, it was discovered that he had left a fine gold watch to be regulated,
"pending my return."

His next in command was Nicolás Gutierrez who,
naturally, took over as acting governor until Chico's return, or until his successor was appointed. Nicolás was a
Californian, and was well liked as a *hacendado*. He was
a stout man of light complexion and reddish hair, wearing
a long beard sprinkled with gray. A peculiar cast in his

right eye gave him the nickname of El Tuerto. On his
rancho he lived a grand, devil-may-care, bibulous, roaring,
hospitable life that he thoroughly enjoyed and that was
but mildly deprecated, for Nicolás was a jolly soul. Chico
had made him a military commandant, much against his
inclination. He had no use for public office. Responsibility
too much interfered with wine, women, and song. In
office his foibles became scandals. His habit of having
his own way with his own became petty tyranny. The
situation was made to order for Alvarado's adroitness.
The *político* had not long to wait for Gutierrez to supply
him with an excuse. Any excuse would do, if it were a good
enough talking point. In no time Gutierrez had tangled
himself up in a row about revenue. Alvarado rode the
country preaching his slogan, California for Californians.
He was disappointed in his hope of immediate support
by Vallejo. Vallejo, with his usual caution, held off. He
waited to see how the cat would jump. Vallejo has been
criticized for this invariable policy, especially later at
the time of the American conquest. The criticism is un-
just. Vallejo followed, to be sure; but his country and
his countrymen were near to his heart, and his wider
vision showed him that it is sometimes better to work
with than against the forces of the inevitable. Be that as
it may, Alvarado came back alone to San José. There he
managed to collect just thirteen enthusiasts, and with this
army he marched toward Monterey!

But Alvarado's political acumen was sound. The hour
had struck. Others joined him en route. Among them, you
may be sure, was Ramón Rivera, joyous at the prospect
of "essport." By the time he had reached the outskirts of
Monterey he had with him seventy-five young *rancheros*,
animated, it is to be feared, less by burning patriotism
than desire for a lark. There they were joined by Isaac
Graham and the miscellaneous lot of Americans, Indians,
and Mexican renegades that hung around his distillery.

This was an unexpected pleasure. They too had turned out for what fun there might be in it.

It was a wonderful army. The Californians were armed with lances and a few old muskets. With Isaac Graham were six American hunters, useful men with the rifle. The rest of the lot, to the number of about thirty, were sailors of all nationalities. These were armed, but not one of them could be relied upon to hit a barn from the inside. On the other hand the army was plentifully supplied with fifes and drums from the mission of San José. Also they had a cannon. The only drawback to that was that there was only one cannon ball, and no one knew anything whatever about cannons. On the other side Gutierrez had a large force of soldiers behind the walls of the *presidio* which was defended by artillery, some of it in a moderate state of efficiency.

Nevertheless the revolutionists entered into the affair zestfully. There was any number of bright ideas. They were carried out with enthusiasm. They marched and countermarched across open spaces—at a safe distance—to give an impression of numbers. They primed Indians to pass the word from mouth to mouth that this was just the advance guard of a force under Vallejo. Nothing like a good rumor or so. They mounted their lone cannon conspicuously. Alvarado and Ramón and Castro and Buelna and Noriega and some others put their heads together to compose a satisfactorily high-sounding *pronunciamiento* of the sort dear to the Latin soul, which they caused to be delivered to Gutierrez under a flag of truce. The messenger put on all the dog he could invent. Envoys were sent to the ships in harbor, soliciting support. The American captains were favorably inclined: their commercial interests were with the Californians. Steele of the *Caroline* and French of the *Europe* contributed powder and ball. Hinkley of the *Don Quixote* furnished no ammunition, but he sent a band of music. That helped. Also a dozen bottles of brandy. The besiegers were about to consume the latter, but Francisco Soto, a citizen of the town, had a better idea, so the drinkables were laid aside for the moment.

All this took time. About dark the leaders woke up to the fact that no reply had been received to the *pronunciamiento*. After earnest consultation it was resolved to stir matters up a bit with the cannon ball. A gentleman named Pina was confident he could get results, as he knew where there was a book on artillery practice. They gave him fifteen minutes to read up. Pina must have been a good student, for he managed to hit the commandant's house. Almost immediately came a note from Gutierrez. It was rather pathetic. He wrote that he had never wanted the command; that it had been forced on him; and he had no desire to fight; but that now Alvarado was using force he would have to stay with it. Which might be considered as the end of round one.

The "siege" lasted until midnight. The investing army took the affair light-heartedly; as why not? They could go home any time they did not like it. In the meantime they did various pranks as occurred to them; so that Gutierrez, sitting in continuous council with his officers, was the recipient of various and alarming reports. The enemy was being constantly reinforced; it was mounting two more cannon; the ships in the harbor were landing their crews to help the attack. None of these was true; merely the exuberant youngsters were staging various shows of countermarching, of log dummies and of boats. However, the actual and provable news from within was not so good. The soldiers were deserting. The wily Francisco Soto was busy with the twelve bottles of brandy he had insisted on saving. As soon as he had a deserter drunk enough and impressed enough and scared enough, he turned him back into the *presidio* to spread the glad tidings. Part of this treatment was a glimpse of Isaac Graham, who was rapidly becoming drunk and disorderly. When drunk, Ike roared. By nine o'clock twenty-nine soldiers had deserted. There were only thirty-five left, and they were strongly for surrender. At midnight Gutierrez gave in. The show was over; except that Isaac Graham was, as the chronicler has it, "turbulent and had to be restrained." Gutierrez followed Chico back to Mexico, together with some seventy others.

All these things Ramón told Andy later with great gusto and laughter.

"But it should be that you were there, *valedor!*" he lamented. "So soon as I hear I send here a message to Fol-ded Heels."

"I know," said Andy regretfully. "I was off after wild horses over in the valley. I'd like to have been there."

Then they both proceeded to forget about it. That was settled. Andy was glad Alvarado had achieved his ambition. From time to time he listened to garbled news from visitors and neighbors that led him to believe his friend was not having too easy a time. He was sorry for that, but it was none of his immediate concern. According to the best informed it was the south again. They pretended to believe Carlos Carrillo had an appointment from Mexico. But there was some mix-up. Alvarado had gone south with Castro and considerable of a force. Some said the *político* was trying to set up California as a state independent of Mexico; others that Mexico had appointed him as soon as she had found out what kind of a fellow was Carlos Carrillo. What was the matter with Carlos? Nothing: nothing at all as a man, they hastened to tell him. But he listened to the one who was near him. Juan Bandini and those of *la otra banda* twisted him as they pleased. The first thing he did was to name Los Angeles as the capital! When Alvarado went south they did their best to keep Carlos away from him. There were a few cannon fired at long range. A valuable mule was killed. The appointment of Carlos was forged—it did not have a proper

seal—it was signed by the wrong official—no one had seen
it: thus came to him the various "stalls" by which Alvarado avoided recognizing the authority of Carlos until
his own agents in Mexico should get results. The record
of intrigue and counter-intrigue; of excursions south
and excursions north; of conference and disruption—was
too much for Andy even to attempt to follow. He knew
that Alvarado finally won out, and was formally appointed as governor, and was glad. He liked the *político*
and admired his advanced and enlightened ideas.

But Alvarado, whatever his enlightenment or his intentions, had no chance. He was kept much too busy by
the upflame of small jealousies and ambitions. He sometimes wished the south would sink into the sea. Apparently they had much more time and inclination for
politics than the north. Perhaps even then there was
something in the climate! They were always, led by that
pest Juan Bandini, thinking up new grievances and conspiracies and proceeding to intrigue together to the most
astonishing results. They seemed to think of everything;
but when it came to the show-down they were none too
bold. Carlos Carrillo was enthusiastic for one or the other,
depending on whom he had seen last. Alvarado kept Castro
for a time at Santa Barbara, which the great personal
influence of Señor Noriega kept neutral or for the constituted government of the north. On several occasions
he had to go south himself, and there were alarums and
excursions and a "battle" or so in which were one or two
unfortunate accidents, so that some of the more careful
parents began to feel the sport was becoming unnecessar-
ily dangerous. But some of the more spirited took foolish
chances. The ranges were extreme and the powder of a
very low quality. It was considered sporting to try to
stop the cannon balls with the hands as they rolled somno-
lently across the terrain.

Then too the business of the missions had come to its

crisis. Alvarado was, on the whole, friendly to the missions. But his hands were tied by Mexico's policy toward them; and under cover of the petty squabbles just described, the grafters, who had at last appeared, were very busy.

Under the scheme each mission had appointed over it a civil administrator. Immediately he had taken possession, one half of all the horses, cattle, sheep, or other animals were at once distributed to the Indians. Which finished that much, and very promptly; for few knew the value of what they received, and fewer still cared to keep it. They sold out to the first man who came along at the first price he offered. Then the most of them wandered off into the hills. That much damage was inevitable, whether the appointed administrator was honest—as many were—or out for his own, as in the majority of cases. Some of them were pretty bad. Strutting in Mexican pomposity, they ousted the *padres* from the rooms they had always occupied, and themselves took over all authority. Everything portable gradually disappeared. Cattle were slaughtered "to pay expenses" and "to meet the demands of the government." Cattle in great numbers were "lent" to friends, of which few were ever repaid. The *padres* themselves, in self-defense, turned their remaining wealth, as far as they could do so, into money, which they concealed beneath the tilings. It had long been the accepted custom that the missions, on demand, supply provisions for the troops. Now many of these requisitions must be denied on the plea of poverty; they could hardly feed their own Indians, said they, and that denial furnished excuse for added oppression, if the civil administrator was unfriendly. Most of the Indians disappeared as soon as they had received their one half; of those who remained, who came back after squandering their shares, the great majority were intractable, mutinous against discipline. The gardens fell into neglect. The surrounding walls, the very buildings, their upkeep withdrawn, crumbled. The construction material of adobe bricks, together with the violence of the winter rains, lent aid to California's speeded time ratio; so that swiftly the missions became venerable as with the weight of centuries, and so took on the ruin of remote antiquity. Their former grandeur, actually less than a decade past, moved sighing through their decaying and grass-grown corridors almost as a tradition.

Such was the picture at its worst and at its ultimate. But the change came to some more quickly than to others. Not all of the administrators were dishonest or indifferent; not all of the friars took it lying down. Even after such important missions as San Miguel, San Luis Obispo, San Diego had been wholly abandoned, even after nine others had been almost wholly destroyed, a few, like San Fernando, Santa Barbara, San Buenaventura, Santa Ynez, managed to hang on, to function moderately well equipped. But the institution, in its glory, had perished. By the time Alvarado had extricated himself from the maze of intrigues and petty revolutions that occupied all his attention until 1839, it was too late. He then appointed an American, Hartnell, as *visitador*, with authority over the various administrators as a body. Hartnell made a tour of what was left; then resigned. Matters had gone too far; the case was hopeless.

It is interesting to know that in all these years of mutiny and desertion, of destruction and pillage, wherein the Indians were allowed to run wild, there is no instance on record of the killing, or even an attack, on any of the *padres.*

3

The passing of so long established an institution was a dramatic enough revolution in the social structure, it might be presumed. It was certainly a change of enormous significance; what would seem an arresting symptom of movement away from a settled order of things. Yet it took place almost unremarked. Those in the center of affairs, like Alvarado and Vallejo and Castro, were fully occupied by the small *opéra-bouffe* conspiracies and revolutions that delighted the idle and the politically minded dilettantes of the *pueblos*. In addition the revolt of Texas and its ultimate winning to independence as the Lone Star State altered the whole situation as to California's policy in respect to foreigners. What to do about them? The sentiment as to the slowly increasing numbers of immigrants had been, on the whole, if not of welcome, at least of tolerant friendliness; provided, of course, the newcomers were apparently of good character. A Swiss named John Sutter had charmed Alvarado with his pretensions and his evident ability; and had been granted much land; and had built himself a fort on the American River; and had so rapidly established his power that the Mexican government began to make inquiries. The place was becoming a rendezvous for wandering hunters and trappers, whom he kept with him without price. At times he showed his teeth in almost open defiance. Matters adjusted themselves for the moment; but Alvarado and Vallejo remembered Texas.

It was all very puzzling and alarming to the few who could see. Alvarado began to break a little under the strain of it. He caused the arrest of Isaac Graham and the miscellaneous lot that had gradually collected about that worthy and his still at Natividad. It was reported to him that Graham was about to stage an "uprising of American settlers," which is doubtful. Alvarado took pains to specify that no one was to be arrested who "had passports or who were married to native women or who were honest and regular in their mode of life"; which was fair enough. Unfortunately for him there happened to be in Monterey at that time an individual of a type familiar enough in our modern politics but strange to the simple *californios*. His name was Farnham, and he was an expert at viewing with alarm. No one knows who had stepped on his toes; nor how hard; but it is obvious in time's perspective that his grouch was personal. He followed the deported "Grahamites" to Tepic, where they had been banished, and there managed to interest the British consul in their behalf. Twenty-six were forever excluded from Mexican territory; but Graham himself, and a score of his fellows, were permitted to return to Monterey and the still. Farnham then went home, where he published a book. Since at that time California was as remote from the world as Mars, he felt he could say what he wished without danger of being checked. So he left us a caricature of Castro and the Dastardly Spanish Tyrant that contrasts nicely with that of the haloed and sainted Graham and his gang. He incidentally describes taking part in a grand buffalo hunt in the Sacramento Valley as a sort of check or control on his general veracity. All of which helped.

Andy Burnett, at Folded Hills, knew very little of all this; and cared less. He had laughingly resisted Ramón's importunities to join one of the numerous expeditions to the south. Undoubtedly it would be good "essport"; but he was too busy at home. He chuckled over the deportation of Isaac Graham and his crew. He knew Ike's type very well; he would not want a better man to back him in the mountains or the plains. But for some years now Graham had been in a different business that gathered all the idle renegades to itself. Andy would not himself have liked that crew as neighbors; he could hardly blame Alvarado for wanting to get rid of them. Not that the "Grahamites" were a wholly bad lot, by any means. They were idle; and drink was handy. Graham when sober was inclined to be reticent and quiet, hospitable and industrious. But with the drink in him he was loud-mouthed,

unprincipled, profligate and reckless. In other words, he
was neither the Noble American Pioneer of some, nor the
Drunken Desperado of others; but a typical frontiersman,
out of place for the moment. Shift of scene would probably
do old Ike good, thought Andy. But when Farnham's
efforts resulted in Graham's return, Andy sympathized
sardonically with Alvarado. He heard of Sutter and
his fort and his other activities, of course; and intended
to ride over there some day and make Sutter's acquaintance and see for himself. But New Helvetia was a long
distance, occupying in men's mental feeling of travel
about what an excursion to New York would represent
now to a Californian.

Naturally he was, like his fellow *rancheros*, aware of the
decline of the missions. Like them he regretted the fact.
Like them, also, he speculated as to whether something
should not be done about it. He was even a trifle indignant
at some of the rumors. But again like them, he failed to
see the picture as a whole. Once more intervened the element of remoteness, of the isolated instance. He, like all
the others, was unaware of change. The surface of the
waters was as placid as ever; but the tranquillity was no
longer that of calm, but of a current smoothed by the
gathering haste of its movement toward the cataract.

4

His nearest touch with such matters was through his
brief contacts with Alvarado on his occasional visits to
Monterey. He liked Alvarado as he remembered him before the governor had reached his ambition. Now he had
sadly to admit that the *político* had changed. His suavity
of manner had vanished; he had become querulous, given
to violent explosions of resentment; suspicious; vacillat-
ing. He had taken to drinking heavily. His appearance
had deteriorated. His health was bad. He complained

bitterly of people and of matters of which Andy had never heard. Andy could not make head or tail of it all. Especially did Alvarado inveigh against the increasing number of foreigners, threatening the most drastic measures—which, however, he did not carry out. Apparently he had forgotten his earlier views. He raged at times against Vallejo, whom he stigmatized as a traitor bent on thwarting him. Indeed, about this time Vallejo departed for a brief period from his usual common sense and attempted, in his capacity of commander, a formal and rigid military discipline quite out of character with the California spirit. To the troops, Alvarado and Castro had always been Juanito and José. The guardhouses became crowded. Castillero was snubbed for approaching the commander too informally. An officer was overheard commenting on this to a citizen. The officer was ordered arrested; the citizen was sued. Castro himself was arrested for not arresting the officer. Guerra was ordered to the command of Santa Barbara. He begged off on the plea of ill health. Vallejo ordered him into custody for refusing, informing him that his duty was to obey without question, and then to petition for relief in due form. Some were angry; some were merely amused. Vallejo was probably merely taking his appointment too literally; had been reading up on the old Spanish discipline. It was not like him; it was a single-mindedness; it passed. There was a great party at Guerra's house, and everybody shook hands, and Vallejo handsomely admitted that Spanish discipline would not work in an army of unpaid relatives. He returned to Sonoma, and Castro resumed command, and all was well. But he carried with him a contempt for his nephew's slack methods, so that thenceforth he and Alvarado were at cross-purposes. Shortly Alvarado married Martina Castro, but Castro was himself too ill to attend the wedding, and had to be represented at the ceremony by José Estrada.

Most of which was, naturally, quite over Andy's head. He knew nothing of the nagging harassments that had proved Alvarado's fiber to be not of the final heroic quality. He was sorry; and just a little contemptuous. Thomas Larkin merely shrugged his shoulders, when Andy asked him what it was all about, and talked of books. Andy returned to Folded Hills as into fresh air from the miasms of a swamp. It was grateful to be back with the old familiar and engrossing affairs of the *rancho*. Carmel, it seemed to him, was more beautiful than ever. Djo was taller than his mother; promised to be as tall as himself. His sister, Amata, had surprisingly ceased to be a baby. At times she startled Andy with a glimpse, just a brief glimpse, of a woman enfolded within the petals of childhood. As Faquita had been when first he had come to the *hacienda*. Faquita had children of her own, had become surprisingly the matron.

The *rancho*, after the swift California fashion, had taken on an air of settled age. It might have stood just so for a hundred years. Its habits and customs had acquired a mellowness as of immemorial tradition extending to far horizons. The horizons were of the future as well as of the past. The surface of the current still ran smooth.

ANDY'S most amusing connection with all this came about through the Micheltorena row. The bickering between Vallejo and Alvarado finally reached such a point that the governor was requested, or urged, or forced, or permitted to resign or retire. Micheltorena was sent from Mexico to take the place. So there they were, right back where they had started from!

Only now there were complications. Mexico had really never done anything for California. Now at last, most virtuously, she announced that she would fulfill her obligations. With Micheltorena was to be sent an army, of regular Mexican troops; a large army for the day and place. The *californios* could thenceforth rest comfortably. The increasing number of foreigners need no longer trouble them. The mother country was about to protect its own! Or even more ornate words to that effect.

This was good news to the Californians; especially to men of vision like Vallejo, who was constantly hammering away at the necessity for rebuilding and garrisoning the *presidios*. At this time Vallejo still cherished the possibility of independence from foreign rule.

This satisfaction lasted until they had taken one good look at the army. Most of the personnel were convicts, liberated from sentence for this purpose. There was a scattering, a leaven, of regulars; but, in the event, these proved to be worse than the convicts. Except for the officers, there was not a uniform among them. Indeed only a few boasted jackets; or even pantaloons. The sole garment of many was a blanket; and a ragged blanket at

98

that. Los Angeles, hopeful as ever that each new governor might designate her as the seat of government, was prepared to welcome this one with open arms. She drew an enormous sigh of relief when, at the end of some months, he and his army departed for Monterey. For once the north was welcome to be the capitol.

Poor Micheltorena! He was a decent soul. The people could not help liking him personally. But that army! It stole everything it could lay its hands on, much of the time purely as a matter of principle. The ragged rascals of *Erminie* had nothing on them! They took food, of course. At the mansion of José de la Guerra the cook left the kitchen for a moment, for a "mere wave of the hand," she said. When she returned the whole meal had vanished. They were very skillful with hook and line, by means of which they hauled in all sorts of clothing, chickens, even pots and pans and kettles—anything that could be hooked or entangled. Twelve of these *cholos*, as they were called by the Californians, were detailed as an especial guard of honor for a party given by Don Vicente Sanchez. By this time Micheltorena had wangled at least a few uniforms, and they made quite an imposing appearance. Don Vicente lost an entire chest of jewelry at that party.

It did no good to appeal to the officers. With a few exceptions they were almost as bad as the *cholos*. The honorable Lieutenant Arguado met a soldier concealing something bulky, under his *serape*, beneath which, however, projected the feet of a turkey.

"What have you there?" demanded the lieutenant.

"My bass viol," replied the soldier.

"This evening we will have music at my quarters," instructed the officer.

"*Sí, señor,*" agreed the disappointed *cholo*.

Micheltorena in despair tried to appoint a grizzled old veteran, a *californio*, the Colonel Garfias, as commander of a battalion. The colonel refused with a scornful laugh.

"They are a bad lot," he said bluntly. "Your very officers are a bad lot. If you send one of them to buy cigarettes, he will 'lose' the coin."

There were hold-ups at night, at the point of the sword. There were even a few murders, and rapes of Indian women or *mozas*, things unheard-of among the natives. The unrest of lawlessness was in the air. The Indians of the foothills resumed their forays on horses. Raiding excursions of Indians, Mexicans, and a few outlaw Americans crossed the deserts from Santa Fe to swoop down in short, swift dashes on the southern country, as far north as San Luis Obispo. They were pursued; but once they reached the Puerto del Cajón they were safe.

Micheltorena did what he could. Frequently he made good from his own pocket the thefts of the *cholos*. He was a pleasant man, with exquisite manners, who honestly liked his neighbors and meant well by them. He restored the missions to the care of the friars; which was a rather empty gesture in view of their condition. He tried to establish better schools. He even married the mistress he had brought with him from Mexico, as soon as he realized the local prejudice. Some of his bitterest critics thought him indolent. As a matter of fact he was clear-sighted and he was in despair. The Americans would surely fall heir to the country, he wrote Mexico, unless clothing and money and proper troops were forthcoming. He could, and would, die, he added; but that "would not restore a province worth four times Texas, the most precious part of the Mexican Republic."

Alvarado, aroused from his retirement, had no difficulty in collecting several hundred men at San José. The *rancheros* were indifferent to theoretical deprivations of political rights, which they did not understand; but they objected seriously to losing their chickens.

Andy rode up to San José because Ramón came over to get him. He was not much interested. In the remoteness

of Folded Hills these affairs were to him much of a muchness with all the rest of the squabbles of the past years.
He was astonished to find that the gathering considered itself an army, and that this was a revolution. He had not even brought the Boone gun; and he had brought Djo for the experience and the ride. Even yet he could not take the affair very seriously; though he tried to appear to do so for the sake of his friends, especially Castro and Alvarado, who were much excited. There was a great deal of dashing about and maneuvering and importance.
Micheltorena at the head of his forces was coming, was at hand. The revolutionists rode out from town to meet the enemy. Andy was puzzled; and a little annoyed at what he had been let in for. They gave him a lance and a musket, in neither of which he had the slightest confidence.
Ramón did not cease reproaching him.

"Always, always before, you take with you that accursed rifle of yours when it get you in trouble!" he lamented. "And now when you need heem, you leave heem home!"

Somehow Andy could not persuade himself that he would need him now, in spite of apparent evidence to the contrary. And he was right. After the forces had dashed around sufficiently, a meeting was arranged. Micheltorena agreed to send his *cholos* back to San Blas. After which a pleasant time was had by all; and in due course everybody went home.

2

But two months later Andy was awakened in the first part of the night by the incursion of a large body of horsemen. They were very much excited. The candles were lighted in the *sala*. The leaders, and as many more as the place would hold, crowded in. Alvarado was there, and Castro, and all the Rivera men, and Carlos Lugo and many another of Andy's acquaintance. For a time he could make nothing of the matter that brought them. Too many talked at once. Andy sensed that they were angry; deeply and thoroughly, with an anger quite different from the usual volatile and passing indignations of the Latin. He felt within himself a genuine stir of partisanship.

Don Andrés recalled without doubt the treaty made by this Micheltorena after the campaign of Santa Teresa?

Andy suppressed a smile at calling the picnic a campaign; but he remembered perfectly the treaty. It was that the governor was to get rid of his *cholos;* and everybody was to go home, was it not?

Exactly. Well, now this governor, by proclamation, had canceled the treaty. Was this to be a man of honor?

Andy shook his head. What reason did he give?

None. And more than this, he named them with whom he had treated—Andy among the rest—as revolutionists and traitors; and he was marching with an army to capture them; perhaps to send them to San Blas instead of his accursed *cholos.*

Andy's jaw set; but he made no comment except to ask what had caused Micheltorena's change of mind. At this question Alvarado, who had remained silent, burst into angry denunciation. He was confused, trembling with the weakness of his ill health; but his spirit flamed high. Andy tried to understand. He cast a glance of appeal toward Ramón, who, in apparent detachment, was leaning against the chimneypiece, a half-amused smile on his lips.

"Why, it is like this, *valedor,*" said he. "My cousin,"— he waved a negligent hand toward the fuming Alvarado— "when he was governor gave much land and many favors to this John Sutter who has made the fort and the *hacienda* up yonder; and now this same John Sutter goes to Micheltorena and says that he will help the governor to capture my cousin, and all us others. My cousin thinks this is ungrateful of John Sutter, and treacherous to one who has befriended him. And indeed, *valedor*, I think I agree with him."

"John Sutter promised Micheltorena that?" questioned Andy incredulously. "Are you certain? One should not trust what may be idle tales."

"We do not need to trust idle tales, *valedor*," replied Ramón silkily. "For no later than yesterday, at Salinas, this John Sutter and this governor joined themselves together. The governor had with him his *cholos*, and Isaac Graham and these worthless ones who drink his *aguardiente* at Natividad." Ramón smiled slightly, "That one need not wonder at: Isaac Graham has cause to thirst for the blood of my cousin. But John Sutter brought with him those many who have collected at his fort, and also one hundred Indians whom he has trained to be soldiers. I think," said Ramón judicially, "that even with the training of John Sutter these are not greatly to be feared. And the *cholos*"—Ramón shrugged. "But these others—these what you call men of the mountains—with their rifles—it is said there are more than a hundred." He shrugged again; and resumed his cigarette.

"This Sutter, who has called me friend!" burst in Alvarado. "He comes to me with nothing—nothing but his tongue and his grand manner. He seems to me *hidalgo*. He is educated; he talks Spanish, and besides that German, English, French. He comes with many letters from great men of the Hudson's Bay and the Russians and many others. He talks much of becoming a Mexican citizen; of guarding the eastern frontier. I give him a wide grant of land: I permit him to buy the arms and supplies of the Russians. I even make him a Mexican officer. He represents the government on the frontier of the Río Sacramento. I permit him to give *permisos* to those who come to him. And now how does he repay me?"

Andy shook his head, his mouth grim. He hated ingratitude and treachery.

"Why does he do it?" he inquired.

"More land," replied Alvarado bitterly. "He wants more land. From this governor he thinks to get it. That is all he thinks."

Andy pondered darkly.

"What do you do now?" he asked at last.

"We ride south," Ramón told him simply. "Here we are too few."

The room was still. No more word was said. All eyed Andy expectantly.

He raised his hand to the long rifle resting on its pegs above the fireplace.

"When do we start?" he asked.

They shouted and crowded about him. Ramón's eyes were shining.

3

They were off within the hour, for Salinas was not many leagues distant, and Micheltorena's forces must be soon upon their heels. It was a busy hour. Though none of the others seemed to be uneasy about their families and properties, Andy was not so sure. The Californians were wholly chivalrous in such matters; and, he was fair enough to admit, Micheltorena himself, and possibly Sutter, were above molesting noncombatants. He was not so certain that the Indians and the rougher elements among the backwoodsmen could be controlled. He summoned Panchito and Abel Means and gave them specific directions: Carmel and the children to go at once to the Rivera *hacienda;* the horses to be driven far back in the hills beyond easy requisition. There was not much else that could be done. After all, Folded Hills was well off the main route of the Camino Real; and if Micheltorena pressed the pursuit he would not be likely to indulge in side excursions.

Having disposed of these matters, he took leave of Carmel. To his surprise she accepted the matter calmly. Her chief lament was that he should consider it desirable to join the expedition at all. Why was he so suddenly interested in these politics? Andy did not explain. There was no use in unduly alarming her. Finding him determined, she accepted the situation.

"You will not take Djo?" she asked. "No? Possibly it is a little far for one so young. But it would be well sometime for him to see the south. The south is very beautiful. Once I made that journey as a girl. The Riveras have *parientes* in the south. You must see them, *amigo*. Ramón knows. And the Noriegas at Santa Barbara; them you must visit, and the Carrillos. You will like the Carrillos. Tell them that the little Carmelita remembers them well. If you were not going in such haste I would give you something to take to them. I shall be very lonely here without you, *amado*. You must think of me much. And you must not look too long on the *doncellitas* of the south. That I shall not like to think of. Some of them are very beautiful. Why must you go? No-no, of course you must go. Men are all the same. It will do you good. But I shall be very lonely; and you must think of me much. Do not be too long on this *merienda*."

She moved about the room collecting what she thought he should have, complaining a little that he seemed to think he must leave on such short notice. At the last she clung to him in a sudden passion of farewell; but her emotion was obviously more at the idea of separation than because of any thought of danger. Even in his very real anxiety, which he concealed, Andy's sense of humor was tickled. Carmel had been perturbed enough when he had set out on his expedition against the horse-stealing Indians. Her present attitude was rather a delicious commentary on California warfare. He took pains to say nothing that would hint that this campaign might be of a different quality; that a hundred American riflemen had introduced into it a new and possibly serious element. He tiptoed in to touch the sleeping children lightly on the forehead; kissed Carmel for the last time; joined the impatiently waiting company. They rode away into the night.

CHAPTER IX

THE miscellaneous little band arrived in the southland days ahead of their pursuers. They were well mounted, with many spares; while of Micheltorena's command by far the greater number marched afoot. Naturally they would have ridden if they could; but the Californians saw to it that no horses were to be had. They did not linger at Santa Barbara, but pushed on at once to Los Angeles. Andy would have liked much to spend a few days in the former place. The sprawled little town commanded by the most imposing and the best preserved of the missions; the flowery rolling half-moon of lowland held within the arms of the mountains; the somnolent sea; the distant islands swimming like mauve and lilac clouds; these, and the soft caress of the air, combined in an impression of quiet and well-being that was accurately mirrored in the manners of the people. They moved about their affairs, if any, with a calm absence of haste that elsewhere might have been described as indolence, but here possessed the spaciousness of dignity. However, Alvarado and his leaders desired as quickly as possible to get to the more populous centers; so the stay was only overnight.

As a Rivera, if only by marriage, Andy was invited to stay that night with the most important people of the place, at the great house of Don José de la Guerra y Noriega, of whom he had heard much. He found the great house worthy of its name, both in size and in hospitality. Señor Noriega proved to be short and stout, with a flat nose and an ugly face; and with, at first, a cold and rather pompous manner. But after the first formal moments the manner thawed to cordiality; and after the first visual impression Andy forgot all about his surface appearance. His native wisdom made itself felt, even before he expressed it. Andy was not surprised to hear from Ramón that at times of the frequent earthquakes the lower classes of the *pueblo* flocked to the great house, there to remain until the earthquake was all over, certain in their faith that somehow Don José's mere proximity would keep them safe. He and Ramón stole a brief interview with the ladies of the family. They were charming. Andy was able to deliver his messages from Carmel, to answer a few eager questions. He felt himself the object of a veiled but vivid interest. He must take his leave; for in the *sala* the leaders were gathered for council.

The room was filled when the young men entered and took their places against the wall. Ramón knew most of them and mentioned in a whisper the most noteworthy. Andy was particularly struck by the appearance of one man of about fifty, for with the exception of a Blackfoot Indian named Walking Eagle, it seemed to him he was the most imposing figure he had ever seen. He was well over six feet tall and must have weighed at least two hundred and twenty pounds which looked to be all bone and muscle. This was, Ramón told him, Teodoro Arellanes; a very rich man, he added. Next him was, by way of contrast, about the homeliest man Andy had ever seen; but his ugliness, like that of Señor Noriega, was somehow pleasing. This was Nicolás Den, a foreigner who had like Andy married into the country. Ramón called his attention to a number of others—Daniel Hill—Isaac Sparks—George Nidever, whom Andy remembered as one of Joe Walker's men, but to whom he had no chance to speak; a half-dozen more. Andy was impressed by their numbers. But, like himself, they seemed all good Californians. He would much have liked to talk to them. There was no opportunity. The business of the gathering lasted far into the night; after

which all scattered at once for a few hours of desperately
needed repose. The northerners were ahorseback and on
their way before dawn.

Andy listened with growing respect to the decisive wisdom of Noriega. He now understood the man's reputation
for sagacity. Without argument or combat of any kind the
hidalgo imposed his ideas. They were elementary common
sense; but, Andy reflected, it takes good eyes sometimes
to see common sense.

Santa Barbara, said Noriega, stood by itself, isolated,
between the population centers of the north and the south.
It could therefore receive effective support only in case
Alvarado had decisively gained the upper hand. On the
other hand, should it declare for Alvarado and the Californians, that fact would furnish Micheltorena a sufficient
excuse to seize it and its resources, which were considerable.

"Therefore," concluded Noriega, "though as good Californians our sympathies are naturally with our people,
we can best serve them by remaining neutral. Thus though
we do not seem to help you, we deprive this Mexican of
the excuse to help himself."

The incisive clear reasoning of the old don pleased Andy,
whom the customary circumlocutions of Latin grandilo-
quence had always irked.

So they rode south, at low tide, on the hard wet beach
around the Rincón toward San Buenaventura, their numbers unaugmented by any of the youth of Santa Barbara,
who chafed restlessly but obeyed the wisdom of Noriega.

2

The south rose to Alvarado, who had for the occasion
shaken off his lethargy and showed again the blaze of his
old genius. In a remarkably well-worded speech before

the Assembly he managed to put Micheltorena legalistic-ally in the wrong. He made much to the Californians of the fact that Micheltorena's forces were largely composed of foreigners. He talked of the character of these forces and of the danger of plunder, and so enlisted a substantial foreign contingent. Men like Lemuel Carpenter, Abel Stearns, John Warner, Isaac Williams—merchants and *rancheros*, who had come early to the country and who had raised families and acquired substantial interests—became seriously alarmed. Andy was astonished at the numbers of these men. He talked to them of the situation, which he himself now considered serious, and was enabled to con-vince them that, what with Micheltorena's superior arms and the presence in his army of Sutter and Graham with their riflemen, this was like to prove a different affair from the usual partisan revolutions of the past. Looked like there might be some real fighting, he said. The Ameri-cans and a scattering of English and French searched out what arms they possessed, and concentrated at Los An-geles. And from all the wide countryside gathered the Californians in great numbers, determined for once, well mounted, but lamentably deficient in arms. For the first time the natives of the north and the south were united in a common purpose.

The *pueblo* was animated with gayly caparisoned horse-men. Ramón and Andy wandered about restlessly. In the town itself was not much to see. The houses were adobe, with flat roofs, a few of them two-storied. There were a church, a *cuartel*, a government house. A few of the dwell-ings were large and attractive: the frame "palace" of Abel Stearns was the most esteemed, as well as the most ugly. But in general there was little comfort, little luxury. Part of the town was mean and squalid, inhabited by a class of people strange to Andy in this quiet land, ragged, dirty, treacherous-looking. After dark the quarter was noisy and even dangerous; a true red-light district to be shunned by one undesirous of a knife in the back. The dust was deep and choking.

The excitement was intense, almost hysterical. Save for a few responsible heads, no one seemed to give any thought to plan or preparation. The *caballeros* rode the streets in little groups, brandishing their lances. The lesser folk gathered in the *tabernas* and got drunk. The women chattered like magpies. Andy surveyed the confusion with misgivings. Save for the lances and *reatas* and a few dozen old muskets, the Californians appeared to have no arms. Most of the Americans possessed rifles, but they were comparatively few in numbers. Castro had unearthed two cannon and some ammunition for them. There seemed to be no attempt at discipline. Andy got tired of it; remembered Luis Vighnes; made inquiries; looked him up. He spent an interesting evening with the French wine grower; next day rode out to Vighnes's place. Andy learned a great deal. He stayed overnight and the following day Luis wanted him to continue the visit. He dismissed the revolution with a snap of the fingers.

"I have seen a many of doze things," said he.

Nevertheless he accompanied Andy back to Los Angeles. In spite of his scorn, the news that Sutter's men accompanied Micheltorena impressed him. He joined the foreign contingent, contributing as personal arms a pair of exquisite dueling pistols.

3

Micheltorena had at last reached Santa Barbara. A messenger brought back word that the governor refused to listen to argument. Whereupon Alvarado calmly declared him deprived of office and superseded him, provisionally, by Pío Pico! It is difficult to decide which most to admire, the *politico's* insolence or his astuteness. He had, of course no authority to depose Micheltorena; no authority except a public sentiment, united for the first time in California's history. He just did; and so much for the insolence. But he shrewdly avoided naming himself as acting governor; as he might well have done. The scene of resistance was in the south. Pío Pico was a southerner. Furthermore, unlike Juan Bandini, he was a man of moderation. If he aroused little fanatic enthusiasm, certainly he would excite little distrust or jealousy. He held the office of senior *vocal*, which gave the nomination some legal coloring. The selection was good evidence that Alvarado's political intelligence was still clear; though a good many people were astounded.

"Ye gods! The idea of Pío Pico with the title of Excellency!" wrote John Jones to Larkin.

But whatever the opinion of the little man's personal qualifications, Alvarado had managed to commit his countrymen. There could now be no compromise, no drawing back.

The morning of February 19th the Californians moved to meet Micheltorena, who was reported advancing down the valley of San Fernando. The night before, the *pueblo* had been visited by a terrific storm. This was an omen of something or other; nobody knew quite what. There was great furore and foofaraw. The *caballeros* pranced gayly, their lances aflutter. Some of the younger and more exuberant dashed ahead and circled back, reining their horses to a plunging halt. The two cannon staggered along drunkenly at the ends of *reatas*. The Americans and other foreigners rode more soberly apart. Castro, who had some military ability, tried, with only partial success, to inject order into the proceedings. The movement resembled a gay-colored and disorderly mob. But on the flat housetops the women, their hair unbound, wept unrestrainedly and prayed to the blessed saints.

Andy was not there to see. The evening before, he had been summoned to Abel Stearns's house, where headquarters had been located.

"You are an old mountain man, Burnett," said the merchant, speaking Spanish for the benefit of the others present, "and you are accustomed to these things. We are going to ask you to act as scout; ride out and spy the disposition and numbers of the enemy forces. Will you do this?"

Andy nodded, his eye lighting up.

"Do you wish help?"

Andy considered.

"I can do better alone," he decided, "—unless there be another among you accustomed to Indian warfare on the plains." He considered further. "I may take one man to act as messenger."

"Select whom or what you wish," said Stearns.

Andy sought Ramón. The latter was delighted. This was a chance for more "essport." But his face fell a little over Andy's conditions.

"No," his friend overrode his expostulations, "it must be as I say, or I shall not take you. I wish to work unseen; and you, my friend, are not skilled. You must remain, concealed, exactly where I leave you until I come back for you or signal you. That is agreed," he insisted.

"But you are *serio, valedor!*" complained Ramón. "You act like the *papá* to the so-little boy!"

He had to agree. He had, moreover, to imitate Andy, who divested himself and his animal of all bright-colored foofaraw that might attract the eye, stripping down to the sober essentials. Ramón's idea of war was to cut a brave figure with, preferably, a few gonfalons and trumpeters.

The two young men rode forth about sunset through what is now Hollywood toward the pass of Cahuenga. They sheltered during the storm in the house of one of the smaller *rancheros;* but as soon as it had ceased were again in the saddle. Daylight found them in the hills. Andy left Ramón beneath a white oak and took up his scouting in the patient methodical manner that had become to him

routine. He did not trouble, however, to exercise the excess
of caution he had employed against the raiding Indians.
He was now looking for a large body of men; and incidentally for any detached scouts, like himself. The presence
of such people would be easy to establish. Except at sky-
lines Andy did not even bother to dismount. Nevertheless
he was deft enough to see another and distant single horseman before he himself had been discovered. After a moment's scrutiny he led his horse to better concealment and
returned to lie flat behind a thin screen of brush. The
stranger was obviously not riding on a definite journey.
He was hunting for something. He might be merely a
vaquero in search of strayed stock. Or more likely he was
out on Andy's errand. If the man was an enemy scout, his
capture was highly desirable.

Luck favored Andy. The stranger was working methodically in his direction. Andy watched his movements
critically. He was not surprised, as the man drew nearer, to
see by his dress that he was no Californian; his maneuvers
smacked of the expert. Probably one of the Americans
brought by Sutter. Andy slipped back of the hill and
moved down through the chaparral to intercept his line.
If he was to capture the man alive he must be very close
to him. So he did not get another good look until the other
rounded the small hog's-back almost on top of him. Andy
stared for a moment; then laughed aloud.

"Harry Mulford! You old horny toad!" he cried. But
he did not show himself. It is as well to give a man with a
gun time to get over his startle. And indeed Mulford threw
forward his rifle with a speed and precision that would
have been dangerous had it a defined object.

"Who calls me by name?" he demanded sharply.

Then Andy stood up into view. Mulford narrowed his
eyes for an instant; then widened them incredulously.

"Andy Burnett, by the 'tarnal!" he cried. "Somebody
told me you were daid!"

He flung himself from his horse. The two men clasped hands. For just an instant a constraint held them. To each came the thought of their last meeting, the day of the massacre at Pierre's Hole and the killing of Joe Crane and Andy's pursuit of Ben Tilton, the murderer. It was Mulford who had promised grimly that none of Tilton's friends would follow to interfere with his vengeance. To both men the scene came back vividly—"See to things, Harry —Joe—and—better get his woman back to her people." "Rest yore mind easy, Andy." Since that day they had not met.

"I done what you told me—about Joe and his woman," Mulford muttered after a moment, looking down.

"Thanks; I knew you would," said Andy, looking away.

A mocking bird in the thicket was pouring its heart out in a flood of ecstatic melody too great for its little body.

"Them birds sure do sing purty," remarked Mulford with an effort.

"They sure do," said Andy.

The tension fell away. They were back in the present, with the bird.

"What you doin' projectin' around in the sagebrush, Andy?" asked Mulford curiously.

"Same as you—scouting," replied Andy, "and," he added with a humorous relish, "I reckon I sort of got the drop on you, old-timer."

"That's right," acknowledged Mulford without embarrassment, "but I had no idee I was goin' out against no mountain man, or I'd a-done things different. I thought they was only these Mexs."

"They aren't Mexs," corrected Andy. "They are *californios*. There's a big difference."

"Mebbe," agreed Mulford placidly, "but they all look alike to me. And they don't know sic-'em about this sort of thing. That's what fooled me. Eff'n they'd told me, now, that they had a white man with 'em——"

"There are plenty of white men with them," interrupted Andy. "Look here, Harry, what are you doing with this other outfit, anyway?"

"Why, I dunno," confessed Mulford. "I was up at Cap'n Sutter's place, and he said come along, so I come along with the rest of the boys."

"Well, you're on the wrong side," stated Andy decidedly.

Mulford was thoughtful.

"Wall," he said at length, "I dunno about that. Cap'n Sutter seems to me like a purty white man. He tuk us in when we come through the mountains without enough possibles left to dust a fiddle. Seems like he ought to know."

"I don't know Sutter: I never saw him," said Andy. "But this time he's made a mistake."

"Let's smoke on it," said Mulford.

They squatted on their heels beneath the fragrant sage. After the storm of the night before, the air was heavy with perfume released by the sun. Before them rolled the modeled hills darkly solid with shadow and the deep green of the greasewood; daintily fragile with the highlights of reflected glossy leaves, and the ghostlike white blossoms of the cascara, and the deep blue of the mountain lilac. Mocking birds everywhere wove their intricate patterns of song: the tiny tree sparrows trilled unceasingly their single notes, thin, high, clear, sustained, like a silver wire of sound. Unseen, the blue, plumed quail chattered in undertones or flung the brisk valiant challenge of their calls from the tops of bushes. Jeweled lizards rustled the drying leaves in short quick dashes. Overhead, against the unbelievable blue, the slow serenity of soaring vultures. They smoked: Andy talked: Mulford listened.

"It's too much for me," the latter confessed, "but this I see: they ain't no manner of use of good white men shootin' up each other in a quarrel that's none of their business.

And you ought to know the rights of things, Andy." He smoked and pondered. "I'll tell you this, Andy: back thar at that *pueblo*—what do they call her?—Santa Barbara, thar's a might' smart passel of men quit us and vamoosed, Mexs and white men both. I thought that a purty poor trick; but mebbe it wa'n't." But that was as far as he would go; though he was plainly troubled. Andy arose to his feet and put his fingers to his lips. "What you up to?" asked Mulford.

Andy whistled shrilly four times.

"I left a friend down there below," he explained, "a Californian."

"Jist one?" queried Mulford, rising quickly to his elbow. He sank back. "No, that's all right," he added, "I know you, Andy Burnett."

Ramón appeared. He looked at Mulford curiously; acknowledged the introduction with courtesy; considered the situation as Andy repeated it to him.

"But this is fine!" he cried. "I think your frien', he is right!"

"Right? How?" Andy was puzzled.

"But look," said Ramón, "it is not this Micheltorena and his *cholos* we fear; nor yet this John Sutter and his *indios*. Pah!" He snapped his fingers. "But these *americanos*. That is another horse. Without them where is Micheltorena? Listen, *valedor;* and you, *señor americano*."

Rapidly he disclosed his plan. It was very simple. Why indeed should the *americanos* kill one another in this quarrel? Let them stand apart—on both sides—and leave the *californios* and Micheltorena to settle matters by themselves.

"What think you, *señor?*" he appealed to Mulford. "Can you so make it with your countrymen?"

"Why," confessed Mulford slowly, "I reckon old Sutter's got no string hitched to us. And I sure reckon I got no use for Andy's sculp—or any other good American's, for that matter. And we none of us got no use for that comical raft of chicken thieves that feller calls his army."

"And you, *valedor*,"—Ramón turned to Andy—"you shall tell these brave *americanos* who are with us that there will be no esstealing and that we shall—what you call?— lick him the pants off these *cholos*."

"Say," said Mulford admiringly, "yore friend can sure talk United States!"

"I talk him like he's my own language," agreed Ramón complacently. "What you look so funny for?" he demanded of Andy.

"Looks like I was quitting on a job; and I've never done that yet."

"That is for me," said Ramón. "I shall myself talk with Señor Alvarado. Is he not my cousin? He is *político*. He will be delight. You shall see. Come; he shall tell you so himself!"

Andy looked inquiringly toward Mulford.

"I'd ruther sit on a side hill and watch the show than be lookin' at the leetle end of that thing," confessed the latter, laying his hand on the Boone gun. "And I've sure got no use poppin' over ary good American for nothin'. And," he added, "I don't believe you have nuther, Andy."

CHAPTER X

THE battle of that day and the next, shifting in terrain from the Cahuenga Pass to the Verdugo Rancho, presented various aspects to various people.

Back in the *pueblo* the waiting people could distinctly hear the sound of the cannonading. There were five pieces engaged, two on the side of the Californians, while Micheltorena had brought the other three. They were grand old pieces, and none of them burst; but as they were fired at the extremest ranges and as the powder was of low quality and old, they were hardly to be classed as dangerous weapons. But they made a wonderful flash, bang, and smoke; and the women in Los Angeles wailed and prayed in a satisfactory emotional debauch.

Here on the field the Californian forces deployed and maneuvered with confidence; while Micheltorena, dismayed by the defection of the element on which he most depended, moved in countercheck and debated what to do.

On the hills, comfortably ensconced as in a grandstand, sprawled the Americans and other foreigners, from both sides, chewing tobacco, smoking, renewing old acquaintance and making new. After the first small hesitation of distrust, the fraternization was complete. Secure in their agreement that they would stick together in defense of their rights whichever side won out, they relaxed to enjoy the spectacle.

It was a good show. Because of the constant and shifting movement it was difficult to estimate the numbers engaged. Andy thought there were at least five hundred, perhaps half as many again, of Californians in the field.

Henry Mulford said he supposed Micheltorena had about the same. The stage-set of hill and plain was beautiful, for the spring flowers were coming out, and the first vivid green of the rainy season had only just begun to darken. The costuming was as colorful as any director could have desired; for, it must be remarked, this was the land of Hollywood where, three quarters of a century later, many just such spectacles as this were to deploy through the selfsame hills. The gayly caparisoned *caballeros* dashed about on horseback, the pennons of their lances fluttering. The cannoneers whammed away at intervals with most satisfactory noise and smoke. Micheltorena's foot soldiers marched and countermarched, and took up positions, and abandoned them. Occasionally they let off their smooth-bore muskets when some of the mounted enemy swooped closer than usual.

Micheltorena was gradually forced back. The spectators on the side hills had to trail along, if they wished to continue to enjoy the show.

Neither Andy nor Mulford could make out quite why the governor was forced back. There had been no real fighting. Indeed, as far as they could see, nobody had been hurt. One horse and rider had tumbled in a heap; but the man had extricated himself and ridden away behind a friend's saddle. Mulford was openly contemptuous of what he called cowardice.

"All he's got to do is to stand tight and let 'em come to him!" he cried. "And," he added, "all these other fellers would have to do would be to ride right in over 'em and be done with it!"

Andy nodded abstractedly. He only half heard the comment. Two lines sketched themselves between his brows. Suddenly his face cleared.

"Got it!" he exclaimed aloud.

"Got what?"

"I just happened to think of Cazador—he's our old dog

at Folded Hills. He's pretty old. He must be goin' on seventy."

"Say, Andy, is this yere sun gittin' you?" asked Mulford solicitously.

"About seventy for a dog," explained Andy. "That's really about twelve years old."

Mulford surveyed him disgustedly.

"What's this yere venerable dawg got to do with what?" he demanded at last.

"With this,"—Andy waved his hand toward the valley. "I was thinking of old Cazador, and remembering how he takes each new pup and plays with him. You've seen dogs play, Harry, r'aring up and growling and tryin' for holts on one another. But it ain't serious. They grab their holts, but they don't bite home; just hang on a minute to show they've really got the holt and then let go. Sort of counts 'em one, I reckon. They ain't aiming to hurt each other; just to get the best of it. Well, that's the way down there. They don't want to hurt each other: they just want to get the best of it!"

"They wouldn't git no best of it eff'n one or the other would reely fight back," said Mulford. "Why, give me a half a dozen——"

"No: you watch awhile and see." Andy was intent on his great discovery. "They maneuver around back and forth till they get one or the other of them dead to rights, and then that feller sort of says, 'All right, you got me there,' and he pulls out of that place and they start over again."

"Yo're seein' things at night, Andy. Who ever heard of ary 'tarnal foolishness like that!"

Andy laughed. He was happy. His mind was cleared of a question that had long bothered him; for he knew profoundly that, in spite of appearances to the contrary, the Californians as individuals were no cowards. Here was an explanation, fantastic enough in all conscience, but an explanation nevertheless. He began to watch the spectacle with more interest. He remembered that most Californian families were interrelated. He remembered Ramón's delight in "essport." Nevertheless the idea *was* fantastic.

"It ain't fightin' at *all!*" complained Mulford.

2

The second day wore on. They moved into the shade, ate the food they had brought with them. Their interest flagged. They talked idly, dozed a little, swapped news of all sorts. Andy moved about among the men who had come with Sutter. He was astonished at the number of them who had settled in the country. He learned much. The life at Folded Hills had wrapped him in an isolation of seclusion. Things had been going on. There was news, change. Dawson's prediction had been fulfilled. The Sierra had actually been crossed. He heard for the first time of the Bartleson-Bidwell party, true immigrants. To be sure, they had had to abandon their wagons, and had packed over the great range, and they had arrived in a condition of destitution at John Marsh's place near Mt. Diabolo, but they had made the crossing on their own, without a guide, and there were women and children. And wheels had tracked in all the way from the east—the Workman party by way of the south, and another lot from the north, from Oregon. Some had stayed with Sutter; some had squatted here and there in the upper Valley, and were farming, on sufferance it seemed. Andy felt very ignorant. He talked to Abel Stearns, to others of his race who had been long in the country. He found them surprised that he knew nothing of these things.

"You are a true *ranchero* right enough," laughed Stearns. "Why don't you get about a little?"

Andy would have liked to learn more; but Ramón came dashing up the hill in search of him.

"Tight up your *cincha* and come, *amigo!*" he cried gayly. "Come quick if you would see!"

He waited impatiently while Andy obeyed.

"Come! Come quick!" he cried and struck spurs to his mount. They raced down the slope and across the plain of Verdugo. Andy drew alongside.

"It is over!" Ramón explained. "Micheltorena, he give up! Now there is a talk and the surrender. Ride fast, *valedor*, if you would see. It will be good essport!"

Andy found the leaders of both parties at San Fernando. Alvarado was there, and Castro, and Micheltorena, of course, and Sutter and many others. Andy looked at Sutter with curiosity. He saw a short stout man with broad shoulders and a large full face decorated with a stubby mustache. His manner was exquisitely courteous but reserved, and informed with rather a theatrical dignity. He had a cold and penetrating blue eye which looked Andy through and through. But in spite of his surface poise Andy detected an underlying worry. He had guessed wrong.

The occasion was suavely polite with undercurrents. If the direct-minded Anglo-Saxon had expected either triumph on the one side or resentment on the other, he was disappointed. Neither in word nor look was revealed a shadow of doubt as to the sincerity of what was said.

Micheltorena announced that he was a true friend of the Californians; that he had been sent to protect and not to destroy; that the Californians were a brave people but ill prepared for war; that he was well aware that their cannon were of no efficiency and their small arms were worse, while he, Micheltorena, was well supplied with all these things, and his army was brave and determined. But that he saw his duty. He had been sent to do his duty. It was not to use force against the wishes of the people. He surrendered merely out of good feeling to the people.

Alvarado bowed. They let it go at that.

John Sutter spoke up. He stated that he wanted his position understood. He too was an ardent friend of the Californians. But he had received a command, a command by the constituted government. In joining this expedition he had merely obeyed orders, as a loyal citizen. He added that he had instructed his men to fire over the heads of the Californians.

This also was accepted politely and without comment. Nobody called attention to the obvious fact that, during the battle, Sutter had no men to instruct. Castro even kissed Sutter's cheek and told him how glad he was to see him again. But Andy noticed a fine bead of perspiration across Sutter's forehead.

The principals retired to draw up terms. Ramón drew Andy's arm through his.

"Was it not good essport?" said he delightedly. "And all so much the *fiesta?* But I think this John Sutter he— what you call?—cook him hees goose!"

The combined armies marched rather hilariously back to the *pueblo*. There was a dinner; and speeches. After the dinner the troops were paraded and a hot-air balloon was sent up. Everybody had a remarkably good time, everybody but the *cholos*. They were too closely watched.

3

Andy attended the celebration. He was surprised and touched to discover how many strangers among the Californians had heard of him and wished to make his acquaintance. He ascribed this to his connection with the Riveras; and especially to the partisanship of his friend, Ramón. But it was more than that; and deep in his heart, whatever his natural modesty might say, Andy knew it. He had been definitely accepted as a *californio*, adopted but true, like these others, many of whom were present—

Daniel Hill, Abel Stearns, Lemuel Carpenter, Thompson, Luis Vighnes, Larkin, Jacob Leese, a long list whose names it is a pity not to record. They had adopted the customs and manners of the country and married its daughters, and here, at this *fiesta* of victory, they moved as though to the manner born. Andy's heart warmed at the thought that he was indeed one of them.

After a time he slipped away from the festivities. The days had been long, and even his iron frame was wearying. But principally he wished to get out of the confusion, to be alone for a little, to think of Carmel and Amata and Djo. He might just as well have brought Djo along, he reflected. It would have been a good experience for the youngster, broaden his outlook and his acquaintance. The boy was well grown for his age, toughened to the saddle, *sabio* beyond his years.

As Andy passed across the plaza, he hesitated for a moment. A group of the trappers who had come south with Sutter, true to form, had built them a useless small fire around which they squatted and sprawled. They were strangers to him, since his day, subtly a distinct type from the men he had known, younger, more hairy, with somehow a different air. He recognized nobody in that group; and was about to pass on, when one of them arose to confront him. He looked down on a young man at least fifteen years his junior, on whose smooth face the beard was but just sprouting. Nevertheless in the straight bold and reckless level of his eye, Andy recognized him as no greenhorn but a seasoned plainsman.

"Yo're Burnett, ain't you?" he asked. In his manner was a trace of embarrassment. "Yo' don't know me," he answered Andy's unspoken question, "but I've heerd tell of you so much I just want to shake you by the hand."

"Heard of me?" repeated Andy.

"Over yander"—the boy jerked his head toward the

east. "I've heerd tell of I-tam-api ever since I hit the plains."

He clasped Andy's hand gravely; hesitated for something more to say. His almost awed admiration was evident. Andy himself was embarrassed, a little overwhelmed. He was not forgotten—over yonder. For an instant a wave of nostalgia for the old life flooded him. He half turned as though to join the group about the fire; but at that moment Ramón hailed him.

The young plainsman slipped away.

"Why do you leave the *fiesta, amigo?*" asked his friend.

"I am tired of it," confessed Andy.

"You think of Carmel," Ramón accused him shrewdly. "Eh? I too: I think of Conchita." He sighed. "Thus it is to be marry and to be happy. These *doñas*, they are ver' beautiful, no doubt." He shrugged. "But they are not so beautiful for me." He paused to contemplate himself, his head comically to one side. "To think that Ramón Rivera should say such thing! No one would believe—but you, *valedor*. Let us go look at the star, and not talk, and think of those we love."

The night was very still and brilliant. The two young men walked in companionable silence through the scattered outskirts of the *pueblo* to the open country, where they paused atop a hill. Undoubtedly Ramón pursued his intention and confined his thoughts to Conchita. But Andy had been stirred by the events of the past few days. His mind returned persistently to the things he had heard. Especially his imagination lingered on what had been told him of the flood of immigration over the Oregon Trail, through that South Pass, of which, only a few years before, he had been one of the discoverers; hundreds and hundreds of them, they told him, with women and children and plows slung under the wagons——

Andy raised his head, startled.

"What is it?" asked Ramón, at the sudden gesture.

"Listen to the surf, how loud it roars!"

"The surf? What ails you, *valedor?* The sea is seven leagues away!"

Andy came to himself, bewildered. The night was still. But still in his ears lingered the echoes as of a rising tide.

INTERLUDE

Djo

THE year following the expulsion of Micheltorena, Djo Burnett celebrated his twelfth birthday. Andy had taken the greatest pains with his son, and in consequence the latter was probably the most carefully educated small boy in all California. He had had every advantage the society of that period afforded. Nevertheless, to a child of our days Djo would seem almost incredibly ignorant. He knew literally almost nothing of history, or geography, even of the continent on which he lived. He had no mathematics; he had never heard of natural science. To be sure, he could read and write; but the latter painfully, inaccurately, and with only such grammar as his ear had taught him. On the other hand, the modern child translated back to Djo's times would in turn have seemed to him most illy instructed.

Let us review his accomplishments.

In common with all other infant *californios*, Djo could ride; and his riding was a rather wonderful performance, quite different from merely staying atop a horse gracefully. He could throw the loop of a *reata* with almost magical dexterity. He was wise in the lore of cattle and horses and their habits, and the rotations of their ranges. He knew all about breaking the one and handling the other. He was well instructed also in the graces of life. He knew the stately and gracious formulæ of society, as also the small niceties. Though on terms of the most delightful and somewhat mischievous intimacy with his uncle, Don Ramón Rivera, the latter was also his godfather, so at each encounter Djo never failed to remove his hat or to utter a short prayer; nor did Ramón, gay and irreverent scapegrace though he was, omit in response to bestow his grave and measured blessing. Djo played the guitar and sang to it very sweetly such old-time songs as *Adiós, Adiós Amores*. He knew and could execute with precision and grace—though as yet with a moderate rapture—such dances as the *contradanza*, the *jota*, the *zorrita*, *los camotes*, and others.

In these matters Djo was not unique. He shared such accomplishments with every well-brought-up *caballero-in-embryo*. But as Djo's parents took their responsibilities seriously, his schooling went further. Not every *ranchero*, even of the better classes, could read and write; not one in a thousand knew anything of Latin, except that it was used by priests in church; very few bothered about the possibilities of growing things in *milpa* or in field, or the mysteries of manufacture even of the simple affairs of everyday use. They left such matters to the priests, the *mozos*, or the Indians, as the case might be. But Djo was surrounded by enthusiastic specialists, each eager to appropriate to himself the *patroncito*, and each secretly a little jealous of the other's influence and scornful of his accomplishment.

Padre Sanchez, the younger, journeyed from the crumbling mission at Soledad to stay at Folded Hills for a week or more at a time. From him Djo, respectfully reluctant, learned that Latin was a language, and not just queer sounds made in church. That did not get him much of anywhere—though Padre Sanchez was piously certain it did—but it was good and needed dumb-bell exercise for that side of his intelligence.

At Folded Hills his preceptors were many. Chief among them was the head *vaquero*, wooden-faced sardonic Panchito, who considered all that did not pertain to horses and cattle either superfluous or beneath the notice of an *hacendado*. But Djo's interests were catholic, and many besides Panchito had a hand in his schooling. There was, for example, gentle moon-faced Benito of exquisite manner, sensitive in the lore of growing things. Or Abel Means, the Yankee millwright, incredibly ingenious at mechanical constructions—he built Djo a water wheel that made all sorts of contraptions operate; and which, in the scornful opinion of every *californio* on the ranch, wasted too much of the youngster's time.

After all, an *hacendado* could hire done for him such things as mechanics. As soon might be learn to wash clothes, like the *mozas*, at the streamside!

But Djo's was an active and inquiring mind. Of a sudden he took up with Pascal, the Indian. Pascal was in charge of what might broadly be called the menial activities of the ranch—whatever could not be done on horseback. Djo was haled one day from the bottomlands, literally plastered with drying mud and full of enthusiasm over the making of *adobe* bricks! Both Panchito, who brought him back, and Vicenta, who cleaned him up, agreed that there was no question but that something should be done. When Vicenta had finished her scrubbing, the two escorted Djo to the cool low *sala* where sat the Doña Carmel, his gracious lady mother.

"It is not," Panchito explained carefully at the close of his narrative, "that the *patroncito* is knowingly at fault, *señora*, for it is the nature of *los niños* to delight in playing in the mud, as all men know. But to associate with Indians and to labor with the hands, that, *señora*, is below the dignity of a Rivera."

The scene was quaint, and just a little ridiculous—to all but its participants—the so-tall and grave Panchito, the so-fat and suppressedly quivering Vicenta, the so-small Djo between them. But unexpectedly the culprit spoke in his own defense.

"I am not a *niño*," he submitted with entire respect, "and, *señora madre*, I did not play in the mud like a *niño:* I learn to make bricks." His miniature formality broke, and be became eager. "It is very interesting that, and not so easy. *Adobe* bricks do not make themselves. See! One crushes the *adobe* fine like powder, and pours in the water slowly, kneading it—as Vicenta kneads the flour; and when it is just-so one throws in the straw with one hand and stirs with the other; and if the mixture is not just right the brick crumbles when it is dry and——" He broke off ruefully. "My brick crumbled," he confessed, "but I think next time——" He subsided, suddenly blanketed by the heavy disapproval at his right elbow and his left.

Carmel's eyes dwelt on him fondly. He was a handsome youngster, with all the dark soft beauty of his mother's race but with something of his father hard beneath like steel. His blue-gray eyes now met hers with a directness that startled her, they were so like Andy's. He said true; he was no longer an infant.

A chuckle from the doorway betrayed the presence of a spectator. Carmel turned her head, startled.

"I did not hear you come, *querido*," said she.

Andy strode forward down the *sala*.

"I have been listening," said he. He stood in the middle of the room, his legs apart, surveying the scene amusedly. Panchito started to speak.

"I heard what you said," Andy checked him. He turned to Djo. "You think that next time—?" he prompted Djo.

"Yes, *señor padre*," said Djo, "I think that next time I can make a brick that will not crumble."

"Very well," said Andy.

Djo could not restrain a glance of triumph toward his rigidly disapproving captors.

For a moment Andy pondered, his eyes on the floor.

"You see," he remarked pleasantly to Panchito and Vicenta, "I think it well for Djo that the more he knows of whatever interests him, the better."

"*Sí, señor*," said Panchito submissively, but with a gleam of disapproval in his eye.

Vicenta, the privileged, was not so pliable. She snorted.

"I will remind the *señor* of that in a few years' time," she stated—"a few years, when the *señor* begins to wish that all *mozas* were born old and ugly."

Andy rested his gaze on her. She subsided, curtseyed, followed Panchito from the room. She knew that when the *patrón* said nothing, it was best to stand from under; but her broad back was eloquent.

"Djo!" Andy halted his son at the door.

"*Señor padre.*"

"Just this,"—for the first time Andy spoke in English. "If you make bricks, they must be good bricks. And you shall work at the bricks until you do make good bricks, firm and hard. Understand?"

"Yes, sir," replied Djo. He waited a moment for further instructions. Receiving none, he bowed from the hips and went out.

Carmel surveyed Andy, her head on one side, the corners of her lips lifted in a half-smile. When Andy's eyes returned to hers, after following the sturdy, straight, little figure through the door of the *sala*, the smile deepened into a chuckle. She lifted her shoulders ever so slightly, and spread her hands apart in a swift graceful gesture.

"And me also!" she cried. "I fall upon the face and hit the head on the floor when you stand up so-tall and look that way. I too have learn!"

Andy laughed and flung his great length into a chair.

"Vicenta is a faithful creature," said he, "but I can't let her run me."

"Can anybody r-run you, *amado?*" speculated Carmel curiously. "That I do not think."

"Nobody but you, *querida.*"

"I think I like it—that nobody r-run you. Not even me," disclaimed Carmel.

Djo went back to old Pascal and the *adobe* bricks. For one week he did little else than mess about absorbedly in the tenacious clay. Other interests, other duties had to him no existence. This was characteristic of Djo. His singleness of purpose was complete. At the end of this period he exhibited with satisfaction a row of perfect *adobes*. Thereafter he made no more bricks.

2

The brick episode is detailed as typical of many things. From Djo's earliest infancy Andy had interfered in just such a fashion. At first the women had protested, but they had speedily learned that protest was useless. As a baby Djo had never cried. Whenever he started to yell, Andy placed the flat of his palm across Djo's mouth and there held it until all symptoms had subsided. Even Carmel had to laugh, though unwillingly, at Djo's streaming eyes staring indignantly above the brown broad hand.

"Indian children never cry, and that is how they train 'em," explained Andy.

"But Djo is not an Indian!" protested Carmel.

"I hope he turns out to be as good a man as some Indians I've known," Andy repeated his customary reply.

The method worked. Djo, like all adventurous children at the tottery age, came some awful bumps. He might yell once, or even twice, but no more. "All gone!" he then remarked; and proceeded about his business.

By the time he was ten years old Djo had acquired several accomplishments unknown to other children of California. He could shoot; he could throw a knife, not by the blade, *vaquero* fashion, but from the flat of his hand; he possessed a strange lore of woodcraft. That part of Djo's education was empirical. He accompanied Andy everywhere—Don Largo's shadow. As they rode together Andy threw off information. Days later, unexpectedly, he would catechize.

"What did you notice near the High Tenaja?"

He would listen, generally without comment, to Djo's reply.

Occasionally he would utter a brief commendation; that was a happy occasion. Occasionally he would shake his head.

"Ride up there and look again," he might command; or merely maintain a disapproving silence; and Djo was abashed.

That was the way Andy remembered, that he himself had learned, and he saw again, across the years, the leafy Pennsylvania forests and the fantastic figure of Joe Crane striding ahead, and almost he could hear once more the slow drawl of the mountain man:

"In Injun country quakin' asp's yore best fire. It ain't got no smoke nor smell. . . ."

These things were delightful to Djo, and in his growing proficiencies Andy took a vast satisfaction; but to the people of the ranch they seemed entirely useless. On his tenth birthday Djo killed a buck with the old Boone gun, which was much taller than he was, and which he had to rest over Andy's shoulder to make the shot. Both he and Andy were inordinately proud of this feat, though nobody else saw any sense or glory in it. Why anyone should climb a high mountain to shoot an animal that was not much good anyway, when there was beef to be had for the roping, was beyond Californian conception.

At the conclusion of the festivities celebrating Djo's twelfth birthday Andy summoned his son to appear before him. He surveyed the youngster with a newly appraising eye. He saw a handsome boy, dressed in the Californian costume of the period. Except for Andy's straight frowning brows, his gray-blue steady eyes, and the determined set of his jaws, his appearance was Spanish. Certain features, considered singly in isolation, were almost effemin-

ate. For example, the long upcurled black lashes, in
arresting contrast to the eyes. His body was straight, with
a hint of whalebone supple strength in its slenderness.
He would stand perhaps three or four inches above the
five feet. Andy's heart swelled with pride and affection;
but no hint of this illumined his face.

Djo stood patiently and respectfully at attention.

"You are twelve years old today," Andy broke silence
at last. He spoke in English, so Djo knew this for a real
conference, man to man. "Back in the Indian country they
used to say that a boy stopped being a child when he was
twelve years old. They let him do a lot of grown-up things,
by himself, that he couldn't do before. Let him play men's
games. Look here, Djo; suppose suddenly you found yourself over yonder in the mountains, without anything, how
do you think you'd make out? Could you take care of
yourself?"

"Yes, sir," said Djo promptly. His father and he had
often played similar games, when riding the country; but
on a smaller scale.

"Now hold on," Andy checked him. "You got to think
this over. Never go off half cocked. Look-a here." He held
up his great hand and checked the items on his fingers.
"You've got no horse; that's been stole. You've got no gun.
You've got no flint-and-steel. You've been stripped clean.
You haven't even got any clothes. Nothing but your two
hands—well, maybe you saved your knife. But that's all
you've got; and," Andy added, "that's more than many
a good man, white or red, was left with in a sight harder
country than this."

Djo considered.

"Yes, sir," he said confidently at last.

"Want to try?"

Djo's correct posture broke in a wriggle of delight.

"It's a game!" he cried. "Let's call it Wildman!"

"Well, yes; it's a game. We'll call it Wildman; that's a

good name. And if you play it you'll have to stick to the rules." Djo nodded. "Well, here they are. You know all you need to know, if you remember what I taught you. You'll have your knife. The game is to see how long you can make out. You can come home any time you want to quit. Any time at all. Just come home. Or we can fix a signal and come and get you. Things might go wrong first time, you know. All right. But while you're out you've got to do it all yourself. No help. Of any kind. From nobody. You've got to promise that, and stick to your promise."

"Yes, sir," agreed Djo happily. "When can I try?"

"Tomorrow, if you want to."

The boy's face clouded with the doubt of an afterthought.

"Will Mother permit—and Vicenta?" he asked.

"They will permit," promised Andy, "—but perhaps we'd better not say tomorrow. Say on Monday."

3

That Andy was able to meet his promise was only because, as *patrón*, he had authority and used it. The idea was fantastic, senseless—even dangerous. There were wild cattle, there were bear, there might even be Indians from the *tulares*. And the cold! the *pobrecito* would die of the cold! Deliberately to expose one's own son to such perils, for no reason at all, would be the act of a madman! Or an *americano*, it was added as an afterthought of loyalty; and it had always been said that *americanos* were mad. Thus Vicenta; and much more; and after her every other dweller of Folded Hills, with the one exception of Panchito, the head *vaquero*. Partly from his hard-bitten conviction that hardship is good for anybody, mostly because of Vicenta, he defended the *patrón*. When it was realized that Don Largo really meant what he said, a dozen petty conspiracies came to life.

Andy could silence the ranch people with a command. But Carmel was another affair. It took some time for him to convince her that the whole matter was not a joke. Andy was patient and gentle; but beneath the gentleness was an inflexible determination against which Carmel's protests beat in vain.

"But it is madness!" she cried. "He is an infant! He will perish!"

"He is no longer an infant. He is grown. He will not perish. He has been taught enough to care for himself, if he remembers what he is taught. And he can come home at any time."

"But he is my baby. This is a foolishness. The season of the rains is not yet past. No: this I cannot suffer. He is mine. I shall not permit."

"He is mine, also," persisted Andy steadily. "You have had him as a child; now I must have him as a man."

Carmel threw out her hands.

"But I ask it of you that you do not insist. I cannot bear it. It is a little thing to ask. You have never refused me anything that I ask."

Andy was troubled and distressed.

"Do not ask me, *querida*," he begged. "I wish this very much."

"But why, why, why?" demanded Carmel.

"Djo is twelve. Back in my old Indian country when a boy became a man in years they tried him to see if he was a man at heart as well. I think it was a good idea."

"Djo is not an Indian. What is it you would try? Is he not strong and brave? Is he not *hidalgo*? Have you no eyes in your head to see? Must you do this madness to prove to yourself that he is your son?"

"It is not that. But Djo must prove it to himself. Yes; that is it. He must prove it to himself."

"I do not understand," wailed Carmel.

Nor did Andy himself quite understand his own obstinacy. There was some mysterious, mystic inner compulsion. Deep within him were subtleties too profound for the
analysis of his simple mind, insistences born of his hard
and savage training, distrusts that were racial, hopes that
were a passion of love. This that to Djo was an exciting
game, to Carmel a dangerous madness, had become to
Andy high ordeal. He could not have explained to himself,
much less to Carmel, the almost tremulous anxiety of soul
with which he awaited the event. She would not have
understood it if he had. Old Abel Means came nearest.

"What's the idee, boss?" asked the millwright. "Ain't
there some other game you can play with the young-un
that ain't so skeery for the women? Looks like you're
carrin' matters a leetle fur, don't it?"

"Doggone it, Abel," burst out Andy, "I've got to *know.*"

"Know what?" asked Means curiously.

"How much guts he has."

"Oh, that young-un's got guts," said Abel, "eff'n that's
all you got to know."

But it was not quite all. It was something besides;
though Andy himself did not know what it was.

4

"There you are, son." Andy reined his horse after a
stiff climb. "This is pretty favorable. There's water and
other things to keep you if you know enough. Scared at
all?"

"What of?" demanded Djo.

"Well, there's nothing to be scared of," admitted Andy,
"if you know how to take care of yourself. And you ought
to: you've been well taught. And it's pretty favorable
here." He looked about at the little basin, or "park."
The new grass was well started; the live-oaks were bril-
liantly mottled with fresh leaves among the old. Birds

were singing ecstatically, and the quail chirked and called
and muttered and twittered, scurrying beneath the chaparral like dried leaves. "Pretty favorable," Andy repeated. He was remembering the Rockies, in winter. "Or
the desert," he said aloud.

"Sir?"

"I was thinking that after the big mountains and the
desert this is pretty soft."

"May I try them some day?"

"Better try this first," said Andy dryly. He became
businesslike. "Climb down," he commanded. "I'll take
your horse. Strip off. Tie your clothes on the saddle. You
can keep your shoes: your feet aren't hard for barefoot."
Djo stood before him, a straight, brown, strong little figure.
Andy's eye traveled over him with satisfaction. "Take
that off," he ordered dryly.

"What, sir? The *botas?*" Djo looked up at his father
with limpid eye of innocence.

"You know better. Hand it over."

Djo grinned, undid his loincloth. Andy grinned back.

"Thought you knew how to use that, didn't you?"

"Yes, sir."

"Isn't in the game. Here's your outfit." He handed Djo
the long-bladed knife. "Now we're going to play fair. I'm
not going to spy on you. See that big flat rock up there on
the edge? We can see that from the house plain, with the
glasses. We want to know you're safe. So every morning
you go up there and put a pretty fair size stone on that
rock. Lay 'em in a row so we can count 'em. Better see to
it, for as soon as a rock is missing we'll come up after you,
and the game is over. And, remember, any time you want
to quit or you can't make it, come right on home. Or go sit
on the rock where we can see you, and we'll come and get
you. This is just a game, you know. You can always try
again, if you don't make it the first time." Andy checked

himself. He was becoming garrulous. This was now Djo's affair, to be carried through, one way or another, by his own inner promptings, without the aid or handicap of suggestion. He gathered up the reins.

"Good luck, son," said he.

At the edge of the chaparral he turned in his saddle. The straight naked little figure stood where he had left it, bronze in the sunlight. Andy raised his hand, palm outward, Indian fashion. He rode slowly down the mountain. It did not occur to him that the situation was fantastic; that this deliberate abandonment by its father of a child to the mercies of the wilderness was grotesque; that there might be pathos in the tiny naked figure. For the moment Andy was all Indian. The solid and actual world had vanished. He, and with him in spirit Djo, had moved apart into a mighty world of shadows, just they two, where awaited the event an enduring truth of spiritual relationship. There lay Djo's heritage, could he find it. Andy sensed it dimly as something bright and glowing and precious, that had illumined the struggle of the Dark and Bloody Ground, a guarded flame held in the high heart of the old woman, his grandmother, in a Pennsylvania farm, a living fire that quickened himself to a part in destiny. His hand tightened on the stock of the long rifle that Boone himself had borne. This was Djo's heritage. But he must find it for himself. Andy could not help him further. While these things resolved themselves in the alchemy of ordeal, he must stand apart. No one but himself understood, and he but dimly, and rather with the heart than with the mind. For an instant the lonesomeness of a complete isolation in space overcame him. He shivered slightly as though with a chill. And then a slow warmth bathed him. It was as though a companionship had drawn near. At certain crises of life this thing had come to him. He felt himself surrounded, upheld.

He gathered up the reins, touched spur, rode on down the mountain, humming half-voice. He was unconscious of the fact that he sang. The song was the Blackfoot song of prayer for the intercession of the Above People.

5

Djo did not come in the first day, as Vicenta volubly predicted. Nor the second; nor the third. Regularly the stones agreed upon as a signal appeared one by one on the flat rock. After Andy had determined this fact with the telescope, each in turn took a peek through that instrument. Each must see for himself. Andy moved withdrawn in his preoccupation with the inner spiritual crisis which, it must be repeated, he did not understand. It was as though the ranch and its people were of shadow substance. In his presence they felt shadowy: his piercing abstracted gaze through them made even the least imaginative *mozo* doubt for a fleeting instant his own substantiality. This was true even of the little girl, Amata; even of Carmel herself.

"Come back," she pleaded. "You have gone so far! See, I am no longer angry. I was foolish to become angry. I do not understand wholly; but he is now a man child and you are a man, and it is yours to make him a man."

With the adaptability of her race when deeply in love, she had swung even beyond Andy's own viewpoint. Reassured by the regular appearance of the all's-well signals, her anxieties were giving way to a truly Spanish pride in Djo's prowess. She thought Andy must also be feeling both the relief and the pride. She could not understand why he did not share them with her, why he remained thus removed.

On the morning of the seventh day of this strange testing, Andy on arising did not as usual take down the telescope from its pegs on the wall.

"Today, when you have arisen, we shall ride," he told Carmel.

She parted her lips, but checked her eager question in a sudden queer illusion that her voice would not carry to the still remoteness in which his spirit poised. In silence she hurried into her riding garments, in silence she piled the dark masses of her hair, and on her head placed the woven straw riding hat with the soft sun cloth weighted with little golden apples. In silence she gulped down the chocolate. They crossed the *sala* together, and out the door into the early freshness. In the half-light just before sun-up the guardian oaks spread wide as though in sanctuary to the last dusk of dying night crouched beneath their brooding. The mourning notes of doves floated through their branches, spaced and slow and soft, like the drift downward of golden flakes. Beneath the oaks were horses waiting, in charge of Panchito; and, surrounding them, the other people of the ranch. They were all there, a notable gathering: the *vaqueros;* the women of the household; the *mozas* who washed clothes at the stream; the very Indians and *mozos* whose affair was the varied menial business of the estate; and the children big and little. Benito had trudged up from the *milpas* and grain fields in the flats below. Abel Means leaned against the trunk of an oak, chewing tobacco. None spoke. They looked.

Andy helped Carmel to the saddle, himself mounted and took the reins.

"We ride alone," he said briefly to Panchito, who prepared to follow as usual.

The assembly watched them ride away. They eyed one another furtively and quietly dispersed. Something in the occasion had awed comment. They feared to voice what was in the minds of all, for each had looked into Andy's face and seen there something he could not understand. Only Vicenta, her eyes following her mistress, crossed herself, muttering,

"*La probecita!* The *patrón* is mad!"

"Silence, woman!" cried Panchito harshly.

And for once Vicenta made him no reply.

6

Andy and Carmel rode up the mountain together, meeting the warm sunlight on its slopes. They topped the rim of the park, and Carmel uttered a joyous cry. Andy laid a restraining hand on her horse's bridle.

Djo squatted before a fire. He was naked, as Andy had left him, except that he had replaced the confiscated loincloth with the skin of some small animal. He was intent on cooking something, and various objects were scattered about on the ground near him.

After a moment Andy relinquished his grasp. The two moved slowly forward.

Djo looked up and saw them. Carmel could no longer be restrained. Her horse leaped forward. She flung herself from the saddle and clasped the little figure to her, laughing and crying at once, babbling endearments and questions, her hands caressing Djo's body in reassurance of her eyes. Andy followed at a footpace. He reined in his horse, and sat, his hands crossed on the broad saddle horn, his eyes slowly and appraisingly taking in the details of what lay before him. He said nothing, and his face was grave. Djo had stiffened in his mother's embrace. He stood at rigid attention, and his eyes met those of his father unwaveringly. Carmel felt the tension. She released Djo and rose from her knees, looking from one to the other in perplexity. And at once she felt herself set aside. It was as though she were not there; as though she had become a disembodied onlooker at this encounter.

"Why do you come, *señor padre?*" asked Djo in Spanish. "Have I then failed?"

"That we shall see," said Andy.

"I have here made me fire," commented Djo, "and I have eaten well, and I have slept warm. If you had not come so soon I would have also clothes, for today, or tomorrow at most, I would have trapped a deer. Could I have done more?"

"You have done this without help?" demanded Andy searchingly.

"Of a surety, *señor padre*. Was not that the rule?"

He looked into Andy's face, hesitated.

"One came offering me help," he said reluctantly after a time. "But that I would not accept, and I made her——" He broke off confusedly.

A cold smile crossed Andy's face without relieving its austerity.

"That, naturally, I know," said he. "The sign was plain on the trail."

"But naturally, *señor padre*," agreed Djo. "But," he added, "surely Vicenta must not be blamed."

Andy smiled grimly. "She is not blamed," he said briefly.

He said nothing further. His eyes again swept over the details of the little camp.

Djo's faced clouded with enlightenment and anxiety.

"These are from the *milpa*," suggested Andy at last; and waited.

"But yes, *señor padre*," cried Djo eagerly. "From the *milpa*, of a surety. But no one brought them to me; I myself took them. Is not that in the game? And I went there, not at night, which would have been too easy and, I think, not in the game, but in the daytime, while Benito and the Indians were there working, and I crept there under their very noses and took them, and I covered my trail so that they never knew." Djo chuckled boyishly, then became grave again. "If they had caught me I would have come straight to you, *señor padre*, to tell you I had failed. Was not that all right?" he asked anxiously. "I remember how you told me of stealing into the Indian villages. . . ."

Andy heard no more. For an instant in his relief from suspicion, he felt lightheaded, a little dizzy, so that he grasped the pommel of his saddle for support. And in that instant he caught for the third time in his life at a rather tremendous inner experience, a sensation as of the uplifting of austere presences outside of and beyond himself; living, actual presences that had shared and which now rejoiced. And suddenly he seemed to himself to be rushed back as on a mighty wind from the remoteness in which he had for the past week poised, and to be free once more of warm and living and human relationship. He flung himself from the saddle with a mighty shout and in his turn clasped Djo in his arms. And between the man and the boy a last thin barrier broke so that thenceforward both knew they were wholly akin.

Carmel threw her hands wide in despair.

"These Burnett!" she muttered. "Never, never shall I know them!"

But in that second she was swept into the general embrace; and strangely enough she forgot all her maternal agonizings of the past week, she even forgot Djo. Passionately she clung to Andy, sobbing.

"Oh, *querido, querido!*" she cried over and over again. "You have come back! You have come back to me! Never, never go so far from me again!"

7

Andy sat on a fallen oak bole while Djo made his report. Or, rather, while Djo answered his catechism.

"How did you get your fire?"

"I found a fire stone and hit upon it with the back of the knife."

"And for tinder?" Andy grinned at him. "That's where

that breach clout would have come in handy, eh? Did you think of that when I made you give it up?"

Djo grinned back.

"Yes, *señor padre*."

"I thought so. Good boy. What did you use for tinder?"

"It was difficult," submitted Djo, "for this is still the season of rains, and all is green, and nothing is ripe, so there is no dry pith in any of the plants you told me. I found some dry rotted oak, but it would not take the spark I could make with my fire stone. It was not very good, not like a real flint."

"What is that yonder next that mariposa?" said Andy suddenly, pointing.

"It's a lizard," replied Djo.

Andy sighed, arose from the bole, made two strides to the mariposa, and picked up a good-sized chunk of rock, which he tossed to Djo.

"Plain sight," he commented.

Djo stared at the fragment.

"But—but there should be no flint in these mountains," he stammered.

"No," conceded Andy, "I put it there. If you'd had that you wouldn't have had much trouble making your fire, would you? Well, why didn't you see it? I put it there for you to see; in plain sight." Djo hung his head. "I'll tell you. It was because you didn't *expect* to see it. Go ahead. How did you get your fire?"

"I didn't, until the next day," confessed Djo.

"Oh!" cried Carmel. "The cold! My poor baby!"

But this was a false note; as she instantly realized, and fell silent, for she saw this was men's business, and Carmel was not devoid of common sense—or of humor.

"There's no cold—what you can call cold—in this country," Andy flung to her. "And next day?"

"While searching up the hill yonder, for a *mescal*, I came upon a cave in which were many bats. There was much droppings which were dry almost like powder, so I struck a spark in it to try. It is much better than tinder, *señor padre*. It takes the fire instantly."

"Now that I did not know!" cried Andy. "That is something worth knowing!"

Djo glowed at the approbation.

"Once I had my fire, there was no more trouble. There are here many rabbits, and quail—and other things. And, *señor padre*, if you had not come so soon I would have had a deer."

"Until then you were hungry?"

Djo made a comical face.

"I ate," he said briefly.

"But what?" cried Carmel.

"The new buds just starting in the trees," enumerated Djo, "the curl tips of ferns, some seeds of the grass—there was one place where the sun was hot where they were ripe, the berries of manzanita. They were not very good; but I was not hungry."

Carmel made a murmur of indignant protest.

"You caught your rabbits and quail with snares?" suggested Andy.

"Yes, *señor padre*, as you had showed me—at the first."

Andy grinned again.

"Loincloth would have come in handy again, wouldn't it?"

Again Djo answered the grin in acknowledgment.

"What did you use for your snares?"

"I climbed to the *puerto suelo* where I remembered we saw mares last month, and I searched until I found where hair from their tails had caught in the brush."

"*Bueno!*" cried Andy, then in English: "That shines!"

He arose from the tree trunk and began to pace back and forth.

"When I had eaten the meat of the rabbit," Djo continued, "I cut leaves of the *mescal* and pounded them with stones and scraped them with the knife until the fibers were bare and wove me a strong cord. Like this,"—he fumbled behind a rock and produced a fragment.

Andy examined it curiously.

"I learned this from Pascal," Djo explained, "while I was making bricks."

Andy glanced at Carmel.

"It is with this that I would catch the deer," Djo continued. "I finished it yesterday, and I made a loop and laid it where the deer come to drink."

"We shall look at that," said Andy. "It is not as easy to catch a deer as a rabbit."

"No, *señor padre*," acknowledged Djo, "and it may be I have not set it well. It is not easy to bend a large enough young tree with no one to help, for I am not very heavy."

"For why do you bend a young tree?" Carmel could not restrain her curiosity. Her interest was kindling. She became aware that her menfolk looked down upon her from superior masculine heights. She chuckled to herself in appreciation.

"The loop catches the deer by a foot," Andy explained patiently, as though the thing were obvious, "but it could easily pull loose. The sapling is bent, like a spring, to lift the foot from the ground so it cannot do so. You are as heavy as a small deer," he told Djo. "Possibly a small deer might be caught—if you set the loop and the trigger properly. We will take a look. What else?"

"I also made this." Djo submitted a strip of rabbit hide, in each end of which he had tied a hard clay ball. "You hold it by the middle and whirl it about your head like a *reata*, and throw it," he explained to Carmel. "Sometimes it hits something. I am not very good with it. But it is fun. And I did kill a quail with it, and two rabbits."

"I did not teach you this," said Andy.

"No: Pascal told me. He said it was better for ducks.

I have not tried it for ducks. Pascal also told me how *los indios* catch ducks with a net woven of *tules*. I was going to try that, but the *laguna* is far, and I wanted to catch my deer first, and I must place the stone each day on the flat rock, as you told me."

"With nets," repeated Andy. "Now there is something I do not know. How can that be done? To strike the ducks with the *bola*, yes, that I see. But nets? How do you do that?"

Djo explained, his manner modest, but his whole being suffused with delight.

"Why, one makes a wide net of *tules*," said he, "and finds a narrow slough with the *tules* growing high on either side, and he sets up the net across the slough on stakes; and he makes some small bundles of *tules* and sets them afloat by the net, so that the ducks flying see them, and come down to swim with them, thinking that they are other ducks."

"Decoys," Andy supplied the English word.

"Decoys." Djo repeated the word experimentally. "One hides, very carefully, close below the net. And when there are many ducks swimming, one leaps out suddenly and some of the ducks dash against the net and fall back, and one seizes them quickly before they recover."

"Well," observed Andy. "I never heard of that!" He ruminated the idea. "It doesn't sound reasonable. Pascal told you they catch ducks that way?"

"Yes, *señor padre*."

"We've got to try that."

"Yes, *señor padre*," said Djo happily.

Andy prowled about restlessly. Djo waited. Carmel watched them both with bright eyes.

"Bough bed's not so bad, eh?" suggested Andy, reverting to English. "Next time put her next a rock and make your fire t' other side of your bed. You'll sleep warmer: rock reflects the heat back.—Hm? Make you any deadfalls?"

"No, *señor padre*."

"Snares good enough, eh? Try a pit trap?"

"Yes, *señor padre*," acknowledged Djo, with a certain reluctance which Andy could not but notice.

"It's quite a trick," the latter consoled the boy for supposed failure. "Animals are pretty noticing. It's hard to hide things from them. Takes practice." He examined his son's face keenly. "What is it, Djo? Out with it?"

"It wasn't that," said Djo. "I caught a skunk," he blurted out.

Andy threw back his head with a roar of laughter; in which, after a moment, Djo joined.

"*Gato montés*," Andy translated the word to Carmel.

Still chuckling, Andy crossed the tiny grass plot to the horses. He untied a bundle from the saddle strings.

"Here, son," he said, "here's your clothes. If Vicenta sees you with nothing on but that rabbit skin she'll have my scalp. Well, what is it?"

"My deer snare," said Djo.

"We'll ride up later and take a look."

Djo still hesitated, the bundle in his hands.

"Come along!" urged Andy.

"*Señor padre*," began Djo, and stopped.

"Well?"

"Oh, *señor padre*, must I go back now?" pleaded Djo in a rush of words. "Cannot I stay just a little, just a few days more? I shall catch my deer, I know it. And I shall make clothes. And—and——"

"And?"

Djo eyed his father doubtfully.

"Over beyond the *puerto suelo* there lives a bear." He stopped.

Andy was eyeing him steadily.

"Well, what of it?"

Djo was embarrassed, unable to proceed.

"What do you think you can do, monkeying with a bear?" demanded Andy in English. "Don't talk foolish."

"If I catch my deer I could make a strong *reata* of rawhide," urged Djo in the more familiar Spanish, "and it might be that I could trap the bear. I have thought of it much, *señor padre*. With another *reata* and a heavy stone to help I could bend down a strong tree, and——"

"And after you have caught your bear—if you did— what would you do with him? Go up and bite his ear?" asked Andy sarcastically.

Djo flushed but stood his ground.

"I have the knife," said he. "I could stand to one side, and if I threw it just so I might——"

Andy surveyed the small figure mockingly, but with a very tender light in his eye.

"Son," he said at last, still in English, "you're a good boy and I'm proud of you. Proud of you," he repeated emphatically. "But there's one thing you've got to learn."

"Yes, *señor padre*."

"Don't bite off more than you can chew. Now you get on those duds and come along."

8

Djo mounted behind his father. They rode slowly down the mountain. All three were happy, though each in a different way. Djo had had a wonderful time, and glowed with pardonable triumph that he had played the game of Wildman well enough to earn his father's praise; for Djo knew that in such matters his father's praise was worth while. Carmel's heart was singing because this prank was finished, and because Djo was safe and well; but above all because her lover had come back to her from across mysterious and terrifying spaces.

But Andy's happiness was a happiness of his whole being, for it was made of the dissolution of something that had long lain heavy in his heart. The fact that he had had no conscious knowledge of it until these past few days had not lessened its effect. Now he saw it clearly; could even put it into words. He was astonished, even a little uneasy, as though at an implication of disloyalty. But with characteristic honesty he now put it to himself bluntly.

In Djo's veins ran the blood of two races. Andy admired and loved the Californian people with whom he had cast his lot. Nevertheless, he did not want Djo like them; not even like Ramón or the stately old *hacendado*, Don Sylvestre. He wanted Djo to be an American of his own breed, the breed of mountain men; and that was something that could not be taught, but must come from the inner spirit; could not be told, but must be tested.

His mind flashed back to the old days. Before it arose a picture of Running Elk in full ceremonial costume watching gravely the initiation ceremony of which his son was part. The boy was dragging about a buffalo skull by means of a cord passed through deep slits in the muscles of his chest. This he must do until by his own leapings and plungings against the weight he could tear the cord through the flesh, and so stand free, nor must he flinch or fail. Andy recalled his own admiration, both for the boy's courage, and for Running Elk's stolid calm, for he knew Running Elk's affection for the lad. The warrior puffed at his pipe with detached indifference; but Andy particularly remembered the fine circlet of perspiration that stood out on Running Elk's brow. Now, many years after, he understood that Running Elk agonized in spirit not so much at the terrible physical torture, as Andy had thought with sympathy at the time, but with a deeper anxiety lest by failure the boy should prove his only in flesh and not in the deeper kinship of spirit. The ordeal had been long and severe, for the lad was strongly

built and his muscles were tough. Even Andy, hardened
as he was by the wild life, had felt a little squeamish, and
would gladly have retired could he have done so without
grave offense. At last the boy tore free, standing rigid
with the last remnant of his strength, hand uplifted, facing
the setting sun, a figure of mingled pathos and glory,
the blood streaming from his breast. And even now in
Andy's ears tolled the deep resonance of old Running
Elk's voice:

"The Above People have given me a son!"

Andy was suddenly snatched back from the high pure
cold of the Rockies to the bathing golden warmth of the
California hillside. Carmel was laughing at him.

"What is it you say, *querido*, in that strange language?"

"I did not know I spoke," said he. "It was the Blackfoot language. I was just remembering."

But he would not tell her what it was. That was between himself and the Above People.

PART II
Foofaraw

CHAPTER I

THE *casa* of Folded Hills ranch stood part way up a gentle slope. Two great live-oaks shaded it. It was low and colonnaded and whitewashed; one corner of the roof line was concealed under a spread of cream-colored roses, reaching out to capture a grape arbor that continued the low straight line of the house. A capacious jar of earthenware, an *olla*, hung from one of the oak's branches, where it swung or revolved slowly, following the caprice of breeze or the stretch of the rawhide by which it was suspended. Its mouth was closed by a wooden cover on which stood a cup.

Close to the walls of the *casa* was a strip of garden in which had been planted the gayest of flowers. A little child threaded her way carefully among tall foxgloves, touching blossoms delicately with the tip of one finger. Near the entrance door stood an earthenware vase in which was so incongruous an arrangement of color and bloom that it was instantly evident as the child's effort. The still air tingled hot to the nostrils; but only just inside the deep embrasure of the doorway the shadow was cool to the eye. Across the flagstone a large dog lay. He was bothered by the flies; kept moving restlessly, snapping at them with a sharp click of teeth. Above him hung a mocking bird in a homemade cage.

It was a nice buzzy morning. The rounded hills were saturated with sun. The day seemed wide, spacious, serene. Under the oak in front of the house stood haphazard a number of benches. A blackened spot marked the site of past fires. The whole surface of the ground had been well sprinkled by water, so that in the warm air was the smell of good wet earth. A filled bucket stood next the bole, in case the dust should anywhere dry out.

The immediate scene was otherwise empty. Across the background, however, moved an occasional gayly clad figure. Someone was singing, a good hearty man's voice. From down the slope, in the direction of cottonwoods that marked the course of a stream, came the sound of women's laughter; but so far away that it was almost indistinguishable as such, so that it was more like little distant tinkling bells. These movements and sounds, somehow, did not disturb the picture of spacious, serene, timeless leisure, in which the only living figures were the child and the dog annoyed by the flies.

2

But now, around the angle of the house, suddenly appeared a man on horseback. He raised his left hand slightly. The horse stopped short in its tracks. This was a grave, lean man, nearing middle age, with steady sardonic eyes and a face set in deep lines as though it had been carved from wood. At his appearance the child paused, her finger-tip still on a rose. The dog forgot its tormentors and lifted its ears.

The man swung from his saddle with the grace of the *vaquero* and stepped forward, the great rowels of his spurs clinking against the baked earth. He swept off a flat wide *sombrero*, exposing a brilliant kerchief bound tight about his head. The horse stood quietly where it had been left, its ears slanted in virtue, champing softly and musically the rollers on the long spade of its silvered bit.

"*Buenos días*, Panchito," the child greeted this new-comer with dignity.

"*Buenos días, señorita*," the *vaquero* returned the greeting respectfully; and waited.

"You desire?" the child inquired.

"The *señor*, your father; with your permission, *señorita*," submitted the newcomer. "Is he within?"

The child inclined her head.

"He but just returned from the *pasear* of the morning," said she. "I will seek him."

"If you will be so gracious, *señorita*," said the man.

She moved toward the door, threading her way daintily between the tall foxgloves. At the door she turned, outspread her skirts slightly between the tips of her fingers, dropped the sketch of a curtsey.

"Be with God, Panchito," said she.

"And His blessed saints," returned the man, bending from the hips.

The Doña Amata, who was but eight years of age, stepped over the dog without loss of dignity and disappeared within, closing the door of the *casa* carefully behind her. Panchito waited impassively, his broad hat against his thigh.

3

A few moments later the door opened again to disclose the tall form of the *hacendado* of Folded Hills. The dog wrinkled his lips back from his teeth and thumped his tail. No line of the *vaquero's* wooden face altered, but his eyes quickened, and the rigid lines of his body relaxed to a more informal ease. A tempo quickened as though a breeze stirred, though the air hung still and sun-warmed.

"Don Ramón is approaching, *señor*," the vaquero stated directly.

Andy Burnett's face lighted with pleasure.

"That is good hearing!" he exclaimed. "Is the Doña Conchita with him? Where are they?"

"I saw them from the hill," replied Panchito. "They were then near the *álamos*. The Doña Conchita is not with him. He rides from the direction of Soledad. There are with him the Padre Sanchez, and two Indians, and with them a young girl. A *moza*," he added.

Before Andy could speculate on this information, the little group of horsemen rounded the corner of the building. There were, as Panchito had said, five of them. Ramón Rivera and Father Sanchez rode together. Close at their heels were two Indians, and between them the girl. The latter was a handsome creature, vivid, vital, with stormy sullen eyes, and a shock of dark hair, unbound and falling about her shoulders. She wore the *camisa* and short skirt of the *moza*, and her legs were bare.

Ramón rode directly to Andy without dismounting. His salute was brief, his face grave. Andy surveyed his friend with secret amusement. Ramón's externals were rarely serious. When he departed from his gay and debonair detachment from the responsibilities, one of two things was certain: either the matter was of the last importance or of none at all.

"The *padre* Sanchez and I have come to consult you, Don Andrés," he stated, after the first formal greeting.

"*Á su disposición, señores*," acknowledged Andy. "Be pleased to dismount." He signed the *vaquero* to take charge of the horses and stalked away to the great oak tree, where he seated himself on one of the small benches and awaited the approach of his guests. This was not discourtesy. It was a part of the rôle he had so long played that he slipped into it easily, as into a garment. The custom of holding a court of complaint and informal justice beneath this live-oak had grown gradually to a settled institution. Its beginnings were in the issuing of the orders and the settling of the small disputes with which every *ranchero* must begin his day with his own people. Andy liked to do this in the open air, rather than in the house. He had a practical frontiersman's common sense, combined with a secret well of sympathy and humor belied by the grave mask of his face. His somewhat picturesque and unconventional decisions and solutions appealed to his people. Shortly this reputation for fair play had spread beyond the boundaries of Folded Hills. He was called upon to arbitrate a dispute between neighbors over a cattle range. The difference was an angry one. In vain he protested; recommended recourse to Monterey. The disputants insisted that at least he listen. He did so; finally, under pressure, voiced an opinion. To his astonishment the opinion was taken for a decision. Furthermore, it was accepted unquestionably by both parties, who rode away amicably together.

From that the thing grew almost to the proportions of an institution. Andy found himself in the position of a sort of informal justice of the peace. People journeyed considerable distances to submit to his judgment not only matters of some import, such as a dispute on the cattle range, but smaller perplexities and problems that involved no dispute at all. And this even when priest or *alcalde* was nearer to come at.

Andy had no authority; he needed none. He continued to look upon his decisions as merely his personal opinions. It took him some time to conquer his own diffidence, to admit the full significance of his influence over these fundamentally simple people. But he could not fail to be touched by it. He accepted the situation finally as a responsibility; and into these small irregular occasions grew certain loose formalities. They too had grown slowly, out of the mountain man's gropings for an atmosphere of attunement.

Andy seated himself on the bench and waited. Panchito, having turned the visitors' animals over to the care of other *vaqueros*, proceeded methodically to kindle a small fire on the blackened spot that marked the site of innumerable other similar fires. Andy liked a fire to sit by when serious talk was forward. He did not himself realize

that somehow the little blaze and the tiny column of
smoke eddying across the shafts of sunlight linked him in
spirit with grave-spaced councils of another adopted
people in another land. He would have been astonished
had anyone told him that it was a symbol: but that is
what it was. Nor, of course, did any of his people understand. They knew merely that Don Andrés wanted a
fire: and theirs was a spirit of charming acceptance.

4

Ramón and the priest followed Andy and sat down
either side. The two Indians and the girl remained ahorseback, where they had been left. Ramón talked: Andy
leaning forward, his forearms on his knees, listened.
Father Sanchez stared straight ahead of him, his face inscrutable, slipping the beads of his rosary back and forth
between his fingers.

"It is the matter of a little difference between the good
padre and myself," stated Ramón. "We have talked long
together, but we cannot agree except on one thing; and
that is to abide by your decision."

"It is not my habit to decide anything for anybody
else," said Andy.

"That fact had escaped my memory," said Ramón,
"but you will at least accord us the benefit of your
opinion?"

"Why, yes," assented Andy. "I will tell you what I
think, if you will tell me what it is."

Ramón raised one quizzical eyebrow toward the priest,
who paid him no attention.

"Will you explain the matter, *padre?*" the *ranchero*
deferred to him politely. In the end they both explained;
each from his own point of view. Wapita, it seemed, was
one of the *mozas* on Ramón Rivera's *rancho* on the plateau
of Jolón.

"Wapita?" queried Andy. "What name is that? That is not a Spanish name. Is it Indian? Is she Indian?"

"No," Ramón agreed to this, "it is not Spanish. It may be Indian. I do not know. She is not Indian. She is pure *californio*. But as for the name, which is indeed a strange one——"

"Never mind. Go on."

Her mother, it developed, had been one of the girls attached to the great Rivera *hacienda* down the valley. She had died. Her father——

"Why, I think she is one of our bastards," admitted Ramón easily. "I have allowed her the name of Rivera."

"Yours?" asked Andy.

"No," Ramón denied with decision. "But there are many Riveras."

She had been raised on the *rancho*. She was well treated. She had no more than the usual tasks to perform. Ramón stressed the details of her circumstances, which should be in all respects happy. But she was continually in trouble; a little devil. She had always been a little devil with respect for nothing and no one. Lately she had taken to running away. Three times in the past year. Always she had been found and brought back. But she was becoming a scandal. His was a respectable *rancho*, Ramón averred virtuously.

Where did she run to? Andy wanted to know.

That was unknown. She had never succeeded in getting very far. Toward the sea.

"What does she say?" asked Andy.

"Nothing! Nothing at all!" cried Ramón. "She will answer nothing."

"Does she seek men?"

"Men!" Ramón exploded. "But that could be understood! That would at least make sense! But let me tell you, I believe on the cross that there is not a *mozo* or a *vaquero* at Los Madroños who has not nursed a broken

head that she has bestowed upon him for his pains!"
He chuckled reluctantly. "She seems to hate all men.
And that is strange, for she is an attractive little hussy
enough, and——"

"Perhaps she hates all men because of one."

But Ramón shook his head.

"She has always been thus: and I have had her as one
of my people since she was a baby; and I have watched
her well, for it is the business of a good *ranchero* to be a
father to his people." He stopped himself short with a
flash of white teeth. "You need not make the joke of
that, *amigo*," he warned.

But Andy, on a trail, was too single-minded to be deflected. Wherein was the difference of opinion between the
priest and the *ranchero?* he insisted.

Very simple. Father Sanchez—whose mission Indians,
by the way, had made this capture and brought the truant
in to Soledad—had summoned Ramón, and now insisted
that the obvious procedure was to put Wapita in a convent and make a nun of her.

"A human soul is in danger of perdition," interposed the
priest.

Ramón did not think she would make a very good nun;
and that something else should be devised; some effective
discipline; or perhaps she could be sent away somewhere.
He was vague, but decided, following obviously some
inner instinct.

"Let me see her," interrupted Andy.

Ramón shouted a command to the Indians, who in
turn spoke to the girl. She shook her head violently and
gripped the horn of her saddle. One of the Indians seized
her by the arm. She shook him off fiercely; and then, as
though suddenly making up her mind, she leaped from
the saddle with a swirl of her short skirts. With a toss of
her head she marched herself across the intervening space
to plant herself squarely before the three men, her hands

on her hips, her eyes staring at them defiantly from beneath her tumble of dark hair.

Andy surveyed her mildly for some time in silence.

"What is the trouble, Wapita?" he asked at last. "Why do you run away?"

She set her lips.

"I am your friend," persisted the *ranchero*. "Why will you not tell me? It is possible that matters might be arranged."

For some moments he continued to question, but without result. Her silence and her defiance were impenetrable. At last he gave over, but continued to study her thoughtfully.

"You see," said Ramón, "It is as I say. She is——"

Andy silenced him with a gesture.

So for a long time the little group remained. The girl's high defiance fell to sullenness, but she did not lower her eyes. The priest stared detachedly into mystic distances. Ramón leaned back against the great tree trunk and lighted a cigarette. After a moment he threw away the cigarette and arose to his feet. The Doña Carmel was coming up the slope from the direction of the *milpa;* and with her Djo. As she moved into the shadow she took off her broad sun hat, exposing her sleek smooth hair. Ramón was the only one, amid these varied absorptions, who saw her and the straight handsome boy. She silenced her brother's greeting by a finger on her lip; glanced at her husband, wholly rapt; rested her eyes for a moment on the girl; raised one eyebrow toward Ramón in quizzical amusement; repeated her gesture of caution; and continued on into the house. To Ramón, looking after her, brother though he was, it seemed that her graceful figure floated, as floats an imponderable on an air current; so it was to him as though a cooling breeze had passed, and a faint perfume. And he reflected that this was a strange thought to be having, and how astounded Carmel would

be that she had inspired it in him, and how pleased; for
his gay spirit had accustomed her to a robust fraternal
teasing. It is because I have been so long away from Conchita, he thought; and his mind wandered to Los Madroños, and how completely it, and its people, filled his life;
and from that another shock of surprise that this should
be so. I am past my youth, he thought; but he thought it
with no regret, but on the contrary with satisfaction. And
that brought his mind back to the girl, for he realized
with a slight astonishment that he discerned in himself
no trace, no flicker of response to the wild and savage
beauty of her. He stopped to examine this, as one stops
to examine any new and curious thing, and he barely
repressed a chuckle at the himself he saw, for he had
never looked at it before. Not that the younger Ramón
—he told this later self-virtuously—had ever excessive
cause to shrive its soul; but it must admit the roving eye.
And this girl, it now came to him, undoubtedly possessed
a certain challenging allurement of vitality. So his thoughts
ran idly, while his friend pondered.

5

Suddenly Andy raised his head and began to speak.
Father Sanchez came back from his mystic distances;
stopped telling his beads.

"Why, this is what I think," said the *ranchero*—"that
you are both wrong. It's your decision, Ramón; but if I
were handling her I'd take her back where I found her
and tell her if she wants to run away, to go ahead and run.
You can shut her up on the *rancho* if you want to. Or
put her in a convent," he said to Father Sanchez. "But
you won't get anywhere, any more than you would bot-
tling up a kettle by sticking a plug in the snout."

"You would abandon this child to destruction, to the
everlasting flames of hell!" cried the priest.

"I don't know about that," said Andy. "You can find those things right on the home ranch if you've got it in you. Nobody ever quite knows the end of the trail he's on, seems to me. I've seen some of the worst of 'em come back, *padre*, from a pretty good scorching—and persecute every young thing in sight with their virtue. Maybe her trail lies that way. I don't know. Neither do you," he added.

"I do not understand you, a son of the Church, saying these things!" cried Father Sanchez. "From another I would cry heresy!"

"Don't, *padre*," advised Andy. "I'm just saying what I think. What do you say, Ramón?"

Ramón was taken aback. His trust in his friend's wisdom was almost childlike. But he had knowledge of the world of men and temptation. To throw to it, unprotected and unguided, a young girl—and such a girl as this! There was on him a moral obligation. It would be a relief, heaven knows, to dump it overboard, to thrust it aside. Ramón had been raised in piety.

"Have we not here responsibility for a human soul?" he asked piously, with a glance toward the priest.

"Plenty," said Andy dryly. "Too much to block its trail." He surveyed his friend with twinkling eyes. Ramón caught the twinkle.

"Very well," he assented doubtfully. "It shall be as you say."

The girl had been looking from one to the other during this colloquy. Andy turned to her.

"All right, *muchacha*," said he briskly. "Climb on that horse and go wherever you like. The Indians can bring it back when you're through with it."

He arose as though in dismissal of the whole affair, expressing no curiosity as to her destination; or if, indeed, she had one. But apparently he thought better of this.

"You've got some place in mind," he stated, rather

than inquired. "Better ride all the way—it's hard going afoot. You needn't be afraid: nobody will bother you. *Adios, y buena fortuna.*"

"*Señor!*" For the first time the girl spoke. Hers was a low-pitched voice, with beneath its smoothness a strange under vibration that was almost a husk.

"Yes?" said Andy over his shoulder.

"May I not stay here? At this *rancho?*"

The *ranchero* turned back to face her.

"So you have a tongue, *muchacha;* and you wish to stay here! Why?"

"For the same reason that I ran away. It is my desire." But there was little of arrogance in the words.

"Well," said Andy reasonably, "why was your desire to run away? If you are to stay here, you must tell me that."

Wapita thrust her hands, palm outward, from her face. "I do not know! I could not breathe!"

Andy did not press her further.

"Very well," said he. "You may stay here as long as you wish. When you want to go away, why, go. No one will stop you. So do not be so foolish as to run away barefoot again."

"No, *señor*," said the girl.

6

The three men looked after Wapita as she disappeared under convoy of the servant summoned by Andy's whistle.

"How long," then speculated Ramón, "do you imagine she will stay here?"

Unexpectedly it was Father Sanchez who replied.

"For as long as she is certain she is free to go," said he. He turned to Andy with a gesture that might have been apology. "My son," said he, "I repent my hasty words."

"*Holá!*" Ramón uttered his great shout, and slapped his

thigh, "But you, my frien', are the sly one!" He spoke English, as always to Andy when he was especially pleased. "You know all the time she would not run away! Your pardon, *padre*," again in Spanish. "How often must we learn over again that this one is *sabio!*"

"*Fuera!*" Andy was embarrassed. "There's no great wisdom in that. It's just common sense. I know the breed: that's all. I've seen them before. They're just made different. They *are* that way. She's—she's——" The almost mystic attunement with reality had passed. Andy was again his inarticulate self, groping for expression. "She's *bronco!*" he cried with sudden relief. "That's it! You know how it is with *broncos*, Ramón. There's some you can break. But there's others you just have to give their heads and let them run until they tire themselves down. No good to shut them in a corral, or tie them up. They fight; and when they quit fighting, they wait for another chance. Every fool *vaquero* knows that."

"He is telling us we are fools, *padre*," said Ramón mischievously.

Andy aimed at him a mock blow, which he dodged. The priest was smiling.

"With permission, Don Andrés," said the latter, "I will pay my respects to the Doña Carmel."

"Inform my sister, *padre mío*, that I follow you to her presence in a little minute," requested Ramón.

CHAPTER II

THE girl Wapita appeared completely to have changed her type. And overnight! Her wild and defiant manner vanished. Even her unruly hair was made to lie down and behave. She surveyed the world from large dove eyes—when she raised them at all. Left more or less to her own devices to find her niche in the *rancho's* activities, she attached herself to the *casa*. Andy was amused. The domestic affairs of the *casa*, and their outside ramifications, were under the direct supervision of sharp-tongued old Vicenta, the "too-fat one." No one in the know would pick out that department as a snap. He even warned Wapita of that fact, though indirectly by suggesting she might find an outside task freer or better fun. But Wapita persisted that she knew what she wanted. Nor at first did Vicenta spare her. Wapita accepted everything meekly. She ended by becoming a sort of maid, or personal attendant, to Carmel.

The latter's kind heart was enormously gratified over this transformation.

"But she is indeed a true *penitente, querido!*" said she to Andy. "It is a miracle of the blessed saints. And," she added piously, "it was wrought through you, *querido!*"

But Andy only laughed.

"Don't holler till you're out of the woods," said he in English.

"What you mean, that?" inquired Carmel in the same language; for her interest always quickened at new expressions in this, her adopted tongue.

"Too sudden; much too sudden," he reverted to Spanish. "People don't change so completely overnight—especially people like Wapita. That *would* be a miracle. And," he added quaintly, "I don't somehow see either of us important enough for any saint to bother with. He'd have to be a very little saint with a lot of time on his hands. And in that case he probably wouldn't be big enough to do such a miracle."

Carmel had a delicious sense of humor about most things; but none at all when it came to a question of religion; and deep in her heart dwelt a very secret uneasiness as to the state of Andy's soul. Andy loved to shock her simple piety with such speeches. They never failed. As always she leaned forward earnestly, her eyes big and round.

"Do not say these things!" she besought him. "I think such talk of the blessed saints is blasphemy; though I do not know. For the soul of the least of God's creatures——"

Andy snatched her to him with a great shout of laughter.

"You are delicious, *querida!*" he cried. "Be consoled: I do not doubt the blessed saints. And I am as delighted as you are that Wapita is so good. But I am a little in doubt that the blessed saints had much to do with it. Wapita, I think, is likely to shock them at any time. They should be warned. Couldn't you do it? That's what I mean."

Carmel freed herself, and smoothed her ruffled plumage, but she could not at once smooth out her ruffled spirit. Andy departed, still laughing at her expression of reproof. As soon as the door had closed behind him, Carmel sought out a candle from the store in the aromatic chest, brought from China on one of the Boston ships. It was a very lovely candle of sperm, quite other than the ordinary homemade affairs dipped from tallow, and was brightly painted. This she placed in a socket before the image of the Virgin that stood on a small shelf against the wall of her bedchamber. Kneeling before the image, she bowed her sleek dark head for some moments in silent petition. Then she lighted the candle. After a moment's thought she again opened the chest and took from it another candle, but a smaller candle and unpainted, altogether an inferior candle to the first. This, too, she dedicated to the aloof, faintly smiling image. She closed the door softly behind her. She hoped she had straightened things out for both Andy and the girl. She was not quite sure.

2

Life went on serenely enough for nearly three months. Wapita's conduct continued exemplary. At first Andy had paid her no great attention. Now he found himself watching her with a quickening interest. He began almost to be persuaded that he had been mistaken.

Then abruptly she disappeared. No one knew where she had gone, or why she had gone. Carmel was greatly troubled and would have search made. To this Andy refused assent.

"I made a promise and I shall keep it," said he. Nor could he be moved by pleadings to do with the girl's youth and inexperience. The only concession he would make was a search of the immediate vicinity in acknowledgment of Carmel's passionate conviction that some accident had befallen her.

"There are so many things!" she cried. "She may have fallen into a *barranca*—one of the great bears from the *sierra*—she may be lying somewhere, right now, while we are speaking, suffering the tortures of——"

Carmel drew a harrowing picture, which she instantly believed as a fact.

"In that case she is at no great distance," Andy pointed out.

So Panchito and the *vaqueros* and Djo rode methodically in widening circles, until they had covered the radius of any reasonable short expedition from the *casa*, but reported nothing, and were then ordered to desist. Only Djo continued to prowl about, apparently on an off chance.

Andy too was troubled; but more disappointed. However, he did not swerve from his original attitude toward the matter. Andy was like that.

Coincidentally with the girl's disappearance appeared a visitor. There were many such to Folded Hills, mostly residents of the country; but occasionally, as now, a stranger. This man was an American. He announced himself as named Seth Murray; and that he was one of a party of immigrants recently arrived in the upper valley at Sutter's Fort. Business connected with his sojourn brought him to Monterey. He had made the deflection up the Salinas Valley to make the acquaintance of the *ranchero*.

The type was not uncommon. Carmel had become used to them and their idiosyncrasies. At first she had tried to play her part of hostess; but she learned in time that this only rendered them ill at ease. They amused her greatly; and sometimes she expressed this amusement to Andy; but desisted when she felt his genuine distress.

"I know, *querido*," she consoled him half mockingly, "I know he's the what-you-call r-rough diamond! Like you when first I mak' you dance *como-el-oso*. So fierce! So *serio!*" She scowled comically. "Afraid to let hees smile go too far! Always ready for the Indians! It ees very de-pend-able,"—she deployed one of her best words triumphantly—"but it ees not com-fort-able. You go talk to heem. R-run along, an' be good boys!"

So Andy would kindle a little friendship fire under the great oak, and then the two would squat and talk and smoke far into the night. With these visitors he relived old times and learned about the new.

But this man, Seth Murray, was more interesting than

most, for he brought what almost amounted to a personal message.

"I got interested in coming west on account of a friend of yours," he told Andy. "Didn't know it till I'd lit in Californy and heerd your name. Though I didn't start for Californy," he added parenthetically, "started for Oregon, same as the rest. But this old feller lived in my town, back Ohio-way, and he'd roamed all over the plains and mountains, and I used to sit and listen to him by the hour. He called your name often. So I sez to myself, I'll just look this feller up."

"Who was he?" asked Andy.

"Kelly—John Kelly. Said he knew you right well. Recall him?"

"He was a partner of mine—more to me than a father," said Andy soberly. "How is he? What is he doing?"

They talked of Kelly, who had married, it seemed; and had children; and was in business. Andy heard the words; but they did not get through to his intelligence. He could not see Jack Kelly as a business man, a husband, a father. The old picture persisted, as he had first seen Jack, in St. Louis, 'way back in the early 'twenties; tall, muscular, clad in fresh buckskins, his hair hanging to hide the broad of his shoulders, his eyes hard and direct, puckered to a keen scrutiny.

"You'd find all of them changed, one way or another, the old-timers," submitted Murray when Andy said something of this. "Everything's changed, I reckon, from what Mr. Kelly told me."

This man, Seth Murray, was a godsend. He was the first wagon immigrant Andy had seen. Vaguely he had comprehended that the trail to Oregon through the South Pass had been worn deep with the wheel tracks of the covered wagons; but the picture had had no reality. Murray made him see it. He had not been one who had followed blindly the trail, insulated by the very dust clouds of his caravan. He was intelligent; observing. He had not only kept his eyes open, but he had taken pains to reach out for acquaintance, to talk, to ask questions. In addition he proved to have a curious background of knowledge unusual in a greenhorn. He appeared to be a man of considerable education, but he spoke in the dialect of the middle border.

Andy was astounded at what Murray told him. The fur business must be all upside down. The beaver days were now almost a thing of the past; that is, as compared with its pristine importance. The trade was in buffalo robes and wolf skins and small stuff. The mountain men no longer met in annual rendezvous. They had scattered; died; disappeared; become hunters for the posts called forts; turned into guides to the caravans of covered wagons that, each year, in greater numbers wore deeper the Oregon Trail. Andy heard the names of a few of his contemporaries; but as to most of them rumor was silent. Fitzpatrick was guiding wagon trains; somewhat scornfully and sardonically, it seemed, for Murray spoke of Bad Hand's reputation for arbitrary methods.

"You can do what he says or go to hell!" said he. "But," he added, "he does get you there."

The ability to get you there, Andy gathered, was highly esteemed and highly prized. Increasingly many, especially those who tried it alone or with incompetent guides, did not get there at all. It was not a matter of getting lost, as might have been the case in the old days. Nobody could possibly mistake the trail. It was in places hundreds of feet wide, for when the wagon ruts had bitten too deep into the soft spring prairie, they were abandoned, and a new set started. You crossed the Kansas now on a ferry, consisting of two boats that held two wagons each. The animals swam. Cost you a dollar a wagon. There were regular stopping places, landmarks where people carved their names or scrawled messages on buffalo skulls for those who followed. Andy recognized some of them by description, though he had not known until now how they had been named—Independence Rock, Pawnee Rock, Scott's Bluffs. Other of the regular stopping places convenience had established since his time: Fort Laramie, Bent's Fort, Jim Bridger's place. Andy was glad to hear of Jim again, to learn what he was doing. He had built him what they called a fort in the Black Fork of the Green. Andy recalled the spot, solitary and wild and beautiful; a pleasant meadow with clumps of cottonwoods; and a small stream full of trout; and fat deer in the bottomlands. The stream divided into three, and on one of the islands Bridger had established himself.

"She's a long way from solitary now," said his informant, "and you'd have to travel for your deer. There's trout there yet."

Andy listened with interest to details: two joining log cabins with sod roofs, surrounded by an eight-foot palisade of pickets, a "fort" by courtesy; the bottomland aswarm with horses and oxen; scattered encampments of Snakes and immigrants; horsemen galloping; Indians squatting motionless for hours before the tents and buildings; pack trains from Taos bringing in trade; a lively barter.

"For furs?"

No; trade in buckskin and buckskin garments; swaps of horses and oxen; buying or selling of provisions; plenty of whiskey. Jim Bridger was doing well.

"He ought to!" commented Andy's visitor bitterly. "He's got no conscience when it comes to a trade. But he'll divide anything he's got, if he takes a notion to," he admitted.

People were always coming and going. Pretty rough at times when the trade was lively and the whiskey flowed. Yelling, screeching, fighting, swearing, drinking. All night and all next day until sundown. Men, women, and children. Running from tent to tent, from lodge to lodge, carrying cups of raw liquor, inviting to drink.

"Too much for me," confessed Murray. "I was scared."

Everybody drank but the dogs, he added dryly.

"I never saw Jim Bridger take a drink when I knew him," said Andy.

"No, he was sober," acknowledged the immigrant. "But he was about the only one. He managed to handle 'em somehow," said he admiringly. "Dozen times looked like there was going to be a massacre, sure." He chuckled. "One time when the Injuns crowded in too thick and he couldn't get rid of 'em, he stopped up the chimney and smoked 'em out. One old coot—they called him Bill Williams; he was guiding for a Massachusetts outfit—got to bragging about his shooting and was so drunk he stuck in two-three loads of powder and when he let her off she blew up on him. Everybody thought he was dead, sure. But he come to. 'No damn gun kin kill me,' sez he. They're too tough; too tough for me!'"

But, he added, Bill Williams was a good guide; a fact Andy did not need to be told. Andy understand only with difficulty the emphasis on the guide's importance. He could imagine well enough the tough problems of the wagon train. He knew well the bogs, quicksands, deserts, mountains, fordless rivers; but that was the business of the bullwhackers, not the guides. He nodded understandingly when told of mutiny, obstinacy, ignorance; but these were matters that, for their handling, required a strong captain rather than especial training and knowledge.

"It's the Injuns," Murray explained.

The plains and mountains were no longer as Andy had known them. They were astir with hostility and the greed for plunder. Each caravan was under scrutiny almost from the moment it started; a scrutiny that estimated very accurately not only its strength but its arrangement.

The vulnerability of a single mistake, a single relaxation of vigilance was pounced upon by savages rapidly becoming expert at this type of raid.

"And then," commented the immigrant dryly, "a massacre and a bonfire. There's a plenty of charred wrecks. They, and horses' and ox' bones, could mighty near landmark the Trail. It takes an Injun fighter, and a heap good one, to do that job right."

Lone travel, or travel in groups of a few, such as Andy had known it, was practically a thing of the past.

Under question Murray added the names of other old-timers. Andy knew them all. A perfume of nostalgia drugged his imagination. Vivid pictures arose before his inner vision, evoked by those names. California Joe! Andy chuckled aloud! The man all but stood before him, taller than himself—at least three inches over the six feet; thin as a rail, all bone and sinew; reddish gray hair and whiskers; freckles; an old saddle, with generally a pair of elkskin hobbles and a chunk of meat dangling; a rusted Hawkens rifle, rusted on the outside, that is; a sloppy army hat, a ragged blue army overcoat, buckskin shirt black and shiny, buckskin trousers shrunk almost to the knee; scratched and tanned bare shanks: he was surely a figure of fun until you looked into his eyes! Or old Bill Williams himself with his short stirrups that seemed to bring his knees almost to his chin! Uncle John Smith; Uncle Dick Wottan; Jim Baker; Tom Tobin—they were all in the game, it seemed, and their services as guides were valued high.

They had been Andy's contemporaries, mountain men of the old regime. Harry Traeb? Bob Campbell? Jim Kipp? Bill Sublette?

The man shook his head.

"Never heard of 'em," said he.

"Surely you must have heard of Bill Sublette?"

"Nope."

Andy pondered, a little sadly, on the evanescence of fame. Or Kit Carson?

Kit Carson! Yes; sure! Everybody had heard of Kit Carson. Lived down near Taos somewhere. Said to be the best Injun fighter of the lot. But he wasn't guiding emigrants. He was with an army officer, name of Frémont.

Kit with Frémont? Andy caught at the name. Why, that party was over at Sutter's Fort a year ago. He had heard of them. Made considerable of a fuss down at Monterey as to what they were doing in this country at all. He'd gone back around south of the Sierra somewhere. If Andy had known that Kit was with that outfit, Andy would have ridden over to Sutter's to see him!

"This Frémont is quite a feller," submitted the stranger. "He was out west in '42 too, but he didn't get to Californy. He wrote a report about it to Congress, and our Congressman sent me a copy. It's really what started me out this way—that and John Kelly. Like to read it?"

"I sure would," said Andy.

3

He sat up later than usual, even after such a conference, reading the report. Like most men uneducated in the formalities of knowledge, he had almost a reverence for them. The exactitude of Frémont's observations and the mysteries of his scientific findings, together with the fact that his descriptions of the country were vivid enough to recall it to Andy's detailed recognition, held him fascinated.

"That fellow shines!" he told Murray the next morning.

"Like it?"

"Sure did," said Andy.

"That's all right. I'll leave it with you. No; never mind if you don't get it back to me. I'm through with it."

"How come you came to California 'stead of Oregon

with the rest of your outfit?" Andy was curious to know.

"I was raised up north in the lake country," said Murray, "and since I was a little wee young-un I've shook and burnt up with chills and fever. I made up my mind I'd find me a place where there wan't any ague. Out there at Mormon town—up near the big salt sea," he answered Andy's puzzled look. "After your time? Well, they's a heap of Mormons made a settlement up there, and she's a great trading post for folks comin' through to Oregon or going back to the States. You trade in what you brought because you're a dam' greenhorn for what the Mormons tell you you're going to need, and you're both wrong. There we happened on two men going back home. One of 'em was from Oregon and the other from Californy. They both tried to tell us the country was no good, and they each tried to outbrag the other as to how tough things was where they had been. The Oregon man allowed as how the soil was so poor up there that fifteen bushels to the acre was called a big crop; that it rained five months of the year without letting up, and the rest of the year it rained only most of the time. He said the whole place just swarmed with fleas and gallinippers."

"Gallinippers?" queried Andy.

"Mosquitoes. That's what we call 'em where I came from. And as for the Columbia River there's so much talk about, it's nothing but an Injun fish pond. The Californy man went him one better on most of those things, excepting that he had it raining half the year and so dry the other half that a man had to prime himself to spit. I didn't take them too serious, though some of our outfit did. I figured they were hoping to get some company and protection back across the Injun country. 'All that's all right, strangers,' I broke in after a while, 'but I'd like to ask you one thing, is there fever and ague in your country?' 'Full of it,' says the Oregon man. 'There ain't none,' says the Californy man."

Murray laughed. "I couldn't make these fellers out," he confessed. "That started 'em going the other way. They switched right around. Each one began to brag up his country. They got real hot about it. 'Specially on the fever-'n'-ague. 'Like hell there ain't no fever-'n'-ague in that country; like hell there ain't!' Oregon kep' saying over and over. 'Look-a here!' yells Californy after a while. 'Thar ain't but one man in Californy ever even had a *chill*, and folks come as high as eighteen mile just to see him shake!' That settled Oregon. But the general result was about half of us decided to try Californy, so when the trail forked we split blankets."

"How did you come in? Over the Sierra?" asked Andy. Murray nodded.

"Followed Bidwell's route pretty close. Tough going. We made her though, and Cap'n Sutter took us in. There's a white man! He gave us what we wanted; and he fixed us up with papers; and he's going to give us grants of land. We're mostly working around his place 'till we settle on what we want. You never been up to see his place? Well, you ought to go! He's got a fort with cannon and a gang of trappers and Injuns and a passel of cattle and hosses and sheep, and he owns most of the country thereabouts."

Andy listened open-mouthed to the man's account of the upper Valley. In the remote life of Folded Hills he had heard little. Murray claimed there must be upwards of three hundred American settlers in the valley.

"And that ain't a patch to what come out to Oregon," Murray assured him. "They say there's been over three thousand took the trail to the Willamette in the last year or two."

Andy shook his head. He could hardly believe these things, for he knew Mexico's exclusion policy as to foreigners, and he had heard that the Hudson's Bay Company had been very jealous of white settlement in Oregon.

"We heard something of that," acknowledged Murray.

"But seems like Cap'n Sutter claims he's some sort of Mexican officer himself, and can make land grants as well as anybody. And I reckon," he added grimly, "that if these yere leather-bellies think they're going to put us off our land, we'll have something to say about it ourselves."

Andy's mind cast back to Sutter's ill-advised interference with the late revolution against Micheltorena, and his consequent loss of prestige, and he wondered. Murray's information gave point to certain rumors that had come to his ears. He must ask his friend Larkin about this.

4

Andy was much interested in an item of his visitor's equipment, a pistol with a revolving cylinder that contained six charges, the barrel of which was grooved like a rifle.

"And she shoots like a rifle; that is, close to," boasted Murray.

He permitted Andy to try it; shot the new weapon with him. Andy was badly beaten in a shooting match; but Murray handled it with a skill that, while it did not quite justify his boast, inspired the *ranchero* with admiration.

"I bet I could shoot that thing with a little practice," said Andy.

"Sure you could," agreed Murray heartily. "It's a knack, and it's got that knife trick of yours skinned a mile." He patted it affectionately. "That little darling makes all men equal," said he.

"I'd like to get one of those," said Andy. He examined admiringly the ingenious mechanism that revolved the cylinder; read the name stamped on the barrel: "Address Col. Sam E. Colt, New York, U. S. America."

"Made for Colonel Walker and the Texas Rangers," said Murray. "Quite a contraption, eh?"

"I'd like to have one of them," repeated Andy. "I surely would! Can't we make a dicker?"

Murray thought not. But in the end he let Andy have the weapon for two good horses.

"I reckon now I'm a farmer I've got more use for horses than for pistols," said Murray.

SETH MURRAY spent two days, mostly out of doors, with Andy; then resumed his journey to Monterey, driving before him the two horses he had acquired in exchange for the Colt's revolving pistol. Just before noon Djo rode in, carrying Wapita behind him. The girl slid from the horse's croup, shook herself, looked about her a moment suspiciously, and marched into the *casa* and through the *sala* into the small room beyond, which Andy used as a sort of office. He was seated now at a rough table, his back to the door, his elbows planted apart, his forehead in his hands, reading again Frémont's report. Andy was at best slow to apprehend ideas through print: only on second perusal did he begin to have opinions on what he read. Now his eyes were traveling slowly along the lines of print; and his mind revolved about the obviousness of what it saw, spinning its webs of surmise and judgment.

This fellow is a great man, he thought; like this man Scott that Tom Larkin lent me the books of; or that other fellow who wrote about Rome. I don't see how a man learns to write a book, thought Andy, so smooth and even and all the words fitting so snug, and just the right words so that what he was talking about came into your mind as clear as though you were looking at it. I know mighty nigh every inch of that country he was in, reflected Andy, and he's got it down so plain I can just *smell* it! And all the little-bitty things you never really notice at all, but you recall them right away when he puts them down! I reckon, decided Andy, that a man don't rightly learn how to write a book: he just has it in him, like I have it in me to shoot straight.

For a moment longer he pondered this aspect until it was complete and rounded in his mind. Then he left it one side; and hit off methodically down another trail opened to him by these printed words.

This fellow, thought Andy further, sure does know a lot. He knows the name of every plant and every bird and every kind of rock. And he's sure a noticing cuss; he sees 'em all and he puts 'em all down. And he puts down their long names too: I suppose that's Latin. I'd like to *sabe* just how a man figgers where he is by the stars. I can see how a man knows by them which way to *go*—we all do that—but not just where he *is*. I suppose he does it with one or the other of those instruments he packs along. And where he tells about mending that busted barometer and bringing her back to read accurate. That shines! I wonder if Tom Larkin knows about these things? I don't know; it takes a man special eddicated to *sabe* that.

Then what was the matter with him? Andy stopped short in surprise at this thought. He had not suspected that there was anything the matter. Andy had been quite naïvely possessed by his admirations. But beneath them had been this other thing all the while, this doubt of the man's wholeness of integrity. Andy, with quickened interest, bent his eyes again to the report. It was at this moment that he felt the presence of someone behind him; and turned half about in his chair to see Djo and Wapita.

"Here she is, *señor padre*," said Djo immediately he knew himself noticed. "I brought her at once to you that she might explain. She did not wish to do this: but it is fitting."

Andy concealed a smile at the lad's dignity. He surveyed the two from beneath the frowning line of his straight brows. The girl's garments were moderately fresh and in order; though Andy's keen frontiersman eye noted various small indications. Her manner seemed to him faintly deprecatory rather than ashamed; but her eye met his. Djo was as always.

"I think," said Andy to Djo in Spanish, "that I will let you do your explaining first. How did you know that Wapita was to be found over by the Big Tenaja?"

Djo looked a bit startled. Andy grinned at him, and indicated by a flick of the eye the girl's short skirt.

"Why," said he, as Djo failed to comprehend, "where else is there sulphur water?" And consolingly as Djo showed dejection, "It isn't a very big spot." He waited Djo's reply to his first question.

"I took her there," said Djo steadily. Wapita started impulsively forward to speak. Andy checked her.

"In the first place? When she ran away?" he asked Djo.

"Yes, *señor padre*."

"Why?"

"I knew it as a good place. That is where we played Wildman, you remember. Nobody goes up there. She could stay there in my shelter. I could bring her food and no one would notice."

"I see," said Andy grimly. "And when I sent out Panchito and the *vaqueros* in search, you told them not to bother with the basin of the Big Tenaja: that you would look there."

"Yes, *señor padre*," admitted Djo wonderingly.

"H'm," Andy repeated. "And you'd promised you would not tell; not even that she was safe. I see."

"Yes, *señor padre*." Djo's admiration for Andy's quick apprehension of the situation was profound.

Andy's habit was to read his trail by the sign, inch by inch. What he saw with his own eyes was so; what was merely told him might or might not be so. Djo would not lie to me on his own account, he thought; but he might throw a smoke on her account. I must get at the rights of this slowly, he thought, or I'll scare 'em off. What I must find out is what this means. Who started this anyway, Djo or the girl? What sort of a prank was it? He looked at the boy closely; considered; dismissed a lurking shadow of an idea; an idea that had come to him, he now realized, because of the thought of what Ramón was sure to say. They came directly, and together, to me, he remembered.

"That is all, Djo," he said. "I'll talk to you later. You may go. Now I shall talk to Wapita."

Djo hesitated; then bowed properly from the hips.

"Yes, *señor padre*," said he, and went out. Andy watched him thoughtfully until he had closed the door behind him; then turned with decision to the girl.

"Now it is your turn to explain," said he.

She returned his look from behind a barrier of what he sensed as a sort of sullen defiance.

"There is nothing to explain," she returned. "You told me that I could go when I desired. I wished to go. I went." Her eyes flamed to life. "You promised!" she cried. "Do you not remember that? Do you make the promise that you do not keep? Tell me that! I ask you!"

"No," said Andy. "I keep my promise. If you wished to go, you were free to do so."

"Then why," she accused vehemently, "did you send the *vaqueros* to hunt me down? Did you not order that? Do you tell me you did not order that?"

"I ordered," said Andy quietly, "that search be made, near at hand. We must be sure that you had not had an accident."

"Oh!" said she.

"I did not order them to bring you back, if you did not wish to come back." He paused for a moment, watching her face. "Why did you come back?" he shot at her suddenly.

She looked up, startled at this unexpected shift of ground.

"He had gone away," she replied.

"Who?"

"This pig of the world who comes riding: this——"

Andy gradually comprehended, to his considerable bewilderment, that her reference was to his late visitor, to Seth Murray, the immigrant. He could make no sense in this. The man was new-come to the country. It was impossible that Wapita had ever before laid eyes on him. He knew positively that she had had no speech with him.

"Did you ever see this man before?" nevertheless he asked.

"Never! Never!" cried Wapita passionately. "If he spoke to me I should spit upon his face! And never do I wish to see him again!"

"Then what," asked Andy, "have you got against him?"

"He is *e'tranjero!*" cried Wapita. "Never shall I remain where I must see these pigs, no-no-no, not if I must live with the Indians of the Tulares!"

Andy looked at her curiously, trying to fathom the cause of this violence.

"This man is *americano,*" he suggested mildly at last. "I too am *americano.* The *señor* Larkin is *americano* and the *señor* Leese, and many such another."

"No, no-no-no!" she shook her head, "you are *californio.* And," she added, "you are *hidalgo.*"

Andy's great strength was that he never butted head-on into a point of view.

"Do you wish to tell me why you object to the *e'tranjero?*" he asked.

"I hate them: I hate them all!" she cried.

"So I see; but why?"

"It is like when I see the rattlesnake, *señor.* The shudder goes through the breast and out of the backbone; and the hair prickles on the head like little needles. But you cannot understand."

Andy threw one long leg over the arm of his chair and leaned back in easy balance.

"Why, I think I do," he replied. "I feel that same way about a few things. No reason at all: just feel that way."

He continued to swing his foot for a few moments in silence.

"Doesn't it seem rather foolish to leave your home where, it looks to me, you are pretty happy, just because one foreigner comes along, who will probably stay no longer than overnight, or a day or two at most?"

"I cannot help it! I shall *not* breathe the same air with these *bellacos!* I should stifle! I——" Her voice was rising again hysterically. "If Djo had not talked to me, I should by now have been—I don't know where. And next time you shall not see me. I shall——"

"*Basta!*" Andy interrupted her. "If one cannot, he cannot; and that is as true as Mother Church. But Wapita, one does not burn down the *casa* to get rid of the fleas." He considered rapidly. "But *next* time, you say— is it not more sensible to go away, if you must; but again to come back?"

"Others will come! And others and others!" Wapita was wringing her hands distressedly. "I can see them— like the locusts that swarm on the trees until they are bare, and the leaves all gone, every one! You shall see, *señor!*"

This girl is a little mad, thought Andy. But no, that is not so, he continued within himself, for in all else, as I have seen her, she is sensible and warm-hearted and loyal to serve. And his parallel of the *bronco* recurred to him; and he recalled a very beautiful chestnut which he had purposed for Amata, so docile was it. He himself had ridden the animal much, gentling it for the child. It was a remarkably intelligent beast, so that it seemed subject to none of the great or small equine alarms. But now

Andy felt again between his knees the shiver of the animal's whole body preliminary to the violent plunge that had all but unseated him, so unexpected was it. He had mastered the beast only with the greatest difficulty, and by the cruel main strength of the long spade bit that had left its mouth bleeding. He, and Panchito, had puzzled long in search of the cause of these occasional outbursts, which had recurred at irregular intervals. They discovered it at last to be the dull sound of wood knocking against wood; though for some time they could not believe, so curious was that. But it proved to be the fact; nor could they ever cure the chestnut of its terrors, though they tried patiently by many repetitions to accustom it. This girl is like that chestnut, he thought; and there is little use hitting trees with billets of wood.

Aloud he said:

"Well, that may be, Wapita; and when that time comes, then we shall see. But for now this is what I say, that when this desire comes to you, that you will tell me; or at least the Doña Carmel, for the Doña Carmel has a tender heart for you, Wapita, and it is not well that it should be torn with fears. Will you do that?"

She burst into a storm of tears.

"No; never, never, in all my life shall I leave the Doña Carmel!" she sobbed. "Nor you, *señor;* for I adore you above the blessed saints in Paradise." Andy sighed in relief. He did not bother with the inconsistency; nor try to understand.

In such matters as these he did not pretend to move with understanding. He groped by an instinct which was, nevertheless, sure. Andy would not have known what the word "psychology" meant; nor, indeed, at that time would anybody else. He faced a complex; and recognized it as such, in essence, but not in name. Nor did he need the handle of a name; though, as his intellect was not incurious, he could have used one with satisfaction. He and Panchito had agreed that something serious must have happened to the chestnut at some time or other in its colthood to frighten it so unreasonably of so simple and harmless a sound; but they could never determine what that might have been. I wonder, he thought, what happened to this girl. In spite of what Ramón had said, there must have been something. I must question Ramón, he thought. This is not reasonable otherwise.

T HE understanding between the two, thus brought to Andy's attention, caused him for a time to watch their conduct together. He found that the boy and the girl were seeing more of one another than he had suspected. In the *casa* Djo frequently encountered the maid going here or there about her simple and leisurely duties. Or she encountered him in his own domain of the out-of-doors, on her way to the stream in the bottomland where the laundry girls splashed and laughed. Whenever this happened they seemed to have plenty of time to linger in long and apparently very serious conversations; in which, however, Wapita did most of the talking. Sometimes, but more rarely, they met as by prearrangement and quite frankly joined forces for an expedition to vineyard or *milpa*.

Andy said nothing to Carmel; nor to Djo. He watched attentively. He was, after his fashion, making up his mind before he spoke or took action. Carmel would at once have forbidden their intimacy on the ground that it was not fitting. She would have confided privately to Andy that it might be dangerous. In spite of herself she would have grown a violent prejudice against the girl, whose situation would shortly have become intolerable.

But Andy continued to watch; and to hold his peace. When he assembled his observations for review he was satisfied that matters were well enough, at least for a while. The two were indeed much together, but always openly. Andy detected no clandestine meetings. He examined the boy and the girl with newly appraising eyes. Wapita was no ordinary *moza*. She had about her a vague something of race. She was superbly scornful of men; all men. Indeed Djo and Andy himself were the only two male humans on the *rancho* she would more than tolerate. Andy discovered in himself a growing interest, curiosity as to this vivid creature.

I'd like to know about her mother, he thought; and I'd like to know what she and Djo find to talk about so much. But I won't ask. Maybe sometime it'll come along natural, so I can find out.

2

Late in the summer he made up his mind to ride down to Monterey. He easily found an excuse for the journey in certain business matters to do with the disposal of hides from the last *matanza;* but his real impelling motive was his desire for a talk with his friend, Thomas Larkin. Matters of interest for such a discussion had been gradually accumulating in Andy's mind. How was Pío Pico making out as governor? How was José Castro getting along as *comandante militar?* Folded Hills was remote from active affairs. To its seclusion came only the customary mouth-to-mouth rumors. Since he had returned from the southern campaign that had ousted Micheltorena, Andy had been out of the current of affairs; and that revolution had left certain interesting tag ends. Andy had no great interest in politics, but he was possessed of normal curiosity. He recalled the expression of Sutter's face when he had realized that he had picked the wrong side in the Micheltorena affair; and the frigid politeness toward him of Castro and Alvarado. Looked like Sutter's goose was cooked. But now Seth Murray said that Sutter had power to issue passports and make grants of land. Andy had heard that the latest from Mexico was that every foreigner—even the old settlers—unprovided with governmental permission, was to be cleared out of the country. Then how come all this immigration described by Murray?

So Andy sent a messenger over to see if Ramón would meet him at Soledad; and, together with Djo and Panchito and a dozen extra horses, set out for Monterey. Carmel, who was amusedly wise in masculine reactions, flatly declined to go along. She knew her place; and that it was unassailable.

3

Ramón joined them at Soledad. They dashed down the valley at full gallop, the dust clouds swirling behind them. As always they enjoyed to the full the exhilaration of the going and savored the slow change from the stinging dry heat of the interior to the fresh coolness that stole inland from the sea, like an infusion. But there was scant opportunity for other interchange than the shouted brevities of speech. Only at the frequent pauses for change of mount the two friends squatted on their heels, smoked cigarettes and talked. At one of these Andy told Ramón of Wapita's disappearance. He did not mention Djo's part in it. But he did voice his surmises, and his curiosity as to the cause of Wapita's violent prejudice against foreigners.

"It isn't sense," said he, in conclusion. "Something must have happened to her. Are you sure she's never been —well, treated badly by some man?"

Ramón considered, rolling his cigarette between his fingers.

"No, never," he said at last with decision. "These things are never hidden, on a *rancho*, as you know. And she is only yesterday but a child. She is," said Ramón astoundingly, "but just past twelve years old."

"Twelve years!" Andy fairly shouted. "You're crazy! You don't know! Why, she's a grown woman if I ever saw one!"

"She look like a woman," assented Ramón in English.

"That came only just this year. I bet, you give her chance, she act like woman, too. But," he stated positively, "she has twelve year. Some Espanish pipple like that."

"But she's younger than Djo!" cried Andy unguardedly.

Ramón looked as though he were tempted to say something. However, he refrained. He glanced sidewise at Andy with carefully concealed amusement.

"But I think, *valedor*," he resumed with complete gravity, "that I can tell you what you would know. I had forget. It was a so-small thing, at which we all laugh, and then forget. It happen so-long ago. One time when this Wapita is a so-small *niña*—five-six years old—I don't know. There came to the *hacienda* a sailor man who ran away from a Boston ship. There were many like that. This man is ver' big, and he has the whisker all over his face, *como el oso*. And he is drunk. He see this *niña*; and he grab her and hold her up high; and then he kees her, and put her down again. That is all. He mean no harm; none at all. But I think now maybe he esscare her much. We all laugh, she look so funny! That time she run away, and we no find her for two-three day. Until that sailor man he go. It was a so-small thing, so long ago. No harm. But maybe-so that is it?"

"Why, sure!" Andy was delighted. His being moved sometimes obscurely, through instinct; but he had a direct mind. It liked things tidy. Now if he only knew what had scared that chestnut horse . . .

4

Larkin lived in a long low *adobe* house overlooking the bay. Unlike most Californian houses, it did not completely turn its back on the outside world in favor of its inner court. A roofed and tiled veranda overlooked the brightly gardened slope toward the plaza and the beach

below. Here, rather than in the patio, Larkin preferred to
sit, smoking his pipe, enjoying the prospect before him.
He loved flowers. On the slope grew the roses, carnations,
hollyhocks, sweet peas brought originally from Mexico
and cultivated in every Californian garden. But here
also were certain native varieties which the *californio*
did not consider, merely because they grew wild—yuccas;
chollas; mariposas; cascara and artemisia bushes from
the mountains; and, scattered as lavishly and irregularly
as stars or little suns, the yellow-gold and copper-gold of
the California poppies. Below the garden, beyond the
custom house was the inner bay, bluer than any sky, where
the boisterous rollers of the outer sea checked to decorum
and stole to the beach with a whisper of warning to those
that followed. Or, as it sometimes seemed to Larkin, it
was as though here the pounded billows raced in to sanctuary and that, once they had rounded the point, they
found quiet and peace, so that on the curving bosom of
the shore they laid them down with a sigh of rest. His
spirit met them, followed them, shared their calming,
flowed with them in high tranquillity to quietude. In a
little while his mind was cleared of all its small irritations.
The vexations of the days' commerce and politics had
been reduced to their proper insignificance.

So he sat, on this afternoon; and he arose with an exclamation of pleasure when the three visitors dismounted
before his gate. At his shout the household came to life.
An Indian servant hastened to take charge of the horses;
another to untie the slender baggage from the saddle
strings. Within the house was a stir of preparation. Mrs.
Larkin joined her husband on the garden path. There
was a great to-do of welcome; for both had a genuine
liking for the tall *ranchero* and the handsome boy, his son.
And Ramón was an old friend.

For a little time they all sat exchanging the gossip of
the occasion and the small personal news of interest

after a long interval. Then Andy and Ramón must tell
of their experiences in the southern campaign that had
ended with the abdication of Micheltorena. To this Larkin
listened with close interest, interrupting only with an
occasional question. He was a dark man, and thin, and
held himself with a slight stoop, his head thrust forward
in a fashion that gave him an air of continual inquiry.
Habitually he held a hand behind his ear, as though he
were a little deaf; but as his interest quickened he abandoned the gesture and appeared to hear well enough. He
seemed especially inquisitive as to Sutter's part in the
revolution, questioning Andy closely, weighing his statements thoughtfully.

"There will be trouble there yet," he made his only
comment. "Castro is bitter, and Castro is now military
commander. Sutter picked the wrong side. What had he
to say for himself?"

"Why, that he thought he had to support Micheltorena
because he was the governor," said Andy, "and he thought
he ought to support the regular authorities."

"And what did Castro and Alvarado have to say to
that?"

"They were polite," said Andy dryly, "but I thought
Captain Sutter looked worried."

But it was not until after the evening meal that Andy
brought up the subject which he had really come to discuss. Ramón excused himself on the plea of visits to make;
he had little interest in politics. Mrs. Larkin shortly left
them.

"I know you men want to talk," said she.

Andy and Larkin sprawled either side the fire which the
evenings of the early season made grateful. Djo sat upright next his father. Larkin extinguished the lamps.

"I like the firelight," said he.

For a time they smoked in silence.

"Had a visitor at the ranch, an American, name of

Murray," observed Andy at last. "Came over the Sierra with some immigrants. Know him? Is he reliable?"

Larkin shook his head.

"Why do you want to know about his being reliable? Does he want cattle?"

"No," Andy disclaimed. "He don't want anything. Just some things he was telling me. I was wondering if they were so."

"What things, for instance?"

"Well, one thing; he claims that Captain Sutter is giving out *permisos* and even making grants of land. That right?"

"So I understand," said Larkin. "You look surprised."

"Well, I am," admitted Andy. "Last I heard Mexico had tightened up on foreigners, especially Americans; and last I saw, Cap'n Sutter didn't stand much with Castro and Alvarado—as we were sayin' this afternoon."

Larkin did not reply.

"This Murray says there's as high as three hundred Americans came in lately. I reckon he's bragging a lot there."

"No," said Larkin, "he's underestimating, if anything. There's more will come. What you laughing at?"

"I was thinking of Castro and how tickled he was when they made him *comandante militar.*"

"One thing I like about you, Burnett," said Larkin, "you've got a way of pouncing on the root of a matter. That's just it. I'm sorry for the man. He is a conscientious officer, and he wants to do his duty, and he genuinely loves California. Yes, I know he's a little pompous and arbitrary, but every Spaniard thinks that goes with being a military officer, like the epaulets. Remember what happened to Guadalupe Vallejo time he was *comandante?*"

"Made a star-spangled *burro* of himself, bossing things around that didn't need bossing."

"Exactly. And Don Guadalupe is about as *sabe* as they come."

"Oh, I like Castro," Andy assured his host. "He and I always got along. It's just his kind of foofaraw, I reckon."

"I'm sorry for him," repeated Larkin. "He's in as tough a place as you could make up. You said a minute ago that Mexico had tightened up. You don't know the half of it. Wait a minute." He arose, lighted the lamp with a long spill of paper ignited at the fire, opened a drawer, and rummaged through a pile of papers. "Here we are: here's the latest orders; that no foreigner can enter without *permiso*, that even a foreigner can't hold land; and—privately—that *permisos* are not to be granted. And," he added, "the *comandante militar*, as an officer of the Mexican government, is to carry out the order."

"I reckon the Texas business scared 'em," said Andy shrewdly.

"What is Castro to do? None of these immigrants, naturally, even had a chance to receive that notice, or even know that it had been given. They just came. And once they were in the valley, what was to be done? Castro is a humane man. It would be sure death to turn them out, in their condition and at that time of year. What could he do?"

"Issue a *pronunciamiento*," Andy chuckled. "And he could send that to Mexico where it would sound good."

Larkin joined him in laughter, but immediately became grave.

"More foofaraw," observed Andy.

"I'm beginning to think you've got the best head on any shoulders in California."

"Shucks," said Andy, "anybody could figger that. So Cap'n Sutter gave 'em *permiso* and there they are."

"There they are. And more coming. And all stirred up over the *pronunciamiento*, for a lot of them have taken up land, have gone to farming; not ranching—farming. You see, Burnett, this is a different class of people than you know of. They've brought women, and children—babies. There's a plow under every wagon. Look here, Burnett,"—Larkin leaned forward earnestly—"suppose someone told you you'd have to move out of Folded Hills, move out of the country?"

"They wouldn't," said Andy sensibly. "I'm a *californio* and I have a grant."

"Yes, but suppose they told you your grant was no good and you'd have to get out?"

"I'd admire to see them try!" said Andy.

"That," observed Larkin quietly, "is how I understand the settlers are talking." He arose from his chair and took two or three steps back and forth. "A moment ago," he resumed, stopping squarely in front of Andy, "you said you were a *californio*. I think the time may come, and soon, when you will have to decide whether you are a *californio* or an American."

Andy looked up, startled. Larkin checked him with upraised hand.

"Wait. Burnett, you've a head on your shoulders. I am going to talk to you freely. I believe you can keep your mouth shut, and I am going to ask you to do so."

Andy nodded. Larkin raised an eyebrow toward Djo.

"Djo don't blab," said Andy briefly. The boy was frowning steadily at the two of them. He made as though to speak; but thought better of it.

"Well, California's not going to belong to Mexico very much longer," continued Larkin.

"No?" Andy turned at a half-strangled cry from Djo. "What is it, boy?" he asked.

"*Nada*," said Djo. Andy stared at him a moment; then turned back to Larkin.

"No," repeated the latter. "For a great number of reasons; the principal of which is that California is a rich country, and several of the larger nations would be delighted to get her, particularly England or France. All any of them need is an excuse. If a man is looking for an excuse he can always find one. You know that."

"Yes, I know that," Andy agreed.

"And the Californian *políticos* do nothing but squabble. Why, right at this minute Castro and Pío Pico are hot at it."

"What about?" Andy wanted to know.

"Oh, usual thing. Power. Pico is governor, as you know, and is a southerner, and makes his capitol in the south, and Castro is military chief in the north; and each claims the other is usurping his authority, and all the rest of it. Usual thing. And all the idle *políticos* are taking sides. When one issues an order the other countermands it. Point is, the best of the *rancheros* and *hacendados* are beginning to get disgusted. That's my job just now."

Andy looked his inquiry.

Larkin reseated himself and drew his chair to face Andy.

"This is confidential. Perhaps you know that I have been appointed consul for the United States?"

"Yes, I know that."

"The day is coming," repeated Larkin solemnly, "when the flag of a foreign nation wiil fly from the staff yonder in the plaza. That flag must be the Stars and Stripes."

Larkin was still speaking, but for a moment Andy did not hear the words. His mind had flown back to his youth. He was seeing another room in another clime, and another man was expressing the same thought in other words.

"One people, one flag, a mighty civilization that shall extend, that *must* extend, from sea to sea."

That was in the long ago. The man was Benton of Missouri. In the many crowded years between, the clean-cut sharpness of the vision had blurred, the straightness of the road had diffused into many trails. And here, with a sudden sharp click, the confusion fell in order, the road again lay straight, and he, Andy Burnett, with his feet still upon it. And as Larkin's voice again became audible to him through the muffling of his preoccupations, that other voice of the long ago, the beautiful resonant voice of the orator, fading again to the land of memory, reached his inner spirit like a little bell:

"More surely than most you play your part in higher destinies!"

To the boy it had been an inspiring prophecy splendid with the fire of inspiration. But in a later life of hardship and wandering and battle and tragedy the prophecy had been forgotten; or, if occasionally recalled, remembered with the wistful indulgence one accords the dreams of youth. And still later, when it seemed to Andy that he had reached his quiet haven of life and love, and when, on his wedding day, he had, in a moment of half-conscious symbolism, hung the old Boone rifle on the pegs let in to the adobe wall, the last glowing embers had grayed, and he had smiled to himself humorously and without regret.

Now! He caught his breath with a sort of awe. Incongruously another forgotten memory pictured itself before his mind: he and Joe Crane in a bull boat floating idly down a stretch of waters of the Green. The surface of the stream was placid, the air was soft; the sun was warm. They were half asleep. And instantaneously, as it had seemed to him, they had been snatched between high dark cañon walls, and the water roared white about them, tumbling along great boulders. For a minute or so they struggled; then Joe with a curse had shipped his paddle.

"Reckon it's the Old Man's job," he had shouted to Andy; and after a moment, "See you Over Thar!"

The bull boat whirled around and around; the spray blinded Andy so he could not see. He was sensible only of rush and resistless power and a sense of snatching hands. The shouting and lurching ceased, and again they floated on quiet waters, and the dark cañon lay behind. He cleared his eyes. Joe was grinning at him.

"Wall," drawled the mountain man, "I kain't figger what the Old Man's a-savin' *me* for, Andy. Must have some use for you."

These things crossed his mind in a flash of time. He missed but the fraction of a sentence from Larkin's speech. He was recalled almost violently to the present by Djo's outburst:

"Never! Never shall that be!"

Both older men now wheeled upon the boy in surprise.

"What is it you wish to say, Djo?" demanded Andy sternly.

Djo recovered from his momentary excitement.

"Your pardon, *señor padre;* and yours, Señor Larkin."

"Why did you say that?" persisted his father.

"California does not belong to the *americanos.* She belongs to us, to the *californios.* And," he added proudly, slipping into Spanish, "she may not be passed from this one to that one without her consent. The *californios* are brave. They can die for her."

Both men were looking at him; his father with bewildered surprise; Larkin with calculating attention, for he now felt he had talked rashly. Djo bore their scrutiny respectfully, but without flinching.

Andy reoriented himself painfully. This was the first time in all his life that Djo had ever asserted his own personality as differing from that of his father. He had always been literally, and in all things, the shadow of Don Largo. And the occasion had fallen flat and cold against his rekindled vision. Nevertheless it was characteristic that, after the initial gasp of the shock, his first thought was of admiration. The young-un's got backbone, he thought; he ain't hiding, and he ain't afraid to stand right up to the two of us for what he thinks. Where in tarnation did he ever get such ideas? Ramón? Maybe: though I've never thought of him as such a rabid patriot. Surely not from any of our neighbors or visitors: fat lot

they care for such things. Nor our people on the *rancho*——
Hold on! Andy's mind quickened with illumination. He
almost laughed aloud with relief at the simplicity of the
explanation. That girl—Wapita—to be sure! Filled him
full as a tick with it all, thought Andy: *that's* what all this
everlasting talk was about. Politics! Those young-uns!
Oh, Lord, thought Andy, I sure want to see Ramón's
face when I tell him that! But at this juncture he could
not forbear emitting a brief chuckle which he instantly
suppressed. He caught Larkin's troubled look.

"Djo don't blab," he repeated confidently. "You
needn't be scared of him. To nobody, Djo, remember,"
he warned.

"I am not a traitor," said Djo proudly. "With your
permission, *señor padre*, and that of Señor Larkin, I will
retire that you may go on with your discussion." Djo
spoke in Spanish. He felt much more grown up in that
stately and formal tongue. But Andy brushed aside that
screen.

"Shucks!" said he. "You'll stay right where you are,
and listen. You may hear something that'll do you good.
I'll talk to you later. Go ahead, Tom. I'll guarantee Djo."
He felt almost light-hearted at having thought of so
simple and childish an explanation for Djo's sudden opposition; for, he now confessed to himself, that had been
for a moment a real shock. Not that it amounted to anything; but it was the first, and so unexpected. The boy's
got to have a mind of his own, acknowledged Andy in all
fairness. What's the matter with me? Wouldn't want him
to grow up talking back at me like an echo from a cliff,
would I?—or one of these yere poll-parrots on a Boston
ship? "What were you saying, Tom?" he urged Larkin
again.

"Why,"—Larkin hesitated a moment, then decided to
continue, "I don't know but the boy's hit it after a fashion.
He's a pretty good example. It's the *rancheros*, the *ha-*

cendados, we will have to depend on, try to influence. The
political *banda* will remain 'patriots' and true to Mexico
—and also pretty noisy," he added dryly. "There's no
use trying to do anything with them. And," he added,
"I am beginning to think we have none too much time."

"What do you mean?" asked Andy.

"You remember the Jones business?"

Andy did. A few years before, an American commodore
of that name had sailed into Monterey harbor, landed a
large force of marines, and raised the American flag.
Next morning he had again landed his marines, replaced
the Mexican flag, fired a salute of cannon, tendered a
formal apology. The apology was accepted good-naturedly
and the incident forgotten in an elaborate champagne
dinner given by Micheltorena when Jones put in at Los
Angeles.

"What did you make of it?" asked Larkin.

"Why, that the laugh was sure on the commodore,"
drawled Andy.

"Yes. But why do you figure he did it?"

"Probably drunk," Andy voiced the popular opinion.

"Here's a secret for you to keep: He had heard that war
had been declared between the United States and Mexico
over Texas. He had also been given to understand that
an English squadron was on the way to seize California.
He thought he had to act promptly. That's why I say we
have not too much time. I've managed to make considerable headway. You might help. That's why I'm telling
you."

"How?"

"With the *rancheros,* the *hacendados.* You have their
confidence. In spite of what Djo says, some of them are
already pretty disgusted with Mexico. Mexico has never
done anything but insult and neglect California, as they
see it. Many of them realize that California in the long
run will pass from Mexico's control; and I think they are

a little glad of it. I've got to—we've got to—fasten that idea in them. Animate them with a desire for freedom."

"Kicking out the Mex's wouldn't be much of a job," said Andy.

"The most intelligent element, especially the older men —like Vallejo and your father-in-law—understand that already. But they realize that California cannot stand alone. They already have a strong leaning toward the United States. They believe—I've told them; and it is true—that what they need is a government strong enough to settle the Indians. Look at the situation, Burnett. Except for a little strip along the coast, and a few fortified places like Sutter's, they range the whole country. And even the coast strip is not free from their raids."

"Give me a free hand and I'd guarantee to stop that. I have stopped it up to my place," observed Andy positively.

"Yes, I know. But Mexico hasn't stopped it. And Vallejo and the few others I've been talking about realize that they'd be better protected under the American government, more secure in life and property. My job, my *instructions*, are to foster and spread this sentiment. Burnett,"—Larkin was very earnest—"I am talking high political secrets. We do not intend to see this country pass to a foreign nation. It is logically part of our country. Her head is in Washington, on the Atlantic seaboard; but her feet are planted on the shores of the Pacific. Sooner or later—sooner, I think—what Commodore Jones did in '42 is going to happen again, for there will surely be a war with Mexico." He was very much in earnest. Both men had again forgotten Djo.

"You think so?"

"I know so. Some other commodore will sail into Monterey harbor to hoist our flag. That will happen. And when it does I want to see it done, not against hostility, or even ill feeling. I want to see it done with joyous consent. I love these people, Burnett; just as you do. They would not have a chance in the world against us, against any conqueror. You know that. I wrote Washington just the other day—here, I have a copy of the letter. Here's what I said: 'If Mexico should send a military force to succeed them,'" Larkin read. "I'm talking of Castro and Pico," he interpolated, "'and they could be agreed, they could bring into the field 800 to 1,000 men. But they cannot unite in anything. If Pico and Castro were united, they could at present raise a force of some 300 to 400.'" He laid aside the letter. "What would that amount to? And, Burnett, you've seen something of their fighting qualities."

"I'm not so sure of that part of it," said Andy slowly. "They've been fighting for fun up to now."

"All the worse, then," Larkin pointed out. "That is what I wanted to avoid, unnecessary bloodshed and ill feeling. And I think we can do it. And I want you to help."

"How?" asked Andy.

"Do what I've been doing, among the *rancheros*—your friend, Ramón Rivera, all the younger men. I'd like to see that choice unnecessary—whether you'd be an American or a *californio* if it came to a showdown. Maybe you could be both."

"I'll do what I can," said Andy simply.

"Good!" cried Larkin. He leaned forward to clap Andy on the shoulder. "If it weren't for men like Castro and his like!" he added. "I like Castro. But he's like a horsefly. He's like a young-un with a wooden sword, runs around waving it and never thinking he might frighten someone. He keeps on writing his confounded proclamations of how the immigrants are here without legal right, and how he is going to put them out of the country, and I don't know what all. Don't mean a thing, but they read well in Mexico City, I suppose."

"Likes to hear his head roar," observed Andy.

"Trouble is, makes the settlers uneasy, too. They don't know. They don't understand. That is, some of them don't. And they remember the eviction of Graham and his gang. They don't stop to think that it was a gang of cutthroats and that most of them ought to have been hung. The more responsible don't pay much attention. But the lawless and wandering, spoiling for a row, make much of it; and some of the more timid are impressed. If Castro would only subside—still, I don't worry much about that."

"Too much foofaraw," Andy applied his formula.

"Exactly. Lucky our people aren't much given to that sort of thing. If there was a Castro on our side too we'd be in a mess in no time." He had a thought, and struck his thigh. "There's where you can help, Burnett!"

"How's that?"

"How about taking a trip up the Valley? Talk to the settlers. Calm 'em down. You understand the *californios;* no man better! And most of them know who you are. At the same time you can look things over. Come back and tell me how things are! By God, it's an idea!" He laid his hand on Andy's arm. "You can practise on Djo," he added with a sudden humor.

"Why, yes," assented Andy thoughtfully, "I think I can. As for Djo: I'll take him along. Do him good. He might learn something." He turned to the boy. "It's late for you, son; you go to bed."

"Yes, *señor padre,*" said Djo.

CHAPTER V

I BROUGHT you a mighty interestin' book, case you haven't seen it," said Andy after Djo had said his goodnight and retired. "This Murray left it with me. It's a book written by an army man name of Frémont. Tells all about the old South Pass country. You read it?"

"Yes," said Larkin. "It's a government report. They sent it to me."

"I brought it along in case you hadn't. What you looking so funny about?"

"Was I looking funny? I didn't know it. Did you know that this man Frémont was in California only last year—over at Sutter's Fort?"

"So Murray was telling me. I'd have gone over. He tells me Kit Carson and Bad Hand—Fitzpatrick—were with him. And," Andy ended, "I'd like to have sized up this Frémont, too."

Something in Andy's manner caught Larkin's attention. "What *you* looking funny about?" he demanded.

"Was I?" it was Andy's turn to ask.

"Didn't you like the report? You know that country better than almost anybody else. Isn't Frémont accurate?"

"I think that's one of the best books I ever read," said Andy earnestly. "I know pretty nigh every inch of that country he was in. Yes, sir, that's a great book, and it's going to be mighty useful, too, if what Murray says about the number of people crossing the plains is so."

"It's so," said Larkin.

Andy whistled. "Don't seem possible—as I remember that country, only yesterday." Larkin glanced sidewise at him, with a humorous lift of the eyebrow. "Yes, that's right," Andy laughed, "I have been here quite a while, come to think of it."

But Larkin returned tenaciously to the point he had raised.

"Nevertheless," he insisted, "you did look funny when you said you'd like to have had a chance to size Frémont up."

"I didn't mean anything." Andy laughed in slight embarrassment. "Not really. But you see I always size people up. Got the habit in the mountains, I reckon, over yander, where it's a mighty healthy idea to size a man up soon as you can. Now I just can't seem to help it, even with people in books. Even when I don't know a thing about them. Take this Walter Scott you lent me those books of. I'd lay a bet he was porely in health, or else he lived where things were pretty dull—or he thought they were."

"Yes? How do you make that out?"

"Well," explained Andy, "I've noticed that a man likes to talk about things when he's far off from them; and he wants to get back to them whether he knows it or not. That's when he sits down and yarns about them; not when he's there and doing them. And he sort of dresses 'em up in foofaraw a whole sight better'n they really are." He laughed shortly. "Shucks, I'm that way myself sometimes about the mountain country. If I didn't watch out I'd get to be as bad as ary of these old windbags around the posts. I have to check up short when I get started and say to myself, 'Andy, you old fool, you know dam' well that ain't so!' A man sort of forgets all the hard scrapes and the mean times and the drunks and the like, and he fixes everything up pretty in his mind. It's human nature, I reckon. I ain't ever really thought of it before," Andy half apologized, "and I'm probably wrong, but that's the way it strikes me. I'm talking a lot. I'll shut up."

"No, go ahead," urged Larkin, "you interest me. What about Scott?"

"Oh, yes, him. Well, I'm probably wrong; but it just struck me that was the way with him. Those were mighty interesting books; but I'd lay a bet there's a lot of things left out of them."

"Such as?"

"It don't stand to reason things were as pretty, as romantic-like in those old times he writes about as all that. Why," said Andy bluntly, "a fellow's going to sweat a lot in all that armor out in a hot sun." He stopped, suddenly helpless. His idea eluded him. For a moment he groped after it, his brows knit.

"In other words," supplied Larkin, "you think Scott was writing about heroic deeds and strong men and romance because he didn't have them himself."

"That's it!" cried Andy, relieved. "Probably all foolishness."

"It's not foolishness at all," stated Larkin emphatically. "But what has that to do with Frémont?"

"Nothing at all. I was just sort of explaining how I like to size people up in my own mind. I'm probably generally wrong, but it seems I can't help doing it. I was saying that's why I was sorry I didn't get to know he was in this country last year."

"I see. Well, how do you size up Frémont? Does he make things pretty, as you call it?"

Andy shook his head.

"No. And I got no right to judge." He hesitated; then decided to go on. "I don't know a thing about him, except that he did a mighty good job. But it struck me his judgment is pretty poor, and that he is bull-headed, for one thing."

"Where do you get that? Go on; I'm interested."

"I've got no right to judge," repeated Andy, "but you

remember, in the book, where they were at Fort Laramie, and the Injuns were said to be bad, and everybody advised him not to go ahead for a while, and he went just the same? You remember that when he decided that, Kit made his will?"

Larkin nodded.

"Well, I know Kit Carson, and he knows Injuns: and ary greenhorn who goes against Kit's advice in those things is bull-headed."

"They had no trouble with the Indians after all," Larkin pointed out. "And he was a government officer under orders to go ahead and do his job."

"No," acknowledged Andy, "they played in luck. But it shows he's bull-headed."

"Or a man of bravery and determination."

"When Kit says a thing is bad, it's bad," insisted Andy, "and a lot they call bravery is just plain ignorance."

Larkin smiled.

"Didn't you ever take a chance?"

"Lots' of 'em," agreed Andy promptly. "And I ain't saying Frémont didn't do right, considering his job, to take this one. I'm just saying it shows he's bull-headed. I was sizing him up," he reminded. "And," he added, "there might come times when being bull-headed isn't so good. They's a difference there . . ." He was groping again.

"Never mind the difference. What else?"

"Well, it sort of looked like to me he hasn't got first-rate judgment. Take that time they got their bull boats wrecked on the Platte, and lost all their instruments and papers and most of the things they'd collected. Remember?"

"Yes, I remember. But they had bad luck."

"And they earned it," stated Andy positively. "Look at what happened. Frémont divides his party up in two. Part of 'em gets in bull boats and goes sailing off down the river, up there near the headwaters, that nobody knows anything about, except that it goes through a rough country with deep cañons and probably lots of rough water. That's all right—they want to find out about it—except that they might just as well have waited and asked old Bad Hand. He'd been through there and could have told them. The other half he sends around by land to meet him down below a ways. Now why in tarnation did he put all that valuable plunder in the bull boats instead of packing them on the horses? That's only good sense. I'd lay another bet if Kit was still with him he told him that. Maybe," concluded Andy shrewdly, "that was why he did it. If a man is bull-headed, he sures hates to do anything the other fellow's way."

"There may have been a good reason."

"Sure," agreed Andy heartily. "I told you I had no right to judge. But if there is, he don't say anything about it."

"Anything else?"

"No," said Andy, "nothing much, that is. Except it strikes me he has a lot of foofaraw in his get-up."

"How do you make that out?"

"I don't know," acknowledged Andy. "I just got that notion. Strikes me he's one of these yere 'been there first' fellows."

"Huh?"

"You know, first man that ever spit in this lake. One of my old friends used to say that being first in a place was only being one man better than nobody." He stopped to laugh. "That's about right. Shucks, there's many a mountain man been all over that country."

"I don't recall that Frémont claimed anywhere he was actually exploring," said Larkin slowly.

"No, he don't," acknowledged Andy, "but somehow he always acts like he does." He laughed again, rather shamefacedly. "I reckon I'm just a dam' fool," he confessed, "now I come to say it. I'll tell you!" he cried suddenly, "the way I get it. He's sort of play-acting with himself, like Djo, here, would. He ain't all grown up."

"That may be his French blood," submitted Larkin. "You know he's part French."

"Is he?" Andy considered this. "Yes, I reckon so. These French are great hands for foofaraw. He sure makes a great point of climbing that peak in the Wind River country. Shucks! There ain't ary peak in the Rockies that ain't been climbed by someone—or could-a been if there was a sheep or something to go up after. If it's the peak I think it is, Joe Walker told me Cap'n Bonneville climbed it eight or nine years ago."

Larkin laughed in hearty amusement.

"In some parts of the world there are clubs formed just to climb mountains," he told his visitor.

"Sho!" Andy opened his eyes. "You don't say! What do they want to do that for?"

Larkin shook his head, smiling.

"It's a harmless foible," said he.

"Sure," said Andy, "foofaraw is."

They smoked for a time in silence.

"If you go up to Sutter's you may get news of your friends," said Larkin at last. "I understand several of Frémont's men stayed in California. No: I don't know their names."

"I'll look them up. I'd like to hear about Kit—and old Bad Hand." Andy stirred. "I've done a power of talking about nothing," said he. "I didn't mean to bother you. I just got started." He glanced through the open window at the stars. "Time to turn in." He faced Larkin with an engaging grin. "You forget what I been saying," he advised. "I got no right to be saying them. I don't know this man at all, and I've got no right to judge. But want to know how it strikes me? That it's a mighty good thing this yere Frémont went back from Sutter's. You remember what we were talking of? You remember what you said? About it's being a good thing there wasn't any Castros on our side or we'd be in a mess in no time? Well, there'd have been the Castro on our side! Now you *know* I'm a dam' fool!" He arose and stretched his long form. "We've had a mighty interesting talk," said he, "and it looks like a job. I been asleep, I reckon. More ways than one."

"Yes, it's a job," agreed Larkin. "You might start in with Djo," he repeated.

2

After seeing that Djo was in the sleeping room that had been assigned them, Andy stepped out for a moment to look abroad over the sleeping town and the quiet harbor. The conversation of the evening had stirred him strangely. The night was quiet, and the age-old somnolence of the Lovely Land hung like a suspension in the moonlight. In the town a few lights shone, dim and feeble. The only sounds were of the numerous dogs, the wash of the waves against the strand, or the occasional cry of the solitary sentinel on the walls of the dilapidated fort.

"*Vigilante!*" he challenged; and from the landing below his comrade answered, "*Vigilante!*" After which, as Andy well knew, both would roll cigarettes and go to sleep.

So it had been for many, many years; and so Andy had looked out upon it many many times, and so it had always seemed to him it must go on forever. But tonight, somehow, was different. It was as though the soft Californian atmosphere had undergone some subtle change. It was no longer soft and slumbrous. It stirred with a certain essence of impermanence, strange to it before, a vibration that quivered to the rhythm within himself. It was somewhat like the difference between still and boiling water. For a long time Andy lay awake, unable to sleep.

CHAPTER VI

ANDY postponed any discussion with Djo until the Monterey business was ended and they were on their way back to Folded Hills. Ramón did not accompany them, announcing that his business at Monterey was as yet unfinished. After the little cavalcade had surmounted the pass into the Salinas, Andy checked its pace and set about his inquiry into Djo's attitude. He found the boy very reasonable, very respectful, very obstinate in his opinion. Andy was surprised to discover that it was an opinion: and really astounded to find that actually, now that the subject had been broached, Djo welcomed the chance to set his father straight! Obviously, it dawned on Andy slowly, Djo had not the smallest doubt that he was right; as obviously he had been secretly solicitous for his father's integrity. Andy was so fascinated and amused by this discovery that he forgot even to defend himself. The lad was delectable; he was so wide-eyed, so serious, so in earnest, so concerned—and, Andy reflected humorously, so completely feminine—or was it Latin?—in his lordly brushing aside of practicalities when they turned annoying.

It was so simple: the Spanish had discovered California; they had settled California; they alone had a right to California. It was their property. Open and shut: just like that! No *e'tranjero*, no foreigner, had any right to it at all.

"How about Señor Livermore? Señor Gilroy? How about me, your father?"

"You are all *californio*," Djo pointed out reasonably. "Are you not citizens of California?"

"That is true," agreed Andy, "but what are you—are we —going to do about all these people, like that Seth Murray, who are coming in from Oregon and over the Sierra?"

"They should become *californio*, as you did, *señor padre;* or they should be sent back where they came from."

"Do you think they would go?"

"They must be made to go," said Djo stoutly.

"Well," agreed Andy, "that might be done—for a while anyway. But how about other kinds of *e'tranjeros* —the French, the English? What could California do about it if one of them decided to sail their ships into Monterey, say? Be reasonable, son: you know the *presidio*. How long could that hold out—against even one ship with cannons?"

Not very long, Djo had to admit. But Monterey was not California. California was of vast extent. Andy, probing curiously in the boy's ardent mind, discovered in it a sublime faith of invincibility. He realized with an impact of surprise that Djo knew literally almost nothing of the size and power of the outside world; and in a flash of clarity he for the first time understood that the boy in that but reflected the simplicity of nine in ten of his people. Andy had not thought of that before. So stupendously qualifying was this thought to his own point of view that he paused to contemplate it. The horses shuffled along steadily at the rapid "Spanish walk," raising small smokes of dust that drifted, golden-shot with sun, across the dry-parched brittle brown grasses, and arose on heat eddies to dissolve against the strong blue of the sky. The little *caballado* of remounts, strung out in single file, followed close, and the greater cloud from beneath their hoofs moved with them, so that the hindmost was almost obscured, and Panchito at the rear had ceased his song and raised his neckerchief across his nose against its choking. Both beasts and man moved in restrained resignation, awaiting the moment of the *patrón's* pleasure, and the release of swifter movement.

"Perhaps," suggested Andy after a while, "all *califor-*

nios do not feel that way. Señor Larkin says that many favor the idea that it would be better for everybody if California became a part of the United States."

"That cannot be!" Djo was aroused. "Ah, no, *señor padre*. No *californio* can be so base! That would be as though—as though—— That would be to—— Such a one would be a traitor!"

"Would you say that the Señor Vallejo is a traitor?"

"The Señor Vallejo!"

"Yes. I am told that he has said it might be better."

"That must be a lie. Yes: it is a lie. They have lied to you, *señor padre*."

Andy examined the boy's flushed face, and the half-amusement died in him. He sensed here a deadly bitterness, that somehow was familiar to him. In this moment of clarity he saw it for what it was. The same thing over again. There was no real difference—Blackfoot, Shoshone, Snake, Sioux, and now *californio;* and the tide of the eager, ruthless of the comfortable establishments. He had lived through the insensate clash of these forces once before; and in despair had fled them to this remote land; and now in the slow revolution of the years again they were overtaking him. He felt hunted; like an animal. And here was this boy, his boy, headed straight into it. It was so useless, this brave high spirit dashing itself against the inevitabilities of the slow compelling years. His soul was stirred with a sudden panic conviction that something must be done about it; that this great blunder must not be permitted to repeat itself, that these forces moving in menace toward one another must somehow be brought to move in harmony with their common destiny, which now for the first time he saw clearly as though in revelation. And the words of Thomas Larkin recurred to him, and he began to talk earnestly to the boy of acquiescences that, one way or another, he perceived must come about. But abruptly, at the sight of Djo's shocked face, he forbore.

"You cannot mean what you say, *señor padre!*" cried Djo. "No, no! It is the *americano* in you speaking. But you are *californio*, now." The boy was filled with a passion that sealed his mind against the rational; a passion not only of his simple and childish prejudice and conviction but, more greatly, the passion of his great affection. He was aghast; heartbroken.

"But, Father, you *must* see!" he pleaded. "I must *make* you see! *Don't* you see? *Can't* you understand? It is *not* like what you say of the Indian country. You did not have a *rancho* to defend, rights to hold, people who looked to you. You were alone then. It was all right for you, but what would all your people think if you did not stand by them? Think of Panchito, Benito, of all the others! Think of those in the Valley, and over the *sierra* of the Sur, who come to you to ask you what they shall do! Can you desert them when they need you the most? Can't I *make* you see?"

Against the boy's passion Andy was baffled, helpless. He could make no reply; for there was no reply that could penetrate it. He tried to soothe it, taking a lighter tone.

"Well, Djo," he pointed out, "seems to me we're raising an awful pother about nothing. I reckon when the time comes we'll all do what's best. Let's ride."

They set spurs to their mounts, dashed away headlong, leaving the smother of dust behind them, to the great relief of Panchito and the loose horses, who were white and choked with it. They rode side by side, but it seemed to Andy that they rode apart. He had a queer irrational feeling that somehow their rôles had been reversed, that the austerities of judgment remained with Djo. This was Andy's first experience with the gloriously assured convictions of youth. Djo was absolutely certain. Andy was not. For the moment that mere fact lent Djo an illusory moral dominance.

2

Andy did not again refer to the subject with anyone until he was alone with Carmel, in the privacy of their bedroom. His dependence on her had grown with the years until her being was inextricably interwoven with the fabric of his existence. Andy never ceased to be astounded at this, whenever he stopped to think of it: which was often. His early history had been so solitary of women and so adventurous that he had come to look upon himself as self-sufficing, a lone wolf in life, as the trappers had it. At first, and for a while, he used to dally with the idea that some day he would go back to the old life. Not for good, of course; but for a season. He might guide one of the wagon caravans, just for the experience; or hook up with Jim Bridger for a while. But he had soon to admit to himself, with a rueful humor, that it could not be done. He would not have admitted it to anybody else, not even Ramón, but the truth of it was that he could not leave Carmel for so many months. He knew perfectly just how it would be; a void, an uneasiness, at first slight but increasingly accelerated until it became all but intolerable. Nice fix for an old mountain man to be in! And him by now upwards of forty-odd years old! But he was in the fix, and there was no use trying to dodge it, so Andy did not try. His was a true mating, help or hinder, weal or woe, and henceforward he must move within its radius.

"Doggone," he muttered to himself, "I've sure got used to having the darn little thing around!"

So it was a distinct shock to him when he discovered that Carmel was inclined to find Djo's point of view wholly natural and reasonable. Her acceptance of it was broadly comfortable. She seemed to think, or she assumed to think—Andy could not be quite sure which—that his whole concern had to do with Djo's relations with the girl, Wapita.

"You need not worry," she laughed amusedly. "I know these thing. I keep the eye on them. Djo is child yet; and she—she too is child. You do not know that, eh, *querido?* You look at the shape—yes, you do! All men the same. And why not? She's nice to look at. Me, I look at the inside, the *corazón.* She's grow-up for the shape; she's child for the *corazón.*"

"I wasn't thinking of that," disclaimed Andy. "But she's putting these ideas into his head. Her influence——"

"Pooh!" Carmel snapped her fingers. "Djo, he did not get his ideas from her."

"Where else?" asked Andy.

"Anywhere," returned Carmel indolently, "from Father Sanchez, from Don Arturo if he come to visit, from Ramón or Ignacio, from the *vaquero,* from the *mozo,* from the bird and the tree and the flower, from anywhere where it is *californio.* Why not?"

It was here that Andy's heart skipped a beat. He checked as he would check at the brink of an abyss. It yawned suddenly before him, unsuspected. He shrank from facing what its depths might contain. He eyed Carmel covertly, seeking to fathom the edge of intention beneath her casual manner. She drew the comb idly through her glossy hair. Her eyes were vacant, as though with the last remark she had dismissed the subject from her mind. Andy tiptoed away from it. He suggested the idea of a round of visits to the north. He said nothing of its purpose. Carmel brightened to the proposal. She approved: welcoming the break in the placid and somewhat monotonous life at Folded Hills. Djo had never been farther from home than Monterey. Amata would be well cared for by the competent Vicenta. She ceased combing her hair and turned squarely to Andy, her face alight with interest.

"Never have I myself been north of the Bay!" she cried. "We shall go to Sonoma, no? To visit with the Vallejos? Many time, at Monterey, the Doña Francisca has beg me that we come. It is said that Don Guadalupe live there like a king. That will be good to see. And there shall be the *merienda* and the *fiesta* and we shall have much pleasure!" She was as eager as a child. "Shall we take with us many peoples? Do you think maybe Ramón and Conchita like to go?"

"I shall take Panchito, perhaps another *vaquero*," said Andy, "not too many people, I think. Ramón is still at Monterey."

His purpose was unchanged: he did not wish to complicate it. But its savor had gone dreary in a formless foreboding. He recoiled from facing the nature of the foreboding; refused to formulate it to himself. It was like a dark cloud rising across the horizon of the long quiet years. She looked up at him quickly.

"What is it, *querido?*" she asked. "Do you not think it will be fun?"

Apparently she had forgotten. Andy aroused himself with an effort.

"Great fun," he agreed.

"We shall stop also to see Don Eugenio and the Martínez," she promised herself. "I shall take my green dress that we buy from the Boston ship. I think, if you like it, we shall take Wapita."

"Wapita!" cried Andy.

"But yes. I must have with me a woman to serve me. That would not be *gentil* if I do not that. Vicenta, she is too fat for that: and she must esstay with Amata."

"But why Wapita?"

"Oh, I think she like. She is—what you call?—r-restless. She like r-run away," Carmel laughed. "I think maybe-so it's good she r-run away with us. You no like?"

"Oh, yes," agreed Andy. "It's all right. Bring her along if you want."

He did not know why the idea made him uneasy. But it did.

CHAPTER VII

THEY rode in the proper dignity of a Californian family of the upper class; and therefore presented a very gay and attractive appearance. The riding horses were the best the ranch afforded, their accouterment ablaze with chased silver, carved brown leather and embroideries of bright silks. The riders were brave in costumes that would have been theatrical in any other place or time. Here they were as apt to the picture as the sun to the sky. The years had not dimmed Carmel's beauty; nor, as was only too common with the women of her people, blurred her form with fat. In Andy's eyes she was in appearance the same girl who had ridden with him up this valley nearly fourteen years ago. On her head she wore a wide straw hat, under which hung the sun cloth for coolness, embroidered at the four corners and weighted with little golden apples so that the cloth flapped and swung about her face with a certain air of coquetry. She and Andy rode together; and Djo at one side, but a half-length behind out of respect. Djo looked exactly like Andy, but in miniature. His dress was the same, down to the smallest detail, even to the small rifle he carried across his saddle as the *ranchero* carried the Boone gun. This latter was not at all Californian; but on a journey the old mountain man would have felt naked without it. It was Don Largo's idiosyncrasy, his trade-mark of personality, so to speak. But Djo's resemblances went further. Consciously or unconsciously his every mannerism of movement and speech was copied from his father; until in result he gave no impression of the child, but was rather the man made

225

small, the shadow of Don Largo. This grave and sober identity of the two amused Carmel greatly. When she thought she could do so unobserved, she embraced them with her eyes in which danced much amusement clothed in tenderness. But Andy caught her at it, and grinned at her in complete understanding, and that made it even better.

Twenty or thirty paces in the rear of *el patrón, la patrona,* and *el patroncito* followed a little cavalcade of seven horses. Three of them were ridden by Wapita, Panchito, and another *vaquero;* the other four bore packs, which contained all the baggage. In his *cantinas* Andy carried only the passport, without which not even a *californio* could stir abroad in his own country. It was encased as usual in a pouch of tanned skin, which in turn had been enveloped in a bladder thoroughly greased against the wet. The packs themselves included a mysterious bundle which Andy himself had made up, and whose contents he smilingly refused to divulge to Carmel's inquiry. There were no loose horses. This was quite different from the arrangement of an ordinary journey from point to point, when the horses would have been twenty or more, and none save the riding animals burdened. In that case the party would have swept through the country at top speed, changing from one horse to another as the animals tired, abandoning any too weary to keep pace. But this was a leisurely excursion, and if fresh animals proved desirable, why, any *ranchero* would supply them gladly as a matter of courtesy. They rode gayly, at a foot pace, savoring the golden bath of sunshine, listening to the larks and song sparrows, sniffing the perfumes of sage released by the warmth, admiring the shadows sleeping in the folds of the hills. There was no haste. Today, tomorrow, yesterday; they were all of a piece. The birds sang; the horses' hoofs shuffled in the easy Spanish trot with a sound as of wind in dried grasses; the silver bells on the harness of the sumpter animals tinkled cheerfully; the younger *vaquero* hummed the minor cadences of a love song.

They stopped at the Rivera *hacienda* overnight and were made much of. They rode over the pass to San Juan and up the valley of Santa Clara, and so to the great bay with its rippled waters, now brown, now blue and sparkling, and with thousands upon thousands of wildfowl, upon all of which Djo gazed with wide eyes. Other people they encountered, people of all sorts: *caballeros*, *vaqueros*, churchmen, Indians toiling on foot. All these greeted them and were greeted in return with a high grave formality. Sometimes they paused to exchange the courtesy of the day, sitting at ease for a while beneath the widespread shadow of a live-oak, separating with a backward reining of the horses and a sonorous *vaya con Dios*. There was plenty of time for these things: time did not exist. And yet vaguely in the background of Andy's mind persisted a queer feeling that with each league forward they drew nearer to the curtain of an unguessed boundary where things endless would end; a boundary to a new land where timelessness would cease. For the moment, however, he resolutely submerged his forebodings and perplexities, and rode in enjoyment without a care.

They proceeded north along the shores of the Bay, turning aside from the direct route when fancy called or interest led. They looked across the waters and saw the far-off huddle of houses at Yerba Buena where San Francisco was to be. They looked upon the islands white and gleaming with the guano of sea birds. Just after this they came upon a wonderful sight, an immense herd of elk swimming vigorously to a landing on what is now Mare Island. There must have been over a thousand of them, and their spreading antlers looked like a forest of bared branches moving across the waters of the Bay. Djo was much excited, for he had never seen wild deer of that size, and he wanted very much to shoot at them, but this Andy would not permit. Carmel thought it a pretty sight; but Panchito looked on the spectacle with the complete indifference of the cattleman. A chance *vaquero* told them these elk often migrated to and from the mainland, and were sometimes caught with the *reata* for the hides and the tallow.

"The fat makes very fine candles to burn to the Virgin or the blessed saints," said he.

After this they turned sharply to the east, and so came to the Rancho Pinole, a great holding belonging to Ygnacio Martínez, whose cattle were uncounted, and who was reputed to own more than a thousand horses. Here they lingered for two days for a *merienda*, after which they and their baggage were ferried across the strait, the horses swimming, and so at last they headed directly for Sonoma.

With all and sundry, as occasion offered, Andy talked guardedly and apart. Nowhere did he discover any evidence of concern over the incoming and increasing number of immigrants. Indeed Señor Martínez surprised him by the expression of a hope that at some future time California might throw off the Mexican rule and rid herself of the constant revolutions.

"And in that case," Andy inquired cautiously, "do you think that California can stand alone?"

His host shrugged.

"*Quien sabe, señor?*" he disclaimed. "But if not, then, so it seems to me we shall be more secure under your own government, if so God wills."

2

Don Ygnacio accompanied them across the strait to say farewell to them on the northern shore. There he issued them a word of caution.

"This land you now enter is not like that to the south," he warned "It is well to ride carefully. The Indians are still wild and treacherous. It is the habit of even our women to carry arms when they ride abroad. But I forget, *señor*,"—he waved a courtly hand toward the long rifle across Andy's saddle bow—"that you need no warnings as to Indians, for you know more of them than any *californio;* though you are so much *californio* that you make me forget," with which somewhat involved compliment Don Ygnacio left them.

Nevertheless they experienced no trouble, nor saw sign of trouble, but arrived safely at Sonoma in due course.

All six of the visitors rode with eager curiosity, for none had been this far north, and somehow—either because of the interposition of the Bay; or, more likely, because of some subtle psychological boundary—this country had a little strangeness as of a foreign land. And indeed, by many untypical details that illusion was strengthened. The mission buildings, the *pueblo* houses and the residences of the *gente de razón* were all grouped rather closely into the loose semblance of a town. This was contrary to Californian custom; but Andy remembered about the Indians. The buildings of the mission had fallen into decay, and cattle overran its neglected orchards. Small buildings were grouped roughly around a sort of plaza scattered untidily with bones. They were undistinguished, indeed almost squalid, and were dominated by a huge barnlike structure which, Andy surmised, must be the *cuartel*, for Vallejo, he now remembered, had conducted a small military establishment. In contrast a number of fine residences ranged themselves across the way. The largest of these, our travelers correctly surmised, must be that of Don Guadalupe. One of the others, a *vaquero* answered their inquiry, was also a Vallejo property; while a third belonged to Jacob Leese, an American, who had married Don Guadalupe's sister.

The travelers were received with even more than the

usual open-hearted hospitality of the country. Andy felt himself rather peculiarly welcome. Andy had met Vallejo casually, at Monterey, on a number of occasions, and his relations with the grandee— for so he appeared in Andy's eyes—had always been cordial. Vallejo was an ideal host. A manner of stately and lofty formality, at first a trifle subduing to new acquaintance, proved to be a genuine sense of dignity rather than arrogance. Andy early discovered that everybody liked the *hacendado;* and that he was interested in all, even the least, of his people, and had for each of them always a pleasant word; though he held himself toward them as beseemed the lord of a principality. Certainly Djo stood in no awe of him from the very beginning, and was soon chattering away to him on all subjects and with all confidence. Don Guadalupe seemed to fancy the boy; reassured Carmel when she would have checked the youngster.

"He is a fine boy; he interests me; he is so different from our own."

Certainly the interest was returned. Djo talked about everything; told about everything; poured himself out. To Panchito's mortification he even exposed that scandal of his earlier infancy when he, a Rivera, had insisted on soiling his hands in the personal manufacture of *adobe* bricks. This exposure was made in the chatter of confidence; and Djo checked short at Panchito's expression.

"I was much younger then," he said primly. "Now I would do nothing to lower the dignity of an *hacendado*."

He said this because he thought he ought to in present company; and Don Guadalupe's eyes twinkled.

"The dignity that can be lowered stands on no firm feet," he stated sententiously. "It is well to know how to make *adobe* bricks. An educated gentleman must know how to make not only *adobe* bricks, but also such things as soap and pottery, to burn lime and tan hides, to fashion shoes and candles and cigars and many other things.

How else can he be sure that his people do these things properly?"

Djo did not look toward Panchito; but he wriggled in his saddle with satisfaction, for he knew that this endorsement of indubitable authority had at last settled the tiresome question.

It was a clear case of hero worship. In spite of himself Andy experienced just a little prick of something over Djo's complete abandonment of his father for the moment in favor of the courtly grandee. He indignantly dismissed the emotion as unworthy—and silly. What more natural? Novelty; Djo's Spanish blood; Don Guadalupe's real charm. And, Andy was astute enough to see this association was in a way a refuge against embarrassment. The boy is a little scared to be alone with me again, thought Andy: he's scared we'll dispute again, like we came near doing on the ride up the valley. He's letting the whole thing cool off again. And, Andy added to himself with comfort, that's because he cares. If he didn't care a heap, he wouldn't mind.

Nevertheless Djo himself was the one to recur to the subject. He could not help it; for he must vindicate his hero. He sought Andy out for the purpose.

"I told you, *señor padre*, it must be a lie," said he.

"What is a lie?" Andy was wide of the reference.

"What was told of Don Guadalupe."

"What was that? What are you talking about?"

"That he favored these *e'tranjeros* that are coming into our country."

"Yes?"

"It is not true."

"You have been talking about these things to Don Guadalupe?" asked Andy quietly.

"No. That I promised you and the *señor* Larkin. But I have stood by when Don Guadalupe has talked of them to his brother and to Solano. His voice was angry, *señor padre*. He says these *americanos* are savages. He called them 'white Indians.' And Don Salvador said they should be treated as Indians. He said every one of them should be swept from the face of the land. So you see what you had heard was a lie." Djo looked at his father a little wistfully; as though hoping this tremendous endorsement must make Andy see the light. But the mountain man was not ready to make the issue.

"I have not talked to Don Guadalupe of these things," he dismissed the subject.

This, however, he intended to do at the earliest opportunity. He had great faith in the *hidalgo's* practical wisdom. In spite of the casual remark reported by Djo and which might well have resulted from some individual irritation reported by his head man, Solano, Andy was not convinced of Vallejo's considered attitude toward the whole question. And he was eager to learn it, for Don Guadalupe was the best exponent he knew of really enlightened Californian opinion. As for Don Salvador, his brother, Andy dismissed him with a shrug. That was a different breed of cats. Salvador was notoriously violent in his hatred of foreigners. He possessed the Vallejo charm of manner; but Andy felt that only his tradition of hospitality constrained him to ordinary courtesy. His manner was reserved, inclined to be sullen. At times he skirted as near the edge of positive rudeness as decency permitted toward a guest of the family.

He had the Vallejo good looks; and, as a former commander, affected military mustaches which he bristled in a fierce and gallant manner. Fortunately, as Andy considered it, he was much too important to bother with a boy. Andy was glad of this. He was inclined, secretly, to return Salvador's contempt. He had heard some queer stories about Salvador, to which, until now that he had seen the man, he had paid little attention. He began to wonder if some of them might be at least partly true. Andy's eyes darkened as he recalled one of these tales. Some Indians or other had stolen a single cow and disappeared. Salvador and the soldiers he then commanded had made an expedition north, arriving finally at Clear Lake. Some Indians, reputed to Andy as gentle and peaceable people, lived on an island. When they saw Salvador and his company on the shores of the lake, some of them crossed to him on rafts. Through an interpreter Salvador had told them that his visit was peaceful, for the purpose of making an alliance, and had persuaded them, with this object in view, to ferry himself and his men to the island. Under the same pretext he induced them to lay aside their weapons. The soldiers then fell upon them with knives, killing them thus almost to the last man. The few who managed to leap into the water were shot. It was said that but one human being survived this massacre; a tiny baby on whom one of the soldiers took compassion. The narrative, as Andy had heard it at Folded Hills, was minute and embroidered with detail. He supposed there might be a slender thread of fact in it, but had discounted heavily those details. No one knew the Indian character better than himself; and he thought he saw the basis of this wild story in a punitive expedition of the usual sort. Even if one could not identify the individual culprit, it was sometimes necessary to throw the fear of God into 'em just to keep 'em from running over you! He'd done it himself! Now he wondered a little whether it might not be true. Sweep every American from the face of the land, eh?

"With what?" Andy muttered under his breath with sneering contempt.

He caught himself up short. He was aghast at himself. For a brief moment he had bristled as though against enemies. A sadness fell upon him; for that instant had

made him realize, as no amount of talk could have done,
how instinctive—and almost irresistible—racial antago-
nisms can be.

3

Andy had difficulty in shaking off the lowness of spirit
that seemed to be growing in him through the accretion
of these small things. It should have been difficult to
remain depressed. Except for Salvador, all were so friendly,
apparently so eager to drop everything in order to devote
their whole time to the entertainment of Sonoma's hon-
ored guests. Don Guadalupe was indeed an overlord of
a true principality. Sonoma itself, with its wide cattle
ranges and varied industries, would have sufficed to justify
the title. But also at Petaluma he maintained a two-story
residence, where he raised much wheat as well as cattle,
and employed six hundred *vaqueros* and laborers. He killed
over eight thousand steers at a *matanza*. None knew how
many cattle he owned. Don Guadalupe had in the past
commanded at Sonoma a military establishment. Many
of the ex-soldiers still lived near, *vaqueros* or small *rancheros*. He still maintained an effective discipline. Andy began to understand how it was that, though these northern
Indians were admittedly fierce and warlike, they had been
held to some sort of order. Indeed Vallejo's right-hand
man was an Indian, a remarkable man, educated, able to
read and write, with a ranch in his own right which he
conducted capably aside from his heavy responsibilities.

But if Señor Vallejo was liked and respected, Señora
Vallejo was beloved by everybody. She was a beautiful
and motherly woman who saw harm in nobody. Of her
a later traveler was to say that he found two things in
California supremely good: the grapes and Doña Francisca Benicia Vallejo y Carrillo; for Señora Vallejo was of
the Carrillos of the south. Over her numerous dependents
she ruled placidly and with understanding. Accustomed

as he was to the typical Californian household, Andy was nevertheless astounded at the apparently numberless servants. They swarmed, men and women; though the women prevailed. He could not make out how so many could find employment.

"Why," said Doña Francisca comfortably, "they are all Indians, as you see, and these people seem obstinate against learning more than one thing. So we must have a many. There must be one for each of my children, and I have two for myself. And fully a score or more—I forget —must do the spinning and the sewing. And since we have many guests—welcome, like yourself, *señor*—there are eight in the kitchen, and also those to wash the dishes; and five to grind the corn for the *tortilla*, for when the house is full, three are not enough. And for so great a number many to wash the clothes and the linen; and other things,"—she waved her hand vaguely. She laughed good-humoredly. "They are Indians, but they are very proud," said she. "One who is taught the cooking will not hear of learning the washing of dishes; and a good washerwoman would be insulted if I told her she must know how to sew or to spin. They are very clever, though; and could be taught to do all things well, if they would," she added with pride.

"But what do you pay them?" Andy was still American enough to ask.

"Pay? But we do not pay them any fixed amount. We give them what they need. When they are sick we take care of them. And when they have children we give the instruction." She laughed again. "And when they have children we are godparents. Oh, we are many, many godparents, I assure you!"

Carmel adored her. The two women spent much time together. Nothing escaped Doña Francisca. She even half apologized for Salvador's withdrawn coolness, though his conduct was correct enough as far as externals go.

"The poor Salvador," said she, "a few years since, as *comandante* of the soldiers, in arresting an American sailor who had deserted, he was forced to shoot the man. There was much trouble, talk of murder. Representations were made to Don Guadalupe. Salvador now hates all *americanos.*"

"But Andrés is *californio!*" protested Carmel.

"*Sí, sí,*" agreed Doña Francisca comfortably. No more was said on the matter.

Wapita, perhaps because the change of environment was so complete, lost much of the wild solitariness of her usual habit. She mingled freely with Don Guadalupe's retainers; attended the picnics and dances and took her part in them. She even, in one case at least, lost something of her aversion to all men. She was a good deal in the company of one Pepe. Andy did not think much of her choice; though he had to admit to himself that Pepe was a fascinating enough rascal, in his way. He was young, good-looking, with flashing white teeth, an ingratiating manner, and an unerring eye for the picturesque. He played the guitar and could sing the love songs of the country. Nobody could lounge against a white adobe wall with quite the same effect. His function in Don Guadalupe's establishment was not clear. Nobody seemed to take him very seriously. Nobody trusted him. Djo openly detested him. Carmel did not share Andy's doubts. She laughed when he expressed them to her.

"But she care not that,"—Carmel snapped her fingers. "He titch her the dance. He's pretty good: he know. He's come from Mexico. He's been see the great dancer in Mexico; and he tell Wapita that if someone titch her, some day she be greatest dancer in California." She laughed tolerantly.

"You believe that?"

"Me? What I believe," said Carmel, "is that this Pepe, he's wise man with a girl. He know better than to esscare her at the first. By and bye he forget about titch the dance and how she will be the great dancer. But he is not so wise as he think. Wapita she will not forget. No! All the time she has been shut up tight, like this,"—Carmel squeezed her hands together—"inside. And this dance she—what-you-call?"

"The dance is her outlet," supplied Andy.

"*Sí*. This Pepe, he bring it to her; so she like heem. That is all."

"You think it's a good thing, then?"

"Why not?"

"This Pepe looks to me like a slippery customer."

Carmel shrugged. Andy was puzzled. He could not decide whether she was very wise or culpably indifferent.

4

Andy had not, of course, forgotten the real business of his journey north of the Bay. If he had followed his own inclinations he would long since have been about it. But at Sonoma he was still subject to the pleasant, spacious leisures of the old regime. None of the Riveras had ever before visited the home *hacienda* of the Vallejos. That event could not be slurred over by small unbecoming hastes. There were ridings, and "little dances," and a ball of a more formal character, and *meriendas*. Until these had been enjoyed, it would have been most unseemly to suggest departure. Awaiting the moment, Andy spent much of his time with Jacob Leese, who had married Doña Rosalía, Vallejo's sister.

It was natural he should gravitate to Leese, for the two men had much in common. Leese was a good-looking fellow with half-puckered, quizzical, appraising eyes, that met one straight and square. His mouth, too, was straight with the determination of one trained in the wild country, and seemed to be set slightly aslant so that the right-hand corner was lower than the left. Two deep vertical furrows between his eyes accented the man's general air of capability. Andy took to him on sight. When he learned that Leese's history and experience were not unlike his own, the bond was complete. Leese too had come to California early, from a life as trapper and trader; he too had married a Californian, become a citizen. They had much to talk about, for Leese's experience had been largely down toward the Santa Fe country. He shared Andy's frontiersman's enthusiasm, even reverence, for firearms. Indeed, to the huge though tolerant amusement of all California he had taught Doña Rosalía to shoot the rifle. Was such a thing ever heard of? And furthermore, Andy discovered, she was really an excellent marksman—or should it be markswoman? And she enjoyed the sport. They had shooting matches. Djo deserted his latest admiration for these. He brought his little Hawkens rifle and acquitted himself very well, but was secretly chagrined at being beaten by a woman; though his vexation was healed by his pride in his father's easy supremacy. Andy had not lost his skill with the old Boone gun. But especially were both Leese, and in lesser degree Doña Rosalía, fascinated with the new six-shooting pistol. Andy had caught the knack of the weapon, but in their hands it jumped about uncontrollably, so that they missed entirely, not only the mark, but the very tree on which it had been placed. Indeed Doña Rosalía refused to shoot it but once. It alarmed her. The bang of the explosion was too near her hand; and she flinched from it outrageously.

"I suppose I might learn to use the thing if I kept at it," remarked Leese, "but right now I'd rather have a club."

CHAPTER VIII

NOT until the fifth day of the visit did a lull occur in the festivities. Andy seized upon it. He had not yet had opportunity to sound out Vallejo's opinions; but that could wait until his return. He described his projected excursion with Djo merely as a sight-seeing trip, with its ultimate objective as Sutter's Fort. All agreed that Sutter's Fort was worth seeing, quite unique. Andy had had no difficulty so far. But it took some arguing to make anybody see the sense in the rest of his plan.

He declined with thanks Don Guadalupe's offer of an escort suitable to his station.

He flatly refused to take with him either Panchito or his other *vaquero;* or any spare animals.

He confined his luggage to one pack horse; and made arrangements to lead that one, instead of driving it, as was customary.

"Djo and I are going to make a little *pasear* after the fashion of the trappers," he explained patiently. "I have always promised Djo that some day we should do so."

They rode out of Sonoma at last, just the two of them, thus equipped. Carmel, and Wapita, and the *vaqueros* were to await their return. As to the simplicity of the expedition, Don Guadalupe was politely tolerant of his guest's idiosyncrasy, as beseemed a host; Carmel was amused; Panchito was deeply mortified; Jacob Leese was understanding, and just a little envious.

Some leagues from the *pueblo,* Andy drew up the horses beneath a convenient white oak tree, took off the pack, and from it extracted a mysterious bundle which he had

239

carried unopened from Folded Hills. It proved to contain two plain-cloth hunting shirts, one large, one small; and two pairs of fringed leggings, ditto, ditto.

"There," said he, surveying these things with satisfaction, "that's more like it!" He cast a humorous eye toward Djo. "Might have put 'em on before we started: but I thought we'd handed 'em about all they'd stand. Snake off the clothes you've got on and put these on." He proceeded leisurely to divest himself one by one of the various and numerous items of his Californian costume. As he did so, he continued to talk to Djo, as to an equal; as he had always done, even from Djo's earliest childhood. "They'd look on all this as foofaraw," said he. "And back in the mountain country they'd call these duds we've just taken off foofaraw. It's a funny thing, Djo; but nobody *sabes* foofaraw, unless it's their kind of foofaraw."

He began one by one to fold the discarded garments; watching Djo warily from the corner of his eye. The boy's defensive tensions were obviously relaxing with relief. Andy methodically bestowed the completed bundle in the pack.

"Where are we going, *señor padre?* And what are we going for?" Djo inquired at last. It was evident that he had brought himself to the question only with effort.

"Why, I don't know," Andy said easily, as he threw the hitch, "I thought we'd go nowhere in particular. Just sort of marvel around for a good time together. See what we can see; camp where we want to; sleep out, or maybe stop at any *rancho* we happen across. Kill us our own meat. Live on the country. Just fun. Anywheres particular you got in mind? No? Well, let's get going and see where we land up." He swung into the saddle and turned to survey Djo's figure with approval. "Doggone, Djo," he grinned, "if you don't make a pretty good-looking mountain man." He caught up his horse's reins, laying the long rifle across the saddle in front of him. He glanced at the sun.

"I tell you," he proposed, "let's angle over toward the marshes along the river and try and see if we can catch any ducks with nets made out of *tules*, like Pascal told you. What say? I'd sure like to try that. What say?"

"Oh, yes!" cried Djo. "And where can we stop to-night?"

"Oh, wherever we happen to be," said Andy indifferently.

2

They worked absorbedly, like two small boys together, weaving a high net of the *tules* which they placed on stakes across the water of a narrow reed-bordered slough; and constructed a number of small bundles of *tules*, which they set afloat below it as decoys. Then they hid themselves in the grasses near by to wait. When they thought sufficient ducks had alighted near the net, they leaped forth with loud shouts. In theory at least a few of the ducks, in the panic of flight, should have dashed themselves so violently against the net as to stun themselves. It was enormous fun, but it did not work.

Andy shook his head ruefully.

"Djo," he said, "we're no good. Either that Pascal is a tarnation liar, or these are educated ducks, or else we don't know duck talk. Now which do you reckon it is?"

Djo did not know, nor did he much care. He was happy to the top of his throat in this resumption of intimate and equal companionship. He was even happier when Andy, with a vexed laugh, gave up the experiment.

"Looks like we'd better quit trying to be Injuns, Djo, and get us our supper, if we don't want to go hungry," said he. Unconsciously he was slipping back rapidly into the old familiar vernacular of the trapping days. "You better pot a couple." And Djo's cup of bliss was filled when, with the little Hawkens rifle, he clipped neatly the heads of two fat pintail ducks from the next two lots that came in to the crude decoys.

"That shines!" Andy approved the shots. He waded into the slough, indifferent to the wetting, to retrieve the quarry. Djo waded in, too: though obviously that was unnecessary. Even Andy did not guess at the enormous satisfaction. He did not think of it one way or another, for he had never had a Vicenta to squawk over wet feet.

They trudged back to the higher land, the man and the boy, the ducks dangling between them; and the sky was lucent green in the west; and the distant rim of the coast range was edged with gold; and the broad flat land of sedges lay supine in the dusk of twilight; and glimpses of ponds and sloughs and bayous gleamed silver amid the darkened *tules*. Across the skies long lines of wildfowl slanted. A quietude of still peace lay over the land, as though of silence. And yet there was no silence. From the marshes arose a busy gabbling of ducks and geese; a medley of the voices of blackbirds, gallinules, bitterns, herons. Smaller feathered peoples talked in undertones in the grasses near at hand. The air was clamorous with them all; a mighty chorus of thankful happiness.

Soft darkness took the world. The lucence faded from the sky. Stars came out. The tiny fire under the white oaks gleamed ever the more brightly until at last it became the focal point in the simplicity of night.

Andy raised himself from his elbow to poke an experimental sliver at the breast of one of the roasting duck.

"All set, son," said he. "Might have dug us a few wild potatoes if we hadn't been so busy with that fool net. Never mind: straight meat's good for provender."

Djo ate his duck with relish. He copied Andy's disposition with the saddle gear for the night. He said nothing of his satisfactions. They were many. The chief of these was, I think, that not once did Andy evidence the slightest interest whether or not his garments had dried. They had;

but Djo almost wished they had not. Djo would, at the moment, have welcomed almost any discomfort appropriate to his rôle of hardy pioneer.

3

For some days they wandered, apparently at haphazard, but always in a generally easterly direction. Andy's purpose with Djo was in a fair way of accomplishment. His trust in the power of the open, and of things shared, was shrewd. Djo's withdrawal in spirit was over, and the more quickly because of the boy's subconscious thankfulness that such should be the case. Once more the two saw eye to eye in happy and thought-free companionship. If they had turned back or gone at once to Sutter's, once this communion had been reëstablished, all might have been well: or at least the ground would have been cleared of prejudice for a fresh start in understanding. But Andy's shrewd native wisdom had its limitations.

At the end of the fourth day he swung northward toward the settlers' country. After all, Andy's business was to find out for Larkin how matters stood with them. But especially he was eager to see some of these people. Curiously enough the mountain man had built up in himself a profound admiration for them that was not unlike Djo's small-boy hero worship of his own old-time trapper companions. The amazing hardihood and resource of the latter were understandable to Andy. He was one of them. He knew all about that. All a man had to take care of was himself; and if he didn't, he got rubbed out, and that was all there was to it. He rode a horse, or he went on foot; and he lived on the country. And he learned the job by years in the country. But these fellows started out green, most of them; and they had women with them, and little children; and they had to get ox wagons through the country; and when they got here they had to start from nothing to make a living and keep their women and children. Tough on the women and children, too. Took a stout man to tackle that! Took guts! I'd have been scared to tackle it, admitted Andy. He saw them solely from the point of view of this inner quality which he was thus prepared to recognize. Externals were unimportant, almost nonexistent. He forgot that this insight beneath externals was a thing of his own, developed by his experience.

Once in the settled country, the travelers moved slowly. Andy stopped at every little shack, turned aside whenever he met anyone with whom to talk. He was intensely interested, for he was getting acquainted at first hand with the phase of pioneer life that had succeeded his own. He forgot Djo; or if he half remembered him, it was to assume that the boy, like himself, must be sensing the heroic spirit of this movement.

Djo made no comments. He sat quiet and listened. His face was expressionless; his eyes wide. But in their depths was growing an incredulous scorn.

He had never seen anything quite like these people; or the places in which they dwelt. The men were, most of them, dirty, unshaven, uncouth in speech and manner. They lived in tiny single-room shacks, many of which were made of mud, of crude lumber, even of *tules*. The women were clad in dresses without shape or beauty; some of them looked bedraggled, overworked. The children, obviously, ran wild. A small patch of ground had been plowed; orchard trees like switches were half choked with upspringing weeds; rude fences; crude contraptions; few of the conveniences and none of the graces of life. The disdain within him grew, until it penetrated even Andy's absorption. Andy came to himself with a shock of annoyance. I've been a fool, he said to himself. He tried to repair the damage, after his own fashion.

"You don't think much of these people," he stated, as they rode away after one such visit.

"No, *señor padre*, I do not," returned Djo honestly.

"They look rough," acknowledged Andy, "but they're better men than they look."

"They live worse than the Indians of the Tulares," said Djo, "and these are not Indians, so it is worse. I do not wonder that Don Guadalupe calls them 'white Indians.'"

"You must remember, son, that they've just come, and that they do everything themselves——" He stopped at the sight of Djo's face. It's no good to argue, thought Andy with a sigh: I ought to have remembered—how should he know, raised as he was? Aloud he said, "You can't judge, son: you've no right to judge. You come back in ten years; then if you find these same people living in these same shanties in this same way, you'll have the right to stick your snoot in the air." He checked a slight impatience and continued more gently, "It's this way, son. You've been sizing up the outside of these folks; and what you've got to size up is the inside. That's hard to learn. These folks are just starting. From nothing. And they've had the guts to git here. Each one of 'em, man and woman, is doing four men's jobs. They ain't got time to stop and spit. You ain't seen ary one of them with his tail down, have you?"

He flung his leg back over the saddle and touched spurs to his horse.

"Never mind what you see that you ain't used to, Djo," he advised. "Size up your man. Never mind if he's a rough customer. Notice if he's got his tail up. *Sabe?*"

"Yes, *señor padre*," replied Djo dutifully, but with an entire lack of conviction.

Andy glanced at his face; sighed. It was no good. They were back where they had started from. Might as well get on to Captain Sutter's; get it over with.

CHAPTER IX

SO THEY went directly to Sutter's Fort, which was the best thing they could have done; for the novelty reduced Djo to the status of a tourist. All his faculties other than those of curiosity and observation were wholly submerged. Everything was so different, both in physical aspect and in life and custom, from anything he had ever seen, that he walked about with his eyes and mouth open.

The fort itself stood near the edge of a live-oak park, very imposing, very simple in plan. An immense rectangle was enclosed by two thick adobe walls, one inside the other, and about twenty-five feet apart. By stretching a roof over the space between these walls, and then inserting partitions, rooms could be provided to suit any need. The inside wall, being a little lower than the outside wall, provided a parapet for defense; which was further assured by bastions. The walls themselves were not pierced. The whole place turned a blank to the outside world. It concentrated itself on its own life, as compassed by the spacious parade ground, or plaza, within. Except for an adobe corral at the south end and, a curious wooden trough that ran along the base of the walls, there were no structures outside. The walls and bastions were armed with brass cannon. They were properly mounted, shone with care. They looked businesslike, pointed somewhere, looked as though they might shoot; a marked contrast to the guns at Monterey on their decaying carriages.

Djo's impressions were at first too confused for coherence. It would take time to sort them. The place swarmed with life and activity; Indians standing sentry,

armed and in uniform; trappers; mountain men, such as
his father had described to him, with their strange garments and their long rifles and their swaggering devil-
may-care manner; recent immigrants, like Seth Murray,
still subsisting on Sutter's bounty until they could place
themselves; visiting Indians, admitted a few at a time for
trade or council, wilder than the beasts of the plains,
nearly naked, most of them, with harsh coarse hair falling
about their faces. One that caught Djo's eye was evidently a personage. He stalked about proudly, clad in an
old dress coat and trousers. But he had tied the trousers
around his waist. Evidently he liked hats; or considered
them as badges of distinction; for he had nine of various
sorts, and he wore them all at once, one atop the other. Djo
nudged his father's elbow in delight. But he had no chance
for more than momentary impression, for Andy strode
forward across the parade ground at a pace that hustled
Djo's shorter legs to a trot.

At the far end of the plaza stood a two-story house, the
only one within the enclosure. Here in a sort of office on
the ground floor the two travelers found a quiet-mannered
good-looking young man working at a desk. He named
himself as John Bidwell, at which Andy's interest obviously quickened; for this was one of the leaders of the
very first immigrant party to cross the Sierra. The interest
apparently was mutual.

"We must talk things over," said Bidwell, as he led
them up a flight of stairs in search of Sutter.

They paid their respects. Djo saw a short, stout man,
partly bald, with broad sloping shoulders, a large full face,
a stubby mustache, and a touch of whisker below the lower
lip. His eyes were large, blue, and thoughtfully penetrating, a little cold as though with an inner calculation. His
thoughts were secret; but a suave and courtly manner
concealed that fact from all but the most penetrating.
It was at once obvious that he was somebody; a man who

would be anywhere remarked; one accustomed to wide
affairs. And, indeed, at this moment he stood near the
peak of his powers, for he was veritable overlord of a vast
domain. He himself did not know, nor much care, the
boundaries of his lands. He possessed cattle by the tens of
thousands, and horses and sheep by the thousands. He
raised wheat and other grains on a grand scale. Inside the
walls of his compounds he conducted trades and handi-
crafts—weaving, forging, hat-making, wood-working,
many others. He had purchased from the Russians their
possessions at Ross, including cattle and horses, a launch,
and a formidable armament of guns and small arms. He
was a good administrator. Starting with five white men,
eight Kanakas, and a large bulldog, he had rapidly surrounded himself with an effective force. He knew how to
attach to himself the wild Indians. By treating them
kindly and with scrupulous exactness as to promise or
pay, and at the same time by pouncing on them promptly
and severely for even petty theft or disturbance, he managed early to gain control. Forty of them he trained and
kept in uniform as a military garrison. An indefinite number labored for him in field or craft. In the earlier days he
used, once in so often, to let off one of the cannon from
the walls. The flash and bang and the crash of the cannon
ball through the trees had a grand effect. The Indians regarded him as a man possessed of marvelous powers. The
bulldog was a great help. Sutter defended the natives
against their enemies; fed them in times of famine. It
was said that in addition he held ten thousand wild
Indians at his command, though it is probable that both
the numbers and the degree of influence were exaggerated.

In addition he had gathered a formidable body of wandering trappers and hunters. Any man who came in was
welcomed and kept without price. Many of them stayed
on as permanent fixtures, for Sutter possessed the secret

of attaching men to himself. He would hire anybody who wanted work, whether he needed him or not. He paid in goods; or in a coinage of his own redeemable in goods, bits of tin on which were stamped the number of days the man had worked. There was a great variety of choice in jobs. Besides his cattle and crops and manufactures, Sutter did a heavy trade in furs, in hides and tallow. He ran a flour mill; was preparing to erect a sawmill. Now that the overland immigration had begun, he was making the Fort a rendezvous, a first place of call after the crossing of the mountains. He commanded the routes westward from the States and southward from Oregon. The Bartleson-Bidwell party, arriving destitute and exhausted, were succored and supplied. Bidwell remained with him as a sort of manager and bookkeeper. Subsequent expeditions were relieved from distress, generously and without cost. He sent out rescue parties, at very considerable trouble and expense and apparently without thought of repayment. As a consequence he so gained in power that he was able to warn from the Valley the trappers of Hudson's Bay Company; and he made it stick; and to indite a letter to the *californio* authorities threatening that in certain event, "I am strong now. . . . It is to late now to drive me out of the country the first step they do against me is that I will make a Declaration of Independence and proclaim California for a Republique." "And," he added, "I am strong enough to hold me till the courriers go to the Waillamet for raise about 60 a 70 good men, an another party I would dispatch to the Mountains and call in the hunters and Shawnees and Delawares with which I am very well acquainted, the same party have to go to Missouri and raise about 2 or 300 men more."

Some of these things Andy—and Djo—learned from looking about them, some from John Bidwell, some from the rough trappers and hunters sprawling about little

fires. After a first welcome they were foot-free. Sutter paid
them little attention. It is probable that, at this time, he
was uncertain of his allegiance; possibly he still dabbled
with the idea of his "independent Republique," though
this is unlikely. In any case he did not wish to confide in
a man so close to the *californios* as Andy.

They hunted up Seth Murray, the visitor to Folded
Hills. He still held a position under Sutter, pending his
own land grant. He had become a sort of farm overseer.
He showed them around; explained things. Of course the
cattle work was routine to the *ranchero;* but the wheat
fields interested him. Most of the labor was done by Indians, hundreds of them. Scarcity or lack of implements
was not allowed to restrict the work. Such few plows,
harrows, and scythes as were available were used, of
course. But an immense area further was plowed with
forked sticks and harrowed with dragged bundles of brush.
In the harvesting the grain was collected, not only with
the scythes and sickles, but with pieces of hoop iron, with
willow sticks split to present an edge, even with the hands
struck flatwise! In spite of a certain air of haphazard, a
definite discipline obtained. Bells clanged in understood
signal to direct the general progress. The Indians were
divided into companies, and herded a good deal as were
the work horses of the *caballado*. Most of them were provided with shirts and blankets. They were fed from the
long trough outside the wall. These were, twice a day,
filled with wheat mush. The Indians knelt before them
and scooped up the mush in their hands. But in spite of
the discipline they seemed contented; served Sutter like
so many slaves. After working hours Sutter personally
drilled them as a huge fife-and-drum corps. They appeared
to enjoy this.

The other retainers and hangers-on and visitors fared a
little better. There was always a beef hanging, from which
one could cut a steak at any time. Flour was passed out

as needed. With the exception of the few reserved luxuries, they were free of whatever else happened to be in store. They slept in such rooms or sheds as happened to be vacant or unused; or they bedded down in the open plaza or under the adjacent live-oaks—no great hardship in this climate. Or perhaps they constructed more elaborate shelters of their own in a sort of permanent camp.

Sutter himself lived well, but plainly. Andy and Djo dined with him once in company with a number of other selected guests. The dining room was furnished only with a deal table and benches. Soup was served in bowls of fine China porcelain with heavy silver spoons. The bowls, when emptied, were at once washed and returned to be used as drinking vessels. There was beef, cooked with plenty of onions; potatoes; bread, cheese and butter; delicious melons; wine. That was all; but an abundance of these. Sutter presided with a fine presence and address that a little subdued some of the visitors. He exhibited a great deal of elaborate manner; talked with ease and grace of high matters beyond their experience. He took pains to have it known, but as though indirectly, that he had been an officer of the Swiss Guards at the French court. As a matter of fact he had never even visited the French court, though in his youth he had, for a short time, served in the Swiss army. No one present knew this, however. He managed also to display his fluent knowledge of languages, not difficult in so polyglot a company—German, French, English, Spanish. He spoke casually of the high politics of far-off things. It was foofaraw; but foofaraw with a purpose. Even Andy, specialist on foofaraw, did not recognize it as such. Sutter did not touch upon the politics nearer at home. His guests left him slightly over-awed, with the impression he desired: that of a great man, a man-of-the-world. Andy watched him with keenly appraising eyes, bright with interest. But he made no comment, even to Djo.

2

Andy made inquiry for the men who had been left behind from Frémont's expedition. He found one of them,
working in the blacksmith shop.

The blacksmith, by the name of Hole, proved to be one
after Andy's heart; a mountain man of the old type,
though of a later day, one of the "bearded ones." As soon
as he learned of Andy's identity, and especially of his intimacy with and admiration for Kit Carson, he talked
without reserve. Indeed Hole was one of Carson's men,
joined up with the little group that rode from Taos for
the purpose. He seemed to view the expedition with a
curious mixture of admiration and humorous tolerance.

"Funniest outfit you ever seed," he told Andy. "Eff'n
it hadn't been for Kit and Bad Hand and a few of us
mountain men I don't know what would have become of
them. We started out with a dozen mule carts and a spring
wagon to lug the plunder. All sorts of foofaraw—tele-
scopes, things to measure stars. I don't know what all.
I reckon that was all right, though," he added reasonably.
"The idee was to survey out a rowte to the Pacific; and
as long as we stuck to the wagon trails that was all right.
But we had one thing I bet you'd never guess in a coon's
age. We lugged along a brass cannon."

"A brass cannon!" echoed Andy. "What good was
that?"

"Cap'n claimed she'd be good with Injuns, I believe."

"Man don't want a cannon to fight Injuns."

"I know that. Mout scare 'em, though," said Hole.
"Anyways, we lugged along that cannon. And one hell of
a time we had, too. My God, man, they was times we
darn nigh perished hangin' onto that cannon. I never see
a man so obstinate about anythin' as the Cap'n was about
that cannon. Looked like he was crazy about it. Long
a'ter we quit the carts and the wagons, and had even

abandoned his instruments, and was walkin' to save what hosses we had left, that darn cannon had to go along! Tough doin's, let me tell you that! When we come to pick rowtes it had to be allus on account of that blasted cannon, and to hell with the men and animals!"

"Cannons are no good with Injuns," repeated Andy. "General Ashley and Jed Smith and Bill Sublette tried that out years ago, and gave it up!"

"Sure!" agreed Hole. "Everybody knows that. Kit told him that." He chuckled. "We tried every way we knew to lose the danged thing. No good. Jist made us that much more trouble. Fordin' the Snake we ran her into fast water and had to cut the harness to save the mules from bein' carried down with her. He made us go git her with a rubber boat. We thought we had her lost for keeps once; over east of the mountains thar. It was either quit her and push on or perish the whole outfit. But we had to go back for her when we got fed and rested. And that was one hell of a job, too. Nigh broke the Cap'n's heart when we did leave her."

"Oh, then you did quit her after all?"

"Sure: over the mountains thar." Hole jerked his head toward the rampart of the Sierra. "When we left Oregon we struck down to eastward of them ranges."

"What was the idea?" asked Andy. "Wa'nt the trail from Oregon good enough? There ain't a thing in that country. I know. I crossed it with Jed Smith back in the 'twenties."

"Sure," agreed Hole again. "I heerd some talk about findin' and makin' maps of the Buenaventura River."

"The Buenaventura!" Andy repeated blankly.

That myth had been exploded years ago: the great river reported to break through the Sierra to empty into the Pacific, an easy water route from the high plateau of the Rockies. Jedediah Smith, Joe Walker had put the quietus on that yarn. And there were Gallatin's maps,

and Bonneville's, and, indeed, those of Commodore
Wilkes, though Andy could not have known of these
latter. Andy shook his head. No, that was not reasonable;
there must have been some other idea.

"Well, that's what I heerd," insisted Hole. "We didn't
find no river, nat'rally: we all told him that afore we
started. But we tarnation nigh perished, what with cold
and no water and no game and no hoss feed, and tough
goin'. Got so bad we had to give up the idee of goin' east
from thar. So we crossed the mountains and come here.
And that was a tough one, too. Lost thutty-four hosses
and was dang lucky to git through!"

"What time of year was that?"

"About the first part of March."

Andy shook his head, puzzled. He had twice crossed
that same country, once with Jedediah Smith, once when
he had come to California after the battle at Pierre's
Hole.

"If you'd waited a couple of weeks," said he, "or you
might easy have gone south through that pass Joe Walker
took. Kit's been in this country before."

"You try to tell him," said Hole dryly. "When he gits
an idee, he's got to do it now, *pronto*, right off quick. He
made us a speech, sounded like Fourther July. We jist
sat and didn't say nothin'. Next mornin' we starts, and
next night we was in trouble up to our necks. Snow
forty foot deep."

"Hadn't Kit or Bad Hand scouted ahead?"

"He wouldn't give 'em no time," said Hole. "Well,
we made it! But we lost most of our stock. We had to
tromp trail for them every inch of the way. But"—and
Hole chuckled reminiscently—"we did get shut of that
cannon. Nigh broke the Cap'n's heart; but thar she lays.
Brung her two-three thousand miles, and thar she lays!"

"Did you ever use it?" asked Andy.

"We shot her off just two times," said Hole. "Onct

for Christmas over in the Big Basin; and onct up Oregon
way. We see some smoke off in the distance, and the Cap'n
had her shot off to let the Injuns know how heap-big we
was. Then we lined up and rode all abreast in a long line
over to the village. They were all peaceable and glad to
see us. Thought they'd been a thunderstorm. So we
tucked our tails atween our legs and snuck back."

"You don't think much of this Cap'n Frémont, then?"
surmised Andy.

"I got good and sick of bein' run army fashion," said
Hole, without direct reply, "and bein' ordered around like
a sojer. I reckon that's the main trouble: he's used to
having his own way. We mountain men tried to tell him
at Walla Walla he'd do well to wait a leetle, till spring
broke, afore comin' on down to Californy. Kit did his
durnedest. Yere's exactly what he said: 'I'll show you
fellers who think you know all about mountain explorin'
that I kin go whar I please!' What do you think of that?
They was quite a row about decidin' to go south. Kit said
he'd go anyway, but that he wouldn't ask his men to go
—that's us, who came with him from Taos. The Cap'n
riz up on his hind legs and said he'd put ary man who
didn't go under arrest for insubordination. Kit just
laughed at that. That was funny! 'You got more men
than we have, Cap'n,' says he, 'but I reckon you'd find a
few rifles a lot more dangerous than even a small army
with gov'ment guns and authority.' He wasn't sassy; he
was just laughin'. So the Cap'n puts us under what he
calls 'technical arrest'; allowin' us, as he sez, to retain
our arms. That was a good one!" Hole paused to grin.

"So this Frémont——" Again Andy tried to ask.

"When we started south a'ter all," Hole continued,
heedless, "we Taos men lit out ahead faster'n the Cap'n's
engagees could travel. So the Cap'n stuck a sergeant a'ter
us to keep this yere technical arrest in workin' order. We
run him ragged," said Hole dryly. "Then the Cap'n sent

one of his Delawares a'ter us to tell us to come right on
back and roll rocks out of a cut so that dang cannon could
get through. We sent him back a sassy answer, and kep'
a-goin' so fast we lost the poor old sergeant back in the
desert. Then we stopped and had a powwow. We agreed
that it broke us all up to leave Kit to Frémont's whims,
but they was no help for it. So the Taos men quit thar,
and went back to Taos."

"How come you stuck?" asked Andy. .

"Me? Well, Burnett, I felt just like Kit. Somehow I
couldn't bear to leave the Cap'n. In spite of all the things
I been tellin' you they's somethin' about the leetle cuss
that gits you! You kain't help but like him; and you don't
want to leave him go perish eff'n you left him to his own
devices. You sort of look on him like you woulda small
boy that you got to take keer of. I don't think there's
nothin' he could do that would make Kit quit him. Kit
believes he's a great man; and I reckon, when you come
to it, mebbe he is. Leastwise when he sticks to what he
knows—all this mappin', and his scientific doodads. And
you got to admire his grit. He sticks it out when things
gits tough, when even some of the old-timers mout weaken
a leetle. He's a spunky leetle cuss! And," added Hole
with a laugh, "give him his head, and things will shore
git tough, every time! Eff'n it wa'n't for Kit he'd run
hisself out on a limb ary time he starts!"

"But you quit the outfit," suggested Andy.

"That's jist because I like the looks of this yere kentry," said Hole.

"Would you join up with him again?"

"Yes," said Hole, without hesitation. "And mebbe I
will." He looked about him carefully to see if any could
overhear. "This is jist my own idee," he warned. "I ain't
heerd no talk of it. But I'd lay a bet he'll be back yere."

"What makes you think that?"

"I dunno; jist a notion, I reckon. That there cannon

—and the Taos men. Eff'n he'd got yere with them, I'd bet he'd be yere yet."

"What for, in the name of heaven!" cried Andy.

"Say, Burnett"—Hole apparently veered from the subject—"did you know that Frémont married Senator Benton's daughter?"

"Benton!" cried Andy.

"Jist so. And let me tell you somethin' else that happened: A'ter they'd started out from Saint Louee luggin' their cannon a'ter them, there come an order from Washington callin' off the whole expedition. And Missus Frémont, she got hold of it, and instead of sendin' it to the Cap'n she hung onto it, and she sent him a letter tellin' the Cap'n to git to movin' fast as he could make it."

"How do you know that?" demanded Andy. "You didn't join up till somewhere near St. Vrains, you told me."

"Never mind how I knowed. But I knowed. All the mountain men knowed. Eff'n he hadn't started off on that fool rowte to east'ard of the Sierra they'd have stuck with him. There mout have been some fun."

"Get out, Hole! You're talking wild!" said Andy.

And as he thought it over afterward, this opinion was strengthened in him. The idea that the mountain man seemed to imply was too fantastic. That Frémont and his handful of men could seriously have contemplated establishing themselves as an armed force in the territory of a supposedly friendly nation was, as he had said, too wild to consider. Or was it? He shook his head. These matters of high politics were beyond him. He wondered what Larkin would think about it.

CHAPTER X

THEY left Sutter's Fort for Sonoma in much better frame of mind. Djo's boyish spirit had not been able to resist the romantic picturesqueness of the place. And while it is improbable that Andy would unqualifiedly have endorsed all of the hunters and trappers whom Sutter had gradually accumulated as hangers-on, to Djo they were the heroic figures of his father's past come back to life. He stood about, in his new hunting clothes, and leaned on his miniature Hawkens rifle, and tried to look as little like a Californian and as much like a mountain man as he could. Andy, observing, was much cheered.

But within an hour of leaving the Fort occurred an unfortunate meeting that undid all this. Around a bend in the cottonwoods appeared a tall, buckskin-clad figure, riding ahead of a squaw, a rifle across his saddle and a coonskin cap on his head with the tail hanging down behind. He reined in his horse and for fifteen minutes poured out a flood of talk, punctuating the sentences with a steady interruption of tobacco juice. After a preliminary "Whar ye from?" he exhibited no interest in Andy and Djo, but apparently set out to make himself and his position clear. When he had finished, there was no doubt where he stood.

He was a trapper—and straight Ammurican, by God!

Ammurica was the greatest kentry in God's universe!

An Ammurican could lick any ten furriners—yes, and ary twenty of these yere yaller-bellies!

Interlude for blasting cursing of each and every yaller-belly in California; by which he meant those of Spanish blood. In this cursing was real emotion. The man bared yellow fangs.

"I'd ruther kill one of them than an Injun, and I'd as soon kill an Injun as a tarantula!" he boasted. "Look-a thar!" He snatched an old-fashioned tomahawk from beneath his belt and held it out for inspection. "Every notch is one good Injun, and when she's full up I'll make her longer; and eff'n I git my way I'll put a new handle in her and start markin' her fur Spainyards. Goin' to run us free Ammuricans out of the kentry, be they? Well, I'd admire to see them try!"

"I don't believe they are," suggested Andy mildly.

"You don't know a goddam' thing about it!" shouted the man truculently. "I tell you they be! I lived yere a long spell, trappin' near the coast, and I know what I'm talkin' about! They're gittin' 'em aready fur it right now. Ain't you heerd? Whar you been keepin' yourself? They got a big passel of 'em together right now, and are just waitin' for sojers from Mexico. I hope they make it quick. Quicker the better suits me. I been waitin' three year now to git even with that——"

"I didn't get your name," cut in Andy, suddenly identifying the man.

"Merritt's my name. Ezekiel Merritt, and a good Amurrican name——"

"You are the man who had the run-in with Salvador Vallejo."

"Yo' goddam peak-nosed greenhorn, you!" shouted Merritt in a sudden whirl of violent rage. "You dare to——"

"I just wanted to hear about it," said Andy. His eyes were fixed steadily on Merritt's. He spoke in a low level voice. With the flat of his left hand he quieted Djo, who had reined forward indignantly. The long rifle lay balanced across his saddle bow. His right hand drooped carelessly to his belt, from which depended the long throwing

knife and the new six-shooting pistol. An edge in his voice
checked Merritt's bluster.

"I don't allow no man to throw that up in my face!" he
threatened, but less certainly.

"I wasn't throwing anything in your face," said Andy.
"I was just asking. I heard a little, and I wanted to get
the rights of it."

"And who mout you be?" demanded Merritt belliger-
ently.

"My name is Burnett," said Andy.

Merritt peered at him.

"I've heerd that name," he said after a moment.
"Kain't be the same. I've heerd that feller was rubbed
out." For the first time, apparently, his eyes took in the
details of Andy's appearance and equipment. They
lingered, a little doubtfully, on the Boone rifle and the
throwing knife. "He was called I-tam-api over yander in
the Injun kentry," said he. "You ain't I-tam-api by any
chance?"

Andy nodded shortly.

"Put her thar!" cried Merritt.

They shook hands.

The trapper spat copiously of tobacco juice.

"They was a whole passel of sojers," said he. "What
could I do? But I ain't finished with 'em yit."

His manner had calmed, but as he went on with his
recital his passion rekindled. The account he gave was
circumstantial. He had been trapping in the hills, between
the Bay and the sea, north side where the big mountain
is. A nigger had come into his camp, running away from
an American warship, a cook, he had said. Merritt fed him.
Salvador Vallejo and a body of soldiers had appeared.
He had shot down the nigger; shot him like a dog. Merritt
had called Salvador a murderer. Salvador had struck him
with a ramrod. At this point the narrative broke in
profane threat.

2

They broke away from the man at last and continued their journey. Andy glanced sideways at Djo's face and sighed. It was dark and brooding. For some time Djo said nothing; nor did Andy dare speak. Finally Djo could contain himself no longer.

"Why did you permit him to speak so of our people?" he burst forth passionately. "Why did you permit him to say such lies of the *señor* Vallejo?"

"Keep your hair on, son," Andy advised. "The man was drunk."

"Drunk! And what of that! He is a braggart, a bully. He's a murderer; a dirty, filthy, loathsome reptile!"

"Probably you're right," agreed Andy. "I don't know."

He would have done better to yield the point without comment. But it was a quality of Andy's nature—that sometimes, as now, became a defect—that he must fully express his own honesty.

"Don't know!" Djo checked short in amazement.

"He's drunk," repeated Andy. "You don't know his kind. I've seen a many of them. You can't tell. He might be a pretty able man. You'd have to see him sober before you could judge. Probably you're right; but you must always be careful not to go off half-cock. And what good to quarrel with a drunken man? And what differ what he says?"

"But, Dad," Djo appealed, "he's a liar. Did you hear what he said about Don Salvador? Do you believe that?"

"Yes," said Andy.

"Dad! Don Salvador! An *hidalgo!*"

"I believe what he said," repeated Andy. "Don Salvador undoubtedly shot that nigger, or had him shot. And he undoubtedly hit this man with a ramrod—though I'd heard it was the flat of his sword. But perhaps that wasn't all of it."

"What do you mean?"

"I've heard that the nigger had grabbed a gun. This Merritt didn't say about that. But," Andy added, "Don Salvador was foolish to hit him, no matter what he said. Wa'n't necessary. Should have stopped to think that, what with all the sojers, Merritt couldn't hit back. What do you think of that part of it, Djo?"

Djo hesitated, flushed.

"That was cowardly," he admitted steadily, but with reluctance.

Andy surveyed him in approval.

"That's right, Djo," said he, "face the facts, whether you like 'em or not. But it wasn't so much cowardly, maybe, as that Don Salvador got mad. Don't pay to get mad, Djo. Keep your hair on—when you can," he added. "Getting mad is sometimes as bad as getting drunk to make people get you sized up wrong."

Djo pondered this.

"But, Dad,"—he had a new thought—"wasn't it lying when this—this——" He made a wry face.

"This *roto cabrón*," supplied Andy dryly.

"This man did not tell that the deserter grabbed the gun."

"Why," said Andy, pleased, "that is a good point, too. Djo, you'll be a pretty *sabe hombre* if you live long enough and keep on using your topknot like that. A man can lie by keeping still, that's right. But I don't think this Merritt was lying, not to know it, anyway."

"Why not?"

"Because he was mad. When a man's good and mad, all through, he don't recollect very straight. Remember this, Djo: don't get all het up over any story you hear until you hear both sides of it. Don't go off half-cock."

They rode steadily on toward the willows and sycamores and *tules* that marked the banks of the Sacramento. Djo was silenced, but a glance at his face was enough to convince Andy that he was in no way persuaded. Oh, Lord, thought Andy, what's the use! He's part American, in blood; but he's part Spanish, too; and in bringing-up he's mighty nigh all Spanish. Why should I expect anything different of him? Why should I have bothered to defend Merritt? wondered Andy. He's probably just what he appeared to be; and Djo was quite right. It would have been much better to have let the matter slide; to have agreed with Djo. Much better! And what difference what the boy thought? But immediately Andy knew he could not have done this. He could not let the matter slide as long as there were modifying possibilities which were within his knowledge. He understood the rough frontier type. Djo—or Don Guadalupe, or the other of the Californians—could not. Here was a moral obligation, which Andy could not avoid, even as to the trivial. The discovery dismayed him; for the shadow of coming events was strong upon him, and he knew that he must take his part.

3

These personal preoccupations had not prevented Andy from the accomplishment of his mission. He had by now in mind a pretty clear picture of the state of the Valley. Conversations with the outlying settlers, with John Bidwell, with the various inhabitants of the Fort, had convinced him that here was no uneasiness. Men were going about their business in complete confidence. If they had heard any rumors of eviction, they either had dismissed them as baseless, or possessed so complete a confidence in their own prowess that they were contemptuous.

He had not had much opportunity to gauge the feelings of the Californians; that was Larkin's business, farther south. Most, of course—and naturally—must feel as did Djo and Carmel. Nevertheless, he had talked with a few, like Martínez at *rancho* Pinole, who were far-sighted enough to see that California would be unable to stand alone without Mexico; and were amiable enough to prefer the United States to any other foreign power. This had encouraged him to expect the same attitude in Vallejo, reputedly the broadest-minded of his race. The hope had been a little dashed by Don Guadalupe's hostility to the settlers, his "white Indians"; it had been further enfeebled by the grandee's evasion of the whole subject. He wants to be polite, thought Andy; he doesn't want to hurt my feelings.

But Andy was determined. On the evening of the day set for departure he deliberately drew Vallejo aside and stated his question bluntly. Vallejo listened in silence, drawing together his fine brows. For some moments he made no reply.

"*Señor*," he inquired at last, "do you seek this inquiry as an *americano* or as a *californio?*"

"Why, I think as both, Don Guadalupe," replied Andy. Vallejo nodded slowly twice.

"I think so, too," said he. He surveyed Andy intently; appeared to make up his mind. "I think you are one man to trust," said he. "There are not many. To very few may a man speak his full thoughts safely. I have never done so to any. For that reason many have said many queer things concerning me. You have heard some of them?"

"Yes," said Andy.

"For one thing that I wait to see which side will win in order to join in with it," suggested Vallejo. "You have heard that?" he insisted, when Andy did not comment.

"Yes; I have heard that," admitted the latter.

Don Guadalupe looked pleased at his look of polite protest.

"Well, it is true," said he. "Partly true," he corrected. Then, as Andy still said nothing, he leaned forward. "Gladly, *señor*, will I join with any winning side, *any*— if it prove itself worthy to win!"

He leaned back comfortably and lighted a cigar.

"I am glad to tell you this, *señor*," said he, "though I have expressed it to no other." He smiled faintly. "I do not quite know why I do so now. Possibly because I value your good opinion. Possibly because of my good opinion of you as a man of sense and discretion." He bowed with a touch of formality. Vallejo paused to survey himself with a fleeting surprise. The man is *hidalgo*, he told himself; he is one to trust. Suddenly he rationalized this feeling, which was, however, purely instinctive.

"I am going," said he, "to speak plainly. You told me you sought this inquiry both as *americano* and *californio*. At one time, perhaps, I shall speak to the *californio*, and perhaps at another time to the *americano;* and it may be that each may tell the other, and so both understand."

Andy nodded.

"I would not dare say these things to any other, *señor;* I should not be understood," warned Vallejo. He waited for no disclaimer. "I am *californio, señor*. I am a loyal man, *señor;* but my loyalty is not to any one government, but to California, to her best interests." He paused to draw slowly on his cigar. "Years ago, *señor*, I dreamed of her as a fair province of her mother country. But reluctantly, one by one, I have recognized the figures of that dream as illusions. Little by little I have come to understand a bitter reality, *señor:* that Mexico looks upon California as a cow to be milked, as a convenient banishment for her convicts, and that she will not lift one finger in aid. The thread that holds California to Mexico is too slender. At the first strain it will snap."

Andy leaned forward to catch every word, for Don Guadalupe spoke measuredly.

"For a time I hoped that we might exist as an independent state. But that too was a foolish dream. We are not a people to rule ourselves. We cannot agree; or we are, like our *rancheros*, wholly indifferent. We follow leaders according to our whim. I have watched. I have seen. It makes my heart sad: Castro, Pico, Bandini, my nephew Alvarado, Carlos Carrillo—I name no Mexicans, only *californios*, *señor*, and but a few of many; each eager for power and rule, with thought only of themselves, and with none for California. If any one of them could prove worthy—gladly, *señor*," Vallejo repeated himself, "would I join with the winning side—if it proved worthy to win. But reluctantly I am coming to the conclusion that my old hope—or rather my dream—of independence is false. It has not wholly gone; but it fades. And if we are to look outside for our protection, then among all nations it seems to me that the United States is most to be desired." He smiled at the expression of Andy's face. "That is pleasing to you, *señor*."

"It is very pleasing," replied Andy simply. "Also, Don Guadalupe, I am surprised. It has been told to me that you despised my people, that you consider them as 'white Indians.'"

"Those!" Vallejo dismissed them with a wave of the hand. "Are there not white Indians among my people also? The scum before the wave, *señor!*" He arose. "We speak of bigger things. Now I think we understand one another, you and I. But," he warned, laying his hand on Andy's arm, "these things you must speak of to nobody, nobody at all! They would not comprehend."

"I do not talk," said Andy curtly.

"That I know," said Don Guadalupe.

4

The visitors left Sonoma the next morning. Following the old custom, Don Guadalupe rode with them to the boundaries of his domain. Only after the *hidalgo* had turned back, and the travelers were preparing to cross the Strait of Carquinez, did it occur to Andy that his

promise to Vallejo must include Djo. Nobody; nobody at
all—that is what Don Guadalupe had said. Andy was
vexed with himself. Don Guadalupe's opinion would have
had much weight with Djo. Andy even contemplated
riding back to obtain the *hacendado's* permission. He had
no doubt whatever of obtaining it. It was just like Andy
that he never for a moment considered taking that permission for granted. The strict letter of a promise was all
he knew. His impulse was instantly succeeded by a dead
weight of fatalistic depression. It was not worth while;
things must take their course. This was not like Andy at
all. His eye caught the girl, Wapita. She rode frowning,
raging internally with some obscure discontent. Probably
that scalawag Pepe, thought Andy savagely. He's no good.
He ought to be horsewhipped, monkeying around after
a child of twelve. They both ought to be horsewhipped,
he thought; and caught himself up, a little ashamed. But
the time's about come to use the bit, he thought; I've
promised not to interfere with her, though, Andy recol-
lected. Well, I'll have to keep my promise; but I'll tell
her she'll have to behave as long as she's on my place.
And she's got to leave Djo alone, too. This "child" business is all very well, thought Andy; but if she's old enough
to get Pepe, she's—— He's jealous of her already, thought
Andy, whether he knows it or not. That's a good deal
what's the matter with him. He needs something to do.
I'll set him to breaking horses; that'll keep him busy. And,
his thoughts thus rounding back to Folded Hills, Andy's
mind became occupied with familiar questions, and the
surface of its turmoil settled, though beneath persisted an
uneasy discomfort, like a burr under a saddle blanket.

CHAPTER XI

ANDY returned to Folded Hills as to a sure haven of quiet and peace. The outside world, as represented by, say, the country beyond San Juan Bautista, was filling with a swarm of stinging uneasiness and fears and hatreds and suspicions. Nothing serious, as yet; almost intangible, in fact. But a man walked guardedly, sniffing to right and left; aware that other men, too, were eyeing one with speculation, if not with distrust.

Once across the Soledad ford of the Salinas, however, these things were left behind. Here were all Andy's established confidences. Here were his possessions, his people, his peace. As his horse emerged from the shallow water to the far bank, he seemed to himself to breathe a softer, milder air; to have entered a grateful silence after noise; to have laid aside harsh harness. It was good to be back; to see the smiling welcoming faces of those who had been with him so long: it was good to feel that, no matter how changed the outside world, here lived the old life, simple and gentle, as it had always been; as, it seemed to Andy, it must always be.

He dropped into the established routines gratefully; allowed them completely to absorb him; refused to permit his mind to dwell on anything he could not directly influence or control. In this deliberate avoidance was a psychology of fear; but Andy was not enough self-analytical to realize that. Why he was letting all sleeping dogs lie he could not have told, even if he had realized that he was doing so.

For a time life slid back into the worn grooves of habit.

A number of small arrears in supervision of the *rancho* had to be caught up. Djo was delighted with his new job of gentling the *broncos* and did well at it. Apparently it occupied his whole interest. Wapita had melted back into the insignificance of her domestic duties. Andy caught only an occasional glimpse of her. Indeed she seemed to avoid him when possible. When, occasionally, he encountered her face to face she replied respectfully enough to his greeting, but she did not smile, and she looked after him fixedly when he had passed. Andy was well enough aware of this. It diverted him. He had given over bothering about Wapita's changeable vagaries. She'll get over it, thought Andy—whatever it is. She's a queer one! He grinned amusedly as he recalled her face the afternoon he had surprised her in the oak opening beyond the willows. He had been riding by; had heard something he could not identify; had turned aside to investigate. She was standing there alone, so lost in thought that she did not hear his approach. Suddenly she threw her head up, her body back, flung both arms aloft, and stamped one foot. For an instant she held the pose; then uttered a half-smothered cry of impatience, shook herself violently, and repeated the movement. Andy was puzzled. He watched several repetitions of this performance.

"What are you doing, Wapita?" he called at last.

She leaped to face him a moment. Her face contorted. She turned and ran like a deer, leaving him astonished.

Carmel laughed when he told her.

"She make the dance, the practice of the dance," she guessed at once. "She do not like that you see. She make the dance *serio*. All the *rancho* know that, *querido*. Have you not hear that, and how she shall be the great *bailarina*. But nobody see her dance. Always she riffuse. Everybody beg her to do the dance: it is come to be for a joke. She is so young, and she hold her head so high up."

She needn't be so touchy, thought Andy; as if I cared

what she did! He shrugged the thought of her aside impatiently. And yet he could not rid his mind of her. Vaguely he felt she had some significance or other. His practical mind was not one to tolerate vagueness. Something accompanied her presence in the accustomed tranquillities of Folded Hills that made perceptible other vaguenesses that otherwise would have passed unnoticed and unknown. Andy almost grasped what these were, but not quite. And as he could not grasp them he shook them off angrily. But they returned. He tried to face them. There was nothing to face. The nearest he could come to it was a feeling, a fancy that those around him had moved just a little apart. He seemed to be conscious of a veiled observation, almost a criticism. Of what, for the love of the saints? Was he not one of them, as he had always been? Were they not his own loyal people? Loyal, yes; but the loyalty seemed to have become self-conscious. Sometimes Andy sensed in it something almost conscientious. In certain brief panic moments he felt as though he were being gently but inexorably swept aside by a current. At such moments something shifted out of focus. He thought to perceive all sorts of things that his instantly succeeding sanity told him were ridiculous. Djo seemed to have become painfully punctilious with him; sought him out more than usual; hung around him; the commonplaces rang hollow between them. The boy's eyes seemed to be asking something of him always, to be waiting for something. The old security of his life became thin, precariously fleeting. Like the old Indian days. Only then he had had swift action with which to make life supportable.

Looking about him, he could discern no external reason for this nonsense. But his brief satisfaction had vanished. He wanted to break through. He wanted something to happen. Nevertheless he avoided, walked a-tiptoe. Something was in suspension that a single touch would . . . I'm crazy as a loon! he thought disgustedly.

2

But he must do something; or, he felt, he would indeed go as crazy as a loon. He remembered his promise to Larkin. He ought long since to have reported to Larkin. He eased his conscience by writing to him one of his rather painfully constructed letters telling him simply that, except for a few soreheads on both sides, he had found no one bothering much about the matter one way or another. He added that they would talk things over as soon as he could get to Monterey. In the meantime he would do what he could with his neighbors.

So he took to making short visits up and down the valley, alone, almost surreptitiously, saying nothing at home as to his purposes. He might have felt encouraged by the reception of what he had to say. He was not. He recognized only too clearly the root of indifference from which sprang the facile acquiescences. These were an easy-going people of the old *ranchero* breed. Anything good enough for Don Largo suited them. They had not thought of it before, but now that the matter was called to their attention, there could be no doubt that Mexico had always treated California like a stepchild, that they themselves were very tired of these constant revolutions—let us see: when was the last one? Or is there one on now?—that it would be better to live under the protection of the *americanos* than of the English and French. Was not Don Largo an *americano*? *Viva los Estados Unidos!* And now let us talk of something interesting: saw you ever so many magpies as this year?

That meant nothing: nothing at all. It was not worth reporting to Larkin. The attitude of these people was merely unstable. The next breath of opinion would shift them the other way. And even with them Andy sensed, or seemed to sense, that new and strange aloofness. I'm getting to see things, like a hysterical woman, he told himself. It isn't there. I'm imagining. And then he veered right back to acceptance of it as real. Perhaps it's my clothes, he thought; and the thought, unreasonably, made him angry and stubborn; and so, for the first time, as far as he was concerned, he was actually apart from them. If they don't like my clothes, they can go to hell, said he.

For after his return from his excursion up the Valley with Djo he had not reassumed the gorgeous Californian costume which he had worn now for fourteen years. Up to now he had done so without a thought. It belonged; he felt as natural, as at ease, in it as in the buckskins of his old life. Now it did not belong. An impression of make-believe clouded him; as though he had been, unknown to himself, play-acting all these years. He had become conscious of it as, at a certain age, a child becomes conscious of its naked body. Nor could he analyze this either. Merely he realized he was more comfortable in plainer garments; they were more practical; less fuss and trouble. He could not be moved by Carmel's expostulations.

"You are like a crow!" she cried. "I love you to look well."

"Don't matter how an old fellow like me looks," said he.

She could not understand why he was strongly obstinate about so small a matter; nor did he. But he could do no differently. He wore still the sombrero with its gay band; and, when riding, the *botas;* and he sometimes carried a *serape* across his shoulder. But his ordinary appearance was in the sober broadcloth long coat and trousers, the low-cut waistcoat, the ample linen and wing collar and flowing black tie of the period.

"You resemble thus a Yankee ship's captain," said Carmel discontentedly.

"Or Señor Larkin, or Señor Stearns, or even Don Noriega," Andy pointed out good-humoredly. "But *querida,* I am so much more comfortable thus."

"You do not look more comfortable," said Carmel re-

belliously. "How would you like it if I dress like that woman we see at Monterey?"

Afield, about the business of the *rancho*, he reverted to
the pattern, in stout cloth, of the old buckskin hunting
shirts he had worn in the Rockies, loose, long, so ample
as to fold well doubled across the chest. He justified himself by reciting the advantage of his rig from the practical
point of view. It was warm, turned wind and rain, could
be thrown wide to a cooling breeze, was free in movement,
was not easily soiled or torn. But these were not the real
reasons. Deep within his instinctive areas he felt the
change as an unconscious but apt symbolism.

3

Late one afternoon there swaggered up the hill a band
of five horsemen. Andy recognized their identity and their
errand at once; and within him arose a disproportionate
surge of vexation, which he curbed only with difficulty.
These were soldiers; and, undoubtedly, they had come for
horses. Either they carried a requisition, which Andy
must honor; or they pretended to search lost or stolen
stock. In either case, what it really amounted to was an
irregular tax or graft, as you please. Andy did not object
to the amount of the tax. Nobody did. A dozen horses or
so, occasionally; what did that come to? Nor, ordinarily,
had he troubled himself with the irregularities of its as-
sessment. But he had always been a little irritated by the
method of its collection. At this moment he was in no
mood for forced hospitality. Thank heaven, this squad
was in charge of a sergeant: the *casa* was relieved of the
necessity of entertaining some supercilious officer.

The *rancho* turned out in mass to greet them. The four
men rode double file; their sergeant at their head. Though
the army was small, it made a brave enough show. The
horses were all good; and their harness was resplendent

with carved leather, silver and silk embroideries. The men rode in the soft antelope-skin armor, the *cuero de gamuza;* they carried short muskets slung to their saddles in elaborate scabbards of skin; they bore, tilted jauntily against the right stirrups, long, bright-tipped lances with pennons; they had slung just back of their right legs, against the flanks of the horses, round hide shields, gayly painted. Their hard-glazed hats were tilted at a rakish angle. As a spectacle, they were wholly satisfying; and knew it. The ranch people lined up, and waved things and shouted. Somehow the event managed to inflate itself. This might have been a victorious army returning to the frenzied adulation of a populace. Certain discrepancies of numbers and the like were obliterated by a whole-hearted spirit of make-believe. Anybody, for example, knew well that in real life soldiers were not like these. So far from boasting silvered saddles and gorgeously embroidered *cueros*, the ordinary private was lucky if he possessed a whole pair of pantaloons. But why remember such things, when by the smallest exercise of delightful fancy one could become part in an occasion?

The sergeant was a large burly man with thick frowning brows, long, fierce, upturned *mustachios*, and a condescending swagger of manner. He carried no lance; but wore, attached by long chains to a brilliant red belt, a curved saber of astounding proportions. This weapon swung against his horse's belly and hind leg, so that it was a marvel that the animal could have become habituated to such an annoyance. When the sergeant dismounted—as he did before the door of the *casa*—the saber clanked along the ground, so that it was even more of a marvel how the officer avoided entangling himself.

Andy received his elaborate salutations, which too obviously veiled a military arrogance, with a curtness of manner only just short of offense. He nodded to the man's statement of his name—which was Moraga—his errand;

turned him over to Panchito; reëntered the house. The
sergeant stared at his retreating back with a frown. He
was not pleased by his reception; which was indeed somewhat short of the accepted formula, even though he was
not a commissioned officer. For a moment he glowered
beneath his thick brows, then shrugged his shoulders.
Pig of an *e'tranjero!* But his roving glance had noted the
vineyard and had caught flashes of admiration from bright
eyes. He squared importantly his burly shoulders, skill-
fully rattled the saber against the rowels of his spurs.

"*A su disposición, mayordomo,*" he suggested to Panchito.

Andy retreated to his little office at the rear of the *casa*,
where he intended to remain until this business was
finished. That was his mood. Ordinarily he would willingly
enough have played up his part as *patrón*. The whole
thing was a farce, of course; but the actors in it took their
parts, if not seriously, at least with a certain relish. Feast;
wine; music; dance until dawn; brave and elaborate
toast to patriotism and glory and our invincible army and
what not. A lot of foofaraw that covered the real business,
which was the looting of as many horses as the traffic
would bear. Departure with pennons fluttering, amid the
cheers of the populace. An amusing enough show. Just
now Andy did not find it amusing. He was thankful that
this man was only a sergeant; so that the whole business
could be left to Panchito. He did not want to talk to anybody: about anything. He even contemplated omitting
the usual appearance at the dance: but at the last moment
changed his mind. That would be an inunderstandable
and inexcusable rudeness. He shook himself together and
made his way down the hill.

Outside the range of light he stopped and surveyed the
scene. It was a picturesque enough spectacle. Two heaped
fires illuminated the square of beaten earth that centered
the group of flat-roofed houses in which dwelt the *rancho's*

retainers. A wine keg stood on a low trestle to the right; and grouped to one side of it were men with musical instruments. The rest of the men sprawled on the ground or leaned against the walls of the buildings. The women and girls sat more demurely on rough benches. The only chair had been placed on one side the square, opposite the wine keg, and next one of the fires. In it sprawled the figure of Moraga. The sergeant lolled comfortably at ease, his head bare, his *cuero* discarded, his tunic unbuttoned, his thick legs wide. In one hand he held a cup of wine. His manner was superior, benign, condescending. He was talking; punctuating his remarks with an occasional indolent gesture of the wine cup. The assemblage was attending to him; but idly, almost perfunctorily, with half an ear, as though waiting for him to finish. The musicians sat with their instruments in their laps. The men rolled cigarettes. The women stared at their hands. The four soldiers, obviously, did not listen at all. Only two appeared to follow the purport of what he was saying. Djo stared at him, drinking in every word. By his side stood Wapita, her head back, her eyes stormy, her glance darting indignantly from one to another of the indifferent audience.

Andy did not need to listen. He knew all this stuff by heart. It was a standard routine. Ordinarily it meant nothing, as far as results were concerned: it was doubtful if even the speaker ever expected it to mean anything. Moraga was making the customary recruiting talk.

But as he finished, Andy caught at a variation in theme. In former visits the stress had been upon the delights and comforts of a soldier's life; now Moraga emphasized the encroachments of the tyrant foreigner and the obligation and glory of sweeping him from the sacred soil. He had no doubt that such brave fellows as those who listened to him were already panting to fulfill this obligation, to share in this glory. Let them step forward. Moraga's last words

were almost lost in his wine cup, which he emptied, laid
aside; and then proceeded to roll a cigarette without further glance toward those he had addressed. He expected no
one to come forward for enlistment. That had never happened anywhere yet. His proposal anticipated no answer.
It was of the same sort as the clergyman's request that
someone step up and tell him why this man and this
woman should not be joined in matrimony. The musicians
picked up their instruments. The women and girls on the
benches stirred and sighed. The men came to; some of them
sauntered toward the wine barrel.

"Cowards! Dolts! Stupids! Have you not heard what
he has said? Does it not reach your thick brains? Does your
country mean no more——" The voice choked; stopped in
exasperation and despair. Wapita stamped her foot imperiously. "Music!" she cried imperiously. "You! Music!"
And without waiting for the startled orchestra to respond,
she bounded into the center of the square and began to
dance.

The people of the ranch stared dumfounded, unable instantly to collect their wits against this outburst. The
soldiers snapped to interestedly. Moraga sat up; leaned
forward, his elbows on his thick knees, his head to one
side, his eyes half closed to observant slits. This was
something! He was a Mexican. He had had station at the
capitol itself. He prided himself that he knew dancing—
and women—when he saw them. This was no untaught
rustic performance such as one might expect from the
boorish country people. Nor was the dance itself. Moraga
peered at the performer intently. No: she was *california*
right enough. But where, he marveled, except in the so-
phisticated capital, had she learned this dance? He tried
to attract the attention of one of the men near him. The
vaquero, like everyone else, was staring at Wapita, his
lower jaw dropped.

"*Fuero!*" growled the Mexican savagely, and fetched

the man a kick in the shins. "Who is she?" he demanded
as the *vaquero* turned to him startled. "Who taught her?"

In less distracting circumstances the *vaquero* would
fiercely have resented being kicked by a Mexican. It is
significant that he did not even notice it. He replied without turning his eyes:

"A girl of the ranch. I do not know where she learned.
Never would she dance for us——"

"But these things do not teach themselves! This dance
is one that——" But, perceiving that the man no longer
heard him, Moraga desisted and concentrated gloatingly
on the performance.

The musicians had recovered, had caught the tempo,
at first gropingly, then with growing assurance, at last
with a fire caught from the girl herself. Wapita was dancing
for the first time to music and in public and in sequence
the movements Pepe had taught her. And for the first
time she was giving content to movements which she had
learned and practised merely as a technique. She did
not understand; she felt. She did not even know why, so
abruptly, she danced at all. Suddenly she was drunk with
it. Something was released within her; an overpowering
gush of something that had been pent up. She was hurling
it out, more and more. It swept over her like a flame; and
through her to these others who watched, so that their
indolent lethargy of spirit was burned from them, and
they too were aroused, afire. An hysteria of responsiveness
swept them; the mass emotion of a revival meeting, though
there the similarity abruptly ceased, for the abandon of
this dance was emphatically inappropriate to the latter
occasion.

As abruptly as she had begun, Wapita stamped her
foot, stopped in mid-pose. A storm of *vivas* roared out,
less as applause than as a following flood of response.
A dozen voices clamored for more. The man standing
nearest snatched at her; she turned on him like a tiger

cat. Moraga had dropped back in his chair, was watching her speculatively, trying to guess her out, revolving ideas of his own. Djo stared at her fixedly; his face flushed, his eyes excited.

But Wapita was insensible to these smaller individual cross currents. She felt only the quiver of the sensitization, the breaking down of indolent indifference. Her psychology of these, her people, was sure, even though it was completely instinctive. She burst forth into a torrent of words: and now they listened; the lashings of her scorn fell on bared breasts.

She told them they were blind, stupid, slothful. They could not see beyond their noses. They could not hear a shout in their ears. They only turned over in their sleep. God had given them the most beautiful land save paradise; and they slept. They slept while even now, right at this moment, other peoples, *e'tranjeros*, heretics who denied the blessed saints, were creeping into the land like a plague of locusts on the ranges.

"You do not believe that?" cried Wapita. "Because you have not seen? I, I!"—she beat her breasts—"I have seen! I tell you they are here now; and they creep, creep, creep; and more come, and more. And you shrug your shoulder, and you sleep! And between them and you stand only these too-few brave ones who call to you for help in vain! And when our noble patriots shall be swept aside, shall die for you—in vain—then you shall awake, too late, and you shall find these tyrants standing over you, and their feet shall be upon your necks, and they shall spit upon you and laugh at you because, while there was yet time, you were women who loved your wine and your ease and your blindness and sat at home! Women! Pah! If only the women were men—!"

She blazed at them in a scorn that burned. They kindled back to her, drunk with the extravagant emotion she had aroused. She whirled toward Moraga.

"He has come, this defender of our honor, asking your help in this heroic task. Shall you permit him, and his brave companions, and our great general to die for you in vain? Or are you men?"

She stopped abruptly, her arm extended toward Moraga, who blinked somewhat dazed. But her response from the others was instantaneous. Djo leaped to her side.

"For California!" he cried.

"*Viva! Viva!*" . . . "For California!" . . . "For California and the blessed saints!"

4

At this point Andy came to himself with an angry start. He had been watching the proceedings with a mingling of astonishment and growing impatience. Sympathetic as he was in most things to his adopted people, he had never managed to overcome his Anglo-Saxon embarrassment over naked and unrestrained emotion. He disliked intensely mob hysteria. He disliked the unreasonable. The unashamed pagan abandon of such a dance as Wapita had just executed did not particularly affect him one way or another, but he had seen Djo's face, and he did not like that. But particularly was he disgusted at the final turn this absurd performance was taking. It was high time some sanity was injected into the proceedings.

At his appearance fell a comparative stillness of respect. He could make himself heard. After his first words there was dead silence.

"This sort of thing is silly," said he. "Don't be children! One would think there was an army of invaders just over the hills! There's nothing of the sort. Things are no different than they have been. Why all this hysterical nonsense?"

They looked at one another. The habit of deference to

the *patrón* was long established. The occasion definitely cooled. But Moraga could not resist the chance for a display of his military importance.

"Do you presume, *señor*, to designate as nonsense a call to the defense of our country?"

Andy eyed him in cold contempt of this sophistry.

"I did not, *señor*," he decided at last to reply. "I stated that at this moment there is nothing against which to defend it."

"I suppose you are in the counsels of our leaders," sneered Moraga.

"I suppose I have eyes in my head," said Andy. He turned to the silenced and somewhat awe-stricken people. "Come, *niños*," he said good-naturedly, "drink your wine, and dance, and have a good time. But don't rush off to be soldiers until there's some good reason for it."

"This," said Moraga darkly and with relish, "savors of treason. General Castro shall know of this."

"Treason, nonsense!" Andy was indignant. "If any of these men are fools enough to enlist as soldiers I shall not try to stop them. But I certainly want them to understand what they are about."

"Ah," said Moraga silkily. "Then in your opinion a soldier is a fool. That is well to know."

The man is play-acting, thought Andy, regaining control of himself. He doesn't believe a word of this, of course. But he's having a good time; he's trying to back me into a corner. There's no sense arguing with him. He turned his back on Moraga.

"If any of you want to join with General Castro," he addressed the uneasy men, "go ahead and do so. But there is no occasion now more than there has ever been. I tell you this. You know me. There are many wild stories told. They are not true. I have been to Monterey; to Sonoma; and I tell you they are not true. If a real danger arises I shall know it, and I shall tell you, and if there is fighting

to be done, we shall all do it together. For the love of the
saints, be sensible."

He looked from one to another, smiling half humorously.
They shifted, a little ashamed, their common sense re-
asserting itself as the impulse of emotion calmed.

"*Mucho gozo, señores, señoras,*" he wished them, "*buenas noches.*"

"*Buenas noches, señor,*" they chorused back.

He left them at that and walked back up the hill to the
casa. That immediate crisis was over. He would lose none
of his *vaqueros.* For that he was glad, both for their sake
and his own. But for a number of reasons his spirit was
depressed. For a moment or so he had sensed a distinct
antagonism; and that saddened him, for these were his
people, and he had lived among them for many years.
But it is not an antagonism, he told himself reasonably:
these people are by nature loyal. They wouldn't go back
on me in a pinch. They'd stick to me if it came down to
cases. But, he reflected in a sudden clarity of insight, it
would only be because they *are* loyal to me. They'd do it
against the grain. That is bad for anybody, thought Andy:
and if it lasted long enough they'd hate me, and it wouldn't
be their fault or anybody's fault, but just that—— He
stopped suddenly in his tracks. It would just be that
something bigger than either of them would come between
them. Like the old puzzled conflict of the Indian days
again. The opposing geniuses of two different races. Inevitable—unless they can be somehow blended. And Djo
belonged to, was part of, both!

Andy walked on again more slowly, pondering beneath
the stars. He was seeing again the flushed passion of eager
faces. They are so easily swayed by the moment, Andy
thought; so unthinkingly ready to follow the moment's
impulse! A song, a dance, even a chance irresponsible
word! There lay the worst danger! Or perhaps it could be

a hope? He sighed deeply, for he remembered his helplessness in that other blind surge of tragic injustices and stupidities. He was seized by a sudden panic dread of the historical repetition. There must be something that could be done about it, something he could do! What? He did not know. He had never been more unhappy.

5

He became aware that Abel Means was at his side, was speaking amazingly apropos to all the thoughts that had been passing through Andy's mind.

"I been figgering on talking to you about this for quite a spell," said Means, "and then I figgered maybe it wa'n't my place."

"You've been with me long enough to say what you please," said Andy. "You ought to know that."

"Yes, that's what I figgered," agreed Means, "and now that you've seed what you've seed, I'll just speak my mind and tell you that if you want any peace around here you'll have to get rid of that gal."

"Wapita?"

"That's the one. As a usual thing you know and I know that what you seed tonight don't amount to shucks. These *californios* are great hands to go off half-cock, and holler, and forget all about it come morning. I s'pose," said Abel Means shrewdly, "that's owin' to their not gittin' drunk proper, like a white man. You know that, boss: I don't need to tell you. But this is different."

"How, different?"

"She's got 'em going—that one. She hammers at 'em morning, noon, and night. And I will say," observed Abel Means judicially, "that she's got a sharp tongue in her head, and a convincin' way about her."

Oh, no, Abel Means continued, as Andy questioned him

interestedly, Wapita was not trying to turn the ranch people against the *patrón*. Don't believe that ever entered her head. Not till tonight, anyway. What she talked was the same stuff he had heard; about how the foreigners, the *e'tranjeros*, were on the point of gobbling California; and of how the patriots must rise to drive out the hated foe.

"Funny thing," Abel Means interrupted himself, "these people think they can lick the world. I tried to tell 'em. No use! They actually can't get an idee of what's outside: only what they got right under their noses."

Wapita, Abel Means returned to his main theme, had never talked against Andy. The millwright was emphatic about that.

"Don't believe it ever come in her mind that you are really an American," said he, "and wa'n't on her side." He chuckled. "She lit into me once or twice, regardless. And for nothin'. I hadn't said nothin'. Just on suspicion, as you might say."

But in spite of this forbearance, a feeling had grown. It was not, Abel Means was careful to explain, any spoken disloyalty. It wasn't disloyalty at all. It was more like criticism. It wasn't criticism: it was more like a *feeling*. A man couldn't put his hand on it. Abel Means floundered, trying to express what he meant.

Andy cut him short.

"I know exactly what you mean," said he.

"I think when it come down to brass tacks they'd be with you," submitted Means, "but they don't know whar you stand. They know all about the visits you been makin' up and down the Valley; and they're awful uneasy and sad-like over what they've heerd you been talkin'. Probably ain't got the straight of it; but that's the way it is. That's just a start. Why," Abel stopped to chuckle, "they's a few of the old shell-backs—not our folks, but they drift in and talk—that's begun to chirp up about the

things we've done here—the flour mill, and the wheat
fields, and the irrigation system and the like. They say
those things are out of natur', as you might say; and if
you was a real *californio* you'd do things like they've
always been done, and the *californio* ways of doing things
ain't good enough for you, and I don't know what all."

"That's ridiculous!" cried Andy.

"Sure! They's always talk like that. It don't mean
nothing—usually. Now they're wondering."

"Wondering what?"

"Which side you're on," said Abel Means bluntly.

"But," cried Andy desperately, "there are no 'sides'!
Not yet, anyway. Good Lord, what do they want me to
do?"

"There ain't no sense to it. That's what I been telling
you. And there wouldn't be none of this if it wa'n't for that
gal. She keeps 'em stirred up. You got no idee, boss. She's
kind of—of *contagious*. She gits even the sensible ones,
sort of." Abel Means hesitated. "I think," he said boldly,
"that the *señora* even is—well, sort of worried. Not that
she takes any stock in any of this stuff," he hastened to
add at the sight of Andy's face, "not for a minute. No
more than I do. Just uneasy-like, the way things are
going. Well, that's all I wanted to say, boss. But if I was
you I'd get rid of that gal." Means himself was obviously
uneasy, anxious to sheer off from what he sensed was
dangerous ground. "What do you think of it all, anyway,
boss? Is there really going to be trouble?"

"I don't know—we'll talk of it—if there is, we'll have
to do the best we can."

Means glanced at the *ranchero's* face, hitched up his
trousers sailor fashion, shifted his quid.

"Sure," he agreed. "Well—I figgered I ought to talk
to you."

"Glad you did," said Andy absently. "Thanks. Goodnight."

6

He at once sought Carmel. But in her presence his resolution drained from him. Her first words made his purpose
of discussion impossible. Already she had heard, probably
through Vicenta, of Moraga's appeal for recruits. She was
alarmed. What was this talk of a foreign threat? Was it
war? She was much distressed: asked many questions. And
in them Andy realized with a sinking of the heart how
thoroughly she took it for granted that his point of view
must be hers; and that he was wholly *californio* through
thick and thin against the world. And he saw only too
clearly the hopelessness of bringing her to understanding
without distress and bitter unhappiness, and perhaps discussion; and he shrank from the issue. I am a coward, he
accused himself; we ought to talk these things out. I
must make her see these things in their broader aspects,
as I see them; as Larkin sees them; yes, as some men
of her own race, like Don Guadalupe, see them. She has a
good mind: at the last she will understand, Andy assured
himself. But not at once. Andy looked at her with new
eyes, seeing in her now all California serenely sure in
its old secure tradition. To replace that tradition must
be a distressful task—an uprooting, a tearing down, a
patient, slow reorientation. It must begin, Andy told
himself, with a slap in the face of her profound unquestioning trust. He drooped in a sudden revulsion of weariness.

He forced himself to answer her questions lightly. He
laughed at her alarms. War? What war? Against whom?
Things were as they had always been. Moraga? The usual
thing. Castro wanted men: for his own purposes. He and
Pico were rowing again about something or other. Nothing
new in that. Yes, he admitted, they might get up some
kind of a side revolution of their own; but that does not
concern us.

"The spring is here," said he. "They'll have nice weather for it."

She laughed a little at that. Reassured, she turned again to her mirror and began to brush out the heavy blue-black masses of her hair. Andy looked at her hungrily. Not yet. No, not yet!

She turned to face him, her eyes suddenly grave.

"This Wapita," said she.

Andy stiffened.

"Yes? What of her?"

"I think," said Carmel in Spanish, and by that Andy knew she was serious, "*querido*, that we must send her away somewhere. Yes, I know what you would say. But I have heard of what has passed this evening—of this dance she has danced. I think maybe she does not know quite what she does. It is that Pepe. Do you know what is that dance, *querido?*"

"No," said Andy.

"It is not a dance to know," said Carmel quaintly. "Such a thing must not be." She hesitated, cast her eyes down, blushed faintly like a girl. "Djo was watching that dance," she said in a low voice. "You must send her away."

Andy was silent. Fleetingly he marveled a little over the gentle Carmel's sudden hardness, and at once recognized the ruthlessness of aroused maternity. He knew the things he should say: this was a child: she should be talked to; it was unfair to bundle her off thus; a dozen similar sober considerations. He did not say them.

"We will talk of this tomorrow," he compromised weakly.

He was bitterly contemptuous of his silence, of his relief. A sudden passion of longing arose within him; a longing for something to happen, for action by which he could thrust through this smother of intangibles that thickened invisible about him.

CHAPTER XII

"The spring is here," said he. "They'll have one another for it."

She finished a little air then. Reassured, she relaxed again, taking more and began to brush out the heavy blue-black mass of her hair. Andy looked at her intently; not yet.

No, not yet.

She turned to face him, her eyes suddenly grave.

BUT discussion and decision were taken out of his hands. Before daylight he was called out of bed to receive a messenger. The man had ridden most of the night, from Monterey. His horse was done. He saluted Andy; handed him a scrap of paper, merely folded over, evidently in haste. It was from Larkin:

"I think you can help in this situation. Come as quickly as you can."

Andy read this by the light of the torch in Panchito's hands.

"Do you know what this is about?" he asked the messenger.

"It is said that an armed body of *americanos* have made a fort over in the San Juan mountains; and that General Castro collects men to drive them out. Perhaps that is it," said the messenger.

"A sergeant and some men of the general's are here now," said Andy. "They know nothing of this."

The messenger shrugged.

"*Quien sabe?* I but repeated the rumor. As the *señor* knows, there is always an 'army over the mountains'—whenever some renegade steals a horse. But this I do know: that the *señor* Larkin bade me use haste; and urged your honor to do the same."

Andy nodded.

"Panchito," he instructed, "see that this *señor* has food, wine, and sleep. Then saddle the chestnut. And, *señor*," he returned to the messenger courteously, "rest well, and remain for as long as suits your pleasure. And," he added, "if you could do me a further favor? Do not speak of these rumors among my people!"

He returned to the bedroom; lighted the candles; began hastily to collect a few small belongings.

"I do not know," he answered Carmel's question. "I know nothing; nothing at all, except that Señor Larkin is in haste."

"Is it trouble with the *americanos?*" Carmel was now wide awake and sitting up. "Is it fighting?"

"I do not know," Andy repeated. "I do not think so. There is no great number of Americans this side the Sacramento—nothing to bring any of them this side the Straits—no, that is nonsense. More likely some business that has come in with the ships—perhaps from Mexico."

He spoke half abstractedly, his head in a chest.

"I do not know how long I shall be gone. I'll send back word if it is to be more than a few days." He found what he wanted; caught sight of Carmel's face. "Now, *querida*," he said less hastily, "you must not imagine what is not so. I should have been to see Señor Larkin months ago. I do not wonder he is impatient and angry."

He finished the small package, reached the Boone rifle from its pegs on the wall.

"You said there was no fighting!" cried Carmel. "Then why do you take that, to Monterey?"

"I may need it for Señor Larkin." Andy summoned his engaging grin. He became grave again. "I shall send a messenger," he promised again. "You must not imagine things. I will bring you back some silk from the Boston ships. Give Amata a kiss for me and tell her we'll go see the wild flowers when I get back. Tell Djo to behave himself; and to stay off that buckskin horse until I get back. And now I must hasten if I am to reach Monterey by night." He stooped to kiss her. "*Adiós*." The door closed behind him.

Carmel sat as he had left her. Her eyes were wide and

frightened. She tried to tell herself that her fears were senseless. As Andy had said, there were no settlers short of the Valley; no reason for them to leave the Valley; no reason at all. She listened until she heard the sound of the horse galloping down the slope. Then she arose and dressed hastily. It was impossible for her to remain longer in bed.

She opened the door of the *casa* and looked out. The dawn was graying. Objects were becoming visible. The *rancho*, after the night's festivities, was not yet astir. A single bird chirped sleepily, a note of inquiry, for the day was not yet come. Panchito and a *vaquero*, riding two horses, driving others, rode up, dismounted. There was something calming, reassuring, in his lack of haste.

"What is it, Panchito?" she asked of him breathlessly.

"I am to bring what is necessary, *señora*," said he. "The *patrón* said you would know what he desires."

"But what is this message? What means this summons?"

Panchito shrugged.

"*Quien sabe?* These matters are not for me!"

"But is there trouble? Will there be fighting, do you think?"

Panchito paused in the act of tightening the *cinchas* of the pack animals. He turned to Carmel a blank face.

"Fighting? But what fighting, *señora?*" He appeared to consider, his wooden face expressionless. "*Política,*" he hazarded. "There is always *política.*"

"But what are your orders?"

"To follow with the horses; and what is necessary for the *patrón*. The *patrón* said the *señora* would know." He looked at her. "We follow *paso lento*," he added. "There is no haste. The *señora* must not be troubled. If there were fighting, that would be known. And this messenger knows of no fighting. And this sergeant of General Castro. Would he not know of fighting? *Paso lento, señora.*"

Carmel made a gesture of despair. She reëntered the *casa*, collected such of Andy's belongings as she thought he might need. Panchito made up the packs. He, and the *vaquero*, and the half-dozen loose horses, departed in their turn down the slope at the shuffling slow trot. Panchito whirled idly the end of his *romal*. The *vaquero* sang a song. Daylight had come. The *rancho* was beginning sleepily to stir. Carmel looked after them, her eyes wide. There was nothing to be done.

2

Carmel did not reënter the *casa*. For a time she stood in the doorway. Then she moved slowly to the great oak and sat down on the rough bench before the blackened spot that marked extinct council fires. It was still early. The new day was taking possession of the world, indifferent that still the *rancho* slept. And this fact a little stilled Carmel's anxious mind; that these things went forward just so, clothed in higher majesties, calmly, leisurely, in due deference, like a slow, spaced pageant, though there was none to see. And queer little thoughts came to her in that new stillness, so it seemed to her impossible that this solemn ritual should unfold in emptiness, and that she must sit very small and quiet and decorous and humble because she had been thus privileged to be one with those for whom this had been prepared. And as Carmel's training had been one of churchly reverence, it came to her that these must be the blessed saints.

So she sat in communion; and human beings and their troubles and their fears became small and fleeting.

3

But this reassurance was almost as short-lived as the dawn itself. Before the morning was ended came Ramón riding hard from Jolón, clamoring for Andy before he had even dismounted. He too had received a messenger. This one bore definite news. The rumor was true; the incredible must be believed. A body of American riflemen were entrenched atop the peak of Gavilan. They had raised a flag. They had sent out a defiance. General Castro was gathering men at San Juan. Already he had two hundred; and cannon. Ramón spoke excitedly; his eyes danced. Barely would he pause for a gulp of food, a change of horses. When he learned the hour at which Andy set forth, he was disappointed.

"I shall not be able to overtake him," he admitted sadly. "But I shall join him at San Juan."

Men from Los Madroños were organized to follow as soon as might be. Ramón talked briefly, from the saddle, to Moraga. Many of the *vaqueros* were preparing to go. But Ramón would not wait, even a minute. He was consumed by a fever of impatience lest he arrive too late.

At the last moment came Djo breathless from the hills where he had been searching for horses; and with him Wapita riding bareback, astride, her hair flying.

"Why did not someone come to me with this news!" he cried accusingly. "I might not have known if Wapita had not thought of me! Wait for me, *Tío* Ramón!"

He tumbled from his saddle; darted into the *casa;* returned, carrying his little Hawkens rifle.

"Djo!" cried Carmel.

He collected himself to a brief formal courtesy, but so jumbled that Ramón laughed.

"*Con Dios, señora madre,*" and he snatched at her hand to kiss it. She seized him.

"What are you doing?"

"After my father—with my uncle—to San Juan!"

Carmel clung to his arm.

"Djo!" she cried again. "Ramón!" She appealed to her brother. "Speak to him! He is only a child!"

"He is a *californio*," said Wapita.

Carmel drew herself up and cast on the girl a look of such cold displeasure that she said nothing more. Djo looked to Ramón in appeal.

"He is more a man than many," Ramón responded to this. "Mount, *sobrino*." He spoke with the authority that this patriarchal society accorded the men of its families in such matters as this. Carmel drooped to the decision. "We shall see that no harm comes to him—his father and I," assured Ramón more gently. He stood up in his stirrups, his mobile face aflame with delight.

"*Adelante!*" he shouted.

Djo leaped to his saddle. They struck spurs to their horses.

"*Adelante! Adelante!*" echoed the *vaqueros*, dashing after. Moraga and his soldiers followed, but at a more sober pace. The ranch people waved and clamored.

"*Viva! Viva! Viva* California! Death to the foreigners!" cried Wapita. She stood looking after them, her right arm extended above her head. Behind her the ranch people buzzed excitedly.

Carmel leaned faintly against the doorpost, clasping the round-eyed and wondering Amata. After a moment her arm slipped from the little girl's shoulders. She turned slowly and entered the *casa*. From the *armario* she took candles which she lighted before the image of the Virgin. She knelt and bowed her head. Had she known it, she at that moment moved squarely into a long line of succession, for this was the fate of the women of these Burnetts, to stand unquestioning, watching their men ride away.

ANDY reached Monterey in mid-afternoon and rode at once to Larkin's house. The consul had evidently watched for his arrival. He met the *ranchero* at the foot of the garden.

"Thank God you're here!" he cried. "Hell's popping!"

"What is it?" asked Andy. "They talk of an army—toward San Juan. What army? Is it war?"

"War? No: that's it. It's Frémont."

"Frémont! What about Frémont? Is he back?"

Larkin stared at him incredulously.

"Do you mean to say you didn't know that! Haven't you heard that——"

"I've heard nothing; nothing at all, I tell you," said Andy.

"Oh, Lord!" Larkin threw out both hands. "And you not twenty leagues away! What can a man expect!" His shoulders stooped. "Come, get down," said he briskly, after a moment. "I suppose I've got to tell you the whole thing from the beginning!"

"I suppose you have," assented Andy. He swung from the saddle and dropped the reins of his wearied horse over its head. The two men wandered slowly up the garden path toward the veranda.

They stood there for a while, too absorbed to think of sitting down. Finally they sat, without knowing that they did so. Andy was astounded at his news. The isolation and self-absorption of Folded Hills were borne in on him as never before.

Yes, Frémont was back. He had appeared suddenly at

Sutter's Fort, in December. He had with him only a few men, and had entered California over the Sierra. The main body of his company had turned south. Joe Walker was in charge of them. Joe was to bring them in by the easier route he had himself discovered years ago. The two parties were to rendezvous at Tulare Lake. After a short stay at Sutter's, Frémont had gone south to meet them. So far everything was all right, though naturally Castro and the authorities were uneasy and wanted to know why he had returned, and why he had brought so many men.

"How many did he bring?" asked Andy.

"Somewhere about sixty or seventy or eighty," said Larkin.

"Well, that's no great army. What did he come for this time?"

"Surveying a route for a wagon road, he says. I managed to smooth it over. If he'd stayed over across the Valley, it would have been all right. Maybe he intended to; I don't know."

But things broke badly. Joe Walker mistook the forks of the Kern for Tulare Lake and waited there. Frémont found the right lake but no Walker. So after two weeks he returned to Sutter's. Along the last part of January he left his party there and came alone to Monterey.

"I had him here at the house; took him to see Castro," said Larkin. "The situation was ticklish, but I managed again to smooth things over. Castro was personally inclined to be reasonable, but he has pretty positive orders about foreigners. Frémont insisted that all he was doing was to establish routes the other side of the mountains, that his men were not soldiers, that all he wanted was to winter somewhere across the Valley, and perhaps refit. Castro could not give him official permission; but I got him to say he'd offer no formal objections. It was a long session. I turned in that night feeling pretty good. When I saw Frémont off a couple of days later I felt not quite so good. Talk! Talk! Talk! Why can't people keep their mouths shut! I began to hear all sorts of things that Frémont had been telling. So did Castro. He came to see me. His friends had been telling him that Frémont had bragged that ten thousand men were starting for California from Missouri in the spring! Naturally he was all on edge again. I told him flatly it wasn't true; and I told him flatly I didn't believe Frémont had said any such thing. Of course he wasn't by any means satisfied; but I got him to let it go. But I was mighty glad Frémont was gone so he couldn't do any more talking."

"Drank too much?" surmised Andy.

"I don't think so. That fellow doesn't need drink to talk," said Larkin dryly. "Well," he went on, "I thought that was all settled. And the next thing I knew I heard that the whole kit and caboodle of them were over somewhere in the Santa Clara valley. That is a long way the wrong side of the fence."

"It sure is," said Andy.

"I began to feel like a man in a bad dream. But it wasn't so raw as it sounded. Seems the men at Sutter's got tired of waiting and started out to find their commander; and Joe Walker heard where they were heading and turned off to join them; and they got together. Bad luck it turned out that way. Looked bad. But it could be explained. It was explained. If Frémont had marched right on back to Sutter's as soon as he had joined them, everything might have been all right in spite of it."

"Didn't he?" asked Andy.

"He did not," stated Larkin emphatically.

To understand, as Andy did, what Larkin now told him of Frémont's movements, one would have to know the topography of the country. It is sufficient to say that a direct return to the Valley, and Sutter's, would have taken him east and north, his back turned to the Salinas Valley and Monterey. In place of that he marched his whole force on a wide circle, across the Santa Cruz Mountains, into the Salinas Valley, and to within seventeen miles of Monterey! And he had taken his time about it; a week for a normal day's journey!

And if this were not bad enough, he was conducting himself with an incredible arrogance.

"I warned Frémont against buying horses from anybody and everybody," said Larkin, "but evidently he paid no attention. At any rate, Sebastian Peralta—you know Peralta, a most reputable *ranchero*—thought he recognized three horses that had been stolen from him a while back, and asked Frémont for them. Frémont denied they were Peralta's. Perhaps they weren't; but he insulted Peralta and ordered him out of camp. Peralta complained to the *alcalde* at San José. The *alcalde* wrote to Frémont about it. Frémont answers—no, wait a minute, I want you should get this. I have a copy." He darted into the house, to return with a slip of paper. "Here's how he answers: 'The insult of which he complains consists in his being ordered immediately to leave camp. After having been detected in endeavoring to obtain animals by false pretenses, he should have been well satisfied to escape without a severe horsewhipping,' and he adds later that he can't be bothered appearing before any magistrate 'on the complaint of every straggling vagabond who may visit my camp.'"

"Polite cuss," observed Andy.

"And for God's sake!" cried Larkin exasperatedly, "why did he have to go out of his way to be so insulting? Here he is, in a friendly country, with an armed force, where he has no right to be. He gets permission to rest and recuperate two hundred miles away in an unsettled part of the country where he'll disturb nobody. And he comes deliberately into the most thickly settled part, and then says he's too busy to give the lawful authority any attention. And he uses conduct and language one would hardly use to a gang of genuine horse thieves, let alone a man of Peralta's standing!" He struck the arm of his chair. "And about what? Three horses! Peralta would have given him the horses if he'd asked for them! Or he could have bought any number for a few dollars at most. Unless the man is crazy or deliberately trying to provoke trouble, I cannot understand it!"*

"Perhaps he was," surmised Andy thoughtfully. "If he could get himself attacked—and hollered loud enough——"

"What's on your mind?" Larkin urged him.

"You know he's Senator Benton's son-in-law. Well— this is probably foolish—but ain't it possible the Senator's looking for a good excuse, and this feller's trying to make it? An excuse for taking over California, I mean."

"But I have very explicit instructions from the government. We've talked of that. They certainly do not jibe with any such performance as this!"

"I didn't say gov'ment," said Andy. "I said Senator Benton. When I was a kid I saw him once. Oh, yes, I told you about that! Well, from what I hear he ain't shifted his ideas. And that girl of his, from what I hear of her, is his own daughter. You heard how she held up Frémont's orders not to go on that last trip and sent him word to hustle up and get out of reach? How did that come out, anyway?"

"It raised considerable of a stink. But Benton handled it. By the time Frémont got back it was all smoothed over; and they gave him medals instead of a court-martial."

Andy nodded. "Benton's pretty powerful then, I take it?"

"About the most powerful, I should say; at least about matters to do with the West."

"Well, there you are!"

"There I am what?" demanded Larkin impatiently.

*Larkin shared that inability with future historians.

"If you mean that Benton is resolved on the acquisition of California, I agree. Expansion westward has always been the passion, the obsession, of his whole career. But we shall have California; peacefully; with the full approval of the people. The administration has its plans all made, definite plans." He checked himself, then went on, overmastered by long-pent impatience: "I shouldn't be talking these things to you, or anybody else. But the thing is all arranged. Every navy commander on the Pacific has his orders. In case of war with Mexico they are to seize and occupy the ports. Occupy them: that's all— to keep other nations from occupying them. That's the whole idea. Then they are to use every means to conciliate the inhabitants. A land conquest would gain nothing. And if the inhabitants won't be conciliated, nothing is to be done about it for the present. That can be attended to later. If the ports are safe, there can be no trouble that can't wait. I don't know why I'm telling you these things. I ought not to. They are confidential."

Nevertheless Larkin felt no real compunction. It was a curious fact that everybody talked to Andy freely. There was something fundamentally trustworthy about the man. Vallejo had felt this same quality.

"So why," Larkin concluded, "should the government countenance this man doing exactly the opposite?"

"I didn't say the government," Andy repeated dryly. "I said Senator Benton." He shrugged at Larkin's expression. "Go on. What's the situation?"

"That's why I sent for you. Naturally Castro sent him notice to clear out, that he must retire out of this department. I saw it; and I must say I think Castro was very restrained—for him. Frémont did not even bother to answer it in writing. He sent back word to the general effect that Castro could go to hell. Then he moved his whole force up to the top of Gavilan Peak where he's hoisted the American flag and put up breastworks. The whole

country is aroused. They're mad; and I don't blame 'em.
They're coming in to Castro. He has two or three hundred
already. It's got me worried; worse than worried. I sent
Frémont a letter telling him the people are very much
surprised and excited; and I told him I thought I could
fix it so that he would not be attacked if he'd pull out, and
that he'd be allowed to remain if he'd behave. It would be
a job, but I think I could have done it. Castro doesn't
really want trouble, and sixty riflemen behind breastworks atop Gavilan would be a tough proposition. Frémont
answered that 'we will fight to extremity and refuse
quarter, trusting to our country to avenge our deaths.'
What can you do with a man like that?"

"Foofaraw," said Andy.

"What?"

"Foofaraw. That's how I sized him up. And," he
added, "I have a kind of notion that that's how Benton
sizes him up, too."

"What you must do is to go over there and stop this
thing, somehow," said Larkin, disregarding the last remark. "No, I don't care how. You know Carson—your
name ought to have some weight—I don't know. You've
got to go."

"All right, I'll go," said Andy.

"You've had a devil of a ride today—and yet——"
Larkin hesitated. "Could you possibly make it tonight?"

"Sure, I can make it tonight." He arose at once and
strode down the path, Larkin following close at his heels.

"Don't you want something to eat first? How about
horses?" asked the latter.

"I'll get horses. Eat? No."

CHAPTER XIV

A NDY reached the crest of Gavilan long after dark, guided to the camp—or the fortification—by the gleam of fire. A sentinel challenged him sharply while he was yet several hundred yards from the top. Andy, whose usually placid temper had been shortened by his reflections, and perhaps by the long fatiguing day, was in no mood for military folderol.

"Oh, go to hell," he answered the challenge contemptuously.

"What is it? Who is it?" a guarded voice behind the sentry was inquiring.

"Sounds like a friend," said the sentry doubtfully. "Leastwise he talks United States."

"That you, Kit?" called Andy.

"Who is it?" the second voice demanded sharply.

"I-tam-api."

Ensued a brief pause.

"Dismount and step up where I can see you," then ordered Carson. —"By the 'tarnal powers it is! I'd heard you were rubbed out. Where did you drop from? Come along. You don't know how glad I am to see you!" He was wringing Andy's hand, pounding his back, dragging him toward the light of the nearest fire. "Is it really you? And alive? Here, you," he called to a young fellow, "take this horse."

"They tell me it's me," said Andy. "I ain't really never been dead; not what you'd call dead."

For the moment he was conscious only of the pleasure

301

of slipping back into old association. It was, to him, a sort of brief escape.

"But where have you been? What you been doing all these years?" Carson wanted to know.

"I live up the valley yonder: got a ranch and cattle."

"Married?"

"Yes."

"Any young-uns?"

"Two."

"Boys?"

"One of 'em."

"How old?"

"The boy's about thirteen. The girl is eight."

"California woman?"

"Yes."

The questioning snatched him back from the past. He answered curtly, with reluctance. Carson perceived this, and thought he understood. He said no more, but turned away toward the fires. Andy thought how, in other circumstances, Djo would have welcomed this chance. Kit Carson had become to him, through Andy's stories, a sort of hero. He might have been disappointed, thought Andy. Kit was not much to look at. He was small, rather stoop-shouldered, with mild blue eyes, reddish hair, a freckled face. And this reminded him of how much he missed Djo tagging at his heels; sharing things with him. He followed Carson. The elation of his spirit, induced by the relief of swift direct action, had fallen.

They neared one of the fires, about which sat a dozen men, who looked up inquiringly.

"Just an old friend of mine," explained Carson briefly, passing by.

"Hoped it might be the yeller-bellies a'ter all," said one, spitting into the fire.

"Where you taking me?" asked Andy of Kit.

"To see the Cap'n. He'll be glad you joined up. Least-wise, he ought to be."

"He's the feller I've come to see," agreed Andy. "But wait a minute: I want to talk to you first." They stopped in their tracks. Andy lowered his voice. "What's this all about, Kit? What's the idea?"

Carson glanced about him.

"What do you mean?"

"What you aiming to do?"

"I don't know," confessed Carson.

"You can't fight all California."

"I bet we can," said Carson, "give us a chance. I'd like to see ary force these yeller-bellies can git together put us off of here if we don't want to go. The men are jist sp'iling for a fight," he added.

"But what for?" Andy wanted to know. He began, reasonably, to point out the facts of the general situation. Carson cut him short.

"I don't know nothing about that," said he. "That's the Cap'n's business. Whatever he says goes with me."

"Strikes me your Cap'n's judgment is poor," said Andy bluntly, "from all I've heard. Come on, now, keep your scalp on. I've heard a plenty—about your brass cannon and your crossing the mountains in snow time and the rest. You're no fool. You can't tell an old-timer like me. You know better."

Carson hesitated.

"Well," he admitted grudgingly, "mebbe he gits a little off the trail sometimes. But, Andy, he's a great man. He is that. You don't know him. Makes you mad as blazes, but they ain't a man in this outfit that wouldn't foller him through hell."

"And the hell would be handmade, by himself," interposed Andy shrewdly.

Kit laughed, though with evident reluctance.

"That's all right," he insisted stoutly, "but you're going to have a heap of fun doing it. And you're going to land somewhere. I bet you on that."

"Let's go see him," said Andy.

2

Frémont was seated before a small tent, on either side of which stood the tall figure of one of his Delaware Indians. Andy surveyed him with the keenest interest.

He saw a slight man, but well proportioned and sinewy, dressed in leggings of the sort affected by the Westerner of the day, and a blouse vaguely military in the suggestion of a white star sewn on its either lapel. He wore moccasins on his feet. His head was bare, but he held loosely against his knees a broad felt hat, the brim of which had been turned up picturesquely on one side. A little fire burned almost at his feet. He was gazing moodily into it, his eyes somber. The eyes were blue, and very large; so large and round, indeed, as to convey to the beholder a first impression of frankness and candor. Later in the interview Andy caught moments amid the flashes of animation when their blue was as surface and as cold as the waters of a glacial lake But Andy was what might with justice be called a trained observer; and his keenness was sharpened by a definite interest in analysis. To any other Frémont's remarkable magnetism of person and grace and refinement of manner would effectually have concealed such small revelations.

A restraining hand on Kit Carson's arm, Andy paused for several moments outside the firelight. Frémont's forehead was high; the eyebrows arched in such a fashion as to lend to his face in repose a rather appealing touch of childlike surprise; again merely a physical effect, but none the less convincing for that. His nose was thin, aquiline, aristocratic. The lower part of his face was obscured, and at the same time invested with a certain force and maturity, by a cropped beard. Andy would well have liked to see the line of his jaw, the shape of his lips. . . .

He relaxed his grasp of Kit's arm. The two stepped forward. Frémont looked up, the prominent blue eyes traveling from one to the other. He said nothing; waited.

"It's Andy Burnett come to life, Cap'n," said Kit.

Frémont bowed his head, spoke in greeting. Andy discovered he had been waiting with real eagerness for the sound of the man's voice. It was soft, clear, gentle. He spoke deliberately, distinctly. He at once made it plain that he knew of Andy by reputation, even mentioned the *ranchero's* Blackfoot name, and showed a familiarity with some of his history. This seemed to Andy astounding; for he had left the Rockies fifteen years before. For a moment even his coolly sardonic mind was caressed by a sense as of flattery. This feeling was immediately succeeded by a more robust admiration for Frémont's industrious scientific thoroughness. Obviously he carried outside the scope of the purely physical that same faculty of minute and interested observation that enriched his reports with vivid and glowing pictures. Evidently he must collect annals as assiduously as plants and animals and astronomical observations. Impossible to be invincible to the man's spell. For that moment Andy forgot the evidence of preposterous event.

His preconceptions were overturned. The man before him exhibited none of the pretentiousness and self-assurance Andy had expected. He was quiet, well-bred, courteous, listened to Andy with attention and an apparent respect. Remembering the theatrical fight-to-extremity die-in-the-last-ditch bombast of Frémont's reply to Larkin, Andy was a trifle nonplussed. He said his say plainly, in full expectation of a return burst of fiery defiance.

"I've lived with these people, as one of these people,

for a good many years," he concluded. "I know them
pretty well. Don't fool yourself thinking they are cowards.
They are not. They are not much at fighting each other,
but from what I know of them they'll fight. Castro has got
together two or three hundred men already, and some
cannon. He'll get more. News is slow to travel; but he'll
get plenty more. The people are mad. And," said Andy
boldly, "in my notion they've got a right to be." He
paused for the angry response he fully expected. Frémont
made no comment. It was Kit Carson who spoke.

"You mean to say you believe that good American riflemen can't lick ary lot of yeller-bellies in California—or in
Mexico either?" he cried indignantly.

"I'm not saying they can't," said Andy, "but I'm
telling you there'll be a real fight."

"Fightin's jist our dish," said Carson grimly; and looked
at his chief.

Frémont still made no comment.

Andy stopped uncertainly. He had said his say. He did
not know what to do next.

"Do I understand you bring this as a message from
Larkin?" Frémont asked quietly at last.

"No," said Andy. "I bring no message from Mr.
Larkin—that is, not exactly. But he asked me to see you
and tell you what I think. He thinks the same," he added.

"I thank you for your trouble," said Frémont with exquisite courtesy. "You are welcome to remain with us as
long as it suits your convenience." He looked directly at
Andy, his wide blue eyes blank of all expression. He said
nothing more, but Andy felt himself dismissed. He hesitated, bowed, and turned away. Beyond the firelight he
looked back. Frémont's soft large eyes were still upon
him. Andy's perceptions were stopped short by their
surface. What lay beneath it he could make no guess. But
a finer inner sense stirred faintly, apprising him of an
enemy.

3

So preoccupied was he by the thoughts induced by this baffling encounter that he hardly heard Kit Carson at his elbow; except to gather that Kit was being as disappointedly reproachful as his mountain-man loyalty would permit.

"What's got into you, Andy?" lamented the little man. "You've lived out yere too long! If I didn't know ye—— But your heart's in the right place. I knew that."

Andy absently agreed he should spend the night. It was too late to do otherwise.

"Surely you're goin' to stick yere with your own people?" cried Carson anxiously. "We may need every rifle!"

"No, I can't do that," said Andy. "I'm going to pull out first thing in the morning."

Kit stopped short in his tracks.

"You ain't goin' to fight *agin'* us, Andy?" he cried in dismay. "You *kain't* do that!"

Reassured on that point, he led the way again, shaking his head doubtfully. But he gave over further discussion. It was obvious that he was disappointed. The occasion was not very cheerful.

"You et?" asked Carson. "No? Well, come on. We got plenty beef." He stopped again. "You ain't—you ain't going to say nothing to the boys?" he suggested.

"I expect they're just taking orders," said Andy.

They joined the group around one of the fires, were plied with roasted meat and bannocks. Andy gnawed on a rib. In spite of his anxieties his spirit relaxed. He was for the moment at home again. He savored a certain familiar satisfaction in the picturesque romance of the occasion; the mountain top, the log breastwork, the flare upward of firelight revealing the folds of the banner drooping on its staff, the long figures of the frontiersmen sprawling at ease, the stars faint and unsteady through the waver of light and smoke, the dark guessed sea of space below as the steep of Gavilan dropped away. The talk was frankly exultant in anticipation of the morrow. Nothing pleased these men better than the chance of a fight, and they were grandly confident in their own prowess.

Midnight neared. A few were preparing to turn in, though most still sat in eager savor. Out of the darkness one of the Delawares glided to stoop over Carson in summons. Kit followed the Indian. He returned after a short absence, an expression of such astonishment and chagrin on his face that the chatter died.

"Git together your possibles, boys," he commanded briefly. "Saddle up. We move."

A blank silence fell.

"What?" someone asked at last.

"We move," repeated Carson. "Don't ask me. Orders."

They would not believe. Then they had to. A storm of anger and protest broke out. Run away! Never! Carson moved among them talking urgently, low-voiced. Andy realized that he was not intended to hear. Men grumbled, protested. But one by one they got to their feet. He felt himself the object of a hostility only half suppressed.

Swiftly the preparations were made. Andy could but admire the accuracy and discipline of the movement. He knew these men's natural independence. He had to respect the quality of a man who could thus command their obedience.

Nobody spoke to him further. At the last, men heaped the fires high with fresh fuel. Kit rode to the fire, by the side of which Andy still half reclined on his elbow.

"So long, Andy," said he briefly.

"So long, Kit," said Andy.

One of the men fell out from the column, already disappearing into the dusk down the mountainside, and rode

back to reclaim some article he had forgotten. He looked
darkly at the *ranchero's* recumbent form.

"You tell yore friends," said he, "that we'd-a stayed
here till hell froze if—— Damn this gov'ment stuff!"
he exploded. He glowered at Andy, then apparently his
sense of fair play intervened. "I s'pose you had to mind
orders same as us and the Cap'n," he conceded, "but I
wish to hell you'd got lost!"

Something in the words or manner caught Andy's instinct. He detained the man, questioning. So that was what
Kit was telling them in secret! That was how Frémont had
succeeded so promptly in exacting obedience to the command of evacuation! An obedience at which Andy had
marveled, for he knew well the breed. Simple! Andy learned
for the first time that he was said to be the bearer of positive orders from Larkin, as Frémont's superior officer!
What could Frémont do but obey? Andy whistled. Some
of the perplexities with which his interview had clouded
his previous judgments were thinned. Once more he could
stand comfortably on his old formula.

"Foofaraw," he said to himself. For he had borne
no orders: Larkin was not Frémont's superior officer,
and had no authority over him. Frémont had saved his
face.

Andy sat by the fire thinking of these things most of
the night. His interest had been greatly quickened by this
encounter. The man was an enigma. Had he deliberately
planned his performances to provoke the *californio* into
making the first move of hostility that should serve as an
excuse for war and conquest? If so, was it his own irresponsible idea; or were such secret and powerful interests as might be wielded by Benton of Missouri back
of it? Or had he merely acted on theatrical impulse, without consideration of results, and so found himself in a
mess from which he was only too delighted to find a way
out? In that case, Andy reflected, Frémont ought to be

grateful to him; but that was too much to expect. He thought over different aspects of the man. Andy knew them all—separately. But he did not know this man; nor could he guess what he would do next, or why.

4

When daylight came, he caught and saddled his horse. For some moments he stood making up his mind. The obvious thing was to ride over the ridge to San Juan, there to inform Castro that the enemy had gone. But Castro would find that out soon enough. He turned his horse's head to Monterey and thus missed old John Gilroy plodding up the slope as emissary from Castro. He also missed Ramón Rivera and Djo, who had joined with Castro, and were wondering what had become of him, though they supposed him still detained with Larkin at Monterey. They, with many other of the younger men, rejoiced mightily at John Gilroy's report; and they all swarmed up the mountains, and rummaged about, and looked with curiosity upon the nature of the fortifications. The more ardent were eager to be about the pursuit; but most were satisfied with the situation, especially when scouts brought back word that Frémont's party was at last actually getting out of the country. Castro ordered no pursuit. He had, all things considered, conducted his part of the affair with ability and discretion. He was better aware than his men of the formidable fighting quality of such men as Frémont's; and he estimated pretty accurately the weakness of his own haphazard forces. He was immensely relieved. Like a sensible man he dismissed the volunteers. But he could not refrain from issuing one of his typical *pronunciamientos*, in which he described the Americans as "a band of highwaymen who dared unfurl a foreign flag in the department," and told how at the mere sight of the two hundred assembled patriots they had fled, abandoning the camp they had occupied and "clothing and other war material."

This proclamation arrived in Monterey shortly after Andy had finished telling Larkin of the night's adventures. He read it and laughed.

"Some of the men threw away two or three old hunting shirts and some moccasins because they were worn out. That's all that was left. Shucks! He knows better."

"He's talking for Mexican consumption," reminded Larkin. "It's the same old trick. But now let me show you something. Made me pretty mad for a minute. Then I had to laugh. When this fellow first roosted up there and hauled up his flag, I sent him a letter by my own courier, warning him things were getting hot and giving him some advice. Here's what I got back. Listen to this:

"'I, this moment, received your letters,'" Larkin read, "'and, without waiting to read them, acknowledge the receipt which the courier requires instantly. I am making myself as strong as possible, in the intention that if we are unjustly attacked, we will fight to extremity, and refuse quarter, trusting our country to avenge our deaths. No one has reached my camp, and from the heights we are able to see troops—with the glass—mustering at St. John's and preparing cannon. . . . If we are hemmed in and assaulted here, we will die, every man of us, under the flag of our country.'"

"Now," said Larkin, laying aside the paper, "I consider that a prize curiosity, and I'm going to keep it. If you take it for what it's supposed to be—a personal, private answer to a letter sent to him by a friend, then it just plain doesn't make sense. He answers without even reading what I wrote to him. Why? What's the hurry? There's no enemy. He couldn't even get a sight of an enemy without climbing over the range and looking down the other side. And then he'd have to use glasses to make them out. 'The courier requires instantly,' says he. Who in hell is that *vaquero* to 'require instantly'? And what's *his* hurry? Rot! And why write *me*, in a private letter, all that brag and bluster about dying to the last man, and refusing quarter and all the rest? I'll bet you one thing, Burnett, a copy of it is on its way to Washington, or soon will be."

"It's sure a pair of 'em," agreed Andy.

"Well," sighed Larkin, stretching his arms luxuriously, "he's on his way to Oregon; and Castro and Pico can go on squabbling again."

CHAPTER XV

SAVE for brief cat naps atop Gavilan, Andy had not slept since the early morning of the day before. Incidentally he had ridden a matter of a hundred miles or so. He was tired. He shook his head a little over this astounding discovery. I'm getting older, thought Andy; I don't stand grief like I used to. He turned in and slept the clock around.

Panchito awaited him, squatted on his heels against the outer wall. He had followed, *paso lento*, and so had not arrived until late the evening before

"The horses are in the corral of Mendoza," said he. "The baggage awaits the *señor's* pleasure."

"*Bueno*, Panchito," acknowledged Andy.

Panchito waited a moment for instructions, if there were any. Then said he:

"The black, Modesto, turned lame at the lower crossing. I left him at the *hacienda*. As the *señor* said to come *paso lento* we stopped there overnight." Andy nodded approval. "Don Ramón and Don Djo and their men passed us below Soledad," continued Panchito in the same easy tone of gossip.

"Eh?" Andy was startled. "You say?"

"Don Ramón and Don Djo and men from Los Madroños and Folded Heels. They rode fast—to join with Don José Castro. Don Ramón sent you word, *señor*, that he would see you at San Juan. He bade me tell you to make haste, *señor*." He paused for a comment; but receiving none, went on. "But the news is that this bandit has fled. That is good news, *señor*, if it is true."

"Yes, it is true. He has gone," replied Andy.

"We shall not, then, go to San Juan?" Panchito was suggesting.

"No," agreed Andy absently. He only half heard Panchito. He was thinking. Panchito's news had surprised, even a little dismayed, him as he thought what might have happened if Frémont had indeed made a stand. But that was settled. Panchito revolved slowly his wide hat between his hands, awaiting orders. Andy considered.

"You may return to Folded Hills with the horses— *paso lento*," he decided. "You may start when it pleases you. Inform *la patrona* that I follow when my business with Señor Larkin is finished. Leave for me the chestnut horse."

"*Bueno, señor*," said Panchito.

But within the three hours he was reported as back, seeking the *patrón*. Andy went out. He found Panchito afoot, holding firmly by the arm the girl Wapita. When Andy came into view she jerked violently, kicked at Panchito's shins, finally twisted her head in a swift attempt to bite the *vaquero's* hand. The latter shifted his grip in cool avoidance.

"Not so, *diablita*," said he half humorously, and gave her a little shake.

"What's this?" cried Andy. "Where did she come from?"

"Answer the *patrón*, little she-devil," urged Panchito; but as Wapita hung sullenly silent, he took the reply to himself: "It is simple, *señor*. This side of the pass José and I, driving the horses *paso lento*, as the *señor* commanded, encountered this one. We asked her this same question, as was natural. In place of replying she struck spur to her horse and dove into the chaparral like a rabbit. So I thought it best to bring her here that she might explain to the *señor*."

"He caught me with the *reata*," the girl found her voice passionately.

Andy, to his surprise, was called upon to repress a sudden almost uncontrollable impulse to laugh.

"Why should you do this, Panchito?" he asked.

The *vaquero* looked surprised.

"How else, *señor*? She would not stop."

"But why should you stop her?" persisted Andy.

Panchito's surprise deepened. For a brief instant a flicker of uncertainty crossed his saturnine countenance. He recovered instantly.

"She rode one of our horses," he submitted.

"I would have returned the horse! I do not steal horses!" cried Wapita. She jerked again against Panchito's iron grip. "I shall kill you for this!"

"That we shall see in God's own time," said Panchito imperturbably.

Andy pondered. The girl is mad, he thought. No one can guess what is in her mind. There's no use trying to get at what it's all about now. She's wild. She'll do or say anything; and it will mean nothing, because she is wild. He sighed with a sudden great weariness. I'll tackle this job later, he thought. I suppose I've got to. Aloud he said:

"I'm sorry this happened to you, Wapita. It was a mistake. Let her go, Panchito. Let her go," he insisted as the *vaquero* looked doubtful. "It was a mistake," he repeated. "I know you would not steal the horse. You may go now. That will be all," he dismissed her, more sternly as she would have spoken. She hesitated; then turned and marched off down the garden and through the gate. "You, too Panchito," he said, when she had disappeared. "I will talk to you later. No; not now—later."

The *vaquero* looked at him fixedly; bowed from the hips.

"*Bueno, señor,*" said he.

2

Andy had to collect his thoughts. He could make nothing of it. Finally he gave up trying. He strove to dismiss speculation from his mind. Later he would talk to her, when she was in a calmer mood, and find out what this fantastic performance was all about. But he could not avoid speculation. He remembered Carmel's solicitude. Could she have dismissed the girl because of her fears for Djo? There had been some talk of that, he remembered. But Carmel would never have turned her out in such a fashion. There might have been some quarrel, though. That was it! And the girl's quick temper . . .

Andy walked slowly down the garden path and across the plaza, lost in a brown study. His mood was one of impatience. He was thoroughly sick of all this nonsense. It was time something was done about it. The girl had been a nuisance from the first. A disturbing element. Like a buzz-fly amid serenities. He resented the annoyance of it all just at this time. Good riddance! For the moment he shook off vigorously any sense of responsibility.

He paused at the shore and watched for a moment, abstractedly, the small wavelets and the small sandpipers chasing one another back and forth. The rhythmic sound and movement soothed his spirit. There came upon him another of his rare moods of mysticism which had always, beneath the hard swift surface of action, integrated his being. He ceased consciously to think, and began merely to feel. Wapita was no longer merely a willful undisciplined girl, a little mad. She seemed to stand for something. Old California. He was banishing Old California from Folded Hills; and that suddenly came to him as something rather terrible; and he started up as though to prevent this thing before it was too late. And then queerly enough Djo came into it; and led him down a new reverie. Djo was mixed up in it. She seemed to be holding Djo uncompromisingly to the Old California; though Andy did not clearly understand how that could be. And instantly Andy recoiled from this; for that also, he suddenly perceived through the strange dreamlike mystic sense, was a terrible thing to him.

The lower fringe of the sandpiper flock was overtaken by an unexpectedly vigorous surge, and rose with a startled twittering. Andy came to himself. He stared about him as though bewildered at being where he was. He turned on his heel and sought Panchito.

3

Andy saw the *vaquero* off for Folded Hills with an addition to his original message that Wapita was safe in Monterey and would be cared for.

"And," commented Panchito, "I think that there will be none on the *rancho* who will not draw a breath of relief, though the saints are a witness that she can be an appealing *diablilla* at times. Even Don Djo," Panchito added as he swung into the saddle.

"Why do you mention Djo?" asked Andy quickly.

Panchito shrugged carelessly.

"Why not? The sap rises earlier in the sapling that is strong. But, *señor*,"—Panchito leaned from the saddle confidentially—"it is not of the body I think, but of the mind, for little harm comes of the one, but great danger of the other."

"Why, that is true, Panchito!" cried Andy.

He watched the *vaquero* ride away; then squared his shoulders and entered the village in search of Wapita, or news of Wapita. He did so with distaste, compelled only by his sense of responsibility. Wapita was one of the minor annoyances that he could brush aside and forget. But only after certain assurances.

He was relieved then to find that she had betaken herself to the house of the horse dealer, Mendoza, who was a sort of left-hand distant connection of the Riveras. He might have expected something of the sort, for in so doing she had run true to California form, which makes of the *pariente* almost a religious institution. For the moment at least she was cared for: she was not loose on the town. What was more important, the responsibility had passed. Señora Mendoza, fat and comfortable, proved more shrewdly aware of the situation than Andy had expected.

"*Quien sabe?*" She shrugged her plump shoulders. "She tells me she will be a dancer, an entertainer. She is welcome to stay here. I shall do what I can, but she is not a daughter of this house. And," added Señora Mendoza, "if I say Yes and No to her she will not stay, for she is a little mad. But," added Señora Mendoza thoughtfully, "it is, *señor*, *la locura grande*, and whether it is of the devil or of the blessed saints only the good God knows and time will show; but this we do know, *señor*, that it will go its own way, and we can but wait and see." She fanned herself slowly, for the day was warm. Andy looked at her with respect. He had not suspected this placid, almost cowlike woman of such profundities of insight. She seemed to arouse herself. She leaned forward and touched his arm with her fan. "This I know, *señor*," said she, "that the blessed saints are watchful for their own, so that one may walk through fire and it will not burn."

"You are a wise woman, *señora*," said Andy soberly. He pondered her words. There was in them no practical reassurance. Only faith. Yet somehow his mind was eased.

"Why did she run away from Folded Hills?" he asked.

Señora Mendoza looked at him queerly.

"That, I think, she must tell you herself," said she. She arose and moved toward the door of the room. At the threshold she turned. "It is a part of her madness—that leads her," she warned.

4

She is indeed mad, thought Andy, as he talked with the girl. The interview was brief, bewildering. Andy's ease of mind had not withstood it. His common sense had immediately revolted against its fantastic absurdities. Except in his rare moments of mysticism Andy's mind was direct and practical. It liked solid things that could be grasped and held. It rejected with protective anger the bafflement of imponderables. It reacted savagely and blindly when the direct certain course of his own life and relationships was deflected by invisible forces. He understood physical oppositions, even the oppositions of circumstance. Against these he possessed familiar weapons, his two hands, his quick and tempered mind. He resented as somehow gratuitous, unfair, deflecting forces upon which those weapons had no hold.

Wapita had left Folded Hills because she would not eat the food of, breathe the same air with, a traitor to California. He denied this? Had he not joined the enemies of California at Gavilan? Did he think to conceal that treachery? It was known. Everybody knew it. It was known at the *rancho*. And, she added contemptuously, he would discover how Californians looked upon a traitor. The words poured from her in a flood. Andy, sitting back silent, could discover in her no trace of softer feeling. She was as though possessed. He eyed her coldly, detachedly. She was fantastic beyond the limits of sanity; so fantastic that he ceased to take her as anything but what she was, a spoiled child who had, mistakenly, been permitted to run wild. What she needs, thought Andy, is a good rounding up, beginning with a sound spanking that would bring her to her senses. The idea came to him that he would do well to take command and do just that. . . .

"What's that?" his attention was recalled to the purport of her words, which he had ceased to heed.

On her way she had encountered Djo and Ramón
returning from San Juan. They had stopped Wapita: but
when they had heard what she had to tell them, they had
ridden on.

"They had awaited you at San Juan; you had gone to
Gavilan," concluded Wapita theatrically. "Don Ramón
was angry."

"And Djo?" Andy was almost irresistibly impelled to
ask; but he bit his tongue and held silence. He eyed the
girl with cold anger; for at that moment her taunting
hostile attitude, her abrupt, apparently unregretful sev-
erance from those with whom she had lived now for some
years made her almost inhuman to him. It did not matter
about him—though he had always been just and kind to
her, and had even become fond of her in a careless sort of
fashion. But how about Carmel, who had treated her almost like a daughter? Whom Wapita had protested so
passionately to love? Andy's anger heated to indignation
as he thought of that. Rank ingratitude; rank heartlessness! Heartlessness; that was it. The girl had no heart!
Even Djo! It was lucky, of course, that this was finished.
But, paradoxically, Andy's indignation quickened again
at the way she was turning from Djo, without warning,
without a backward look. She must have hurt Djo; and
Andy was angry at her for that. And of course, reflected
Andy bitterly, as an afterthought, she had to go and meet
up with Djo and Ramón and fill them full of this so-called
news of hers! Ramón is my friend, my *valedor*, thought
Andy stoutly; and Djo—a fat lot of attention they'd pay
to what this spoiled brat had to say! He looked up, with
a sudden contraction of his straight thick brows, to give
his anger voice. He was alone. Wapita had slipped away.

And queerly enough, now that she was no longer before
him in the flesh, a little of the impression he had experienced on the shore where the sandpipers played seeped
back into Andy's feeling, rather than his mind; so that

she ceased to be merely the negligible spoiled brat speaking her humors to which none attended. Again, in spite of his robust common sense, Andy, uneasily, felt her of significance. It was as though in her something old and beautiful and doomed were focused and made small, a something that seized her and possessed her, and through her made manifest its instinctive hopeless struggle against the inevitable march of destiny. And he saw that such a struggle must be blind, and unreasoning, for it was a death struggle, and therefore mad. Into his heart crept a hushed wonder that such should be the fate of this girl; so that he could no longer be angry at her, but only pitiful and a little awed.

CHAPTER XVI

WITH his emergence from the dim cool room of the house of Mendoza into the sane clear sunlight of the plaza, Andy's mystic insight into realities vanished once and for all. Its residue was a deep and weary sadness of spirit that translated itself into a reluctance to return at once to the *rancho*. Always, whatever the perplexities of the world outside, Folded Hills had been to Andy a refuge. Now its secure peace was in disturbance. When he went back he would have to face the job of straightening things out. Of course not much of a job, thought Andy. Just an explanation: of why he had gone to Gavilan. But he shrank from the necessity of making explanation. Just for a little while. Until he got rested up. It was queer how formidable just at that moment was to Andy the task of arousing himself. He was too tired to do so—just now. Larkin would keep him; for a few days; until he'd got over this strange lassitude. Queer way to feel, thought Andy. I wonder if I *am* getting old? I'm not old; only forty-five! This is silly. I'll start back tomorrow.

But he did not start back tomorrow. Nor the next day, nor the day after. He did not want to start back; and that was a strange thing too. He felt bemused; in a sort of dream; bound by cobwebs that a single thrust would break. But the power of the thrust must come from without himself. There grew in him a longing, a necessity, sharp as a hunger, the necessity of the man of action trapped by intangibles which he could not understand. If only something would happen! And this necessity grew until it became a sort of prophetic sense. Something was going to happen. It was on its way. He was waiting for it.

He lived those days within himself. He was much alone. Each morning he tramped across the peninsula to the outer coast. There he perched atop the boldest promontory he could find in the low cliffs. Here was the sea. It fascinated him. He had never lived in intimacy with it before. It gave him a certain peace. He liked it; liked everything about it.

He liked the wide fling of an horizon that refused to limit, but slipped below the curves of, the earth. He liked the suggestion of inward hurrying multitudes; and he watched abroad for the momentary uplift of single billows, as though one of a crowd, impatient, had raised himself to see. He liked the way the rush slowed to dignity as it neared the shore; and the majestic uprise and pause of the breakers; and their curling crash downward; and the whirling busy searching of the hissing, white-and-green foam. He liked too the clean sharp wind that herded the sea's intangibles to the waiting land. And there were also so many minor things; the slow graceful kelp rising languidly in the translucent billows; nonchalant little ducks playing an apparently hazardous game on the thunder-edge of disaster; wild sea terns crying; long lines of cormorants going home; or perhaps a gleam of polished black far out and the spout of ghostlike spray where played a whale. The sea was his friend; and from it he expected something, he knew not what.

One day he caught sight of a sail, and a sudden and complete assurance came to him that this was the something awaited. He started back at once to town. By the time he had reached the plaza the ship had dropped anchor. She proved to be the United States sloop-of-war *Cyane*, from Hawaii at the moment. He learned further that she had carried a passenger; and that the passenger had hurried at once to the house of Señor Larkin. Andy followed. The same inner sense told him that this was no mere traveler. He felt an inner stir as though precedent to outer action.

His intuitions were correct. The newcomer proved to be a Lieutenant Gillespie of the Marine Corps. He had crossed Mexico from Vera Cruz to Mazatlán disguised as a Mexican merchant. He had borne an official dispatch to Larkin; but as this was of a secret nature he had committed it to memory and then destroyed it. "My memory, however, is exact," stated Lieutenant Gillespie. Larkin was acting very pleased; walking about; rubbing his hands. The marine officer sat, twirling the stem of a wineglass between his fingers, looking straight ahead of him, speaking dryly and with precision. He accepted Andy on Larkin's designation of him as "my confidential agent"; which was the first Andy had heard of that. At Larkin's request he readily repeated the dispatch he had memorized, and now had rewritten.

Larkin was to exercise vigilance lest any foreign nation should be given legitimate excuse to take over the country.

If California should revolt against Mexico, the United States should remain strictly neutral.

If California should assert and maintain her independence, then the United States should "render her all the kind offices in our power as a sister republic."

In case of actual and declared war between Mexico and the United States, there was to be no aggression against the people of California, except that the ports should be occupied by naval vessels. In such event Larkin and all other officers were to emphasize a policy of conciliation. "Let events take their course," the idea was emphasized; the government distinctly disclaimed any idea of extending its territory, "unless by the free and spontaneous wish of the independent people." But it hastened to warn Larkin that any "compulsion or improper influence" toward fostering the latter idea would be "repugnant."

He might, however, use his influence to "arouse in their bosoms that love of liberty and independence so natural to the American continent."

Larkin was jubilant. With such pacific and conciliatory instructions he anticipated little difficulty in winning over the better element of the Californians, if not to an active desire for annexation, when the time came, at least to cheerful acquiescence if annexation became inevitable to keep her from conquest by some other foreign power. Andy, remembering Vallejo and Martínez, as well as the racial easy acquiescences of his neighbors, was inclined to agree with him. This policy was fair; it was forbearing. If it came to a choice, he did not doubt the Californians already preferred the United States to any of the other powers that hung covetously in the offing. That feeling could be cultivated. This specific disclaimer of overt territorial ambition would help that sentiment enormously. Given a little time. And if nothing foolish happened to stir up antagonism. Andy and Larkin looked at each other. The same thought had crossed the mind of each. This Frémont affair had cleared away just in the nick of time. Lieutenant Gillespie's next words startled them.

"Do you know anything of the whereabouts of a Lieutenant Frémont?" he asked. "A man in charge of a surveying party?"

"You have orders for him?" asked Larkin in a small voice, after a dismayed pause.

But the marine shook his head.

"No," he disclaimed. "But my own orders are to repeat to him, if convenient, and if it does not entail too much trouble, the dispatch I have just delivered to you."

"And nothing else?"

Gillespie looked at Larkin in surprise.

"What else?" he asked. He made it clear. Commodore Sloat had these same orders: General Kearny: Commissioner Slidell.

"There is, I believe, some movement forward looking to purchase," vouchsafed Gillespie.

Larkin sighed with relief. He had for a moment entertained a ridiculous idea. He saw instantly that it was ridiculous. Why indeed should an obscure second lieutenant in charge of an insignificant exploring party be instructed otherwise than were all other responsible officers of the government? This Gavilan episode had made him as jumpy as an old woman.

Aloud he said:

"You will not have to trouble about that. Lieutenant Frémont is well on his way to Oregon on his return journey to the States."

Gillespie pondered.

"I am sorry for that," said he. "I feel an obligation to fulfill the whole of my mission, if that is possible. And," he added, "I carry for him some personal letters, from his family, which were taken from the regular mails at the last moment under the impression that I might be able to deliver them to him." He considered further. "I know nothing of this country," he said. "Would it be possible for me to overtake him?"

"It might be possible," admitted Larkin, "but it would be difficult, and would involve a hard fast journey."

"You say he is returning to the States?"

"That, I understand, is his intention."

"I could accompany him," suggested Gillespie. "Yes, I think I would like to go overland. I think," he decided, "that, if I can be supplied, I would like to make the attempt."

"I'd be glad to act as guide," spoke up Andy. "At any rate as far as Sutter's Fort," he amended. He was himself a little surprised at this offer. Suddenly he seemed to see in this journey the movement, the awaited action, that would enable him to break through the invisible bafflements. Something definite to do. And obscurely, in the

background, his own spiritual loneliness for Folded Hills
came into it. Frémont, for the moment, was to him only
a human being. A man would sure want to hear from his
family, thought Andy a little wistfully. And Larkin, too,
in a different way, welcomed the idea. It crossed his mind
as just possible that Polk—or Buchanan—might know
this young man and his tendencies. It might be as well to
deliver the warning implicit in the government's policies.

It was so arranged.

LEST Gillespie's position as a marine officer might arouse suspicion that his errand to Frémont was official, Larkin advised that he assume the rôle of a tourist traveling for his health and desirous of returning overland with Frémont's party. As, presumably, Frémont's party was on the march, no time was to be wasted. Therefore they set out on April nineteenth, rode steadily, and exercised such diligence that as early as the ninth of May Gillespie had overtaken Frémont on the shores of Klamath Lake. To one familiar with the distances thus covered, it is evident that the "invalid" had not wasted much time.

Andy did not accompany him beyond Sutter's Fort. A number of the trappers and hunters at or near the place proved willing to take over the job. He was not sorry. By this time the journey north and back again had ceased to appeal to him. He did not dislike Gillespie; but the two men were not sympathetic, did not speak the same language. Navy training had conventionalized the lieutenant with a military precision and stiffness of manner that translated itself into arbitrary brusqueness of decision and action, and curtness of speech. Probably he meant nothing by it; Gillespie was young; he would ripen out of it. Indeed Andy derived a secret amusement from the contrast between this brusque brevity and the ardent eager spirit it so evidently restrained. Gillespie was very businesslike, very military, still elevated in that lofty superiority of the Service over ordinary mortals so characteristic of the lower ranks. To which must be added an equally callow contempt for all "foreigners." His pose of the invalid merchant was a joke, and fooled nobody. Fortunately that did not much matter, for Castro and Pico were still too busy with one another to pay attention to anyone else. Indeed Sutter did, in duty bound as a Mexican officer, report to Castro that Gillespie had passed through his place, adding that in his opinion the traveler was no merchant but a government agent.

Certainly that was the opinion of the settlers in the Valley and about the Fort. Finer distinctions of governmental departments were beyond them. It meant nothing to them that Frémont's expedition was officially non-military in character; that though he held a military title, his command were not soldiers, but merely "hired men" to further a—supposedly—purely scientific purpose. They looked like soldiers, they were armed, they had certainly acted like soldiers at Gavilan Peak. They carried an American flag. Under orders from a superior, Larkin—so the common opinion ran—they had withdrawn, had headed back toward home by way of Oregon. But now here was another soldier, pursuing them in hot haste, obviously the bearer of dispatches, of other orders, direct from Washington. Nobody could guess what these orders might be; but logically Frémont's future movements must be considered as in obedience to them.

At this particular moment, John Bidwell informed Andy, genuine uneasiness as to California's intentions toward the settlers was at a low ebb. It seemed obvious that the earlier scares had been baseless. Castro, as *comandante militar*, had issued no more proclamations of expulsion; he had no military force north of the bay, nor did he show any intention of sending any force there.

"Of course there are always wild rumors running about," said Bidwell, "but the more substantial old-timers have learned to discount them. A lot of our people are dispersing throughout the country nearer the coast, where they'd be the first to catch it if there were any trouble. You can bet they'd be streaking it for the Sacramento at the least notice. There isn't a whisper of real trouble. Of course there are always the wild bunch getting drunk and shooting off their mouths. And," he admitted, "the new immigrants have to learn better than to believe all they hear."

2

In the meantime, back at Monterey, Castro had received Sutter's letter voicing his suspicion that Gillespie might be a government agent. Little Castro cared. The "highwayman" was in full march for Oregon; must be by now well beyond California. What orders Frémont's government might care to send him as to his activities on his return journey were nothing to Castro. But he saw here a grand opportunity to put one over on Pío Pico. Pretending alarm at an "emergency," he summoned to Monterey a hand-picked *junta* to "advise" him. It "advised" him that Pío Pico ought to come north; that in the meantime he, Castro, ought to establish headquarters and take all necessary steps to utilize the patriotism of the country. Castro, with great relish, followed this "advice." He announced he would defend his department at all hazards. He failed to point to any enemy against which to defend it.

As Castro had hoped, this elicited from Pico howls of rage over usurpation of authority. Castro blandly explained that he was forced to call the *junta* because the governor had failed to come north to assist him in the "crisis." Pico called an assembly of his own, at Santa Barbara. This one, also hand-picked, authorized him to raise troops, ostensibly for the general defense, and also on account of the "crisis." This was one on Castro, for raising troops was usually the *comandante's* official job, not the governor's. To make it complete they removed Castro from command; but as this was in secret session, and nobody—not even Castro—knew it, it must be considered merely as a personal satisfaction. Castro, being now one down, retaliated by announcing his department in such danger that he felt justified in declaring it in a state of siege and under martial law.

It was the gay and merry springtime. Beautiful weather for another nice comfortable family revolution of the old-fashioned sort. Quite a number of the younger idle blades rode in to join up for the fun, and for as long as it amused them. The elders—including Vallejo—smiled tolerantly or disgustedly, as the case might be, and kept on about their affairs. *Políticos* will be *políticos:* boys will be boys.

No one was seriously disturbed; except possibly some of the mothers of some of the boys. California, north and south, went leisurely about the business of the spring *matanzas*. The settlers in the Valley congratulated themselves on a ripening wheat crop. A few of them talked with Lieutenants Arce and Alviso, on their way to Sonoma with eight *vaqueros* to collect some government horses for which Castro now had use. The *californios* made no secret of either their movements or their errand. Indeed they stopped overnight at Sutter's.

3

Andy was in much better spirits by now. Conditions had very considerably settled down since his former visit. No disturbances seemed to be in the offing. Nothing appeared to stand in the way of the policy of forbearance and conciliation. Larkin would be relieved. As for himself, he had thrust himself into the clear, freed himself of the entangling cobwebs. He was inclined to laugh at the morbid state in which he had been. He was humorously ready now to return to Folded Hills.

But he could not do so immediately. Sutter wanted to establish a sawmill, back through the foothills of the Sierra. It must be near timber, of course; and must be reasonably accessible. But it must also be located on water power; and that water power must be intelligently used. John Bidwell was to look for such a site. He wanted Andy to go with him. Andy protested that he knew nothing about sawmills.

"Nor does anyone else," said Bidwell, "but you have a flour mill at your place; and it uses water power. And you do know country."

So Andy went along, not very reluctantly, in spite of the delay to his return home; for it seemed good to him once more to breathe the mountain air. They did not accomplish much, but they had a good outing, and improved acquaintance. Some years later James W. Marshall, another of Sutter's men on the same errand, discovered gold.

The two returned to Sutter's in less than a fortnight. The whole atmosphere had changed. They were deluged with rumor detailed as fact. The Mexicans were on the move. It had been decided to eject all settlers from California. Castro was raising an enormous army. He was inciting the Indians to burn the grain fields. He had six hundred in his command and more were gathering. Already an advance army was on its way, destroying crops, burning houses, driving off cattle—all this, and much more, by men worked to a high fever of excitement.

Andy was perplexed. What had caused this sudden, violent panic? Had anything *happened*? Were there any eyewitnesses of any of these astounding preparations?

"Look here," he argued, "it don't make sense. There ain't any such army in California. There never was much of a one; but just now there's even less." He went on to tell them what he knew; that there were no real military establishments in California; that the *presidios* were practically deserted—the entire garrison at San Francisco consisted of an officer and ten men, no more than two or three of which were ever present at one time; that

Sonoma had been long since abandoned. Castro, Andy told them, had some twenty officers under him, but he could not from anywhere have assembled four times as many soldiers. As for arousing the Indians, when did Castro—or any other white man than Sutter and Vallejo —ever have the slightest influence or control over the Indians? The exact contrary was the case. "I know what I'm talking about," argued Andy reasonably. "I've lived in this country a good many years."

They did not seem to hear him; although most of them waited for him to finish. Many of the old-timers were calm enough; sometimes laughed a little at the wild-eyed excitement. But the inexperienced newcomers and the "floating population," as John Bidwell called them, "the landless men of no fixed dwelling place, trappers, deserters from ships, precious rascals," were only too delighted. They had the will to believe, for they loved excitement and hated the Californians with the hatred of ignorance. These would listen to no reason; and looked upon Andy with hostility, though no one openly challenged him.

To him came John Bidwell and drew him aside.

"Frémont is back," said he briefly.

"Frémont! But he is on his way overland, to the States!"

"He was. He is not now. He is encamped near the Buttes. I have sure advices."

"But why?"

"I do not know; unless your young marine brought him orders to do so."

"No; I saw the orders."

"He may have had others, for Frémont alone."

"No. Larkin asked him; he said not."

"He may have lied."

But here Andy felt on firm ground. Gillespie was young: his judgments were callow and intolerant: he had an exaggerated idea of the importance of the Service. But, by that same token, his standard of honor was high. He would not lie.

"Well," said Bidwell to this, "everybody thinks he brought Frémont his orders; and that is why he is back; and they're waiting to see what he's going to do next. And," he added, evidently unconvinced by Andy's disclaimer, "if you're right, why *did* he come back?"

"I wish I knew," said Andy. So, indeed, did Sutter, who was most troubled. He could not guess which way the cat would jump, or why.

4

Obviously Andy could not leave now. Not until he had some sort of notion of what it was all about. He pondered much on this, but got nowhere. It occurred to him that it was unfortunate that all this baseless excitement should be coincident with Frémont's change of plan. They might play in with one another dangerously. He stopped short in his tracks; smiled indulgently at the thought that had stopped him; moved on. The thought was this: that possibly they might have something to do with one another. Or was the idea so ridiculous? Frémont would not dare! Or would he? Andy remembered Gavilan. Yes, Andy agreed with himself, but that was before he had specific and positive orders.

His mind lingered with Gavilan. That had been an extraordinary performance: the act of a madman far gone in egotism. Unless he had assurances of backing. What backing? Not the government: not unless it had changed its policy, or was playing a secret and rather disreputable game under the surface. Andy's loyal soul stoutly refused to believe that. Well, what then? Had the man merely gone off the handle, crazy-drunk with vanity and self-importance?

"Shucks!" observed Andy aloud, "he's sure got a lot of foofaraw about him, but not as much as all that!"

He had a way of breaking out into speech at certain high peaks of his inner explorations.

"Jehosaphat!" cried Andy.

He was remembering several things of which he had not thought, which had heretofore no especial significance. Frémont had married Jessie Benton. Benton! Benton of Missouri! With his dream of "manifest destiny"! Why, he himself, Andy Burnett, a youngster raw from the farmlands of Pennsylvania, had felt the great heat of that ambition in the long ago, before, as one might say, people knew there was another side to the continent. That fire had endured through the years; had become— what was it Larkin had called it?—an obsession. Andy recalled well his impression of Benton. That too had endured all through the years. No room in that driving fanaticism for patience, for faith in, for understanding or tolerance of, the slower, cautious waiting policies of diplomacy. Andy understood through the kinship of men of action, for he was essentially a man of action himself. Make the opportunity: then strike! Strike quickly! Strike decisively before the opportunity dissolved; before some bolder, prompter rival might seize the chance! For this second of illumination Andy sensed the fine wavering line that separated the patriot and the traitor.

By golly, thought Andy, that makes sense! It explained Gavilan, anyway. Let's see, thought Andy, how does that work out? A clash at Gavilan; an excuse for war with Mexico; annexation. But at the last moment Frémont had given way. Nerve gave out, thought Andy. Pretty big job. A gamble, and a big one. If it worked—why, fine. But if it did not work, if the powers of the government refused to upset its whole policy, if Benton's influence proved overrated—where would Frémont be then? Nerve just plain gave out, repeated Andy to himself; he turned tail and started home. And now something had happened to change his mind again. What? Secret orders through

Gillespie? Andy still refused to believe that. It was too raw.

His common sense rejected the idea that every official of the government, from the secretary of state, the admiral of Pacific forces, the general in command of land forces down to the especially appointed confidential agent, should be definitely instructed to one policy, and that an obscure lieutenant in charge of a small exploring expedition should be instructed exactly to the contrary. And he too was still confident that Gillespie had not lied.

What then? Why, it was as plain as the nose on his face! The letters, the "private mail," the "family letters" Gillespie had carried for the young officer from Jessie Benton, from Benton himself. What had they contained? Instructions, possibly. Sufficient assurance, perhaps, of Benton's ability to swing the thing. At any rate, Frémont had found in them something that stiffened his backbone. In that case there was trouble ahead.

So far Andy on the flood of inspiration. Then the clarity of his insight clouded. There swarmed upon him the confusing obfuscations of common sense. Many things might have forced a temporary return—Andy's experience furnished them in abundance—accident of travel, condition of route, horses, supplies, dozens of commonplaces of this difficult wilderness. Well, the event would tell.

One thing, thought Andy, I've got to go up there and see what I can find out. Maybe Kit will tell me what it's all about, or Gillespie. He remembered his reception at Gavilan. I reckon, thought Andy, they won't be any too glad to see me. He grinned. Well, they can't any more than kick me out, thought Andy. He determined to ride next day to the encampment at the Buttes.

5

But that evening a man named Martin rode in to the Fort after tobacco. Andy sought him out. He soon discovered that Martin could tell him nothing as to the reasons for the change of plan. He took it for granted, as did everyone else, settlers and residents of the Fort alike, that the movement was official, whatever its purpose. Anybody with the brains of a grasshopper could figure that out. Look at the facts. Frémont, an army officer, had withdrawn from armed conflict. Some said he had done this on his own decision; others that he had been ordered to do so by Thomas Larkin. Anyway, he had gone. Now comes Gillespie, also a United States officer; Gillespie follows him; delivers dispatches. He returns. That could mean but one thing: that he had orders from Washington to stand by its citizens in California. Indeed there could be no fault with that logic. It was inescapable on the premises of what was known. But at least he gave Andy a clear idea of the externals of the trip north and back. Andy liked little of what he heard.

At Peter Lassen's place on Deer Creek, it seemed, certain settlers had come in asking help against the Indians who were gathering at a near-by point. Frémont replied that he could give no aid officially; but added that he would discharge his men and they could do as they pleased. This suited them exactly. There might be good sport. To the old Indian fighters of the plains it was like shooting mudhens.

"We killed a hundred and seventy-five of 'em," boasted Martin, "and lost nary a man!"

Andy's face darkened. He questioned Martin closely as to details of the Indian disposition. It was as he had thought. There was no slightest evidence of any hostile intention. The occasion of the gathering was probably one of their yearly councils and dances. But Andy made no comment.

After this refreshing interlude the men were reënlisted back into the fold.

They stayed at Peter Lassen's about two weeks.

Frémont sent men out in all directions to buy horses. From the Indians, said Martin; other Indians, from the Tulares, it was said.

"Captain Sutter told Captain Frémont every horse in the Tulares must have been stolen from the *ranchos*," observed Andy, who had this from Bidwell.

"Hell, what of it?" laughed Martin. "Wa'n't we going north?"

Got hold of a hundred and eighty-seven of them, he added; gave a knife and a string of beads apiece for them.

The journey north was leisurely.

"We followed up the Sacramento," said Martin. "Game was plenty, and we killed a heap of it. Got an Injun every once in a while, too. We made it a rule never to let ary buck get away."

They were camped on the north shore of the Klamath Lake when two horsemen rode in with the news that a United States officer carrying dispatches was behind trying to catch up, and that his escort was so small he was in danger from the Indians, who were strangely hostile. So Cap'n Frémont had taken some of his Delawares and Kit Carson and a few others—nine in all—and turned back from the main body. They met Gillespie that night. Frémont must have received the dispatches and discussed them. At least he and Carson and Gillespie were awake in conference until very late. An hour after they had turned in, the camp was surprised by Klamath Indians. Three of Frémont's men were killed.

"I wasn't there," said Martin, "but from what I hear they was lucky not to be all massacreed."

But the little band had beaten off the assailants; killed a chief.

"Kit Carson done that," said Martin.

"What was the matter with the sentry?" asked Andy. "Did they get him?"

"I wasn't there," repeated Martin, "but from what I hear, they wasn't no sentry."

With difficulty Andy was at last convinced that the camp had been completely unguarded; that even the fires had been left burning. Were they all drunk?

"The Cap'n allows no likker," Martin said briefly.

Andy shook his head. This was beyond him. He did not know these other people, but he did know Kit Carson. If they weren't drunk, the thing became incredible. But his guess was not so far off at that. Though Frémont's discipline allowed no liquor, there are other more subtle wines of the spirit. Around one of the fires, a little apart, the three had sat late, quaffing it deep. They were heady with it when at last they turned in. It was Frémont who talked; Gillespie who kindled to enthusiastic support; Carson, the fighter, who listened until his mind was so full he forgot his cunning.

They rejoined the main body next day. The combined forces hunted up an Indian village and destroyed it and its people; any old Indian village. After which they had all marched south to the camp at the Buttes. Martin did not know why. How should he know?

ANDY left Sutter's early. A *tule* fog hung thick over the bottomlands. It obscured everything. Objects a hundred feet away were invisible, showed tenuous and ghostly as he passed, melted again into the mist. Voices came to him from all about, disembodied voices, of ducks and geese, of blackbirds, and the hoarse craking of the marsh birds; but he could see none of them. Occasionally a splash and a sharp prolonged whistling of wings told him he had alarmed the wild fowl to flight, so near at hand, so clear-cut in sound that it seemed impossible that the sun-shot white translucence could conceal the hurtling bodies. Overhead the sky was clear blue.

And then the sun prevailed. The fog vanished, instantaneously, as though withdrawn into a fourth dimension. He rode again in the familiar world.

About ten o'clock he drew rein at a settler's cabin. Its owner, who named himself as Hal Stowe, came out to greet him. While they chatted an Indian rode up. He handed the settler a paper, and at once rode away, ignoring the questions the man shouted after him.

"Now what in tarnation do you make of that!" complained the settler.

He unfolded the document, read it slowly.

"I'll be damned!" he exclaimed, with a trace of excitement.

He handed it to Andy.

"Notice is hereby given," Andy read, "that a large body of Spaniards on horseback amounting to 250 men have been seen on their way to the Sacramento Valley, destroying the crops, burning the houses, and driving off the cattle. Captain Frémont invites every freeman in the valley to come to his camp at the Buttes immediately; and he hopes to stay the enemy and put a stop to his . . ."

Andy turned the paper over. It was unsigned.

"I ain't paid no attention to the talk that's been goin' around," said the settler. "And that thar proclamation—I'm too old a hand to think they mean much. But this yere is different. Wait till I catch me up a hoss, and I'm with you!"

"What proclamation?" Andy caught at him.

"Bill Loker had it. It read that yeller-bellies ordered all American settlers out of the country and said if they didn't git, right away, they'd be druv out into the mountains, or made prisoners; and if they wouldn't git they'd be shot."

"You saw this?"

"Well, I read the translation. That's what Bill had. I didn't see the original dockyment."

For the very good reason—though, naturally, neither he nor Andy knew it—that there was no "original dockyment." No such proclamation had ever been issued by any California authority. The "translation" in the hands of Mr. William Loker was a forgery.

Emanating whence?

2

They rode toward the Buttes together. Shortly they were joined by another settler, who also had this news. Andy had met this man before, on his expedition with Djo. He remembered him rather vividly, not only because he was a most peculiar character; but also because he had been a subject of especial discussion. And this reminded Andy of his many excursions with Djo; and he sighed, for he missed the boy very much. He had tried to make Djo see the good points of this man, but without much success, for at that time the lad's prejudices were strong.

His name was William Ide. He was a kindly person, deliberate-moving, slow-speaking, about fifty years of age. As long as nothing in particular aroused him he was likely to pass unremarked. But if one touched certain buttons, such as religion, or patriotism, or a twisted sort of abstract idealism, he was off in flights of the most highfatulin, spread-eagle type of oratory. Then one was, for the first time, likely to notice the fanaticism of his eye, and a certain meek obstinacy in the set of his lips. He had been, among other things, Andy learned, a schoolteacher and a carpenter. Some told Andy that the man was a Mormon; though no one was certain of that part of it. "Obstinate as a mule," others informed him with exasperation. "Harmless old crank," said still others, with a laugh; "he'll never git anywhar!" It was on that point that Andy had argued with Djo, hoping to enlarge his tolerations.

"He might get somewhere," Andy had objected to Djo, "if the chance was built to order for him. Notice the set of his eyes? No? Well, one of the first things you want to look at, sizing a man up, is the set of his eyes. This feller acts mild, but he's blind-obstinate, I should say. When a man's blind-obstinate and headed the wrong way, he's a fool. When he's blind-obstinate and headed the right way, he's a hero."

"Yes, sir," had said Djo, noncommittally.

"And," concluded Andy, "in my time I've seen some of the worst fools just happen to get headed the right way!"

When they had reached Sutter's, Andy was interested enough to inquire further. From John Bidwell he had learned that Ide and his family had come overland by wagon train. The Sierra had been crossed by the Truckee River. Near the summit even the experienced mountaineers in the party gave up the task of getting the wagons and the oxen over the divide. Ide knew nothing of mountaineering, but he refused to quit. The wagons and oxen were successfully crossed, dragged up one at a time by ropes over obstacles that any sane man would have pronounced wholly impassable for wheeled vehicles.

"You see, Djo," said Andy, "that time he was headed the right way!"

Now here was William Ide again, flopping along excitedly on a horse, his long coat tails flying. He flung himself into the company of Stowe and Andy. He was, as he at once expressed it to them, "stirred to the quick." He had seen Castro's alleged proclamation. He had received the summons to Frémont's camp. The occasion had thrown him into one of his oratorical fits. Andy listened to him incredulously; he had never, in all his wide experience, heard anything like this before. But Hal Stowe was more typical of his time in that he had been trained to "oratory."

"Are we to risk our lives, and the lives of our wives and children, in the fathomless snows of the Sierra Nevada at the behest of a tyrant hand?" shouted Ide. "Oh, no, sir, no! The brave hearts of our people answer the call! You may be sure there was no hour of deliberation when the news reached our hand—not a moment. The horse bounded back to the cabin; the rifle, pistols, and ammunition were, by every inmate of the house, produced at the door; one brief sentence gave parting advice to the fond wife and listening, excited, and wondering children while the blanket was being lashed to the saddle. Our people rise! Posterity shall be proud of them!"

Andy's face was wooden. He made no comment.

"That's the ticket!" approved Hal Stowe.

3

They arrived at the Buttes near sundown. Frémont's camp was arranged with military precision. His men lounged before their shelters, or stood about in obviously studied aloofness from the swarm of visitors. For nearly a hundred men had preceded our travelers. They also had come in answer to the summons, which had been widely published; a mixed lot, some armed with rifles, many only with pistols, or even shotguns. All were much agitated; and nobody seemed to know what it was about. They questioned Frémont's men; one another. The former refused to talk; or answered questions in monosyllables. Andy looked about for Kit Carson; for anybody he knew. "Somewhars about," they grudgingly vouchsafed. He gave it up, and resigned himself to awaiting developments. Frémont's tent, marked by a pennon, remained closed.

Time went on. Darkness fell. Still nothing happened. Among the newcomers was much talk, but no decision. Some were getting angry. A few of the more philosophical fell away, searching camping places; but most waited, eyeing the closed flaps of the tent.

They parted. Carson peered from the opening. His eye traveled rapidly over the gathering, which instantly fell to expectant silence. He saw Andy, and his face registered surprised recognition; but he made no other sign. He named five names. Andy's was not one of them; nevertheless he followed uninvited into the little tent.

Frémont was seated. One of his party stood at his right hand, Kit Carson took his place at the left. Frémont surveyed the visitors coolly, apparently waiting for them to speak.

"Well, gentlemen," he said at last, "I shall be glad to serve you, if you will state what errand brings you here."

They gasped, and looked at one another in uncertainty.

"Why, you sent for us, Cap'n," said Ide.

Frémont neither acknowledged nor denied this. He continued to gaze at them inquiringly from his prominent blue eyes. Andy was watching him closely. He's playing checkers, thought Andy, he's trying to make 'em take first move. But burly, bearded Hal Stowe would not stand for evasions.

"You know our errand mighty well," he stated bluntly.

Frémont appeared to deliberate. He looked up at them, his blue eyes limpid.

"I have heard of your predicament, gentlemen," he acknowledged with an air of candor, "and I can understand your anxiety. I am myself an American citizen," he reminded them. "I am also an officer of the United States and bound in duty, as well as by personal feeling, to assist you by any means in my power. It distresses me that that power is limited by the—the *unfortunate*—fact that technically our government and that of Mexico are at peace. But my advice is at your disposal."

The visitors looked at one another in dismay. This sort of thing was not at all what they had expected. Advice! Why, they had come to—what had they come for, anyway? Even Stowe could not find his voice.

"What *is* your advice, Cap'n?" ventured Ide at last.

Frémont spoke up briskly, as though he had been waiting for just this question.

"Earn the support of your government," said he. "Make it possible for me, for any constituted officer, to render you all the aid in his power."

He glanced keenly from one to the other examining the effect of his words. For an instant his eye lingered on Andy, whom evidently he had not before noticed, with a mild surprise. He turned to whisper to Carson. Andy felt himself the subject of a whispered colloquy between the two.

"It is very simple, gentlemen, and easy of accomplishment." Frémont turned on them. "There is needed only a dozen men, who have nothing to lose, resolute enough, and willing to suffer a certain small inconvenience to gain great ends. There surely should be a dozen such; men foot-free, patriotic, who have as yet nothing in goods or land or family to sacrifice, heroes in a great cause. Let these men set forth, in full consciousness of the right. They should do two things." Frémont paused once more to survey his silent auditors. "First, they must raid the enemy country and run off enough horses for a march back to the States. Second, they must make prisoners of some of the enemy's principal men."

He waited. They stared at him, wholly confounded. Again it was Stowe who found his voice.

"Hell!" the settler cried out indignantly. "You call that givin' advice! What then? What's a dozen men goin' to do agin' all Mexico? Where do the rest of us come in? Whar do you come in?"

"They do not fight Mexico," said Frémont smoothly. "They can, once they have done these things, escape over the mountains to await the event. Must I explain? Such an action must provoke Castro to strike the first blow against our people, and hence against the United States. For these men, these heroes, you must remember, are acting, not for our country, but on their own initiative. And can any American doubt that his country will protect its own, by war if necessary?"

He examined again his dumfounded auditors, awaiting the action of their slow minds. In spite of the fact that his own earlier surmises were more or less in this line, Andy could hardly believe his ears. Nor, apparently, could Ide.

"You mean to say you are proposing that you want an irresponsible gang to commit an outrage, and then quit the country and leave others to take the consequences?" he cried.

"You asked my advice," said Frémont, "out of your present difficulties. This is not a matter for theory. It is a practical situation. That is the best solution I can offer. Can you think of any other?"

"Well, you'll see me in hell before I'd join up with any such dishonorable shenanigan!" shouted Ide heatedly.

"I resent that implication," returned Frémont sternly. "I resent the aspersion on my honor. You are in danger of your own honor, of your property, of your very lives. Have you never heard, or have you forgotten, what happened to Isaac Graham, and the others of your fellow countrymen? Do you doubt if it had not been for the very government whose good faith you, sir, seem to distrust, they would be to this day rotting in the dungeons of San Blas? Do you dare maintain to me that in a time of such imminent peril any measures of safety are unjustified? Do you mean to tell me that you yourself, sir, stand ready to sacrifice to your ideas of so-called honor the lives, the virtue, of your wife and dear ones, the lives of your neighbors, your own fellow countrymen? Do you profess to believe that if you settlers wait much longer all hope of resistance will then not be in vain? You come here, of your own free will, asking advice in your present dilemma. I give you the best in my power. And you impugn my honor!"

Frémont's eyes flashed. His figure seemed to expand, to vibrate, aquiver with the full power of his magnetic personality. Ide was confused, a little abashed.

"I didn't mean anything personal, Cap'n," he half apologized. "You're an American officer, and I suppose you know what you're doing and have your orders. But," he said stubbornly, "just the same, I don't believe any good comes from treachery, and that's what it looks like to me. And I'd rather take a chance, myself."

Frémont hastily arose, his face dark with exasperation.

"I will not suffer such language in my camp! It is disorganizing!" he cried, and left the tent, followed by Carson.

4

Almost immediately following Frémont's angry exit, and before the astonished and somewhat bewildered settlers had exchanged more than a first word of comment, a stranger briskly entered the tent.

"My name is King, gentlemen," he introduced himself suavely. "Would you be good enough to follow me to my tent for a further discussion?"

King was a direct and businesslike person, of polite—almost too polite—manner.

"Now, gentlemen," said he, with an air of confidential intimacy, "let us abandon our cross purposes. You are among the responsible men of the Valley. These are difficult times; and Captain Frémont, between his sworn duty as an officer and the generous impulses of his heart, is in a difficult position. It is impossible for him to speak freely——"

"Spoke freely enough," grumbled Stowe, under his breath.

"Let us understand the situation. Let us suppose a case. Let us suppose —as may well happen," King warned —"that some of your number should happen to provoke General Castro to retaliation. What would you in that case propose to be done?"

They looked toward one another for support.

"If we were all in the same boat it would be foolish to jump overboard," said Stowe at last. "We'd have to stick together, of course; and to hell with how we happened to git there. How about it, boys?"

"We are certainly too few for division among ourselves," agreed another thoughtfully. "We'd be in it for the whole man."

Ide and the others nodded agreement.

"But that don't mean provoking war; that's plain self-defense!" Ide warned King. "And that's our own affair. The United States may or may not have cause for war against Mexico. That's nothing to us. We are peaceable settlers and intend to remain peaceable if we can. But we

aren't going to flee the country as long as we can fight."
He spoke quietly and with sincerity. Andy looked at the
man with a new admiration.

But suddenly Ide slid into his oratorical manner:
"While there is an arm to fight, or a voice to cry aloud
for Independence!" he cried. "But let truth and honor
guide our cause! We have cause of war and blood—such
as it is impossible for the United States to have received!
We shall stand clear in the eyes of posterity!"

To Andy this lapse into rhetoric was flattening; but the
other settlers kindled to it; for that was the day of "oratory," and these men might almost be said to have been
trained to respond to it.

"Good!" cried King heartily. He had what he wanted.

He threw aside the tent flaps and ran out into the camp
where the settlers who had gathered in answer to the supposed summons awaited the result of the conference.

A cheer arose as King made known the sentiment of
Ide's outburst.

"Good!" "Good!" men cried. "Hurrah for Independence!"

Frémont had returned to his own tent from wherever
his anger had carried him. He stood before its flaps, surveying the scene. Andy, watching closely and detachedly
all that was going on, thought to catch a gleam of triumphant understanding between Frémont and King. It was
instantaneous; he could not be sure. Kit Carson and
a number of men rushed forward, begging to be discharged
that they might join the new struggle for independence;
at which Ide and the other members of the conference
looked slightly bewildered. Matters had moved swiftly
beyond their understanding. A highly theoretical supposi-
titious case, as proposed by King, had suddenly taken on
body of actuality. Everybody seemed to accept the idea
that such a struggle for independence was a settled fact;

worse, that it had been decided on and approved by the settlers' own representatives. Ide tried to protest. His voice was drowned, he himself was hustled aside.

Frémont peremptorily refused Carson's request. He had become brusque, military in manner. He spoke very distinctly.

"I cannot permit this," said he loudly. "I am not at liberty as a government officer to offer assistance to these men. Nor am I at liberty to permit any of my men to do so. I cannot consent to discharge any man. My men were engaged for a definite purpose. I need them all for my overland journey to the States. In spite of my precarious position I have not asked aid of my fellow countrymen here, nor shall I do so. I feel that my party can take care of itself against Castro or any other, if it has to do so; but I shall make no move unless I am first assaulted by him. My only delay shall be to wait until I have received sufficient supply of provisions for my journey, which I shall then undertake without reference to what may take place here. Your request, sir," he said to Carson, "is unwarranted."

Andy listened with growing amazement, Carson and the other men fell back in apparent chagrin at this lofty rebuke; but Andy could not avoid a feeling, which, however, he did not examine, that the request and its denial had been staged, that Frémont's refusal had been intended not so much for them as for the record.

At that very moment, almost as though it had been timed to the second, a great shout arose from those on the outskirts.

"They're coming!" came the cry. "The horses are coming!"

And out of the darkness became audible the sound of hoofs shuffling, and the restlessness of a multitude, and the cries of men. A moment later a single mounted figure rode into the firelight and drew rein.

It was Ezekiel Merritt, tall, lank, soiled, chewing away on his tobacco, his long trapper's rifle resting across his saddle bow. His manner was exaggeratedly casual, but the nonchalance obviously overlaid a deep satisfaction.

He spat elaborately.

"Well, Cap'n," said he, "we got 'em, nigh two hundred on 'em. Thar they be!" He waved his hand toward the darkness.

He dismounted leisurely, tossed the reins of his horse to a bystander, and strode forward into the full light of the fire. The first hubbub of cross excitements had died to silence. Andy, with the rest, leaned forward, eager to know what it was all about. Merritt looked about him calmly, spat again. Evidently he thoroughly enjoyed his dramatic prominence.

"Slick as liftin' ha'r off'n a dead Injun," said he. "We followed your advice of instructions, Cap'n; and thar they be, every hoof on 'em. And nary a man hurt; and nary a shot fired, worse luck! They wouldn't fight. Doggone!" he cried heatedly. "I offered to give 'em back their arms and fight it out with 'em at fifty or a hundred yards jist for f'ar play. They was a dozen of 'em same as we. But they wouldn't do it!"

"What happened?" asked Frémont eagerly.

"We came up to 'em airly in the morning, right a'ter they'd crossed the river, down near Knight's place. They give up; and we took the hosses. That's all they was to it."

"What became of them?"

"I give 'em back their arms," said Merritt contemptuously, "and a hoss apiece, and turned 'em loose." He squirted another stream of tobacco juice and grinned. "I told 'em to go to Castro and tell him eff'n he wanted his hosses to come and git 'em!"

At this statement Frémont uttered an exclamation of vexation. Merritt watched him placidly. For a moment Frémont was lost in thought; then his face cleared.

"I congratulate you, Captain Merritt," said he. "You have acted promptly and boldly."

"I only done what you said," disclaimed Merritt.

But Frémont slurred this over as rapidly as he could. "Men," he cried to the gathered settlers, "you are fortunate that among you are a few who do not hesitate to act. These horses which Captain Merritt and his brave companions have so valiantly captured from the enemy were intended for the use of General Castro to raid your homes! Already, report says, he is on the march at the head of a force of four or five hundred. Captain Merritt's prompt action has gained for you the breathing space of delay!"

Andy looked about him at his companions. He sought Hal Stowe's eye; then Ide's. Neither showed the least comprehension. For the love of heaven, what's the matter with them! thought Andy. Can't they see that the whole thing is cooked up? He recalled the interview in Frémont's tent, and the latter's "advice." Shucks! thought Andy, that proposal's just a bluff. He wasn't taking any chances. He'd already fixed it up, thought Andy. Didn't particularly matter whether they fell in with the plan or not. He'd already found and sent out his "dozen men who have nothing to lose." That described Ezekiel Merritt and his ilk perfectly. I bet poor Arce was flabbergasted, thought Andy. That *must* have been a surprise! In spite of himself, Andy's lips quirked a little. Couple of hundred horses, a dozen unarmed *vaqueros*, riding openly through the country where everybody could see them. Wouldn't Arce be astonished to learn that he had commanded an "army," and that he had delivered up "arms"? And wouldn't he be mad if he knew he was rated as such an idiot?

Frémont was issuing more "advice of instruction," as Merritt had called it. The die was cast, said Frémont. Captain Merritt (Captain! thought Andy swiftly) had seen fit to release his prisoners. The act was chivalrous.

But it was not good strategy, for Arce would carry the news to Castro. There was but one thing to do. Strike first. Seize Sonoma. There was a foothold in the enemy's country. There were prisoners to be seized, men of prominence, hostages! But swift action, surprise, was the only safety. The thing must be done before the news of Captain Merritt's victory reached the garrison at the fort. (There is no garrison: there is no fort! don't they know that, thought Andy.) They were all cheering: even Ide, who apparently had forgotten his outburst in the tent. Every man jack of them was red-faced and excited, swept fully into the current of this ingenious conspiracy. Except for Frémont, Carson, King, and one or two others, everyone present, including the exploring party itself, seemed caught in the mob hysteria.

"And how about the hosses, Cap'n?" asked Merritt.

Frémont calmed abruptly. His manner reverted to its former detachment. Again he spoke slowly and distinctly, that none might fail to hear.

"They are the rightful property of you and your brave men who have so valiantly captured them," he told Merritt. "I have, of course, nothing to do with them."

"But eff'n we go to Sonoma, what's to do with them?" objected Merritt.

"I will take them, for safe keeping," conceded Frémont. "But they are not mine. They are yours."

So obviously did he emphasize this point that for a brief instant it seemed to Andy that surely now these idiots must see the drift. He thought he saw it plainly enough. They think he's going to lead them to Sonoma, thought Andy: well, I'd bet all I own he ain't! He's making it plain enough that this is none of his doing! Andy's eyes narrowed. Surely they must see that! But Frémont, having placed his disclaimer on record, had no intention of permitting it to be recognized as such. He took Merritt by the arm.

"I will talk further with Captain Merritt," he told them. He led Merritt into the tent.

5

Before Andy had an opportunity of saying a word to anybody, Kit Carson glided to his side.

"Didn't expect to see you here, I-tam-api," said he.

"Same to you," returned Andy. "Thought you were on your way to Oregon."

"Injuns hostile," said Carson. "Couldn't make it."

"No?" said Andy. He waited guardedly. He's been sent, thought Andy. What does he want of me?

"Looks like trouble this time," ventured the scout at last.

"Needn't be," retorted Andy dryly, "—unless it's made." He waited; but as Carson had no comment, he went on. "There's no California army anywhere," he stated. "There's no fort at Sonoma. There's no soldiers there. There's no movement against these people. That's all poppycock."

"I don't know nothing about that," said Carson. "Looks like they think so."

"Yes? And why?"

Carson did not answer this. He seemed to be casting about in his mind.

"Which side you on, anyway?" he asked bluntly.

"Me? I'm on the side of common horse sense," said Andy.

"Well, what you aimin' to do?" demanded Carson, losing patience.

That's what he's been told to find out, thought Andy. Only he was supposed to worm it out of me. But Kit's no *politico*. He was even a little amused at Kit's simplicity. And sorry. Kit was too good a man to be mixed up in this kind of shenanigan. Aloud he said:

"Why, 'tend to my business, I reckon."

"Better watch your step, I-tam-api," warned Carson.

So that's it! thought Andy. I wonder, thought Andy, just what that means. Might as well find out. As a matter of fact, Andy did not know clearly what he did intend to do. No use trying to head off these angry fools if they do make up their minds to go to Sonoma, thought Andy. They ain't drunk, but they might as well be. Won't get anywhere argufying; just throw 'em off me complete. He might be able to slip away; and, by hard riding, warn Vallejo. But, he shrewdly suspected, Carson was there precisely to see that he did not do that. Just fix myself so I wouldn't be any good at all, thought Andy; especially if I got myself took prisoner. Frémont would hardly dare order him into custody, just on suspicion; that would be taking sides. But he'd find some excuse. The fellow's smart, thought Andy. Better trail along, he decided; watch how things go; grab a chance if it offered. If this gang gets loose in Sonoma unrestrained by someone responsible, it might be pretty tough on people and property. Especially if this man Merritt has anything to do with it. Andy remembered Merritt's feud with Salvador Vallejo, and his dark threats. Hell of a mess, thought Andy anxiously; don't know as I'll be able to do anything, but I'd better lay low and try. Aloud he said to Carson:

"Reckon if they decide to go to Sonoma, I'll join the parade."

6

From Frémont's tent emerged Ezekiel Merritt, swaggering confidentiy, spitting his tobacco juice right and left.

"We got her all fixed, boys," he shouted. "We're goin' to Sonoma to ketcn us a few Vallejos and such. Ketch yore horses. We're startin' right now."

The announcement was greeted with a ragged cheer. But some of the more sober-minded wanted to know more.

"Is Cap'n Frémont going?" someone voiced this sentiment.

"He'll be along when the time comes," stated Merritt confidently.

For a moment Andy had a hope that at last these men must see what he was now confident was the fact: that their rôle was to be the cat's-paw of the accomplishment. But the hope was immediately dashed. The moment produced its orator; and before the oratory doubts vanished.

This was not Ide, but another of Ide's type, a man named Robert Semple. Andy had seen him before; again in the course of his trip with Djo. At first sight one would have taken him for a specimen of the old-time mountain man. He was actually just six feet six inches in height, but looked even taller because of about a fifteen-inch diameter. He was clad in full buckskins and wore a fox-skin cap, and walked with the peculiar rolling swagger of the plainsman. But Andy's practised eye was not deceived; and a word of inquiry proved him right. The man had but just arrived, only a few months before, with an immigrant train. At home he had been by profession a printer and a dentist; by avocation an orator; and had played at a succession of parts—editor, teacher, writer, statesman—into each of which he had entered with entire earnestness and sincerity, savored with a mighty flow of spread-eagle rhetoric. Just at this moment he was carefully subordinating other rôles in favor of that of hardy pioneer. He was the logical precursor of the hair-pants tourist playing cowboy on a dude ranch. Andy had been amused, but tolerant, for he sensed the underlying, glowing idealism of the man, appealing in spite of its emptiness. This righteous occasion called it forth in a flood of mighty rhetoric.

"If we conquer this country," he cried, "we have no prince to claim it or to dictate laws for its rule! No tyrant hand is laid upon us, but the glorious American eagle will spread her wings over even a conquered people, and afford them protection and freedom! Tyrants tremble on their thrones, and wrong and oppression are hiding their deformed heads!"

The waverers were swept away. These, it must be repeated, were the days of oratory. Andy, with a shrug of despair, joined the volunteers in the search for their horses. His mind was now made up. At the first opportunity he would slip away; ride like the devil; reach Sonoma before the raiders.

Ezekiel Merritt suddenly confronted him.

"You comin'?" demanded the trapper.

"Yes," said Andy.

"You comin' as a friend or an enemy?"

"As a friend—of both parties," replied Andy.

"We don't want no sneakin' halfway yaller-bellies," said Merritt truculently.

"I'm going," repeated Andy.

Merritt glowered at him for a long minute.

"You better behave," he threatened darkly. "Eff'n yo're goin', yo're goin' with me. I'm yere to see that you do! *Sabe?*"

Andy looked into the man's narrow blazing eyes.

"All right," said he; and meant it, for he knew Merritt's kind, and that even I-tam-api could not readily slip away from a mountain man.

THE settlers took it for granted that Andy was wholly one of themselves. Andy did not attempt to disabuse them. Nor did he consider taking any desperate risks to escape. What for? Such an attempt, at this late hour, would merely destroy his any possible usefulness. But perforce he had to submit to Merritt's bragging and his half-concealed triumph. He realized that the trapper had him at a disadvantage and would make the best of it. He realized only too well, also, that Merritt would be glad of the excuse to disarm him of the Boone gun. So he held his peace; and used his eyes; and sized up, as well as he could, the quality of the men with whom he rode. He concluded them, on the whole, fundamentally a pretty decent lot. He came to a resolution.

This was at Barnard's ranch, where they had stopped to rest. The party had by then been asaddle all one day and one night. Merritt ordered a halt. Ide and Semple and a few of their kind objected. They were bone-weary and red-eyed, but their spirit was still strong to get to Sonoma before the alarm might be given. However, Merritt was firm. Barnard contributed a bullock to the cause, but "postponed" joining the enterprise. The raiders ate heavily and slept—all but Semple and Ide, who rushed about the country hollow-eyed but indefatigable, haranguing the scattered settlers. By evening they had drummed up nearly a score of volunteers, who rode in prepared for some large vague enterprise whose exact purport they did not understand, and as to whose authority they had but the vaguest notions.

Andy put into effect his resolution. He chose a time when the men were all assembled for a final attack on Barnard's fat beef. His tall figure commanded instant attention.

"I reckon," he said, exaggerating his slow trapper's drawl, "that we all know what we're after and what we're going to do. Leastwise, I hope so." His voice became faintly ironical.

Merritt had suspended gnawing on a bone. He growled in his throat. Andy raised his hand and hastened on.

"That's all right. It ain't what I want to say. But there's one thing ought to be understood by everybody before we get there. We got to see to it that these people we're going to take prisoner are treated right and proper."

He turned his shoulder toward Merritt, who was stirring uneasily, to address directly that portion of the group that included Ide, Semple, and Grigsby.

"I'll tell you plainly why I say this," he said. "I don't want to see any grudges paid out. If we take any prisoners they must be treated right. And I'm going to see that they are. And I want you men to understand that before we go any further."

"I suppose you think you're running this show," growled Merritt. "Who are you, anyway?"

Andy turned on him.

"If you want plain speaking, you're the man I mean," said he. "I've heard you talk about what you were going to do to Salvador Vallejo if you ever got hold of him. Maybe you have cause; I don't know. I've got nothing to do with running this show. But I am going to see that it's run right as far as this one thing is concerned." He returned to the other group. "You men are biting off a mighty big chunk, and a lot of people are going to hear about it before you get through." His drawl slowed; the corners of his mouth quirked faintly with a private and concealed humor. "How about that posterity you been talking about?" he suggested. "Got to watch mighty careful where you're walkin'."

Andy's shrewdness had hit the right note. Ide and Semple flamed instantly to this appeal. Andy sat down and lit his pipe, content to let them talk of "children in generations yet to come" looking back "with pleasure upon the commencement of a revolution carried on by their fathers upon principles high and holy as the laws of eternal justice." There was something just a little touching, a little pathetic in the spectacle of the simple carpenter and the unlettered dentist from the backwoods of Kentucky lifting for a brief moment this absurdly aimless and unwarranted raid into the pure though empty idealism of knightly emprise. Andy was insusceptible to that aspect, however. His only feeling was of sardonic satisfaction that he had gained his point. Indeed he had gained it more completely than he had hoped. The discussion terminated in the swearing of a solemn oath by all present that the prisoners were to suffer no unnecessary violence; an oath taken by the orators in an exalted spirit of dedication, by the rank and file in slight bewilderment, and by Merritt and a few others of his ilk in sullen reluctance.

And one other thing Andy's interposition, unknown to himself, had accomplished. Though Merritt ostensibly continued as leader of the little party, in actuality its command had passed from him, not perhaps to Ide and Semple, but to the faintly fantastic spirit of quixotism of which they were high priests. A strange situation for a group of solid matter-of-fact American frontiersmen!

That was all right: Andy had gained his point. But he had accomplished still another thing which he no more than Merritt desired. He had got this spirit all stirred up again; so that, instead of a sound night's sleep—with possibly more sanity in the morning—midnight found them once more in the saddle on the road to Sonoma.

This, Andy admitted to himself, would have been good strategy if it were strategy—and if there were anything to offer resistance—for it would bring them to Sonoma about daylight. But it was not strategy. Indeed the little band seemed to have gone fey with an ether of unreality. They were not acting as grown men, but as boys playing out an elaborate and zestful game. They performed with the relish of boys. Instead of taking the direct and easy trail, they stumbled and groped over a rough by-path through the hills, that they might appear from an "unexpected" quarter; though the regular road was certainly deserted enough at night. They were about, heroically, to invest a "fortified post," so they must set about it in due order.

Andy would have liked better an arrival later in the day. It would have been less startling, to say the least of it. But that was a minor consideration. At least the safety of the people was assured. Andy believed these men would do as they had sworn. He was not so sure of the property. And he knew—no more than the others, indeed—nothing of what "advice of instruction" Merritt had received as to the disposition of the prisoners. He was much troubled.

But his uncertainty did not exclude from his mind a little quiet amusement over the show. Having elaborately appeared from the "unexpected quarter," the capture must be properly made. The first thing, obviously, was to surprise and capture the garrison. This occasioned some slight delay. The *pueblo* was sound asleep, and the garrison could not be found! At length he was discovered a "little way out of town," and exhibited gratifying surprise, not to say stupefaction. By this time it was broad daylight. The other searchers for the garrison having been recalled, the whole body of horsemen moved to the open plaza before Don Guadalupe's house.

2

Someone dismounted, thundered appropriately on the door of Don Guadalupe's residence, and scuttled back to his saddle. For a short interval nothing happened, though Andy's sharp eyes caught a moment's agitation at an upper window. The men, becoming impatient, stirred into noisy discussion. There seemed to be various ideas as to what should be done next. Merritt wanted quite simply to break in; but Merritt was out of favor. One cheerful soul suggested that they let this particular matter rest for the moment.

"They kain't git away!" he pointed out. "Let's divide up the spoils!"

But, to the credit of the company, this proposal was cried down, and indignantly. Andy glowed with relief and with satisfaction that his estimate of these, as fundamentally honest and well-meaning men bemused in Wonderland, had been correct.

The confusion was suddenly ended by the appearance of Vallejo.

Don Guadalupe's dress showed the signs of haste; but his manner was composed.

"To what am I indebted for this visit?" he asked courteously.

No one replied. Ide and Semple possessed no Spanish. The few who understood hung back uncertain, ill-at-ease. Vallejo looked them over one by one, his eyes resting with a slight surprise on Andy in the background.

"Do I understand this is a capture of this place?" inquired Vallejo smoothly, after a pause.

"Sí, señor—that's right," at length someone managed to mutter.

Vallejo turned on his heel, reëntered the house, but returned immediately, buckling a sword belt about his waist.

"In that case, *señores*," he said, "it is evident that I must render my sword. Who will receive it?"

His brilliant eyes searched their faces. No one moved. Merritt sulked. Ide and Semple evidently did not understand. Vallejo waited. After a moment he smiled ironically, unbuckled the sword belt, carried the weapon back into the house, again returned.

"My house is yours, *señores*." He swept them a courteous gesture. "I am at your disposition." His eyes rested again on Andy.

Some of the settlers were stirring uneasily.

"What's he say?" they wanted to know. "You, Bill Knight: you know the lingo. What's he say?"

"He wants to know what it's all about. And I don't blame him," said Knight bluntly.

"Tell him he's a prisoner and he's got to come along," suggested one, whose common sense was beginning to reassert itself.

But this was much too informal a proceeding. Both Semple and Ide protested. Things should be done in an orderly fashion. The garrison had been captured. Next on the program must be the formal surrender. Articles of capitulation must be drawn.

"Well, git 'em drawn, then," urged the settlers impatiently.

Semple beat Ide to it in accepting Vallejo's invitation to enter the house. He took with him William Knight. Knight accepted with some reluctance. He wanted it distinctly understood that he was going only as interpreter. Merritt trailed along sullenly. He was disgruntled; for he felt that command was sifting through his fingers, and he did not know what to do about it. As a gesture of waning authority, he snarled at Andy, who was preparing, uninvited, to join the conference.

"You stay whar you be," he snapped. "We'll 'tend to this!"

There was nothing for it but to obey. Andy swiftly considered the advisability of searching out Jacob Leese. In the absence of Merritt no one was likely to question his movements. He decided against it. Nothing could be done until matters developed further.

Ensued a long period of waiting. The men talked low-voiced among themselves. Jacob Leese hurried along the plaza from his own house, entered that of Vallejo, and was lost to view. The square was empty, except for the horsemen. At windows and doors, around corners, furtive heads peered briefly. The sun mounted; grew hot. The house stood silent, inscrutable, as though unoccupied. No sign came from within, either of voice or violence. At length patience broke.

"Oh, for God's sake!" cried someone at last. "We going to stay yere all day! Let's have a captain of our own!"

"That's it! A captain! A captain!" several agreed.

They chose John Grigsby for the post. Grigsby dismounted and was also lost to view. Time went on. Another hour passed. The sun grew hotter. The horses were restless; the men were restless. No one had either drunk or eaten. Yet they continued there to sit, if not with patience, at least with restraint, held by the order of their fantastic dream. But at length they could stand it no longer.

"For the love of heaven, Ide!" they cried. "Go on in—*and come out again*—and tell us what's going on!"

This time there was no pretense at designation of an officer. The carpenter dismounted eagerly. His hour had come! Andy dropped the reins of his horse to the ground and followed. No one stopped him.

3

Within the deep embrasure of the door into the *sala* he stopped, the better, unobserved, to size up the situation.

Vallejo, flanked by his brother and Jacob Leese, sat at

one end of the long table, which had been dragged to the center of the room. Behind them, and a little removed, another, whom Andy recognized as one Victor Prudhon, Vallejo's secretary, leaned against the wall. Next to Vallejo, and at the side of the table, the tall, buckskin-clad figure of Semple bent over a mass of papers which, Andy rightly surmised, were the celebrated "articles of capitulation." Semple was busily interlining and amending, while Don Guadalupe looked on sardonically. Salvador sat back, an expression of disdainful disgust on his handsome face. Jacob Leese examined his fingers as though bored. Farther down the table John Grigsby, the newly acclaimed captain, sat bolt upright, staring straight ahead of him. Andy looked at him twice to see if he was awake; but his eyes were open. Merritt's head was buried in his crossed arms. Knight, the interpreter, was on the opposite side of the table. He also stared, somewhat glassy eyed; without a muscle's motion, as though an effigy in wax.

The table itself was littered with glasses and with bottles partially or wholly emptied.

Andy was little given to imagination; but for a fleeting instant the fancy caught his mind that Ide's headlong entrance broke the inertia of a slowly gathering spell; a spell that would hold these figures about this polished table exactly thus through the long enchantment of a timeless somnolence. It was but a momentary impression.

"They're all drunk," he told himself. "All but the Spanish," he amended, "and Jacob Leese."

"What's all the delay?" cried Ide impatiently.

Merritt raised his shaggy head from his arms to turn bloodshot eyes on the newcomer. Grigsby seemed to gather himself to a difficult focus. Semple fixed upon his colleague a gaze ponderous with intoxication.

But Ide did not await his slow reply. He snatched up the papers and held them toward the light. And at once his impatience subsided. He began to read their contents, aloud and with relish. These were matters after his own heart. Andy listened, at first with perplexity, then with growing amazement.

It was a noble document, with a formal acknowledgment by the Vallejos and Prudhon that they were prisoners, this acknowledgment in exchange for a writing to be signed by their captors that nobody would be hurt as long as he made no opposition. This was Article I. After reading it, Ide paused a moment for comment. None was spoken. Andy reflected that the fact was self-evident, and that opposition in the circumstances was impossible.

There were other articles duly numbered. The undersigned declared themselves to be members of "the republican party in California." They enumerated their grievances: their purposes: their intentions. All these were vague, high and noble; in the best Semple manner. They were comprehensive, and most solemn. The situation was fantastic enough, to be sure, but not wholly unsatisfactory. These elaborate and high-sounding articles of capitulation were absurd as applied to the surrender, to the raid, of a one-man garrison and these inoffensive private citizens. The tail was most vigorously wagging the dog. But it was a surrender. If the articles signified anything at all, they meant that Vallejo and his people were in no danger. Andy tried to catch the *hidalgo's* eye: but Don Guadalupe disdainfully refused to look in his direction.

The document was signed. The meeting arose, somewhat unsteadily, and all adjourned to the veranda.

But the waiting horsemen had sat too long unbreakfasted in the hot sun. They were in no humor for the elaborations of these stately politics. Ide attempted to read his document. They would not listen. They had, as far as they knew, come for one simple purpose, and they could see no sense in all this highfalutin nonsense.

"Let's git goin'!" they cried.

Get going at what?

"We come to git these people and take 'em back to Sacramento," stated someone decisively. "We got 'em; now let's take 'em back!"

Semple protested, waving his signed articles of capitulation, babbling that under their terms Vallejo had been assured of his personal liberty as long as he——

"To hell with that!" shouted Stowe roughly.

"But we've signed!" cried Semple.

"And who told you to sign?" demanded Stowe. "Ain't we got nothin' to say?"

The horsemen crowded close, growling approval.

"You tell 'em we want fresh horses, and we want 'em quick. And we want some grub. Whar's Knight? Knight, you tell 'em."

But Knight was in no condition to tell 'em. He was propped against a pillar of the veranda, smiling vaguely.

The party was in confusion. Men shouted. One, probably the same who had wanted to "divide up the spoils," suggested that a search of the house might produce something worth taking. This idea caught the fancy of some of the rougher element. Others expressed their disapproval of such riotous conduct. Quarrels broke out. Several shouted to Grigsby to settle matters.

"Yo're cap'n," they pointed out. "Take holt!"

"We've got to obey orders," replied Grigsby. "That's all there is to it."

That was common sense. What were the orders? They appealed to Merritt. Where were his orders? Let's see 'em.

Merritt exploded a bombshell. He had no orders.

At this statement a dead silence succeeded the turmoil.

"Ain't you got orders from Cap'n Frémont?" demanded Stowe incredulously at last.

"No," said Merritt.

"Who from, then?"

Nobody.

"Whose authority are we here on, anyway?"

Nobody's, it seemed.

"My God!" cried Grigsby. "Look here, you mean to say we haven't got Captain Frémont's name in black and white? Isn't there *anybody* here who has some sort of orders? Written or spoken?" he pleaded. "Haven't you, Stowe? Or you, Semple? Ide? *No* one?" He stared at them aghast. "I've been deceived!" he cried. "I resign! I back out of this scrape!" He looked about him. "I can git my family to the mountains as quick as ary—I resign! Hear me? I resign!"

For a moment panic seized them.

"We're going to have our throats cut, sure as shooting!" cried one. "Whar'll we find fresh horses?" urged another. "Damn if I'm going to stay here and guard ary prisoners!" shouted a third. "We're in for it: let's git!"

Andy leaned against the side of the house, surveying the confusion. He had attempted to draw near the group of Californians for a word aside, but desisted when he caught Merritt's bloodshot eyes fixed upon him. Merritt was drunk, but in possession of his faculties. The trapper too stood aloof, surveying coolly enough the course of events, unmoved by the excitement and indifferent to the re-proaches and questions hurled at him. He, of them all, would best bear watching.

Such of the party who had dismounted were again climbing into the saddle. It was every man for himself.

Suddenly Ide strode to the edge of the veranda and held up his hand. Andy looked at him with surprised respect, for the carpenter's awkward form was instinct with a dignity so authentic that it commanded instant attention. For the moment, Ide moved from the fantastic into a focus of reality. Its power was brief, but its genuineness lent him authority and a true eloquence.

"We need no horses; we want no horses!" he cried. "Sad-dle no horse for me! I will lay here my bones before I will take upon myself the ignominy of commencing an honorable work only to flee like a coward and a thief when no enemy is in sight. In vain you will say you had honorable motives. Who will believe? Choose ye! Choose ye this day what ye shall be! We are robbers, or *we must be conquerors!*"

He turned his back as though in despair. No other gesture could have been so effective.

"Ide! Ide!" they shouted.

The "revolution" had another leader.

THE panic was over; though no one knew what was to come next. Andy seized the moment of hesitation to slip to Vallejo's side. The *hidalgo* gazed at him with cold displeasure. Andy did not heed this.

"Feed them!" he murmured urgently. "Tell your people to get food to them, as quick as they can. If they ever moved fast in their lives, now's the time. And you'd better send them out something to drink right now." He remembered the little table in the *sala*. "That is, if you have anything left," he added dryly. He caught Don Guadalupe's hesitation. "I'm doing my best to help. Believe me, it will be best to do as I say."

Vallejo bowed in acknowledgment, issued his orders to Prudhon, who turned away to execute them; only to be halted by Merritt. Andy had sensed the lessening of the man's authority; now at last he saw his opportunity.

"Señor Vallejo is sendin' this man to get food and drink for us all," he said disdainfully to Merritt; but loud enough for many of those nearest to hear. "If you want to be fed, you'd better let him go."

Merritt still looked obstinate; but the raiders most emphatically wanted to be fed. Merritt's influence was on the wane. He yielded grudgingly: but, with the tenacity of his type, he insisted on accompanying, guarding, the secretary on his errand. This suited Andy. He turned swiftly to Ide, who was still standing at the veranda's edge, blissfully surveying his army.

"Señor Vallejo wants to see his family. They must be

purty skeered," said Andy in his broadest trapper's dialect. "That all right? I'll go along and guard him."

Ide nodded absently. He only half heard.

"Come along—quick! Get out of sight," Andy urged the Vallejos and Leese toward the door.

They slipped into the *casa;* up the stairs. The women of the household rushed upon them with lamentations and questions; all but Doña Francisca and Doña Rosalía, who held themselves with dignity as beseemed *la nobleza,* but whose fine eyes betrayed the keenness of their anxiety.

"All is well," Don Guadalupe hastened to assure them. "You are safe. These are not bandits who seek plunder. War has come, as we have feared, and these are soldiers of the *capitán* Frémont who have taken possession. All is in order. Papers have been signed. There is nothing to fear."

"What is to become of us?" asked Doña Francisca calmly.

"That I do not know as yet. Perhaps Señor Burnett, who has so kindly arranged the privilege of this interview, may be able to enlighten us." Vallejo spoke measuredly, without looking toward Andy. But Andy had no time for formalities or misunderstandings, nor the stately Californian indirections.

"Listen, Don Guadalupe," he said rapidly. "There is no war yet, as far as I know. This may be the beginning of war, but there is no war. These are not Captain Frémont's men. Captain Frémont has nothing to do with this— officially."

Vallejo turned to him keenly enough at this. His mind was as direct as Andy's in a real emergency.

"Then this *is* a raid?" he cried.

"They call it a revolution," said Andy. In swift short sentences he tried to convey the situation as he saw it. But with only partial success. It was difficult to make them understand; nor did he feel there would be time to enter into full explanations. He could see that Vallejo was aghast at discovering that he dealt, not with a responsible officer of the United States government, but with an uprising of the "white Indians" he had long despised and secretly distrusted. The women clustered, with little subdued outcries, close to the two gentlewomen. Jacob Leese sat very still, waiting, saying nothing.

"We'll all have our throats cut," predicted Salvador gloomily. He was thinking of Ezekiel Merritt.

Andy tried to reassure them. Articles had been signed; an oath had been sworn. He attempted to impress them with some idea of the sincerity, the underlying idealism he felt beneath this movement: but that, too, was difficult, for he did not clearly understand it himself. The settlers were a wild-looking lot, their type beyond the Californian's comprehension.

The door was snatched open. It framed the uncouth figure of Ezekiel Merritt.

"Yere you be!" growled the trapper roughly. He cast a menacing eye at Andy. "Git you aready. You travel."

"What's this?" demanded Andy.

"Nothing that consarns you," retorted Merritt. "It's not yore business." He turned his shoulder on Andy, deliberately excluding him.

But Andy thrust himself forward.

"I'm making this my business," he stated. "You're dealing with me. Understand that. Merritt," he said slowly with deadly emphasis, "I think some day I'm going to have to kill you. If it wa'n't for these women I'd as lieve do it right now. You git out; and you stay out. When we git us aready, we'll come downstairs. Not before."

Merritt was unarmed, except for his knife. He eyed the Boone gun. Andy meant business.

"I'll be back," he threatened. His small eyes blazed.

Only Vallejo and Leese understood the words; but all

could grasp the purport of the action. They looked toward Andy with new eyes.

"What are you doing in this, Burnett?" asked Leese bluntly. "Are you a friend or an enemy?"

"Of course I'm a friend," retorted Andy impatiently. "I'm trying to do the best I can to help. It's a bad mess. They'll be back."

"Where do they take us?" asked Vallejo.

"How should I know?"

The door opened again, this time to disclose not only Merritt, who had now recovered his rifle, but also John Grigsby and two others. Andy was relieved to see that Grigsby had recovered somewhat. Food had steadied him.

"What's all this?" demanded Grigsby. "What's the matter, Burnett? Are you takin' these people's side? Resistance is useless."

"There is no resistance," returned Andy promptly. "I'm telling these people it is useless. I'm just trying to see they get a square deal. This man comes up here scaring these women to death and refusing to tell us what it is all about. They have a right to know."

"Sure; that's fair," acknowledged Grigsby. "Well, we've talked it over, and there's no manner of doubt that Captain Frémont wants us to take these people to his camp. So we're going to do it, that's all."

"Who—the women too?" asked Andy.

"No, no, no!" Grigsby was impatient. "We don't aim to bother women—or anybody else as long as they behave and don't make trouble." He glanced towards the stately figures of Doña Francisca and Doña Rosalía, and belatedly took off his hat. "You tell 'em they'll be all right," he said. "Just sit quiet. And there ain't no harm coming to anybody. But these men have got to come along with us."

"How about those papers you all signed?" suggested Andy.

Grigsby shrugged them aside impatiently.

"I got fooled into this thing," he stated emphatically, "and I'm going to know where I stand. Or get out. And the only way to do that is to go find out."

"Who are you taking, then?" asked Andy after a moment.

"Just the Don, here; and his brother; and this other feller," indicating Prudhon.

"How about me?" asked Leese.

"You ain't included," spoke up Merritt bluntly.

But Grigsby interposed.

"You're not a prisoner," he decided, "but you can go along if you want to."

Andy glanced toward Merritt.

"Who's taking them?" he wanted to know.

"I am," said Grigsby.

"Who else?"

"I git your idea. I'll handle this. There'll be no trouble."

"I'll shoot any damn yaller-belly that tries to git away!" blustered Merritt, and spat a stream of tobacco juice on the polished floor.

"This is a violation of faith!" cried Vallejo indignantly.

"If you're thinking of those papers, Don Guadalupe," said Andy to him with a rueful grin, "looks to me as though you'd wasted a lot of good drinks."

"Talk United States," growled Merritt. He was as surly as a bear.

"There is nothing for it, Don Guadalupe," said Andy, paying no attention to this. "You must go. I would advise no attempts at escape. On account of the people here. I think you are safe enough." He pondered a moment, insensible to Merritt's impatience. "I might go with you," he submitted, "but with your permission I think perhaps it would be better if I stayed here to keep your people quiet and to do what I can for your family and your property."

"For that I shall always hold you in my heart, Don Andrés!" cried Vallejo earnestly.

Andy warmed with the first satisfaction he had experienced in all this sorry affair. Don Andrés! The familiar address of trust!

2

After the departure of the prisoners with their guard, Andy roamed about the *pueblo* reviewing the situation, reassuring the people, advising them as to their conduct. They knew him, from his former visit, and trusted his advice. Solano, the headman, nodded comprehension.

"And if anything happens, do not resist," concluded Andy. "Come to me, and I will see what I can do. Tell everybody what I say; everybody. One man could make a lot of trouble. By the way," said Andy, in a natural transition of thought, "what's become of Pepe? I don't see him about."

"Pepe is no longer one of ours, *señor*," replied Solano. "He has gone to Monterey. A good riddance. He can play his guitar and entertain the drunkards in the *pulquerías*."

Monterey! Wapita! Entertainer! Here was a coincidence that would bear examination! But Andy's mind was too full of the immediate to be concerned with that now. It was time, now that he had reassured himself as to the native population, to examine the conduct and intentions of the "conquerors." He bent his steps toward the plaza where the raiding party still lingered. For a while he stood a little apart from the main group, trying to get the hang of events.

It was not surprising that he found this difficult. Everything seemed to be hind-end-to. The first things to do in such a situation—whether you called it a raid or a revolution—it seemed to Andy, would be to see about shelter and food and water; to make fortifications for defense or provision for retreat, as the case might be; to search out arms, and see to it that the natives of the place were not preparing reprisals; in short, to organize. Nobody was doing any of these things. The entire personnel of the expedition was gathered in a compact group absorbedly manufacturing a flag!

Andy joined the outer fringe. It was immediately apparent to him that the task was monumental, for the reason that no one knew how a flag should be made. But there was plenty of good will. Somebody had found a length of stout, unbleached cotton cloth. Somebody else had begged, borrowed, or stolen sewing materials, a bottle of red ink, and a pot of red paint. So far, so good. But what was the flag to be? And who was to make it?

"Bill Todd here used to be a house painter," suggested a voice.

Todd, slightly reluctant, was thrust forward.

"All right, boys," he agreed. "I'll do the best I can. What'll she be?"

With the example of Texas in the immediate past, a lone star was obvious. Todd, breathing heavily, carefully outlined one in ink, five-pointed as the easiest to draw, in the upper left-hand corner. Then he proceeded to fill it in with the red paint, muttering to himself disparagements as to the size of the brush and the tendency of the paint to "run." What next? Someone in the background had a happy inspiration.

"What's the matter with a b'ar?"

That was a good idea. Everybody, even the most recent arrival, was familiar with the huge California grizzly, admired his size, feared his ferocity. He was a noble animal, a fighter, a fit emblem. Todd doubted whether he could draw a good bear; but he could try. He inked in an outline of an animal on all fours facing the star, and filled it in with the red paint.

"Looks to me more like a pig," said someone doubtfully.

But the enthusiasm of creation submerged criticism. Of course it was a bear: anybody could see that!

Todd had done pretty well up to now. But in fulfilling the next part of his task he made a bad blunder. It had been determined that the words "California Republic" should be lettered in below the bear. When he had finished it was discovered that he had omitted the "i" in "Republic." Todd was abashed and humiliated. The company wrangled disgustedly whether to begin all over again or let it stand. Finally, as a compromise, Todd inserted the missing "i" above the "c." It would do; but there was a distinct lowering of enthusiasm. The majority were inclined to let the thing stand as it was. Others seemed to think there was something lacking. Needed a border, one man said; and backed his opinion by stripping off his red flannel shirt.

"She'll look fine, sewed on all around the edge!" he contended.

"Wall," said Todd definitely, "I ain't going to tackle no sewing job. I'm through!"

"I'll do it," offered the owner of the flannel shirt.

Andy watched with a growing feeling that he was asleep, in a dream. These were sane, practical, hardheaded men, of little imagination, and with the sufficiency of humor typical—and necessary—to their kind. They had to be in order to be in this country at all. Yet here they were, having got themselves into what was probably a serious mess, playing away like a parcel of small boys. It was of a piece with all the rest of it. There was a sort of madness in the air. Andy could not rid himself of the feeling that he must hold onto himself with both hands to keep from being sucked into its influence. Things were not real.

The first fine creative fervor of the occasion was lagging. The volunteer was slow with his sewing. He had accomplished only the lower strip of the border.

"Aw, she's good enough. Call the Cap n,' urged impatience.

For the first time Andy noticed Ide's absence. The Cap'n? He was inside, writin' out the Constitution—the Constitution of the Republic. It was amazing. Andy looked about him, almost distrusting his own senses. For an instant, so strong was the contagion, his judgment nearly wavered to see this thing as Ide saw it, magnified until it marched with the stately trend of history. But his common sense steadied to the solid facts. He clung to them: repeated them to himself until his vision cleared from its momentary dizziness. Here were less than two score men on an adventure no one appeared clearly to understand. This tiny and unsupported force had made an unwarranted raid on the private possessions and person of an outlying *ranchero*. That was all there was to it. Andy took a deep breath.

Ide appeared. All adjourned to the flagpole in the plaza, where they hoisted the bear flag aloft and cheered. Ide, very busy and abstracted, hurried back into the house. It was by now mid-afternoon.

3

In the absence of the fantastic commander a young fellow by the name of Ford began to do, somev.hat belatedly it seemed to Andy, a few of the sensible and obvious things. Lodgings were assigned; the horses were cared for; food supplies were searched out and distributed; tools were found and utilized in the beginnings of rough fortifications. To Andy's relief these things were done in an orderly and sober manner. It became evident there was to be no looting. For whatever was taken Ford gave written promises of payment by the new "republic." The Californians brought some of them to Andy, asking what they were; and when he tried to explain to them, inquired very sensibly with what payment was to be made, since obviously these people had no money or property. He secretly agreed with their doubts on this point, and could offer them no satisfaction. In that, however, he did not reckon with Ide's schoolmaster knowledge—or ingenuity. No private property was taken without one of these promises to pay in return. But in Vallejo's warehouses remained a quantity of old arms and supplies, mementos of the period when Sonoma had been a military post. These Ide solemnly declared to be public property, belonging to the "republic," taken as spoils of war, to be, as he expressed it, "held in trust for the public benefit." This public property guaranteed the scrip issued in exchange for the private property looted from the inhabitants and from Vallejo's stores. It was an admirable arrangement, just like a great big grown-up government, and it enabled the "purchase," with a clear conscience, of all sorts of things on the grand scale: ten thousand pounds of flour, barrels of salt, a formal contract for beef. The army of two dozen did not intend to stint. The distinction, however, was not entirely clear to the Californians. Nor was the "public property" back of the scrip much of a guarantee. It made quite a collection, such as it was: a number of old brass cannon, some muskets, shot and ball, lead and copper; a variety of such things. They were not of great immediate utility, due simply to an unfortunate lack of gunpowder, but they made a brave show; especially the brass cannon.

Ford's next action Andy did not like, though he admitted to himself its theoretical soundness. All the male inhabitants of the place were rounded up and confined in one of the larger buildings. Andy ventured to expostulate.

"They're peaceable," said he. "I'd be willing to guarantee they'll make no trouble. It's a hardship."

"Maybe not," returned Ford. "But I don't want none of them spying and carrying news."

"If any of them wanted to get away for that, they'd have gone long ago," Andy pointed out.

But Ford was obdurate.

"Well, I'm going to keep 'em locked up till the Cap'n says different," said he.

Andy tried to reassure the prisoners. The Californians had made no objections: offered no resistance. They herded together impassively, wondering what next, resigned in the fundamental fatalism of their race. Toward midnight Andy was able to advise Doña Francisca that all was well, and himself to turn in satisfied that there was to be no disorder, for the present, at least. The *pueblo* was dark, save for the lighted windows of the *sala*, where Ide devotedly toiled at his pen, building the vast and reechoing—and almost empty—halls of government, as he understood it. He divided the force into two equal parts. One of these he named the First Artillery; the other the First Rifles. To each he assigned officers; which did not leave too many privates, but it all looked well on paper. At the top he wrote his own name; and opposite it the words "Commander in Chief": and opposite them the "four departments of government," which, as a matter of expediency he assembled in his own person. He surveyed this framework with satisfaction; laid it aside, drew to him a fresh sheet of paper.

For some moments he sat, lost in thought, then leaned forward and again began to write. Before him burned a single light. It threw into relief the harsh features of his face, the growing welter of papers at his elbow. It gleamed on the polished surface of the table. It cast fantastic shadows across the dimness of the wall.

The hours passed. The stars moved across the skies. Still Ide wrote on and on. There was so much to do. He could not rest.

The proclamation was finished. It stated grievances— from which as yet no one had actually suffered; it pledged amnesty to all Californians who would lay down their arms; it invited all good citizens to resort to his camp without delay to assist in the establishment of a free government against tyranny. It purported to address all California; to be issued by the Commander in Chief of the forces assembled at the Fortress of Sonoma.

No government should be without one treaty. So Ide drew one as between the new government and "whom it might concern," guaranteeing no division of public property; free commerce; no imports; no salaries for public officials; no involuntary taxation except for the punishment of crime; no compulsory military service.

Finally he inscribed a letter to Commodore Stockton, whom he supposed to be in San Francisco Bay. It informed that officer—and through him the government of the United States, and the "world in general so far as it was interested"—that a new nation had been born.

The dawn was by now faintly graying the windows. Ide sat back with a sigh. The edifice of government was finished, complete to the last detail. Ide's spirit was freed for the moment from its labors, to wander exultantly in the grandiose corridors of its construction. To him its structure was solid with reality; for the carpenter was typically American in his belief that putting a thing down on paper accomplishes it. What matter that the twenty-six men sleeping outside comprised the entire population of this new republic? What matter that the clear and testing day was even now graying the eastern hills? What matter that its light must disclose again the inexorable realities, must dissolve into their component shadows the substance of his dream? This one brief hour, between night and dawn, was wholly his. It was ridiculous: it was pathetic: it was magnificent.

CHAPTER XXI

IT IS uncertain whether Ide slept at all that first night. At any rate he was early about: for Andy was summoned soon after he himself had arisen. Thus he came to knowledge of Ide's documents; for he found himself called upon to translate them into Spanish. This he did, after a fashion, with Ide hovering impatiently at his elbow. Andy was no expert with the written word, especially with this kind of written word. He did his best. When he had finished, Ide snatched the sheets and rushed to the calaboose where were herded all the male inhabitants. To them he declaimed the gist of his sentiments in what he took to be Spanish. The soft-eyed Californians listened in bewilderment; which was deepened when, at the conclusion of the address and without apparent reason, the doors were opened and they were turned loose.

But Ide had no doubts of the success of his harangue. He rushed up to seize Andy's hand, babbling enthusiastically.

"Did you note the glow of feeling in their eyes when I pronounced the great name of Washington?" he cried. "When the day of battle comes we shall enroll them in our ranks as friends!"

He dove into the house. For the most of two days he was lost to view, unless one took the pains to enter the *sala*. There he was to be seen, scribbling away industriously, tracing copy after copy of the proclamation, purposed eventually to be published the length and breadth of the Californias. This seemed to him the only important thing to do.

2

This complete absorption had one salutary effect. The heady influence of his oratory withdrawn, the citizens of the new republic began to stir dazedly back to normal, as though emerging from anæsthesia. They began to talk things over. Andy was able to get in a word of common sense occasionally; and they listened to him gravely, and weighed his words, though obviously they were not inclined to believe all he said. This was largely because they were afraid to. The bald facts of the situation were plain enough. They had, a few dozen men, seized Sonoma, made prisoner three prominent Californians, and hoisted a flag. If they were not to be backed up in this performance, then, quite simply they were in one hell of a mess. They could not afford to think they were not going to be backed up; that was all there was to it. They reiterated to one another stoutly, with complete outward assurance, but with secret misgivings, what they would like to believe. They put defiant questions to Andy, thus bolstering their confidence.

Frémont *must* have planned this; he *must* be acting on secret orders brought him by Gillespie; he *must* be biding the proper time to act. How else explain all that had happened? How else did it all make sense?

Ide *must* know what he was about. He'd sent Bill Todd off with a letter addressed to Commodore Stockton, or some naval officer or other, in the Bay. What could that mean, except that the commodore too was waiting for word to act?

They pressed Andy for answers to these questions, daring him to deny their hopes. He shook his head noncommittally; refused to encourage them. He said nothing of the proclamation, which Ide had not yet divulged to them. Andy kept his own counsel. He could not himself guess how this was to turn out. He did not want to stir things. He was satisfied that these men were orderly. That must do for now. He considered the advisability of sending a message to Larkin, but gave up the idea. Whom could he send? What could he say—yet? Better wait, with the rest, and see.

It was an uneasy situation. There was nothing to be done. Just wait. Something must happen soon. The news would reach the Californians. There must be some sort of word from Frémont, once the prisoners were delivered into his hands. Bill Todd should be back within a day or two at most with a message or support from the navy authorities.

"We got the b'ar by the tail," said Hal Stowe gloomily. "Just got to hang on and see."

But Ide's stock was going down; and some of the more outspoken cursed themselves openly for getting into this thing, and began to figure on flight to Oregon or over the range.

In the meantime, and since there was nothing else to do, "Lieutenant Ford" organized his little force. He did a pretty good job, for an amateur, with the materials at hand. Day and night watches were appointed. Half the men were on duty at a time, while the other half slept. The seized muskets were cleaned and put in some sort of order. Fatigue parties cut and brought in wood and provisions, cooked and cleaned. Ford himself reconnoitered the country adjacent, spotted the elevations from which Castro's mythical force might plant his mythical cannon, assured himself that no enemy or spy was in the offing. He despatched Cowie and Fowler to Bouile's ranch on the Russian River to obtain a supply of powder. There was not much else to be done; but at least his activities kept them all busy; and so, to a certain extent, took their minds off their predicament.

No word came from Frémont, but toward evening of the fourth day Bill Todd returned. He was accompanied

by a young naval officer, at the sight of whom the men's
spirits rose. The officer looked about him curiously,
glanced aloft at the Bear Flag. He returned no greetings,
made no comment, and his face showed no trace of
expression. He sat his horse while Todd ascertained
Ide's whereabouts; then dismounted and accompanied
his guide into the house. Andy followed. At the door
the officer, becoming aware of that fact, turned to face
him.

"Are you William Ide?" he demanded.

"No," said Andy.

"My business is with William Ide," stated the officer
uncompromisingly.

"I represent the Vallejos," said Andy.

The officer hesitated, turned away. As he made no
further formal objections, Andy slipped into the *sala*.

Ide looked up from his papers; sprang to his feet.

"You are welcome, sir!" he cried effusively.

"Lieutenant John Misroon of the United States sloop
of War *Portsmouth*, Captain John B. Montgomery commanding," he introduced himself with cold formality.

"I certainly am glad to see you, Lieutenant!" Ide was
beaming.

Misroon bowed.

"You are William Ide?" he inquired.

"That's me!"

"Captain Montgomery wishes me to acknowledge your
communication. He instructs me to say that, as an officer
of a government at peace with Mexico, to interfere in any
way with any revolution going on in any country in which
he might be present would justly subject that government
to a charge of dishonorable dealing and himself to dismissal from the service. Therefore it will be impossible for
him to recognize any insurgent party or to render assistance as requested even to the extent of a single charge of
powder. These opinions are fully expressed, sir, in this

letter, which I am further instructed to deliver into your hands."

"But, Lieutenant," protested Ide earnestly, recovering from his dismay, "the captain has mistaken my request. I did not intimate that we asked for or desired assistance. I wrote him so that, in due season, he might notify the government of the United States that we claim the right of self-government as a sister republic. My letter was simply a notice, recording our establishment, notifying our seizure and possessions, lest the well-known desire on the part of the United States government to possess itself of the country should tempt its officers to commit an unwarrantable and inglorious interference in our affairs."

Misroon stared at him.

"Really," he said dryly. "Well, I know nothing of that. I fulfill my instructions. May I ask, sir, what other steps you have taken along these lines?"

"Our position is fully stated in our proclamation, shortly to be issued."

"May I see a copy?"

"We have no clerks, sir, to perform our writing," returned Ide, "but I shall myself prepare one for your use. You shall have it in the morning. Undoubtedly"—Ide became eager with an idea—"undoubtedly your ship's clerk could copy and circulate it for us?"

"Undoubtedly," agreed Misroon with an irony lost on Ide,"—if Captain Montgomery saw fit to order it."

He took his leave formally; but as he turned to quit the room his eye caught Andy's. He hesitated.

"Will you accompany me, sir?" he then invited.

Misroon did not again open his lips, nor indeed even look at Andy until the two had walked down the outside corridor beyond earshot.

"Would you kindly give me your name and station and what is your exact status in this place?" then demanded the lieutenant briskly, and with authority.

Andy flushed. He was not accustomed to this voice or manner. He looked more intently into the officer's face. The boy was young enough to be his own son. His vexation died. "I reckon that's just another kind of foofaraw," he reflected. Looked like a nice boy.

"My name is Burnett," he replied equably. "Andrew Burnett. As for my station, if you mean what do I do, I'm a *ranchero* from over Soledad way. I told you I was looking after the Vallejos here—as many of 'em as are left."

Misroon's manner underwent a slight change.

"Are you the man who is Thomas Larkin's confidential agent?" he inquired swiftly.

"Come to think of it, I *am* Larkin's agent," assented Andy, "and I *did* have an idea it was confidential."

For the first time Misroon's face broke from its correct severity to a smile.

"Don't worry. It's still confidential. Of course we officers know—but no one else, as far as we are concerned. I want to talk to you. Isn't there some place we can go and sit down? And incidentally get a bite to eat? I'm starved."

"I reckon the cares of state set too heavy for Ide to think of little things like that," said Andy. "You come with me."

3

They sat together in an inner room, and the servants of the Vallejos brought food and wine. Lieutenant Misroon had definitely laid aside his formal attitude, became a human likable young man; but withal, as Andy soon discovered, a shrewd though perplexed observer. He confessed freely that his real mission was not so much the delivery of Montgomery's reply as the finding out, at first hand, if he could, what it was all about.

"Is the man crazy?" he asked concerning Ide. "Are they all crazy? What do you make of it, anyway?"

He listened to Andy's account of events with the

closest attention; but shook his head doubtfully over Frémont's supposed connection with these affairs.

"That is not reasonable," said he. "We would surely have heard something of it. Our advices are later than his departure from the East. Why, less than a couple of weeks ago Lieutenant Gillespie visited us and got supplies from the ship for Frémont's return journey overland. By way of the Río Colorado, he said. We gave him some letters to take back. It's nonsense. These people are deceiving themselves."

"Probably. But that's what they think; and you can't make them believe different," said Andy.

"It is nonsense," repeated Misroon. "I happen to know that Captain Montgomery has just written General Castro that Frémont's mission is purely scientific and that it is in no manner whatever, either by government authority or otherwise, connected with any political movements of these people. It is unfortunate, most unfortunate, that Frémont has not yet begun his journey. He should issue a formal disavowal.—Good Lord!" cried Misroon. "You don't for a moment suppose there is anything in it? What a position we would be in! Nobody in the world would believe us sincere!"

"I don't know," said Andy.

But Misroon's momentary alarm passed.

"It can't be," said he. "But tell me: is it possible that all the rest of these men are as mad as their leader?"

"It seems to me they're beginning to wake up a little."

"I think I'd better talk to them," Misroon arose. "Will you come with me?"

"Better not. I'm not one of the elect."

"I understand. I congratulate you. If you will show me where I am to sleep, I'll not trouble you further tonight. But I'd like to see you in the morning for a moment. Early. I must get back to the ship. Sun-up too early?"

"Sun-up is late for a *ranchero*," said Andy.

4

The morning discovered Misroon in better spirits. As the two broke their fast, by the light of candles, the lieutenant expressed to Andy his relief.

"You're right. They are waking up," he told the *ranchero*. "And beginning to get a little scared. They're beginning to wonder how they got into this thing. Tell me, is this man Ide a Mormon?"

"Not that I know of," said Andy.

"Well, a lot of them say he is, though no one will speak up in meeting. I had to talk to them one at a time. There's a sort of an idea that the whole thing is a scheme to turn the country over to the Mormons. They tell me there's ten thousand of them getting ready to come West. What do you think of that?"

"Sounds pretty wild to me."

"To me, too. But a lot of them believe it. They'd like to pull out, if they could; but they don't dare. They are all equally involved. But they don't want to get in any deeper. One thing, they don't want any proclamations. They don't want to stir things up any more than they have, wave any red flags at the bull. They are angry that Ide turned loose the natives here. I don't know how they expect to keep this thing dark; but that is their present attitude. They seem to me, on the whole, a sensible enough lot of men. I can't imagine how they got into this thing in the first place. I can't help but feel sorry for the poor devils. They have a pathetic sort of confidence that the United States officers are going to protect them somehow."

"What did you tell them?"

"I could not tell them anything without orders," said Misroon. "I have no authority one way or another. I am talking to you now in confidence. The best I could do was to hint at results."

He arose from the table.

"Let us interview the chief," he suggested.

They walked together down the corridor. Misroon shook his head sadly.

"I am sorry for these people," he repeated, "desperately sorry."

As they reëntered the *sala* where Ide awaited them eagerly, his manner reverted to its cold formality.

"Good-morning, sir," he greeted Ide. "I have been talking with your men. I agree with them that it would be most unwise to issue any proclamation at this time. Such a procedure would result in your indiscriminate destruction. It's a bad enough business as it is. Something might be done, individually, to relieve this situation. What, I do not know. Rest assured we shall try to do what we can, within our proper powers."

"The proclamation is already published, sir," returned Ide. "And as you say the men of the garrison so seriously disapprove, it is very proper that they should know what it is. Will you be so kind as to take it up to the garrison and read it to them?"

Misroon stared at the carpenter incredulously. He reached his hand for the copy of the proclamation. This he proceeded to read carefully. As he read, his face cleared. Ide, watching closely, drew a deep breath of relief at what he thought a sign of approval.

"You say this has already been published without the knowledge of the men?" the naval officer demanded.

"The full authority of all four departments of government has been confided to me," said Ide. "And I have used my discretion. In the rush of pressing business I have had no opportunity to consult others. But undoubtedly the men should know its contents——"

"I should think so," Misroon interrupted crisply. "Call them together. At once!"

He continued to stare at the document for several seconds after Ide had left the room.

"Are you familiar with this thing?" he asked Andy.

"I translated it into Spanish."

"Of all the highfalutin idiotic nonsense I ever laid my eyes to—— It is high time these men knew the quality of their leader; and I'm going to show it to them."

"What do you aim to do?" asked Andy.

"I can't give them any direct advice as to their policies: I have no orders," repeated Misroon. "But I *can* read them this precious proclamation, and let them see what manner of insanity they are following before it goes any further."

5

When destiny has a certain end in view, she twists the most obvious out of their sequences in order to bring about her purpose. It seemed to Misroon—as, indeed, it seemed to Andy—that the mere reading of the proclamation should be sufficient. It was, in his mind, as though he continued the conversation of the evening before; as though he said, in substance:

"Here; you agreed heartily enough that you did not want *any* proclamations. Well, one has been issued, without your knowledge or consent. Here it is. Listen to it. See what you are supposed to have endorsed!"

After which, he was fully confident, he could leave matters to their own common sense. It never crossed his mind that anyone but Ide—or perchance the Spanish—could take such a document seriously. Lieutenant Misroon had never seen a tail wag a dog; nor did he credit its possibility. It certainly never occurred to him that his personal reading of the document could be taken by these men as an official endorsement by the navy of the United States. But that is exactly what happened. A word of concluding

comment would have clarified his meaning. His rigid sense
of duty did not permit him to utter it; nor, indeed, did
he dream it could be necessary. He rode away, bearing his
copy of the proclamation for the edification of his superior,
satisfied that for the moment he had done all he could.

ANDY was too wise to attempt to set right this impression of official endorsement. No one would want to believe him; so, naturally, he would not be believed. The result would be distrust; a lowering or wiping out of any influence he now possessed. At any rate, it would make little difference. Misroon's visit had enabled Andy to see this whole thing in perspective for what it was: a small local disturbance, unsupported, which could not possibly last long. His preoccupation was to minimize its damage while it did last. He had not much anxiety, now, as to the behavior of these most exemplary and worthy revolutionists. But he wanted mightily to hear from the direction of the Sacramento, if only to allay the natural anxieties of the Vallejo women. No direct word came of the prisoners: no more of Frémont or the other settlers in the Valley. Such news was overdue. Its lack caused everybody great uneasiness. If nothing was heard within two days more, then a messenger must be sent.

But Andy had tidings that very evening. Solano signaled him, drew him aside.

"The man has returned," he whispered.

"What man?"

"The one of ours—whom I sent when the *patrón* was taken away—to learn what happens."

Andy looked at Solano with admiration. He had not thought of that obvious expedient; and his whole training was to think of expedients. Solano led him to where waited the spy—for that, Andy reflected, was actually his status; with attaching penalties. The man was one of the *ha-*

cienda's Indians; but of the more intelligent class, trained under Solano, able not only to make his way about unobserved, but to use his eyes and ears, and to report what he saw. Andy listened to him attentively.

The guards and their prisoners had journeyed to the American River without haste and without incident. They had stopped over night at Vaca's *rancho*. Vaca had quickly arranged for a rescue; and began at once, secretly, to gather many people. The rescue would have been very easy, for the *americanos* set no guard at all. Indeed, a rescue would not have been necessary, for at any moment Vallejo and his companions could have walked out and mounted their horses and ridden away, and no one the wiser. But Don Guadalupe had told Señor Vaca he would have nothing to do with it.

"This I leaned from Señor Vaca," explained the Indian, Tomás.

They came to Frémont's camp only after some search, for its location had been changed. At first he declined to receive the prisoners; even to see them. His men held the party at a distance. Then he changed his mind.

"His manner was cold and distant, *señor*. He would talk but briefly. It was as though each instant he would retire into his tent."

"How know you this?" asked Andy.

"I lay near. I know well that place where the camp was made," said Tomás simply.

Andy looked at him with new respect. The skill and resource implied in this bit of scouting he could appreciate.

At this Jacob Leese had become very angry. He had demanded to know on whose authority, if not Frémont's, the party was held.

"Then," said Tomás, "the *capitán* Frémont called Señor Leese a bad man, and ordered that he too should be arrested as a prisoner, and that all four should be taken to the *portaleza* of Señor Sutter and locked up. I did not understand their English, *señor*," he added in explanation, "but always I took pains to learn afterwards, when I could, what had been said."

"You are a *sabe hombre*, Tomás," approved Andy.

So they had marched on to Sutter's Fort; and Sutter, apparently much surprised, had received them as guests.

"But that same day," said Tomás, "the *capitán* Frémont sent word at once that if Señor Sutter did not learn how to treat prisoners, he would have the *señor* Sutter himself arrested and hanged."

"What said Señor Sutter to this?" asked Andy.

"I think Señor Sutter was afraid," replied Tomás, "for men came with the message to see these orders carried out; and so Don Guadalupe and these others were locked in a room and kept there. It was not fitting that an *hidalgo* like Don Guadalupe should be thus confined without comfort, *señor*. Even some of the *americanos* were angry at this. One Señor Moore spoke freely and was placed in a dungeon beneath a bastion. Then the *capitán* Frémont came to the Fort. Señor Sutter objected again. Again I was present."

"How did you manage that?" asked Andy curiously. "That would not be easy."

"It was simple," disclaimed Tomás. "I know well the *capataz*, who gave me service in the house. At first the *señor* Sutter was angry; and said that he was surprised the *capitán* approved the rebellion. That was brave of Señor Sutter, I think, for the *capitán* had said he would hang him."

"Did he say so again?" asked Andy.

"No, *señor*. What he said—and he said it not angrily, but cold as winter rain—was that he considered Señor Sutter as a Mexican, and if Señor Sutter did not like what he was doing, he, the *capitán* Frémont, would set him across the river and he could go join the Mexicans. But he did not set Señor Sutter across the river."

"You have done well, Tomás. And is there more?"

"Nothing, *señor*. So matters rest. Don Guadalupe is safe, but is locked in a room. The *capitán* is at the Fort. I thought it time to return and tell of these things."

"You have done well—very well," repeated Andy. "And now I think it best that you say nothing of all this —except that Don Guadalupe is safe."

"*Sí, señor*," assented both the Indians. They looked at one another.

"What is it?" Andy asked.

"Why, *señor*," submitted Solano, "how is it that, after the *capitán* says he has nothing to do with all this, he goes to the Fort and delivers orders as though he commanded?"

"I don't know," said Andy. This fellow is pretty cute, he thought; he can see a hole in a millstone. And Tomás: that fellow's got a head on him, too. Doggone if I thought these California Injuns had it in them!

He followed his own advice. To the women, waiting anxiously for news, he merely said that Vallejo and his companions were at the Fort, and safe. He added that they were under the personal care of Sutter.

2

In the meantime something had happened. Cowie and Fowler, who had been sent to the Russian River in search of gunpowder, were long overdue. Bill Todd and another, an Englishman, set out to hunt them up. They, likewise, failed to return.

This was alarming. Ford dispatched a third expedition under Sam Gibson, seasoned trappers who could take care of themselves. They rode directly to Bouile's ranch without incident. Bouile was glad to see them; supplied them with the powder. But he had seen nothing of the other four men.

Considerably perturbed, they started back at once for
Sonoma. But now they were suddenly attacked by a
small body of horsemen. The trappers, accustomed to
Indian warfare, had no difficulty in beating off the inexperienced Californians, killing one and capturing another
whose horse they shot under him. They returned to
Sonoma with their prisoner.

The latter narrowly escaped immediate hanging. Finally
he was allowed to speak. He had not seen any of the missing men, he assured them earnestly: nor had any of his
comrades in the engagement. They were all small *rancheros*, of the neighborhood, who had felt impelled to take
the field to do what little they could in what they conceived to be their own defense. That was only reasonable.
Men of spirit do not sit idly by without raising a hand to
protect their property and their families, he pleaded. But,
he added, he had heard of these others: it was known.
And, he stated emphatically, that was not the work of the
californios, but of bandits, *ladrones*, against whom was
the hand of every true man, be he *californio* or *americano*.
They watched him impassively, from beneath lowered
brows.

"What's become of them?" growled Stowe at last.

"The first two are dead. The other two are prisoner,"
said the captive.

Cowie and Fowler had been taken, he told them simply,
by a party of well-known outlaws under the leadership
of one Juan Padilla. They had been tied to a tree. While
deliberations were forward as to what was to be done
with them, a desperado known as Three-fingered Jack had
slipped away and had knifed them.

"How do you know all that?" demanded Stowe.

"All the country knows it." The man spread his hands.
Todd and his companion?

They, also, Padilla and his men had caught. But, added
the Californian, it was understood that these were still

alive and unharmed. He did not know what was to be
done with them. Murdered undoubtedly; or perhaps held
for ransom.

It seemed to Andy that the man was frank and honest
enough. He even offered, as a guarantee of good faith, to
go along with a rescue party. He knew the country, said
he; and where these *ladrones* were supposed to frequent.
After some discussion Ford and Gibson accepted this
offer, with a warning. They were busily selecting the personnel of the expedition; which must, of course, start as
soon as possible. There was a good deal of excitement
augmented by relief that something was happening. Even
those to be left behind shared in this relief. They had something immediate and definite to occupy their minds. So
they squeezed all the drama out of it they could.

Ford designated Andy as one of the rescue party. The
latter was pleased at this evidence of confidence. Nor was
the chance for a little action of the sort he knew and
enjoyed unwelcome: he had no objection to fighting bandits at any time, or of any race. But he begged off. He
wished no identification with the arms of these people;
and besides, his reason for being here demanded that he
stay on the job. Otherwise he might as well go home, as
by now he desired mightily to do. But he did give Ford
some advice.

"I'm an old hand at this sort of thing," said he. "Ride
slow. Don't tire your horses. When you come up with this
lot, don't pile into them. From what this *ranchero* says
they outnumber you. Just show yourselves. As soon as
they get in motion, get yourselves into the nearest clump
of trees. Dismount your men. Pick you some marks not
over a hundred yards away, and have it understood that
no man fires a shot at any enemy beyond those marks. And
don't let them all fire at once. Otherwise they'll rush you
before you can reload. Tie your horses fast; and don't
make any calculations for mounting your horses or for

running away, no matter what happens. These Spanish can outride you, so don't try to fight them running. If you try that you'll be wiped out, sure as shooting. And don't you take one man you wouldn't trust your life with."

Ford listened attentively. He was a young man, but not too young to heed. Andy liked Ford. He thought it was a pity Ford was mixed up in this business.

"How about Bill Todd and the other fellow?" he asked, however. "How we going to get them loose if we do as you say?"

"Yes," agreed Andy, "there's them. But I don't think they'll be tied up—if they are still alive. And if I know these Californians, every man will be so excited they won't think of them at the time. Hope so. Anyway, it's up to Todd to make his break. You can't do any different; not with the force you have. If you try it you'll be massacreed."

Ford was back next day, jubilant. The thing had worked, just as Andy had outlined it; like a machine. The *ranchero* had proved reliable; at least he had been able to lead them into the general neighborhood of Padilla's haunts. But the actual encounter had been a surprise to both parties. The Americans had been chasing horses for fresh mounts, and had run into the bandits eating breakfast. But Ford did not lose his head.

"We took to the trees, like you said," laughed Ford, "and they charged, like you said they would. We killed one or two of them, and they didn't come back for a second try. And Bill Todd and the other fellow ducked out in the excitement. That's all there was to it."

Andy congratulated him. But a little while later Solano came to him, saying that the prisoner wished to talk to him. As no one made any difficulty, Andy was able to see the man. The *ranchero* was not troubled about his captivity; that was a fortune of war, and he realized fully that he had narrowly escaped execution. But he had news he wished to impart.

"Those were not all the bandits of Juan Padilla, *señor*," he countered Andy's felicitation. "Juan Padilla leads less than a score of men. These were near a hundred."

"Some of the *californios* had joined him," suggested Andy.

"Yes," assented the man, "but they were not *rancheros* of the country. They were soldiers. *Señor*, I saw their leader. It was the *señor teniente* Joaquin de la Torre!"

Here was news indeed. De la Torre was one of Castro's regular officers.

"Near a hundred, you said?" asked Andy.

"Counting the *ladrones*."

Not many. Not enough to be effective: even against the original Bear Flag party. But they might be only a portion of the forces north of the Bay. Or possibly an advance party: or a scouting party. Impossible to say. But important as indicating that Castro was beginning to bestir himself; as, indeed, why should he not?

"Why do you tell me this?" he asked suddenly.

The *ranchero* smiled at him slyly.

"It is well known, *señor*, that you are not of this *banda*," said he.

3

Evidently the news of these happenings had spread up the Valley, with the customary incredible rapidity. Settlers began to pour into Sonoma. They were much alarmed. The story they told was not at all the version narrated by the captive *ranchero*. No mention was in it of bandits; Cowie and Fowler had been captured and done to death by a force of Californians, Castro's men. The fact that Three-fingered Jack had committed a murder entirely on his own was also forgotten; they had been executed by official command. Furthermore, the yarn had been ornamented by gratuitous and gruesome details of mutilation and torture. The curious part of it was that the garrison, the men who had heard the original narration with their own ears, not only did not deny these stories, but seemed actually to have come to believe them. Their forces at Sonoma had been increased by a hundred armed men. And that number was likely to grow as the rumor spread.

Andy began to doubt if his place was here. He disliked deserting Vallejo's affairs: but this matter had grown. Better perhaps go to Monterey—or to Sutter's. He debated the point with himself, worried and puzzled. The scouts sent out by the energetic Ford reported no other forces than De la Torre's north of the Bay. Plans were already forward to move against him. De la Torre would be well advised to get out before they closed off his retreat. They could do that easily enough. Unless he was merely an advance guard? That might be.

But before he had come to a decision a man rode in, his horse alather, to report that Frémont was approaching with all his men.

The sudden relief from uncertainty threw the garrison, even the most hard-headed, almost into hysteria. For the first time they fully realized what the strain had been. Each had stoutly maintained, even to himself, that matters were proceeding according to plan; and that, when the proper time came, their government would stand behind the movement its officer had instigated. By their government they meant the government of the United States. It is doubtful if, by this time, anybody but William Ide took seriously the new "republic." But that proper time had delayed alarmingly. But here was Frémont; and all was well. They gathered in the plaza; and when the first dust of approach was sighted they began to cheer and throw aloft their hats and fire guns. From balcony and window the Vallejo women looked down on the spectacle.

Frémont's men, and the settlers with him, were also in high spirits, answering hilariously the yells and cheers. He rode a little in advance of the main body, with Kit Carson at his right hand; and his four Delaware Indians, his personal and devoted bodyguard, immediately behind. But Frémont did not appear to share in the hilarity of the occasion. He rode somberly, looking neither to right nor left, making no acknowledgment of the salutations. At the base of the staff from which drooped the Bear Flag he dismounted. He glanced disdainfully aloft, stared about him. The noise died. The bystanders did not understand this mood of obvious irritation. What was wrong?

Frémont appeared suddenly to become aware of Ide, who, at first all pride and smiles, hovered near for his attention.

"Who wrote that proclamation for you?" he demanded. Ide's smiles froze in astonishment. Frémont stared him down arrogantly. "Hah! Your name is to it," he said; and turned on his heel. His face was dark with vexation. But Andy, watching interestedly, saw it twist in a powerful effort at control, set in the lines of concentrated thought, clear to a decision taken. The sequence was definite; yet it passed in so brief a time that with hardly a click of pause Frémont was again facing Ide, his hand extended, his whole being irradiated with that charm of personality of which he had so sure a command.

"I am happy to greet the author of so distinguished a document," he said heartily.

The carpenter, recovering, purred in gratification.

"It is," said Frémont, "all that it should be—as far as it goes. In style and diction it holds its own with the best writers in the States." But, he insinuated gently, did it go quite far enough? Had it not, in its recital of grievances, omitted one of the most telling of all.

"What is that?" asked Ide.

That an officer of the United States, on a peaceful errand, had been harried and insulted and abused until in sheer self-respect he had been forced to entrench, to resolve to die in honorable defense, so that only the cowardice of a pusillanimous foeman had enabled him to extricate himself with honor. Had Ide reflected that the recital of that outrage would have been one of the most potent of arguments to incline the sympathies of the world, to arouse the ardor of his countrymen in support of his brave adventure?

It did not matter, Frémont smoothly interrupted Ide's instant agreement and dismayed regret at the omission. Castro could not fail to issue some reply, perform some overt act to occasion another manifesto. In the latter Ide would find opportunity to set forth the insults Frémont had endured at Castro's hands. He spoke familiarly, his hand on Ide's shoulder. Ide, pleased, flattered, mollified, agreed eagerly that this should be done. They moved slowly away together.

Andy stared after them thoughtfully, for the moment insulated from the hullabaloo of fraternization this brief episode had but momentarily interrupted. His brain was busy. He didn't like the situation, thought Andy—something about it. But he is a quick one, thought Andy with reluctant admiration: he can shift ground with the best. He's nobody's fool—in some ways, anyway. Lord, how he fed Ide the soft soap! Had him sized up, all right! Anybody else would have gagged on it. Andy chuckled. He's a slick one, thought Andy: getting Ide to tell his side of all that Gavilan botchery. Takes a good man to keep from doing fool things, reflected Andy, but it takes a better man to make 'em count for him once they're done. Something about that cuss; doggone if there ain't! Andy was recalling the strange fascination of charm with which Frémont had dazzled Ide into instant forgetfulness of his evident first irritation. For a moment Andy glimpsed an understanding of why men like Kit Carson, whose judgments were otherwise sure, were so blindly loyal in spite of everything.

Frémont had stopped at the veranda, was facing the *plaza*, awaiting silence.

"I want to say," he pronounced distinctly, "that I have not come here to take any part in this matter. I've come to see the sport. And," he added, "perhaps to explore about the Bay a little." He turned to Ide. "I'd be pleased to have your party accompany me."

They cheered and laughed.

"Oh, we'll go with you, all right!" someone shouted.

There was more laughter. Nobody seemed to bother much with this disclaimer. They did not try to understand it. They had heard one similar before. But here he was; and his men. Some kind of official monkey work; red tape. Frémont stared at them a moment; then linked his arm with Ide's, and entered the house, closely followed by Carson and the four Delaware Indians.

ANDY sought out Kit Carson, tried to talk some sense. He got nowhere. Kit was in a shell. Andy could not make out just how much he knew; or, indeed, if he knew anything. Kit listened with an air mingled of stubbornness and stupidity. But Andy discovered, to his chagrin, that the little scout took in what he said, and utilized it for his own ends. Or rather for the ends of Frémont. Among other things Andy had tried to explain the row between Castro and Pico, and to point out that, if there were any military preparations, they had been intended as a threat to Pico, and not for use against the settlers. Kit had evinced a trace of interest at this.

"What they rowing about?" he wanted to know.

Andy had patiently explained the situation. He had thought it worth while; for he knew that Carson had Frémont's ear. The inveterate rivalry between the north and south. Pico, the governor, persistently lingering in the south; though the capitol was at Monterey. Castro of the north. Each infringing on the jealously guarded prerogatives of the other.

"For instance?" asked Kit.

Pico, civil governor, calling out troops, which was solely Castro's job. Excuse: the disturbances in the valley. Castro, military commander, convening a *junta*, which was solely Pico's job. Excuse: the same.

Carson drifted away in the direction of the *casa*. An hour later all the uncertainties were over. Frémont, who had backed and filled, dawdled, postponed, and equivocated, at last came out flatfooted for action. Next morning was to begin a movement combined of Frémont's men and settlers. But not against California, nor yet against Mexico, with which the United States was at peace! Certainly not! Even Frémont's ambitious spirit had hesitated at such a step. Against whom, then? Against Castro, the *usurper!*

"I wish someone would kick me *good!*" said Andy disgustedly to himself: for he saw that it was he who had, inadvertently, suggested this way out.

Carson was seeking him again. The scout seemed embarrassed, reluctant to come to some point. He's had orders, thought Andy shrewdly; he don't like 'em.

"Spit it out, Kit," he said aloud. "What he tell you to say?"

"Why, nothing." Carson's face reddened slowly. "But he says yo're to go along with us tomorrow. I reckon he thinks yo're too good a man to stay yere in Sonoma and . . ."

Andy was surveying him so intently that his voice trailed off into silence.

"You mean he wants to keep an eye on me," supplied Andy crisply, "so I won't light out and tell the Californians, or maybe the American officers, all I know. Or perhaps warn Lieutenant de la Torre to get out while he can. Strike you I don't have to take orders from him?"

"I do," said Carson.

"And your orders are to see to it I don't."

"It's a pretty plain trail," muttered Carson. "Me, and the Delawares," he added.

"Am I under arrest?" asked Andy.

"No," said Carson. "I-tam-api," he pleaded, rather miserably, "act reasonable."

Andy laughed shortly.

"Rest your mind," said he. "I aim to go. I aim to see how far this is going. But I'll tell you this." His voice slowed to the trapper's drawl. "Eff'n the time comes when

I want to go anywhar, I'm goin'; and I'd admire to see you or ary Delaware Injuns stop me. I don't want no trouble with you, Kit Carson. I'd shore hate to turn my hand agin' ary mountain man, ary American. But I'm my own master. And I ain't growed so soft that I ain't still I-tam-api, with a trick or so in my possible sack and a word or so left for this to say." He struck with the flat of his hand against the stock of the long rifle. His anger was apparent through the surface deliberation of manner.

But Carson avoided the challenge. He was obviously distressed.

"We'll be startin' off in the morning," said he.

2

They left Sonoma early and marched to San Rafael a hundred and sixty strong. Andy's cooler judgment had returned to him. I'm a plumb fool, he told himself; going off half-cock like that. Lot of good I'd be landed in the calaboose. He was a little surprised that he was still free; and reflected, with some satisfaction, that Kit must have kept to himself his rash outbreak. That was decent of Kit. But he realized that the little scout would carry out his orders. He felt himself under surveillance. He must watch his step; make no false moves; keep his freedom to act.

But his anger had not cooled. He rode in bitter contempt for the whole performance. His resolution had hardened. In his own mind he had at last definitely taken sides. He waited only to see clearly what he could do that would be most effective. Should he slip away and warn De la Torre to make his escape before his retreat was cut off? Andy was still confident he could do this, in spite of Carson. Should he hasten to Monterey? Or might it be better to get in touch with those United States officers, on the ships, who had so categorically disclaimed this movement? Now was the best time, before Frémont might order him into custody. As yet he was free. But he did not know. He must risk it, and wait.

However, there was now no question in his mind that Frémont had at last taken definite command. He had made no announcements; but he gave orders, and the orders were obeyed. And there was no doubt of Frémont's present objective. He was after De la Torre. Scouts were even now abroad searching for the whereabouts of the little band of Californians. He knows well enough now there's no army north of the Bay, thought Andy; but if he can catch De la Torre it'll be something to talk about. It ought to be easy. All they'd have to do would be to watch the crossings. Wonder what he's in such a sweat about?

Andy's shrewdness had guessed a part; but not all. He could not know all that was happening. He did not know, for instance, that Frémont had already despatched Gillespie to convey to the dismayed Montgomery that he had "joined the Bears." He did not realize that, to justify this, he needed desperately an enemy, and that he must have it right away. Only an enemy, a flesh-and-blood enemy, would do. Not an abstraction. There must be action; so that Frémont could seem to have moved on generous impulse to save fellow countrymen from danger. Otherwise he had no leg to stand on. Andy did not understand this; nor the growing impatience curbed beneath Frémont's external calm. Unless De la Torre could be found, the show was in danger of flattening out. Andy could not realize this; nor the leap of welcome with which the man snatched at the tidings a breathless runner brought to him, pacing back and forth in the corridors of the mission at San Rafael.

"They's four Spainyards crossing over the Bay in a boat!" cried the messenger.

Frémont snapped excitedly into action.

"Go get them, Carson!" he cried.

Kit, a Canadian, and another trapper who happened by seized their rifles, mounted, struck spurs to their horses. Carson wheeled and rode back.

"Shall I take 'em prisoners, Cap'n?" he shouted.

"I've got no room for prisoners," returned Frémont in a burst of impatience.

"Fair enough!" Carson waved his hand and raced away.

Andy seized his chance in the bustle of excitement. He could not guess what it was all about, but he wished to be prepared. Unobserved, he mounted his horse and rode out of town to the partial concealment of a clump of live-oaks overlooking the slough. A small boat was leisurely making its way to the edge of the mudflats. It contained four men. The oarsman beached his craft. His three passengers stepped out, lifted their saddles ashore, then proceeded afoot slowly in the direction of the mission. The boatman shoved off and rowed away.

Carson and his men rode up slowly until within fifty yards or so of the new arrivals, dismounted, and without a word shot them down. Then they remounted and rode away, leaving the bodies where they had fallen.

3

For a moment Andy saw red, and he fingered the rifle in his hands. But instantly his lifelong habits reasserted themselves. He raised the muzzle of the Boone gun. Nothing could be gained by shooting one of the murderers; and much might be jeopardized. But Andy was no longer a mugwump. A mugwump is often merely a man who is acting solely from intelligence, and so sees too clearly both sides. That had been the case with Andy. Now his anger over this wanton outrage erased such intellectual niceties. He was freed for wholehearted action; and he proceeded at once about it.

His status had changed. He was in an enemy country. His first job was to get away before the change of status was sensed. This was child's play. While this excitement lasted, he had a clear field. He slipped down the hill toward the slough. It was probable that he would not be missed for some time: it was unlikely that he would now be considered of sufficient importance for serious pursuit; it was even more improbable that Carson or any of the others knew the hoofmark of his horse. Nevertheless Andy took all precautions, confusing his trail whenever opportunity offered; and heading, not toward the south, but toward Sonoma. He knew perfectly that these rough expedients would not long deceive any of the competent scouts; but each would result in delay, and delay might later prove valuable. He did not, however, attempt to ride under cover, for complete concealment was impossible, and he did not wish to arouse suspicion in the mind of any chance wayfarer.

So when, to the eastward of the *pueblo*, he met Jasper O'Farrell, he did not avoid an encounter, although he might possibly have done so, but rode steadily toward him raising his hand in salute, and made as though to pass. O'Farrell, however, drew rein.

"Have you heard what's happened?" he demanded.

"You mean the shooting of those three men over yander?" replied Andy. "Yes; I saw it."

"That was the most outrageous murder I ever saw in my life!" said O'Farrell heatedly.

"It's war, I reckon," said Andy, as though carelessly.

"War!" repeated the young man. "It was just plain murder. The poor devils didn't suspect a thing. They were going right up to the mission!"

"Know who they were?" asked Andy, with studied indifference.

"Certainly I know them!" O'Farrell was explosive.

"One was old Don José Berryesa. The other two were the Haro boys. They were unarmed. They were no more soldiers—no more, by God—than I am!"

"Probably spies—carrying dispatches or something," said Andy unconcernedly.

"Oh, sure!" sneered O'Farrell. "And walking right into camp with them, in broad daylight!"

"Well, probably Carson was a leetle drunk," drawled Andy.

O'Farrell looked at him disgustedly; jerked his horse's head. Andy watched him ride away. He was human enough to regret the impression he had felt it wise to leave with this generous young man. But he considered his strategy sound. If he had sympathized with O'Farrell's indignation, it was probable that the young man might have quoted him in support. Now he had aligned himself with the work of these marauders, it was unlikely that O'Farrell would mention the chance meeting.

He continued on the road to Sonoma. If it were not for De la Torre he would have cut directly for the Strait of Carquinez. It was taking long chances to fool around in this country. But Andy felt he must do something about De la Torre, and he had an idea. At Sonoma he managed to get hold of Solano without being seen by any of the small garrison. The Indian listened to what Andy had to say.

"It shall be done, señor," said he; and his grave face relaxed into a grin of understanding.

"Haste is necessary; great haste," warned Andy.

He procured a fresh horse from Solano, and started at once for the south, though it was near sunset. He had done all he could. Not until a week later did he learn of the success of his plan.

Frémont's scouts had captured an Indian. In his moccasin was found a letter addressed to De la Torre, purporting to carry orders from General Castro. The lieutenant was commanded to deliver an attack on Sonoma the next morning; and stated that Castro's entire army would be there to join in the assault. Frémont, alarmed, had hastened back. De la Torre, instructed of the situation by another of Solano's Indians, had taken advantage of the withdrawal to slip back across the Bay.

4

As he rode, Andy revolved in his mind what he was going to do. The situation was at last perfectly clear to him. This thing was a revolt, a rebellion. It was to be put down by the constituted authorities against whom it was instigated. The fact that the rebels were Americans had nothing to do with it. They might have been French, or English; or, for that matter, Indians or Chinamen; the case would have been the same. All right: that was plain. The catch in it was that the constituted authorities were no good at putting down rebellions of this caliber. If it depended on Castro and Pico and their *políticos*, these revolutionists were perfectly safe. But—and this was the illumination that had come to Andy in the full blaze of his anger—the *políticos* were not California. Not by a jugful! said Andy to himself, emphatically. Ramón Rivera, Carlos Lugo, José de la Cuesta, the *rancheros* and their hard-riding *vaqueros*, hundreds and hundreds of them; and the adopted citizens, like himself, good and loyal men, every one of them. That was California! And in such a California was real power; power enough to blow this Frémont and his followers away like chaff, were they double, treble, in numbers. Nobody had ever been able to get that power together, before, to handle it. Well, I can do it, thought Andy. He thought of Vallejo shut up in a room at Sutter's Fort, he thought of Frémont's arrogance and double-dealing; he thought of the three bodies

of Berryesa and the Haro boys sprawled in the mud of
the tide flats. You bet I can do it, he repeated to himself
savagely.

Frémont early noted Andy's absence; but he did not
now think a pursuit worth while. He was disgusted at
being so fooled by the false dispatches. He hastened back
toward Sausalito in time to see De la Torre bobbing across
the Bay in a lighter. There were no boats with which to
follow. Finally he managed to borrow one from a trading
vessel at anchor in Richardson Bay. It was too late to do
anything about De la Torre, so, with twenty men, he
rowed across to Fort Point where for many years the old
abandoned Castillo de San Joaquín had been placidly
rotting away in the sun and rain. At this time it was
defended by sea gulls and terns; and its armament consisted of ten forgotten cannon, eaten to a shell by rust,
dismounted, and lying about on the ground. Neither the
birds nor the cannon made any resistance. The latter
were sought out from their concealment and solemnly
spiked, which was quite a job, for the touchholes were
closed by corrosion. The party then rowed back to return
the boat to its owner.

In place of this performance—which was foofaraw, if
you will!—he would have been better advised to bend his
energies to the capture of the solitary man, by now near
the Strait of Carquinez. Frémont's foofaraw, however,
was rarely without some use. He was able to write to his
father-in-law, Benton of Missouri, an account of the
"campaign," so far, which the Senator could put to good
use. On paper, and at a distance of some thousands of
miles, it sounded like quite a campaign. "Three of Castro's
party, having landed in advance, were killed on the beach.
Beyond this there was no loss of life"* was what Frémont
had to say of the Berryesa murder. It also appeared, on
paper, that De la Torre and a large force had been de-

*My italics. S. E. W.

feated and driven across the Bay; that the fort of San Joaquín had been "captured" and its guns—"large and handsome pieces," Frémont added—had been spiked, though he failed to mention that the garrison of gulls and terns were still at large; that all the territory north of the Bay, from Sutter's Fort to the sea, had been swept clear of the enemy and freed from Mexican authority.

CHAPTER XXIV

ANDY was back in his proper element at last. He saw a plain course before him. As he rode, his mind was active with plans, concrete plans. He felt as though he had been let out of jail. He was entirely confident.

No trick at all to get out five hundred volunteers from the *ranchos* of the north. That would hold the rebels north of the Bay until the south could get there. Then the combined forces could cross over and wipe things up. Probably fifteen hundred, thought Andy; maybe more. He dismissed contemptuously the popular legend that the *californios* were cowards; would not fight. Shucks! thought Andy, they'll fight like wildcats if they're shown how. Got the makings of the finest cavalry in the world! Andy remembered Ramón facing the grizzly with only his rapier; there flashed before his mind dozens, hundreds, of feats performed on the cattle range as part of the day's work. Like to see some of these renegades tackle that! thought Andy grimly. Give 'em a reason for fighting; and let 'em do it their own way, and someone is going to be surprised! thought Andy with confident satisfaction.

Then, of course, there were the naturalized citizens like himself. Why, there were enough of them to handle the situation themselves! They won't be such hesitating dam' fools as I was, thought Andy. They can see a hole in a millstone as well as the next fellow. Andy ran them over in his mind,—John Gilroy, John Price, Lemuel Carpenter, Jack Murphy, Abel Stearns, John Warner, Dan Hill, Henry Mellus, Isaac Williams—dozens; nay, hundreds of them—all substantial solid citizens, commanding men,

415

money, and influence, and withal formidable with the
American weapon, the long rifle, men with a stake in the
country and sober judgment in their heads, quite a different class from the rabble of squatters and adventurers
north of the Bay. That is how Andy now lumped them in
his own mind; "white Indians" as Don Guadalupe had
called them. His anger had hardened him wholly to the
intolerance of partisanship. Then there was Sutter, who
would undoubtedly jump with the cat, once he was convinced the cat was going to jump.

His mind raced, planning it out, like a thing released.
There ought to be, first of all, a demonstration somewhere up toward the American River, a screen of skir-
mish and threat behind which to gather the strength of
attack: then a movement in two sections—he could see
it plainly; by September at latest the thing would be
finished!

Names, more names, of the men on whom he could depend. Nicolás Den, Alfred Robinson, William Richardson,
David Spense, Robert Livermore—his mind kept returning to the long roll of those naturalized Americans who
needed only the call to gather solidly against the filibus-
tering anarchy of revolt. Then his tense mind relaxed. He
grinned. The name of Uncle Bill Rubottom had popped
into his mind. What was it someone had said to him of
uncle Bill?

"Uncle Bill? Sure, I know him. Met him in the mountains when his mule fell off the trail. Why," said this one
dryly, "he swore 'till the bark peeled off an oak tree; so
thunderously that the mountains shivered and great frag-
ments came crashing down into the river. One of the
listeners' hair turned gray and the others were stricken
bald-headed! Sure I know him!"

But Uncle Bill was a good man for all that.

"We'll turn him loose against Ide and Semple," thought
Andy. "I'll bet he could handle them both."

2

Immediately south of the Strait, Andy received whole-hearted welcome and support. This was only natural. These were the people nearest the source of trouble, who would be the first to suffer invasion if this new *banda* should turn southwards. They were scared as well as angry. To a few of the older men, such as Don Ygnacio Martínez, of the Rancho Pinole, he had to give certain assurances. These men, either persuaded by Larkin or their own native wisdom, wished to be very sure of one thing: that they were not fighting the United States. With them the sentiment in favor of annexation was strong; strong enough to have survived even the sense of outrage Frémont's activities had aroused. Evidently Larkin had made a good start on his job of conciliation. Andy pledged himself that the filibuster acted under no official orders. His own conviction that such was the case was now profounder than any mere reason. But to a still larger number, mostly the younger men, such a consideration made no difference. They were angry, through and through; would as soon fight the United States—or the universe, for that matter: and they leaped at the chance for competent leadership. Andy had to restrain them: persuade them to await mature action.

"I'll send you word," said Andy. "Just keep ready."

He rode toward home eastward of the Contra Costa Hills. This was slightly out of his way, but he wished to stop at Los Méganos. He wanted to sound the ideas of Don Juan Marchet, alias John Marsh. He desired this for two reasons. The first was that this was the first non-Latin citizen in his route: the second was that he was curious to see the man himself.

Andy had been hearing about John Marsh for years; mostly unfavorably. The *californios* did not like him at all. They told all sorts of stories about him. He had, they

said, lived some months with Señor Leese at Yerba Buena
and once in that time had paid fifty cents for fish toward
the general larder. When he left, he asked Señor Leese
for the fifty cents. He squabbled over pennies in all his
trading, so that even the Yankees on the ships called him
a "sharper." He had driven so shrewd a bargain with
Noriega that he had possessed Los Méganos for the
absurd sum of five hundred dollars. There were no cattle
on the holding, but so unpopular was he that the *rancheros*
did not stock his land for him in the usual lavish fashion.
Someone—"an *e'tranjero, señor*," Andy's informant hastened to add—had suggested he "marry some cattle."

"Me marry a greaser!" Marsh had sneered. "When I
marry, it will be with one of my own kind!"

After which, it was said, he took a squaw for a mistress.

These stories were told, and many more like them. Andy
had been hearing them for years; but he had never known
how much of them to believe. Certainly the Californians
believed them. Once when Marsh hauled some hides into
one of the *pueblos* he had to sleep under his cart. Not one
of the hospitable *rancheros* would offer to take him in.

Were this all, Andy would have estimated the man as
only another of the worthless vagabonds not uncommon
even at that early day. But it was not all. Marsh was
neither a vagabond nor worthless. He had made his way.

And some of the stories, Andy had found, were subject
to discount; and some of the traits that repelled the easy,
hospitable Californians, he understood very well. The man
did not want visitors: seemed to resent them. It turned
out that Noriega was eager to get rid of the land because
of hostile Indians: and that Marsh had taken it, cleared of
cattle, and had lived on it defiantly. He had ended by
making friends with the Indians. They had moved their
village to Los Méganos: they had built Marsh an *adobe*.
They had laid him out a vineyard; an orchard of pears,
figs, almonds, and olives; they even plowed him a wheat

field, and trapped for him in the mountains. Marsh in return gave them part of their food and some coarse clothing—and a genuine kindness which he never showed to any white man. It was enough. They became almost literally his slaves. This appealed to Andy. He was Indian-hearted himself.

And Marsh had got his cattle. He set himself up as a doctor.

That would not, at first glance, look very promising. Los Méganos was a long distance from even the thinly settled centers of population. And this was a healthful country. There was some malaria in the great valleys of the interior—where were few but Indians. In California-proper childbirth, occasional smallpox, knife wounds, and accidents about covered it. Marsh made a start by curing his own Indians of malaria. He procured from the ships cow pox for vaccination. And he had the nerve to tackle anything with the scalpel.

It seemed impossible; but he built up a practice. Whenever he could he forced his patients to come to him. But he never refused an outside call, no matter how distant: and he went at once, whatever the weather, at any time of day or night. So he made some fearful journeys.

He exacted his fees invariably in cattle. They were high: sometimes appallingly so. Two doses of salts cost one man twenty-five cows. A child delivery set the proud father back fifty head: a journey to San José cost the husband of Señora Sunol two hundred. He was deaf to pleas of poverty or of exorbitance. If they were not prepared to pay, they should not have called him. They cursed him, and hated him; but they continued to send for him. The Californians were a people at once improvident and excitable, easily thrown into a panic by the most trifling ailments. Once only he had his come-uppance. On this occasion he was called to ride some distance to examine a child suffering from a slight headache. Marsh gave it two or three doses of a simple cathartic, and presented a bill for fifty cows. In vain the Californian protested. He was no *hacendado*, not even a *ranchero* as the title was understood. He was a poor man. His entire herd was only a hundred and fifty.

"That is nothing to me," said Marsh positively. "I traveled a long distance to see your child. The child is cured. I have been kept from my *rancho* and my regular business for several days. I am entitled to this fee."

The father of the child turned ugly. It looked like trouble—and Marsh, it was said, never avoided that. But now the mother interposed. She was a well-favored woman, comfortably fat and placid.

"The *señor* is right," she placated her husband. "And he shall be paid his fee. But *señor médico*,"—she turned to Marsh—"I have, you will remember, washed for you two shirts while you have been stopping at our *rancho*, and for this it is just that I also be paid. My price for the washing of shirts is twenty cows apiece."

Marsh fumed and grumbled. The *señora* was firm. At last he departed for Los Méganos, driving before him his diminished stipend.

Andy pondered these things as he rode. This man is no fool, thought Andy. He may be all they say, thought Andy —and he may not. He's not their sort: they never could understand him in the world. But he's got a head on his shoulders.

3

Andy approached Los Méganos late, guided by a half-Indian *vaquero*, who happened to be traveling his way, and who claimed to know the road to Don Juan's.

"Though one cannot miss it, *señor*," said the *vaquero*, "for one has the mountain yonder to go by, and as the *señor* may observe, it stands high and apart and cannot be mistaken." He glanced somewhat fearfully at its serene symmetry. "It would be well to spur on, *señor*," he suggested, "for the dusk approaches, and this mountain is the abode of an evil spirit. Nay, *señor*, you need not laugh, for this spirit has been seen, and not by Indians alone, but by *gente de razón*."

"Who were these?" asked Andy idly.

"Spanish soldiers, *señor*, who ventured up the mountain in pursuit of horse thieves. To them this evil spirit appeared. It lives in the rocky defiles near the summit, and it wears plumage of the most grotesque. The soldiers saw it, with their own eyes; and crossed themselves, and fled; and no man in his right senses has since then ventured upon that mountain, which is named, therefore, El Monte del Diablo." He reined in his horse. "So I advise haste, *señor;* before the dark falls. Here I must leave you. Follow the *cañada* yonder. *Vaya con Dios*."

Andy arrived at the *rancho* at dusk. He was greeted only by the barking of dogs. He was aware of human beings lurking in the background of dusk; but no one came forward to take his horse. Andy dismounted. The adobe building before which he had halted was a huge affair, of two stories—or more accurately a story and a half. Its roof was thatched. Its walls, high up, were pierced with loopholes. Except for doors, there were no other openings. Andy hammered on one of the doors at random.

"Come in!" cried an impatient voice in Spanish.

Andy thrust open the door. He saw a large but bare apartment furnished with two tables, several benches, and a shelf that ran halfway around the room. One of the tables was bare. The other bore a welter of papers, writing materials, magazines, and books. The shelves were crowded with more books. One end of the chamber was devoted to a commodious fireplace, an unusual thing to see in a California ranch house of that day. A fire of pine knots threw its brilliant flames high up the chimney. This was the only, but sufficient, illumination. A tall man lay

flat on his belly in the middle of the floor, his chin propped
by his elbows, reading a book by the light from the pine
knots. He did not look around, but as Andy said nothing
he at length exclaimed impatiently:

"Well?"

"A visitor," replied Andy in English.

"What do you want? Are you sick?"

"Do I look sick?" asked Andy with a laugh.

The man rolled slowly on his back.

"No," he agreed: and waited uncompromisingly.

"I want a talk with you," said Andy.

"What about?" demanded Marsh. "Who are you?"

"The state of the country, among other things," Andy
answered the first question.

Marsh continued to stare at him appraisingly, his head
supported by his cupped hands.

"Who sent you?" he asked finally.

"Andy Burnett," replied Andy, who was hugely amused.

"Burnett," repeated Marsh. "You mean the *ranchero*
over in the Salinas valley?"

"That's the fellow."

"H'm!" said Marsh. He sat up. "Where is he?"

"Right here," said Andy.

"Are you Burnett?"

"That's the fellow," repeated Andy.

Marsh sprang to his feet.

"Come in! Come in!" he cried. "Don't hang around that
door! Why didn't you say so in the first place?"

4

From that moment Andy could not have complained as
to his reception at Los Méganos. Marsh bellowed into the
darkness, and men ran to take the horse. Indian women
stirred into flame the banked fires in the cooking shed.

Food was brought. In his host's almost eager hospitality Andy could find no trace of justification for the numerous stories he had heard. Nor was there anything in Marsh's manner or conversation to bear out his reputation for either taciturnity or rudeness. On the contrary, he seemed to be exerting himself to be as charming and entertaining as possible. Obviously Marsh liked Andy; or for some reason desired to make on him a good impression. The *ranchero* was slightly puzzled, watched his host appraisingly, trying to make him out, to "size him up," following his custom. He failed. Marsh conversed easily and entertainingly on all sorts of small subjects. It was evident that he was a man of wide knowledge, of wide reading, of education. He talked of things he had read; of things he had seen; of people he had met. Incidental to the development of the West, he showed an astonishing familiarity with Andy's own personal history, of which he spoke as detachedly as he did of the fur trade; so that for the first time Andy saw a clear picture of how closely his own career had knit with greater destinies; and was astonished. But of his own past Marsh said nothing. And over all his apparent frank cordiality was a hard and brilliant surface that effectually concealed the man himself. Only when he spoke of the massacre at Pierre's Hole, wherein Andy lost the last of those he held dear in the world, and of Andy's flight from memory to California, did this shell seem momentarily to crack; so that, for a brief instant, Andy thought to sense a glow of warmth. And for that brief instant an intangible hint of understanding crossed his own spirit. Almost he seemed to himself to grasp the solution of this man's nature. But the impression vanished before he could seize it. His host was still as complete an enigma as possible. Why not? Could Andy guess that Marsh also was a refugee from tragedy of the frontier?

And yet Marsh did talk of himself. He spoke freely

enough of his ambitions as a *ranchero* to become the prince of a great holding. He chatted a little of his tastes and interests.

"I read," said he, "those books there: they wait, patiently, there on the shelves, ready at my whim to take me into men's minds and to distant places. There is in the printed word, Burnett, the magic of the fabled carpet." He laughed. "It is a passion, a vice with me, Burnett; almost a vice, like wine. Anything will do. An old newspaper, a pamphlet on any subject under the sun, anything between covers, anything printed—or written. An almanac will do, if there's nothing else. Why," he said, a trifle shamefacedly, "if I get started I sometimes lie abed, or on the floor as you found me, all night and all day. I doubt if I'd stir to defend an attack by Indians!"

They arose from the table. Marsh threw more pine knots on the fire, led the way to the bookshelves. The books were a curious collection. Andy knew none of them. Some were in Greek: he peered at their strange characters with puzzled awe. Many were in Spanish. There was much of poetry—*The Odes of Anacreon*, Paine's *Verse and Prose*, Johnson's *Lives of the English Poets*. Andy handled a fat medical book, attracted by its size.

"Got that off a ship; it's handy," said Marsh briefly. That was his only reference to his activities as a physician.

He possessed four Bibles, one in English, one in French, one in Spanish, and one in Greek.

"Help to brush up your languages," observed Marsh.

Only when he spoke of personalities did his charm, but not his interest, lessen. His comments were invariably shrewd and penetrating; but they carried the sting of biting sarcasm. Andy could not completely make him out; but he understood enough to confirm him in his first instinct that this man's opinion was worth while. He was glad he had deviated to Los Méganos.

5

Marsh listened attentively enough once Andy began to talk. He frowned over the *ranchero's* account of the doings north of the Bay.

"I had heard a little of these things," said he. "Frémont summoned me to come to him; but I refused to go. I felt that Frémont's actions were leaving the Americans south of the Bay unprotected and under suspicion."

Andy began to say something of his plans: but Marsh cut him short.

"Just a minute," he interrupted. "We'll come to all that presently. What about this man Frémont? I've never seen him. What is he like? What do you think of him?"

Marsh paid alert attention to Andy's reply, questioning, pouncing upon each of his statements, defining it, sharpening it, clarifying it, extracting from it the last drop of significance before he would permit his guest to go on. It took a long time; and Andy, toward the last, grew restive under the terrier-like cross-examination. But when Marsh permitted him to finish, the two of them had evolved a clear picture of the young adventurer—as Andy conceived him.

"I see," said Marsh, refilling his pipe. "Now go ahead with what you were saying."

For some time he listened to Andy's exposition of his plans without interruption. Those plans became more definite to Andy himself as he talked. The mere expression to another of his own race and language clarified them. By now he knew what was to be done down to the smallest detail. When he had finished he looked toward Marsh inquiringly. The latter puffed a cloud of smoke.

"What do you want of me? To join your American riflemen?"

"And bring the best of your *vaqueros;* of course," said Andy, "when the time comes. That would be the best

answer to your complaint that all this leaves us Americans
below the Bay unprotected and under suspicion. Wasn't
that what you said? But what I want now is your
opinion."

"As to what?"

"As to the whole thing."

For some moments Marsh was silent, puffing his pipe.
Then he knocked out its ashes and laid it aside.

"Politically you're right," he said. "Such an action
would definitely outlaw all this business. Just now the
Californians think the American government is secretly
back of the move. I agree with you that it is not. The
surest way to prove that is to do what you propose—give
these fellows a good licking as rebels and outlaws. Then
when the Californians observe that the United States
does not intervene, they will see that its government is
not an enemy, as they had thought, and would designate
this for what it is, a mere outbreak of filibuster. And
we'd be back on the ground that friend Larkin has been
scratching so industriously—that of peaceful and willing
annexation."

"I hadn't thought of that part of it," said Andy admiringly, "but I believe you're right."

"And as for your sentiments in the matter, there you
are right also," continued Marsh without heeding the
comment. "I'm ready to agree with you that the whole
thing is outrageous. As I get your account, less than two
score persons, but recently—and illegally—arrived in the
country, who have as yet no holdings or what might be
called fixed property, seize a man who is not their enemy
who has always been friendly to their sort, even against
Mexican policy, who has a known inclination to the
United States. They confine him and his close followers
like convicts, grab much of his property, and sequestrate
his family. An officer of the United States, on a supposedly peaceful mission, in the country illegally, injects

himself into the situation, together with the men assigned
to him on this peaceful mission. He promptly murders—
or causes to be murdered—an old man and two young
boys who are in no way connected with any of these doings.
I may add—and you probably do not know this—that
his actions in the matter have been repudiated by the
naval representatives of the United States. He has, by
those actions, made of himself an outlaw, a filibuster, who,
in event of disaster, can expect nothing but court-martial.
The whole thing is a clear case of rebellion and wanton
outrage which, as I say, fully justifies your own feeling
in the matter, and the action you propose. Is that a fair
statement?"

"It's the whole thing in a nutshell!" cried Andy.

"Very well. Then you are right politically and ethically.
You are also right strategically and tactically. Here are
the practical elements; correct me if I am wrong: These
outlaws, or rebels, or what you want to call them, would
number about two or at most three hundred, all told.
Sixty are Frémont's men, and may be considered experienced and effective. The rest are trappers, hunters, and
settlers, most of whom are pretty handy at taking care
of themselves, but some of whom are merely farmers,
and not so well armed at that. As you detail your plans
—and I believe you can carry them out—there can
shortly be brought into the field against them a force of,
say, two hundred naturalized foreigners and anything up
to a thousand or so Californians. I agree with you as to
the fighting qualities of the latter, if properly led. I gather
you do not consider Frémont a competent military commander."

"You can fool him with a white rag," said Andy, thinking of the plainsman's trick of luring antelope within
range by fluttering a bit of cloth on the end of a ramrod.

"But there are competent fighters under him; almost
as competent as yourself."

"Better," said Andy. "I'm no Napoleon Bonaparte. But this fellow is bull-headed and won't listen, and——"

"All right," Marsh stopped him with raised hand. "I'll admit that it wouldn't be too much of a job. I'll admit that you are right in all you've told me."

"That's what I wanted to talk to you about," returned Andy with satisfaction.

"But," continued Marsh quietly, "it won't work."

"Won't work!" cried Andy, checked short. "Won't work! Why not?"

"I don't know," confessed Marsh, "but I'd lay a bet on it."

"What'll stop it?" demanded the *ranchero*.

"Frémont," said Marsh.

For a moment Andy stared at his host in blank amazement.

"Frémont!" he repeated at last incredulously. "What do you mean? How do you figure that? Ain't we just said ——Why, what in tarnation can *he* do?"

"I don't know," repeated Marsh.

"Then what reason——"

"None. That is, none but Frémont." Marsh refilled his pipe, lighted it leisurely. "It's the man himself, as you've made me see him. Burnett, did you ever read history?"

"Mighty little," acknowledged Andy.

"Well, history is full of them—men like him. There's something about them you can't get away from. Call it luck; call it personality; call it the idiocy of the rest of mankind—it doesn't make any difference. They've got something. They may be the most empty-headed, ungrateful, selfish, dissipated scoundrels in the world. They may commit every idiocy and every crime in the calendar. They may knife their best friends in the back—fly in the face of everything that is reasonable and decent.

Did you ever," he asked abruptly, "hear of the Stuarts of England?"

"They were kings, weren't they?" asked Andy doubtfully..

"Yes, they were kings. They were about as rotten a lot of kings as you could invent. As near as I can make out they had not one redeeming solid trait. Personally they were a thoroughly dissipated and immoral lot, even for their time. They were wastrels and spendthrifts and lechers and drunkards. They oppressed and looted their subjects for the benefit of themselves and their favorites. Personally they were cowardly and completely ungrateful and treacherous. They were so bad that even conservative old England, with all its reverence for royalty and the rest of it, cut off Charles Stuart's head."

"Well!" observed Andy.

"Well!" retorted Marsh. "You'd think that would settle it: that men would wash their hands of such a lot, and that their name would be a symbol for contempt. Not at all! That was a couple of hundred years or so ago. Now all the sensible decent men that cut off Charles Stuart's head are in men's minds just sober-sided, roundhead plow horses; and these Stuarts get to be more and more picturesque as time goes on. To this day—and for many a day to come, I'll venture—men cry in their drinks and get sentimental over 'bonnie Prince Charlie.' Why?"

Marsh shrugged his shoulders; rose to his feet; kicked the pine knots together in the fireplace; and flopped again to the floor.

"If you'd read history, Burnett," he continued, "you'd see that repeated again and again. The worthy New Englander who made his harsh way against a formidable wilderness is just a drab background for the gay 'cavalier,' who gambled and drank and quarrelled while his convict slaves worked for him. That classical drunk and pic-

turesque spouter, Mark Antony, with his asinine pearls
and his dozen banquets all going at once so one would
be ready when he wanted to sit down, and his Egyptian
'world-well-lost-for-love' nonsense—Cæsar hadn't a chance
—in men's imaginations. And Petronius—— You don't
know what I'm talking about, do you, Burnett?"

"Can't say as I do," confessed Andy.

"Well," said Marsh, "it's just this: you can fight
against rifles and men and win against big odds. But
there's one thing you can't fight against, even if the odds
are in your favor; and I believe this man's got it."

"I don't get the cute of your meaning," said Andy.
"What is it?"

"I don't know," repeated Marsh, "but you'll see. Even
if you lick him up there north of the Bay, even if he is
repudiated and discredited by his government, he'll come
out on top somehow. But you won't. Something will
happen. I don't know what it is: but it will happen. If
you and I could be here a hundred years from now, we'd
find him big in men's imaginations. We'd find things
named after him—bridges, and mountains, and rivers
and things. He'll be a dashing and romantic hero, and
even he himself, no matter what more idiocies he com-
mits, can't stop it."

Andy shook his head.

"It's too much for me," said he.

"Too much for you!" Marsh laughed sardonically. "Of
course it is! It's too much for me; too much for anybody!
But you try to get around it!"

"But what can he *do?*" demanded the practical Andy.
"What *can* happen?"

"How do I know?" retorted Marsh. "But you mark
my words. Something will. I tell you he's got it."

"Got what, for God's sake?" cried Andy, exasperated
beyond all patience at this ungraspable vagueness.

Marsh's manner calmed to the judicial.

"Got what?" he repeated thoughtfully. "Why, that is hard to say. It's—it's—" he groped for a word; found it in his visitor's vocabulary—"it's a certain magnificent foofaraw of the spirit. That's it. You cannot fight foofaraw; not that kind of foofaraw!"

ANDY left Los Méganos only just after sun-up. Marsh did not appear at all until his guest was ready to mount; offered a limp hand and a lackluster eye; nodded curtly to Andy's words of farewell. As he dipped to cross the *cañada* below the house, the *ranchero* looked back. Marsh had already disappeared.

It was only just after sun-up. The day was but newly lighted atop the rounded low mountains toward the 'Bay, and poised there as though waiting, wings raised, for night's slow and sinister withdrawal from the country below. Up the cañons and *barrancas*, and even the tiny ravines and folds in the hills, breathed small cool airs toward the summits, and thin mists trailed after them as though struggling out of lethargy. The great shadow of the Mountain, night's partisan, retreated grudgingly, inch by inch, as though yielding against pressure. As yet it darkened the whole lower country through which the traveler moved. He shivered. In spite of himself Andy felt this as something more than physical; as some subtle and evil emanation breathed from the Mountain, held in suspension by the chill of its shadow, that stained the fiber of all things through and through. Marsh's dark and elusive subtleties were part of it. They persisted in the back of Andy's spirit, no longer as thoughts or conclusions, no longer as prophecies to be feared, but as a disquiet, like the dismissed voices of conscience. El Monte del Diablo . . . and dwelling in its shadow . . .

Andy shook himself impatiently, struck spur to his horse. He dashed away, plunging into mists that blanketed the lowlands. And then, all being prepared, came the sunlight, with the assured calm dignity of ordination. Instantly the mists and the chill and the shadows were whisked away. And with them vanished the plaguing unease evoked by Marsh's vague predictions. Andy laughed aloud at himself for having been bothered by them at all. The world was palpable again, a world of action. Andy understood that sort of world; he only felt the other. He almost reached out physically to touch it with his hands.

By the time he had reached the Salinas Valley he had stopped briefly at a half-dozen or more *ranchos*, including that of another Anglo-Saxon, Don Roberto Livermore. Each interview added details of certainty to the enterprise. Indeed so eager was the response that, if Andy had been of different type, he might well have dallied with the idea of becoming a dictator in his own right. Certainly no man had ever a better opportunity. But the idea did not even occur to him: and if it had been suggested he would undoubtedly have dismissed it with a laugh of genuine amusement. He was no *político* after power; but he was very much in earnest in what he was definitely about, and therefore was the more dangerously effective. He had genuinely liked Marsh; and now he was puzzled to find that his residuary impression of the man was of a dark spirit dwelling in shadow—the shadow of Diablo, the Devil's Mountain. The influence of Marsh's brilliant talk had almost vanished from Andy's mind. Only occasionally, late at night, or just as he awakened in the morning, a faint shadow of unidentified disquiet flitted across his spirit like a bat. Before the light of full consciousness it flapped away, down to mysterious depths below cognition. But though unseen, its presence unfelt, it was not destroyed. It lurked, awaiting a shadow across the sun.

In due time he topped the ranges and looked down again upon the valley of the Salinas. He had been away a long while; and so many things had happened that the time seemed longer than it really was. He reined his horse. The valley was spread below him like a map; and opposite the dark mountains. There, nearly beneath him lay the mission of Nuestra Señora de la Soledad. Andy could not see Folded Hills, but he could make out its location well enough. Down to the right the river-like flow of the valley melted imperceptibly, so that it was doubtful where the valley left off and the brown haze began. Behind the haze was the sea; but that was far away. The specks and brown blotches were cattle, singly and in herds.

A man who lives out of doors, at close touch with the primitive, either develops a curious mystic susceptibility or becomes brutalized. Andy was of the former type. Now as he sat atop the mountain, on his horse, the old accustomedness of what lay before him arose to him so strongly that he had to fight, as though against a drug, to hold in reality what he had seen and what he was to do. He was again in lotus land. And the larger things were crowded aside by the many little things; so that, as his horse plunged and slid down the steep slope, his mind was filled with them, and with an impatient eagerness to wipe out the leagues that still lay between him and Folded Hills and Carmel! He had intended to stop the night in Soledad; but he changed his mind. They would let him have a fresh horse. He pictured her surprise—suddenly he hungered for Carmel; and Djo, and little Amata, and all the friendly accustomed faces of the ranch people, and the friendly accustomed things. He could not stay with them long: he resolutely thrust this from his mind.

A horseman rode from the sycamores to intercept him. It was Ramón.

2

Andy was overjoyed. For the moment he forgot the misunderstanding.

"*Holá!* Ramón!" he cried, spurring forward. "But what luck to find you here. How are all at the *ranchos?*" he cried eagerly.

"All are in health," replied Ramón.

He did not return Andy's greeting in kind. His usually laughing face was grave. Andy thought he understood; was inwardly delighted with the thought of how quickly Ramón's reserve would melt at a few words of explanation. It amused him to delay.

"What ails you, *amigo?*" he teased. "Are you ashamed to greet the traitor?"

Ramón looked at him with an expression of surprise. Finally he comprehended; he brushed the whole matter aside.

"I would never mistrust you, *valedor*," he cut Andy short.

"Something is wrong," persisted Andy, his elation falling.

"Many things have happened," said Ramón.

"Why, of course!" cried Andy. "That is why I am back." He spoke of his projected change of horses at Soledad; that he would ride on that night to Folded Hills. "You must come with me," said he. "There are many things I would tell you. We shall talk of them as we ride. This is a lucky encounter."

"I was awaiting you," said Ramón. "I rode to meet you."

Andy turned in his saddle.

"Awaiting me?" he repeated after a moment. "Why, how could you know I was coming?"

"It was reported," said Ramón, "and I have been watching, from the *pueblo* at the mission."

A chill of foreboding again gripped Andy's heart. He noticed now that Ramón was speaking in Spanish. He has something to tell me, Andy thought, something very serious.

"What is it, Ramón?" he urged. "If you have news, you must tell me at once."

"It is this matter of Djo, *valedor*."

Andy took hold of himself.

"What has happened to Djo?" he asked in a controlled voice; and then, "Is he hurt, or ill, or—dead?"

"No, no-no, *valedor!*" cried Ramón contritely. "No! He is alive, and well." He reverted to English. "He is in —what-you-call?—the esscrape; and I had to talk to you before you talk to him."

Andy said nothing for a moment: then he laughed, rather wildly.

"You must not scare me like that, Ramón!" said he.

But Ramón did not join his laughter.

"I am sorry, *valedor*," said he quietly. "I am esstupid. I did not think of that."

"Well," said Andy cheerfully, "what's the youngster been doing?" Then his rebound of spirits failed him, for the matter must be pretty serious after all to have brought Ramón so far. And Ramón's apparent reluctance to come to the point was ominous.

"What is it?" he repeated sharply. He seized Ramón by the arm. "What's all this about? Where is the boy? Is he safe?"

"We have him safe. No, no, *valedor*, he is safe. He can do nothing. The Father Sanchez is very *sabio*. At once he locked him up until he could send for me."

Locked him up! Djo locked up! But where? Why?

At Soledad. At the mission. No, no-no; Djo had done nothing; committed no crime.

"But," said Ramón earnestly, "he is yet too young to kill anyone. A boy. To kill someone, that is bad."

Kill? Djo kill? Who should he kill, in the name of all the saints! And for what reason? Andy was exasperated almost beyond words.

"Why,"—Ramón appeared mildly surprised—"this

Pepe. I would gladly have killed him myself," he added. "And at one time I thought I would do so. But I reflect. This Pepe is not like the common *cholo;* and to kill him would make trouble with the government of Mexico."

Did not Andy know that Pepe was an agent for the government of Mexico? A spy, one might say? No? Well, said Ramón unexpectedly, neither did anyone else, until this girl Wapita found it out and wrote the letter to Djo.

Heaven give me patience, groaned Andy to himself. But his mind darkened with anger, for he thought he saw dimly what it was all about. Damn that girl! She had made trouble from the first moment of her appearance. And now to drag Djo into a jealous quarrel. How far had the affair gone? It's about time I got back, thought Andy. For the moment larger matters of rebellion and reprisal were swept from his mind. He was going to do something about this girl at last; something swift and immediate——

"She will not trouble you further," Ramón interrupted him.

"Why not?" demanded Andy. "I've thought that before."

Ramón crossed himself.

"She is dead," said he.

"Dead!" repeated Andy, taken aback.

"Pepe stabbed her," said Ramón simply.

Andy with decision turned his horse aside toward the fringe of sycamores and willows along which they had been riding.

"We shall stop here," he said, "while you explain to me all these things that have happened."

"Why," agreed Ramón with a faint surprise, "but it is just for that I have awaited you, *valedor*."

3

Pepe, began Ramón, had come to Monterey. "That," interpolated Andy, "I knew; I have been at Sonoma," he added. At Monterey he had at once made connections with Wapita. Wapita was staying at the house of Mendoza, the horse dealer. "That also I knew," nodded Andy. Wapita had at once left the house of Mendoza. She had gone to live in rooms connected with the establishment of Da Gama, the Portuguese. Andrés knew the establishment of Da Gama? Andy nodded. There she had become one of the regular entertainers. With Pepe. They danced. And, observed Ramón parenthetically, they were good, very good indeed. The girl had a talent; a genius. This Pepe was a clever fellow. "I have seen them," added Ramón; "it was indeed the *danza noble*. Too good for the establishment of Da Gama. In the capital, in the city of Mexico, these two might well——"

"Yes, yes, get on," urged Andy impatiently.

It was assumed, naturally, that Wapita was the man's mistress as well as his partner.

"But that," said Ramón surprisingly, "I do not myself believe; though it was the opinion of all others."

"Why not?" growled Andy, interested in spite of his preoccupations, for this did not seem to him like Ramón.

"I do not clearly know," confessed Ramón. "It is a feeling here,"—he touched his chest with the tips of his fingers. "That one was wild, was a flame of fire; yes. But it was like a fire that burns before an altar." Ramón groped, fascinated by his own imagery. "Besides," he concluded lamely, "this Pepe have already a girl, another dancer, a Mexican."

"All right; go on."

"He is not her lover." Ramón restated this with more confidence, in English. "But he boss her, and she cannot help it. It is like the snake and the so-little bird. She hate it; but she cannot help it. Now, why is that?" He shrugged. "*Quien sabe?* It may be because she is mad: it may be because she is true *artista*: it may be that she have the ambition to be the *bailarina* at the City of Mexico."

Ramón held his head one side, captivated by his speculations.

"If you don't quit maundering and tell me what *happened!*——" broke in Andy dangerously. Ramón looked at him startled.

"Forgive me, *valedor*," he said hastily. He told the rest of it succinctly enough. Presuming on his influence, Pepe had attempted to utilize her in his secret mission. "That," said Ramón, "is how it became known to me that he was a spy. That was in her letter to Djo." Evidently the Mexican had taken some of her talk at its face value. At any rate he had disclosed to her that he needed more evidence to send Mexico with his "list of traitors"; and that Wapita could help him get it.

"It was then she write this letter to Djo," said Ramón. "You see, *amigo*, you were on this Pepe's list of traitors. It was this that he ask of Wapita. She have live long at Fol-ded Heels. What do she know? He is sure from the way she talk wild that she hate you," explained Ramón. "This Pepe is clever; but he is a fool." He cocked his head sideways in his attitude of considering. "I think," said he judicially, "that she also think she hate you; but when this Pepe say these thing, then she find she do not hate you, and she write Djo all these thing. Yes, that is it!" Ramón looked pleased with his astuteness; nor this time did Andy show impatience at his side excursions into analysis.

"The poor little devil," he said thoughtfully.

"It is all there—in the letter," explained Ramón. "She write it all out. I burn it quickly when I have read."

"Why did you do that?" Andy was aroused. "I wanted to see it."

"It had in it too many things," said Ramón. "It was not a good letter for someone else to read."

"What things? About her—and Djo?"

"No, no-no! Lies. Lies about you, *valedor*, that this

Pepe think he know. But the way he tell it is bad—that you make the plan with Señor Larkin, that you go to Gavilan with this *renegado* to make the revolution and, then to Sonoma, and much more." Ramón grimaced swiftly. "Nobody in California believe those thing. But maybe in Mexico . . ."

Wapita had despatched the letter. Then evidently she had made up her mind to follow it to Folded Hills. Possibly something had happened. Possibly she was merely panicky. At any rate she had started. Pepe had followed her; had caught up with her; had stabbed her.

"The first I know," said Ramón, "I get word at the *rancho*, from Father Sanchez, that I must come at once to Soledad. I go. There is Djo. He has had this letter. He is going to Monterey. At Soledad he find what happen. Father Sanchez lock him up because he is wild, and he want to go for to kill this Pepe; and so Father Sanchez send for me. So here we are, *valedor*, and the blessed saints have brought you at the right time; for Djo does not seem to listen to the Father Sanchez, nor yet to me, and I am at the end of the wit to know what to do."

They arose to mount their horses. Andy paused, his hand on the saddle.

"Carmel? Does she know of this?"

"By the grace of heaven Carmel make the visit at the *hacienda*."

"And Pepe?"

Ramón smiled grimly.

"I think there is only one man who will know about Pepe," said he. "He do not talk."

They swung into their saddles.

"Panchito?" asked Andy.

Ramón nodded.

"Now you know all there is to know," said he. "Let us go to Djo."

But Andy did not yet know all there was to know. The

swift twilight of the southern latitudes was passing when they entered the compound and relinquished their horses to the Indian neophyte. Nuestra Señora de Soledad was in externals one of the ugliest of the missions, a grim fortress-like structure. Now, however, it borrowed a certain majesty from the night. Like all the other missions, its church towered high above its living quarters, which were attached to it by colonnades. Andy and Ramón passed the church door, which was open. Andy stopped short as he glanced within.

"You did not tell me it was near here," he said to Ramón.

He removed the broad flat sombrero from his head and stepped inside the portals. Nothing was to be seen of the interior. It was only a great darkness pointed by eight tall candles.

Andy looked down on the dead girl, and the darkness drew closer behind him, so that he was alone with her.

And his first thoughts were random, like bubbles welling up with his pity. How quiet she is, he thought; and he remembered her in all the tempestuous movement of her wild moods, and how her tumbled hair would fly, and the whirl of her skirts, and many such small matters, and so marveled a little—but gently—that so vital a thing could become so still. He studied her face; for he had never seen it in such complete repose. She is a child, a little child, he said to himself, astonished; but then instantly it came to him that from what he was looking down upon something had been withdrawn; and a faint unreasonable indignation passed across his meditation, like the shadow of a cloud, that so young and helpless a thing should have been constrained as the vessel of such turbulence.

Andy was standing very straight and quiet, his broad hat held in both hands before him, alone in the shell of candlelight with this girl. Nothing else existed. It came to him that nothing else could be permitted to exist until

the accomplishment of this occasion; that time had
stopped, so that he stood in a moment of eternity, and
all things had stopped, too, pending his comprehension.
So he stood, waiting in tranquillity for what was to come
to him.

And when he had entered this quiet possession, certain
perceptions presented themselves before him, in the dignity of order and clarity. He saw them, not as thoughts,
not as symbolisms, but as realities, so that no longer was
this that he looked down upon the stilled body of a child.
He saw it as an emptied vessel; a vessel too small, too
frail, for what it had contained, an embodiment of something so much greater than itself that its blind struggle of
expression must have destroyed it. This perception faded
into a curious thankfulness. The sadness of futility that
her wild free vitality had come to such an end was lifted:
and a more lofty pathos replaced it, the pathos that the
gallant blind stand of an old order, an instinct of race,
should have sought its focus here. And so now Andy
seemed to himself at last to be looking upon a symbol
indeed. He saw, not the mere human remains of a child
foully murdered, but the last earthly abiding place of
something old and beautiful and doomed, done to death
by its own in the term of its destiny.

The moment was too big to last. It broke on the tinkle
of a tiny bell. Andy crossed himself and knelt. Ramón
was beside him. An acolyte, unobserved, had lighted the
altar candles. Father Sanchez, in the robes of his office,
was about to say Mass. At its conclusion Ramón touched
his arm. Andy nodded. They left the church, crossed the
compound.

"I think I'd like to talk to him alone," said Andy.

CHAPTER XXVI

THEY rode, the three of them, Andy, Ramón, and Djo, down the valley on the way to Monterey. Ramón exulted in anticipations, for to him, in due leisure, Andy had disclosed his plans, which at once, to Ramón, became certainties. Djo too had now apparently submerged the past beneath an eager interest in this immediate and exciting future. For the moment at least he appeared to have forgotten the tragedy and the humiliations of only yesterday. Andy rode for the most part in silence. This was his son. He must try to understand.

He covertly studied the boy's face. Was Djo as heartless, as superficial as this would seem to indicate? Was it the self-protection of youth: and was Andy getting old? He groped back across the years to his own boyhood. Partly, he acknowledged in all fairness. He cut harshly across the chatter of war with a mention of the dead girl; and was pleased to see the sudden emotion in Djo's face, and reproachful of himself that he had called him back to recollection. But he could not forbear, for he must know certain things before his mind could be at rest. He caught Ramón looking at him with astonishment.

Andy found himself talking of things he had buried deep in his heart, he had thought forever. They had ceased to hurt him only because he had buried them so deep. Now he told of them, in simple brief statements; and because they were a living part of him, they themselves lived, so that Ramón and Djo hung on his words. Andy told of the young Blackfoot, Kiasax; and Nit-

443

o-ke-man, his wife; and the Little Warrior; and his life
with them.

"Kiasax was my blood brother," said Andy. "He was
one of the best men I ever knew."

He told of Joe Crane, the mountain man; and somehow
they saw Joe Crane; not perhaps very clearly in the flesh,
for this sort of man must be strange to both of them, but
as he lived in Andy's heart.

"Joe was like my father," said Andy. "He taught me
all I knew. You're named after him, Djo," he added.

Somehow he made them understand.

"I was really all alone in the world, except for these,"
said Andy.

He had all their attention. Even the volatile Ramón
offered no words of comment.

The horses shuffled along at their own gait. The Camino
Real passed beneath them slowly, unobserved. Simply
Andy went on, his voice deliberate and tranquil. Through
his words they were made to see, and clearly, the growth
and unfoldment of hatreds and rivalries and fierce tur-
moils; and so came at last to the summer meeting at
Pierre's Hole. Without emotion he narrated the death of
Joe Crane, shot through the forehead by a man with
whom he had long been at enmity.

"It was supposed to be a fair fight," said Andy, "—a
duel, you know. I found out afterwards that this man
had managed to empty the priming from Joe's rifle. It
was really just plain murder."

Andy passed at once to the coming of the Blackfeet to
the Rendezvous.

"They came in to trade," said he. "They had always
before been hostile, you see. But Joe and I had got them
to come in. So they came. But there was a mistake. The
trappers and hunters, the mountain men, did not wait
to find out if they were friendly. Or else they didn't want
to find out. They ought to have known. The Blackfeet

had their women and children with them. But anyway they fired into them at once. The Blackfeet took to the woods. There was a battle. By the time I got there they were mostly all killed. A few got away. I went in to see, and all I found alive was Nit-o-ke-man. She had not gone with the rest because her husband, Kiasax, was dead. She was with his body. A Nez Perce Indian came up, and, before I had a chance to stop him, he shot her. Afterwards I was almost glad of that.

"That," said Andy, "is why I came to California. I wanted to get away from it."

He was sensible of Djo's regard, and something stirred in him, for it came to him that in the course of this narration the boy, in some mysterious fashion, had at once moved closer to him and grown nearer to his stature. And for a moment he wondered, for he had had no idea of why he had been impelled to say these things, except that the time had come to say them. He stopped to ponder this; and dimly he sensed that all things have their use at last in one way or another. But, thought Andy, it is not reasonable to imagine that men and women must be killed and lives broken that an unborn boy might grow; though it is uncertain, he continued presently, what the boy is to become or what part he shall play. And there crossed him momentarily a vision of the intricate web of life, and how no man can know the pattern of it, but must follow as he sees his way. He aroused himself from these speculations, in which he was becoming confused.

They rode on more rapidly for a while, for they wished to reach the Rivera *hacienda* before dark. Ramón, who after all was the least directly affected by the girl's death, had quickly recovered his spirits and his enthusiasm for the enterprise. He saw it whole; as a thing already accomplished; and his confident imagination swept events to a gorgeous and triumphant conclusion.

"You shall be a great man, *valedor!*" he cried, "the

liberator of our California! You shall free her, not from these *ladrones* and this so-foolish one, but from the littleness of her own peoples. She has been asleep, the sobeautiful one, while these many *políticos* crawl about her like *las pulgas*—how you say?—the flea."

"Pretty picture," Andy grunted.

"But it is so!" insisted Ramón. "And now you come to awake her so that she shall——"

"Scratch off the flea," suggested Andy.

"But that is the picture that is not pretty!" Ramón reproached him. "Just the same, it is just so." His animation recovered itself. "You shall see. Always it is a esscandal to me, and to all other of true *californios*, that so she essleep; for we know her, and that she is beautiful in the esspirit; and that, if she do only be awaked, she can act with honor and with esstrength so that the world will look on her with the good eyes and not with the eyes of reproach. The *californio* is not the coward, *valedor;* he is not the lazy in the honor of the mind. He just do not know. He essleep."

"I thought it was a lady," ventured Andy.

Ramón shrugged this aside.

"I—and all others,"—he was earnest now—"have waited long for one to come who shall—what you say?—bring us together." He stretched forth his open hand and closed it tight. "You come, *valedor*. You shall be the great hero of California. All men will follow, *valedor*, where you shall lead. And California shall kiss you the feet!"

"Shucks!" Andy was embarrassed. "I don't want my feet kissed. All I want is that everybody get together and do this, right now, *pronto*, and not *mañana*."

"That they shall do," said Ramón, "now that you do lead. You may say your 'shucks,' *amigo mío;* but all true men will follow Don Largo. For why? For that they know Don Largo, that he is something to follow, and not a shadow. And they will do what you say; and you shall be proud of them. They are good, brave peoples."

"I know that," agreed Andy.

He was amused, as always, by Ramón's vehemence; which, as always, he viewed with no great seriousness. Nevertheless, beneath it was a comfort for which he was glad.

"Of course there's Castro and Pico," he suggested, voicing a thought that had a little bothered him.

"Castro and Pico!" Ramón dismissed them with a gesture. "We have before now told these *políticos* their steps!" He pondered and shook his head. "You know what I think, *valedor?*"

"What?" asked Andy.

"I think this *capitán* Frémont has got himself into one hell of a mess. What he going to do? He get kill; or he get sent to San Blas. Or maybe we give him to the ship of the United States, very polite, and say, 'What are you going to do with your officer that act so rude to such a nice peoples?' Perhaps that is better. No," said Ramón, "I do not think I like to be the *capitán* Frémont!"

"I don't much think I would myself," said Andy.

Ramón turned to him a face of impish delight.

"What you call it? I think he learn,"—he enunciated the phrases painstakingly—"not to go off half-cock, and not to bite off more than he can chew. See, *valedor*," he cried triumphantly, "how I learn to say the English like you!"

Ramón had worked himself into a state of complete satisfaction. Andy looked toward Djo to share his own amusement. Djo was riding somberly, utterly unaware, lost in thoughts of his own. He's thinking of the girl again, said Andy to himself; that won't do. He cast about for something to distract the boy's mind. But Djo caught his father's eye upon him.

"I would not talk to you last night, *señor padre*," said he in Spanish, "and you were kind, and sat with me, saying nothing. For that I thank you, *señor padre*. Now I would like to talk." There was in his speech a new quality of grave authority, so arresting to the two men who had known him from a baby that instinctively they reined their horses to a stand. The three clustered motionless, as though in council.

"I listen," said Andy.

"The Father Sanchez locked me in a room," said Djo directly. "At first I was angry at this. Then after a while I was no longer angry. And then at last I was glad the Father Sanchez had locked me up."

"Hah!" Ramón could not repress the exclamation.

Djo turned to him gravely.

"Not for the reason you think, *señor tío*." He turned again in to Andy. "Tell me, *señor padre*, did you kill this man who murdered the *señor* Crane?"

"Yes," said Andy.

"And for that were you sorry?"

"No," said Andy.

"Nor," said Djo, "would I have been sorry—no, never, never!—if I could have killed this Pepe; no more than I am sorry to kill a rattlesnake. And you, *padre mío*, loved the *señor* Crane—you have said it yourself—as though he were your own father, so that you had the more reason not to be sorry."

Ramón stated bluntly the question from which Andy shrank.

"And you did not love Wapita?" he asked.

Djo looked at him for a moment with surprise.

"But surely, my uncle," he answered at last. "Everybody loved her. How should they not? But not as one loves a father."

The men exchanged glances.

"Go on, Djo," said Andy.

"Why, then, were you glad the Father Sanchez locked you up?" suggested Ramón.

For a moment Djo looked puzzled; then recovered the thread.

"After I was not so angry, I must think, for there was nothing else to do. All that night I could not sleep; so I think. I think over all those things Wapita has told me."

"What things, Djo?" asked Andy.

"Of the *e'tranjero*, of——"

"Oh, yes; go on," said Andy.

"I found this strange, *señor padre*," said Djo, "that all this had been on fire; but now it was cold. It was not," he explained carefully, "that I was no longer *californio;* but I was not so excited. And that made me wonder again."

Shock numbed him, thought Andy: he wouldn't understand that. "Wonder what?" he said aloud.

"How much it was me, and how much it was her," said Djo simply. "Being so excited about it, I mean. A man does not think very straight when he's excited," added Djo. Andy strangled on a laugh that almost caught him. The boy's getting a grown-up mind in him, he thought contritely. I must look out I don't head him off.

"Why, that's so, Djo," said he. "What did you find you hadn't been thinking straight?"

Djo turned his eyes gravely on his father.

"You, *señor padre*," said he.

"Yes?" said Andy. "What were you thinking about me?" Djo's gaze did not waver. Andy smiled reassuringly at his son. "Never mind. I knew. That was natural." He switched to English. "All the sign p'inted that way," he drawled in his trapper manner. "Ain't I taught you to follow the sign, good mountain fashion?"

Djo smiled faintly in response; but his eyes were unconvinced.

"No," he replied, also in English, "I did not read the

sign." Suddenly he reverted to the boy. "*Señor padre!*" he cried passionately. "How could I have ever——"

"Shucks!" Andy interrupted. "Forget it. Let's get going. We'll never get anywhere at this rate. We've got things to do." His manner was gruff; but he leaned from his saddle to squeeze Djo's arm. The boy's face lighted. Ramón looked amused; though his eyes were misted.

2

Jacinto, the *mayordomo*, welcomed them to the *hacienda*. He was in sole charge. Don Sylvestre and Doña Engracia, together with Carmel and Ygnacio, who was now the only son left at the *hacienda*, had the day before departed for Monterey. Why, he did not know.

Don Sylvestre had received a message. Jacinto was ignorant of its purport. There were many rumors, but no news, the wise old man distinguished scornfully. Like all rumors, most of them were absurd, tales for *niños*. Such as? Why, for example, that the *americanos* north of the Bay had risen and made the Señor Vallejo a captive; and that with them was an officer of the United States. Heard ever anyone a tale so ridiculous?

"But the tale happens to be true, Jacinto," observed Ramón.

"True, *señor?*" cried Jacinto, crossing himself hastily. "That Don Mariano is a prisoner? Then the United States makes war against California?"

"No," interposed Andy with decision, "that is not true. These men are rebels, outlaws, and shall be treated as such."

"But this American officer—this *capitán* Frémont——" Jacinto hesitated.

"He is a rebel also," said Andy, "a rebel against his own country." He had not before thought of it that way, but ti was so. He turned to Ramón. "You are right. When we capture him, we shall give him to his own country for punishment." The thing was clear. Not for a moment did Andy's direct simplicity doubt that country's rigid good faith. Jacinto was shaking his head. "You question that?" Andy demanded of him haughtily.

"No, no, *señor*," the *mayordomo* hastened to disclaim, "it was not that. Doubtless the United States will do all that is most honorable. Indeed, Don Sylvestre has told us that it will be better for California if she is herself United States, and that so we rid ourselves once and for all of these robbers of Mexicans."

Ramón and Andy glanced quickly at one another.

"Don Sylvestre told you this?" asked Ramón.

"Why yes, Don Ramón. Me, and the other *seguros* of the *hacienda* who are wise enough to keep their own counsel."

"When was this?"

"Some months ago. Soon after the visit to him of Don Largo—your pardon, *señor*—Don Andrés."

"Don Largo is good enough," said Andy. "But why did you shake your head thus?"

"It was a thought." Jacinto shifted in reluctance.

"Speak up, man!" commanded Ramón impatiently.

"Why, this then, Don Ramón, with all respect. To be sure, Don José Castro is said to be gathering men together—some of his people visited the *hacienda* seeking horses. They are always seeking horses," observed Jacinto in impatient parenthesis. "But we supposed him occupied with another revolution, perhaps against Don Pío." Jacinto spread his hands in deprecation. "These matters are not for us, we understand, *señores*, but we observe and we talk. With all respect, *señores*."

"Go on; go on, man!" urged Ramón.

"Well, then, *señores;* I think it will be difficult to make men believe that Don José intends to do anything except against Don Pío. By his messenger who sought horses he

sent also a summons for the men of the *hacienda*. Not one
answered that summons."

Ramón leaned forward in his chair.

"What if Don José and Don Pío had nothing to do
with all this? What"—he paused, and went on with im-
pressive slowness—"what if it were known that Don
Andrés made the call: that Don Andrés will lead the army
against these rebels?"

The old man stared at Ramón, estimating his sincerity.
After a moment his form straightened, his eye flashed.

"Then," said he with great dignity, "*rancho* and
hacienda—nay, the very *rancherias*—will be left to the
women and children. Even I, *señores*, whose beard is white,
as you see, will forget my years to answer if Don Largo
calls me. For, Don Ramón, I think there is in all California of the north no *gente de razón*, no *mozo*, no *indio*
even, who does not know that what Don Largo says, that
will he do."

Ramón uttered a great shout.

"Holá!" he cried. "What said I, *valedor*? Are you
satisfied? And this Jacinto here, is he not a man of sense,
sabio to be the *mayordomo* of a great *hacienda*?" He struck
the table violently in summons. "Wine! Wine!" he cried
to the servant who came. "Sit you down here with us,
Jacinto. Nay, I insist! Sit you down! Here we are all Californians together." He lifted his glass. "To Don Largo,
the savior of California!"

"The savior of California," repeated Jacinto, and
raised his glass to his lips for the smallest and most respectful of sips; after which he arose at once to his feet to the
greater comfort of his sense of the proprieties. But he was
much pleased.

And Andy too was warmed at heart; though he too was,
in his Anglo-Saxon soul, a trifle embarrassed by Ramón's
flamboyance. "Savior of California" was putting it on a
bit thick. But from the practical standpoint this evidence

of adherence and confidence from a man of the people
was greatly heartening. As he walked down the dim corridor of the *patio* to his old room in the west wing, his
thoughts turned back many years in remembrance of the
time he had first come to this house, a fugitive and friend-
less, save for Ramón; and a glow of gratitude filled his
heart that now he was to repay.

CHAPTER XXVII

ANDY arose early the next morning. For the first time
in a long while he felt both energetic and content. The top
of his mind was busy with the immediate things to be
done. He and Ramón picked the men of the *hacienda*
who were to join the expedition. Strictly speaking, this
was unwarranted in the absence of its owner: but Ramón
took the responsibility. These were to ride to San Juan.
Ramón himself would return up the valley; collect the
rancheros; send summons to those Andy had already
interviewed; despatch reliable men to arouse those who
were distant. They decided together who could most intelligently do the job; rehearsed how the project must be
presented.

Andy himself, and Djo, would go to Monterey. There
was plenty to do. Arms from the ships. Larkin. The south.
Castro. Pico. A wide scattering of power to be grasped
and coördinated. And quickly. It would take some doing.
"We can do it!" cried Andy with conviction. He was completely happy in all this brisk necessity for action. Ramón
was a tower of strength. He had laid aside the gay surface
of his irresponsibility: had become as intent and serious
as Andy himself. The two bent together over the polished
table in the *sala*. Andy surveyed his friend with growing
satisfaction. Here, in the person of Ramón, his faith in
California was finding its justification. Djo sat by, listening eagerly, saying nothing. Andy, glancing up from his
absorption, caught the boy's eyes fixed upon him.

These things detained them at the *hacienda* for all of

that day. The following morning they parted at the ford of the river.

"All is understood," Ramón said, still grave and thoughtful. He pondered for a moment, evidently running over in his mind the numerous details of their plan. Then he straightened in his saddle. "*Vaya con Dios*," he saluted; and then: "Give to Carmel for me the kiss of a brother." His face lighted mischievously. "She is yet in Monterey, I believe?" he inquired with mock solicitude. "Or have you forgot? No?"

He laughed aloud at the flash of self-consciousness in Andy's face; leaned to clap him on the back; then sobered to contrition, for he saw that he had for some obscure reason made Andy uncomfortable. He could not, for the life of him, see why. Ramón did not pretend to understand these Anglo-Saxons, even yet. But his intuitions were quick. He laid his hand on Andy's arm.

"I will tell you secret," he said confidentially. "But you must not tell. Just so it is always when I come back to Conchita. And all the time I know that I am the old *papá;* and Conchita"—he looked about him bright-eyed as though to detect an eavesdropper—"I know this," he lowered his voice to a whisper. "I know that Conchita she is become the too-fat one. But, *valedor*, that is all the outside. Pouf!" He snapped his fingers. "That for the outside! We are two old fools; no?" he cried aloud. "Just alike. But we shall tell that to no one. I think, me, it is good to be two old fools together! No?"

He rode away laughing, without further farewell.

As the leagues were few to Monterey, and as Andy and Djo were provided with no *caballado*, they rode slowly. Andy was content. He felt at home again and comfortable. There might be outside vexations of one sort or another, but they did not matter, and could be attended to in good time. He had again his friend; he had his son; even now he was shortening the miles to his wife and daughter.

Estrangements were over, if estrangements there had been outside Andy's own imagination. He was Don Largo still to the *californios*. They loved him; and Andy was faintly surprised to discover the depth of his love for them.

In this new-recovered warmth he talked to Djo as they rode. He had always, from the lad's earliest childhood, treated him as an equal, both in years and experience. Shrewd as always in the reading of character, he was struck by the change in the boy. He pondered over this change, but could not solve it completely. Djo was less emotional, more cerebral. He had been before nearly all Latin; now he was more Andy's own.

The two discussed the situation; and their discussion was sober, analytical, without the prejudice of too partisan emotion. So now Andy rose to a real happiness; for here at last was his son grown to hold council.

They paused together atop the ridge of the low pass through the hills across the Bay from Monterey. Andy never wearied of savoring this first sight of blue water.

"Lot of ships in, Djo," he said at once. "Don't believe I ever saw so many at one time." He sighed in slight disappointment, for undoubtedly there must be a *fiesta* in honor of so notable a gathering; high and ceremonious doings at the Mansion; low and unceremonious doings at the Portugee's. Andy had at the moment no taste or time for *fiestas*. "Make out any of 'em, Djo? Boston ships or whalers?"

The two squinted their eyes.

"I think one or two are ships of war," ventured Djo presently.

Andy looked again: shook his head.

"Too far for me," he confessed. "Which ones?"

"I don't know: but there's the flag up on the *presidio*," said Djo.

"That shines!" cried Andy, obviously pleased. "You

can use your head as well as your eyes, Djo. Must have got hold of some powder," he added.

Djo nodded. He understood the allusion. Ships of one sort or another were always coming in to Monterey—traders in the Boston ships, whalers, and more rarely an occasional warship of one nation or another beating up the coast on business or patrol or survey. The commercial ships were received on a strictly business basis: but the warships must be treated punctiliously. Always, on dropping anchor, they sent ashore a young ensign with a polite offer to salute the Mexican flag—if the officials would hoist it! And invariably the governor, or his deputy, sent back as polite a refusal. No reason was given; though everybody knew the salute was declined simply because there was no powder to return it!

"Shucks!" said Andy. "That settles it. There'll sure be a *fiesta.*"

"Without doubt, *señor padre,*" agreed Djo. "See," he pointed out, "there are people coming to it down the valley." He indicated through an opening in the pines a slowly moving cloud of dust. Andy grinned at him.

"Reckon you ain't sorry, at that," he accused. "Well, maybe it ain't so bad. Save us some bother, maybe. People will all be together. Get us what we need from the ships. Better be getting along." Andy was suddenly impatient.

With a last glance at the blue-and-green-and-gold prospect that never failed of its charm for him, he turned his horse into the open pine forest that fringed the curve of the bay. In spite of his impatience he restrained his animal to a walk. Andy could never resist the pines. In the pungent aroma released by the sun warmth from their dried needles he breathed a faint nostalgic memory of another land and another time. His horse's hoofs sank into their yielding surface without sound. Their shadows were still: their straight-spaced columns stood in a quiet reproof of haste. The brief short flittings of birds seemed the only privileged movements. Even the wind—though today there was none—but touched the tops of the forest. One could hear it going by, high up, hurrying atiptoe. Below was guarded stillness, with only a drowse of bees and a sweet rare chirp of bird and the austere dreaming hum of the trees. Nothing ever touched more surely the hidden, strange, and unrecognized streak of sensitiveness in Andy's practical make-up than the pines.

On this day that touch was not lacking, for it was strangely without surprise that he looked upon the spectacle that disclosed itself when he and Djo emerged from the forest on the outskirts of the *pueblo*. This possibility had never crossed his mind. He did not understand how it could be. Nevertheless, now that it confronted him, it was as though he had expected it all along.

The slight delay in the pines had permitted the concourse he and Djo had inferred beneath the cloud of dust up the valley to converge with our travelers. Beneath that dust, which rose in a choking cloud, eddying in the warm air against the intense blue of the sky, marched a long cavalcade of mounted men, two by two, as far as the eye could make them out. Two by two, at a slow and stately footpace. At their head, dressed in blouse and leggings, his felt hat caught up at one side, his gauntleted hands crossed on the pommel of his saddle, his head high, his eyes fixed straight ahead, rode—Frémont!

3

We have many eyewitness accounts of that spectacular entrance. Lieutenant Walpole, of the British flagship, the *Collingwood*, was ashore at the time. His youthful imagination was much stirred. "Here were true trappers," he wrote. "These men had passed years in the wilds, living on their own resources. They were a curious set." He described the great cloud of dust that had drawn Andy's attention. "Thence in a long file emerged this wildest wild party. Frémont rode ahead, a spare, active-looking man, with such an eye! . . . After him came five Delaware Indians, who were his bodyguard; they had charge of two baggage horses. The rest, many of them blacker than the Indians, rode two by two, the rifle held by one hand across the pommel of the saddle. . . . The dress of these men was principally a long, loose coat of deerskin, tied with thongs in front; trousers of the same, of their manufacture. . . ." He was here referring to the thirty-nine men of Frémont's original party. We can imagine the open-mouthed wonder of the natty and correct young naval officer. "The rest of the gang," he adds, "were a rough set; and perhaps their private, public, and moral characters had better not be too closely examined." He mentions one other besides Frémont. Of this individual he says: "One man, a doctor, was six feet high and an odd-looking fellow." This was Semple, though how he got to be a doctor is obscure. Lieutenant Walpole adds a pious hope: "May I never come under his hands!"

A companion, likewise a sailor on shore leave, Walter Colton, of the American ship, the *Congress*, was also impressed by the stage setting. "They defiled, two abreast," says he, "through the principal street of the town. The citizens glanced at them through their grated windows. Their rifles, revolving pistols, and long knives glittered over the dusky buckskin which enveloped their sinewy limbs, while their untrimmed locks, flowing out from under their foraging caps, and their black beards, with white teeth glittering through, gave them a wild, savage aspect."

There must have been quite a shore party from the various ships in the harbor, of both nationalities. We have scattered comments from officers not only of the *Collingwood* and the *Congress*, but also from the *Savannah* and the little sloop of war *Cyane*. Probably their youngsters gravitated together by the attraction of their common age and profession. All in all it was quite a show, with a thoroughly appreciative audience: "a spectacular entrance," as Zoeth Eldredge dryly remarks, "which must have satisfied even the theatrical soul of the young conqueror."

4

Andy watched the long procession file past. It did not enter the town, but took its way up the slope of the hill behind. He made no answers to Djo, and the boy too fell silent. Only when the last pair of horsemen had passed did he return to the boy.

"What is it all about, *señor padre?*" Djo then repeated his question.

"I do not know. I must find out," said Andy crisply. "Do you," he ordered, "seek out the *señora*, your mother. Tell her I am here; and that I will come to her as soon as possible."

"Shall I then return for you?" asked Djo, who was secretly dying to be about this exciting business.

"You will remain with your mother and sister," said Andy. He spoke with an edged decision to which Djo was a stranger, and which silenced any protests the boy might have made. "I don't know what this means," he relented to explanation. "I may have to get out in a hurry. Don't tell your mother that. I'll let you know."

He rode forward into the plaza. Sailors were everywhere, both on shore leave and on duty. The customs house was guarded, sentries paced before the gates of the *presidio*, on the walls. Two marines stood at the base of the flagpole. Andy stopped his horse to gaze upward at the Stars and Stripes; but he said nothing, and his face was inscrutable. The seamen of the pleasure parties were drifting in one direction, following in curiosity Frémont's men up

the slope of the hill. Their wide glazed hats with hanging
broad ribbons were thrust far back on their heads; their
wide trousers flapped about their feet. They rolled along,
legs wide as though still bracing against a heaving deck:
and their eyes roved, avid for anything that promised
interest or excitement. They spat copiously of tobacco,
and shouted to one another in bellowing weather-hoarsened
voices, and looked with lofty and swaggering contempt on
the marines, with their tall visored kepis and their crossed
belts and their trim tight-fitting uniforms of blue. The
marines paid them no attention, remote in a stiff-collared
secure pride of their own. From the direction of the Portugee's *pulquería* came a confusion of singing and shouting
that presently swelled to an uproar, but instantly died
again to decorum when a compact provost squad of sailors,
under command of a petty officer, dog-trotted to the scene
of disturbance and disappeared within. Out in the harbor
lay the ships, great and small; their sails in the symmet-
rical taper of a neat furl, their yards accurately squared,
the white rectangles of their ports checkered against their
dark sides. Small boats bobbed at the ends of booms; or
danced on the slow swell making into the bay, their oars
rising and dipping in exact and beautiful rhythm. In their
motion was a light and buoyant gayety, in contrast to the
austere immobility of the ships. From the deck of one of
the latter sounded the exultant lilt of a bugle call.

Andy's eyes took in all these things, examining them
gravely and deliberately, one by one. The setting was
to him familiar by a score of visits and hundreds of associ-
ations; but it had become strange. There were the customs
house by the shore, and the wide dusty plaza, and the
presidio, and the low whitewashed houses, and the spacious
gardened residences on the slope of the hill; and the slum-
berous curve of the beach embracing the blue bay; and the
glimmer of the distant dunes across, and the pines behind.
Overhead was the deep clear blue of the sky. Around the

point, unhastening, untarrying, shouldered the spaced slow ground swells from the open sea. Just as it had always been. Nothing really had changed. And yet to Andy, sitting there on his horse, looking about him at it all, it was as though he had come into a strange land. The outward seeming was the same, but the animating principle was different. Something rare and beautiful had gone; something too shy and gentle to contest its place with this new sharp bustle of purposefulness.

5

To his surprise Andy found Larkin well satisfied with the situation. Yes; war had been declared between the United States and Mexico. Things were going according to plan. Commodore Sloat had raised the Stars and Stripes.

"Any trouble?" asked Andy.

"None at all. Not even an objection. Everybody knew it was going to happen, of course. The commodore was here a week before he did it."

"What was he waiting for?"

"He's the sort that can't make up his mind; though don't say I told you so. I had a devil of a time convincing him he'd better act before Seymour—the Englishman, you know—got here and beat him to it. Finally he sent ashore a formal demand for surrender." Larkin stopped to laugh. "There was nobody to receive it. Castro was off somewhere; nobody knew where. The *presidio* was empty. There wasn't even a flag to haul down. So after a decent interval small boats were manned, and two hundred and fifty armed men were landed, who marched up to the plaza, and they ran up the American flag, and presented arms, and after that a band from the flagship played patriotic airs. Everybody turned out to see the show and listen to the band. It was a good show and a good band.

I think they enjoyed it. We had a big party that night; and that was a good show, too. The whole *pueblo* turned out. I saw your wife there, and your father-in-law and Doña Engracia."

"Where's Castro?" asked Andy.

"Last I heard he was over Santa Clara way where he'd got together a few recruits to act against the Sonoma outfit. As soon as they heard of the change of flag most of them quit. They say Castro went south. Do you know," said Larkin, "I very much doubt if there'll be any trouble at all—give them time."

Andy was more doubtful.

"Glad you think so. But I've been back country, and folks are pretty stirred up over this Sonoma business and this Frémont. He's here, you know; with all his outfit," added Andy, remembering that Frémont had but just arrived.

But Larkin was undisturbed.

"Yes, I know," he chuckled. "Sloat sent for him. The commodore wouldn't believe me when I told him Frémont was acting without orders. That young man is in for the surprise of his life. I wouldn't miss that interview for anything in the world."

"You think he won't countenance——"

"I know he won't," Larkin interrupted emphatically. "He told me so."

"Well," said Andy, rising, "that's good! I feel better." He meant it. He had no passing regret for the scrapping of his own plans. He did not even think of them. They were unnecessary. "I'll get on. I haven't seen my family yet."

CHAPTER XXVIII

IN THE joy of reunion with his own it was not difficult to forget, temporarily, the whole matter. He and Carmel had never before been so long separated. Andy was glad Don Sylvestre and Doña Engracia and Ygnacio were there. Amata seemed to him visibly to have grown. Even the comely broad brown face of Lisete, who had come as nurse-maid to the little girl, was grateful as another link with Folded Hills.

There was so much to tell, so much news to exchange. All were deeply shocked at the affair of Wapita. They listened with soft cries of pity and lamentation to what Andy and Djo had to relate.

"*La pobrecita,*" mourned Carmel, "so young! And yet——" She glanced toward Djo secretly; did not finish the sentence; crossed herself surreptitiously.

"It may be that thus the blessed saints saved her for themselves," suggested Doña Engracia gently.

Ygnacio's concern was largely quieted when he learned that Panchito had been despatched on the trail of Pepe. "These Mexicans!" he muttered.

They were all eyeing Djo covertly. Their real interest was in Djo; how this affected him. Djo was wooden. They could not tell. After a decent interval they edged relievedly into other topics.

Andy must tell his story. They listened with little cries of indignation as they heard of the doings in the valley of Sonoma and at Sutter's Fort. But he could not avoid seeing that their interest was in the personal; that Don Guadalupe had been imprisoned; that Don Guadalupe's

464

property had been stolen from him, though Andy tried conscientiously to point out that there had been no looting. These things were Don Guadalupe's, were they not? The murders on the mud-flats darkened the brows of Don Sylvestre and his son.

"I had heard something of this; but I did not believe," said Don Sylvestre. "Surely these men will be brought to answer!"

But these matters too, after a decent attention, they permitted to pass; and fell with relief to an eager narration to Andy of the small easy gossip of personal and familiar things. He had been gone for a long time.

He relaxed to it, yielding himself to it in a grateful comfort as a man drowses in the warmth of an enclosed room after battling the elements, remote from the storm outside. He had said nothing at all of the plans, now useless, that he had made. But in the back of his mind stirred a faint wonder and curiosity. Nobody had seemed particularly concerned with the momentous changes that had taken place. Only Don Sylvestre had touched upon them casually; and that in answer to a direct question.

"Why, I think everybody knew this must happen," said he. "I think that most people are glad it is the *americanos*, and not the English or the French. I do not think there will be much trouble. Though," he added, "it seems to me unfortunate that these things you tell of at Sonoma had to happen. That is very bad. If it were not for that I think there would be no fighting at all."

"There will be fighting?" Carmel asked quickly. "You must not fight," she pleaded with Andy.

"No; I shall not fight," said Andy with decision.

She returned to her embroidery. She seemed with that assurance to have lost interest again. Andy looked at her with curiosity. As though she sensed his wonder, she looked up at him.

"The grass will still grow at Folded Hills," she said quaintly.

Why, that is true, thought Andy; and as he stared at her sleek bent head, he seemed to see in her, as before he had seemed to see so differently in Wapita, California itself, so that these changes became, strangely, at the same time momentous and very small. Aloud he said to Don Sylvestre:

"This Frémont acted without orders. Señor Larkin tells me that the *señor comandante* of the *americanos* has summoned him and his people here to call them to account."

"That is well, that is very well," said Don Sylvestre with gratification.

2

Early the following day Larkin sought him out. The consul was thoroughly pleased: rubbed his hands with satisfaction.

"You should have been there!" he cried. "It was as good as a show. Frémont reported on board; and the commodore asked him point-blank whether he had been acting under orders. Frémont was evasive, made a lot of talk about his 'plan of conquest' as he called it. The old man was thoroughly put out: kept repeating that it was impossible he should do such a thing without orders. Seemed to believe it. I suppose that was natural. Must have been inconceivable to a man like Sloat. He flew into quite a rage. Told Frémont he would not have raised the flag here except on the faith of Frémont's operations across the Bay. That wasn't so, of course, but he was pretty mad; and that's what he said."

"How did Frémont take that?" asked Andy interestedly.

"He had to take it," chuckled Larkin. "He was pretty mad himself, but he was in no position to show it. He tried again to explain his 'plan of conquest.' The old man would have none of it, repudiated it completely. Frémont said something about his 'battalion' as part of the United States forces. The commodore fairly snorted. 'Battalion'! said he. 'What battalion? Do you mean that mob of cut-throats you've brought with you?' Frémont tried to plead with him to use them somehow, for guard duty, anything. I imagine he was thinking what figure he was going to cut with his men. He was singing pretty small. Sloat categorically declined to have anything to do with them. I didn't know the old fellow had so much backbone. I think," said Larkin shrewdly, "that the commodore was even yet none too easy in his mind that he had not exceeded his own authority in taking Monterey. He's had no *official* news of war, you know; only private advices. He probably remembered the pickle Jones got himself into in '42."

"The private advices were reliable, weren't they?" asked Andy.

"Yes," replied Larkin, "but you don't know Sloat. He hasn't got lime enough in his backbone to whitewash his head. Sounds pretty good, doesn't it?"

"It sounds pretty good," agreed Andy. "What's he going to do with them?"

"I guess he wishes he knew," chuckled Larkin.

Andy walked on. He was as pleased as Larkin. Unexpectedly he found himself face to face with John Marsh. The master of Los Méganos was eyeing him quizzically.

"So here we are again," drawled Marsh.

"Didn't expect to see you here," greeted Andy, clasping his hand.

"Me? Oh, I joined up—with Frémont. Wanted to see the fun. How's the great uprising coming on?"

But Andy refused to be baited.

"Oh, that's all useless now, of course," he acknowledged carelessly.

"'Bonnie Prince Charlie,'" Marsh quoted himself. "Something always happens. I told you it did. Nothing *can* happen. Nobody would guess it. But it does. You can't beat it."

"No?" returned Andy. "You think not?"

"Can't you see that flag?" Marsh was slightly impatient. "The one thing nobody could guess: the one lone thing in all the infinite universe of possibilities that could pull this fellow out of the hole he'd dug for himself. I told you it would. You can't fight foofaraw. Foofaraw wins."

Andy grinned in his face. "You better go back to camp and get the news," he thought to himself.

Marsh looked at him sharply.

"If I were you I wouldn't take this matter too lightly, Burnett," said he. "You are in this pretty deep. I'd advise you to stay out of sight as much as possible. Or get out, up country."

"Thanks," said Andy dryly; then, as he saw Marsh really meant well by him, "Thanks," said he in a different tone.

The doctor at once returned to his detached cynical manner, from which he had for that one instant departed.

"It's a pity, though, you can't come up to see us. You'd envy us. We are very, very military. You know some of our specimens already; but we have some fresh ones. Did you know that Ezekiel Merritt has been elevated to the proud rank of major? And we have another with us whom you would enjoy—a recent recruit. There, too, is an admirable specimen for your collection. He wears his foofaraw in the guise of importance. His bearing is that of a man with wooden underwear." Marsh paused to laugh gently at his conceit. He stopped and laid his hand on Andy's arm with informal familiarity. "You should have been there the other night. He was standing sentry, and strutting up and down his beat a good deal like a

puffed-out old turkey gobbler. Suddenly an owl hooted
in a tree, 'Who! Who! Who!' He must have thought it
a challenge by another sentry, for he boomed out, 'Lieutenant Colonel William H. Russell, suh, a bosom friend
of Henry Clay!'" Marsh laughed again. "Did you ever
read Shakespeare, Burnett?" he shifted the subject unexpectedly.

"Shakespeare? I? No," Andy was surprised at the
question. "Why?"

"You should. I advise it. He too was a great observer;
and I think he was also greatly amused. He wrote plays,
you know." Marsh was idly tapping the ground with the
ferrule of his cane. "In one of his plays he utters a profound truth that sums it all up: 'What fools these mortals
be.' There is nothing more amusing in life, Burnett, than
to go along with the crowd and so to prove to one's self
how true that is. So naturally I joined up."

"I see," said Andy vaguely. For some instinctive reason
he was again on guard. Marsh did not need to excuse or
explain his actions.

"What do you make out of Commodore Sloat?" pursued Marsh.

"I haven't been out to the ships," said Andy.

"My dear fellow!" Marsh appeared surprised.

"I'm not interested." Andy was restive.

"You should be. There is great interest in these beautiful engines of war. Little worlds in themselves. You have
not, then, you say, met Commodore Sloat?"

"I have not."

"You neglect your opportunities. Nor his lieutenant,
the excellent Captain Mervine? Nor"—Marsh's speech
slowed, became silky—"nor his second in command,
Commodore Stockton, who but yesterday joined the
squadron with his ship, the *Congress?*"

"I tell you I've not been near the ships," repeated Andy.

"But you must certainly make the acquaintance of

Commodore Stockton," insisted Marsh. "Even if you persist in your apparent attitude of seclusion, upon that I must insist. I must arrange this for you."

"Why must I meet Commodore Stockton?" Andy challenged impatiently. "What have I to do with any of these people? What have they got to do with me?"

"Nothing, I suppose," conceded Marsh. "Nothing. Except as a matter of interest. I think you would find him interesting."

"Why should you think that?" demanded Andy, almost rudely.

"Perhaps you might not," conceded Marsh, "but I was remembering our talk—at Los Méganos. I got the impression there that you were more or less a student, a connoisseur, of foofaraw." He raised his hand in a salute of farewell.

Andy stared after him. He's got a surprise coming to him, Andy repeated his thought to himself. But the thought seemed to him to have lost substance. He could not rid himself of the impression that somehow Marsh had had the last word.

But Marsh isn't a bad sort, thought Andy, as he continued his way. He meant well by me. Came down on purpose to warn me to keep cover. He grinned at his own recollections. I'd sure have to, he acknowledged; I bet that fellow would like to skin me alive. Lucky he stepped in his own trap.

3

, But the next day came Larkin, breathless, stepping into the house unannounced, almost too excited to remember his greetings to the ladies of the household.

"You've got to get out of here, Burnett," he cried. "Have you been seen today?"

"No," said Andy.

"That's good. You can slip away. There's no time to lose."

Andy waited steadily to learn in good time what had happened. No sense asking questions. His fiber stiffened to alertness. But Carmel cried out, wide-eyed, alarmed:

"What is it, *señor*? What is it that my husband has done? What will they do to him? Why is it——"

"Steady, Carmel. Let the *señor* Larkin speak."

"Sloat has quit," Larkin told them bluntly.

"Quit?"

"Quit: relinquished command. He sails for home at once."

"But why? I don't understand."

"He says that his health is poor, that he's sick," said Larkin bitterly. "Sick, yes: sick of the whole situation. I told you he hadn't any backbone."

"Well!" Andy exhaled a deep breath. "Then——"

"Then the authority passes," said Larkin dryly, "to Commodore Robert Field Stockton. Have you seen Commodore Robert Field Stockton?"

"No," said Andy. "I've heard of him," he added.

Larkin leaned back in his chair.

"Commodore Stockton," he said with an air of false deliberation, "is a good-looking man, curly hair and big eyes. He has personality, enthusiasm, energy. Popular." He leaned forward again. "He and Frémont have been all over the place, arm in arm, thick as thieves, for the past two days."

"I get your drift," Andy nodded. "And so you think he will——"

"I don't have to think," interrupted Larkin. "He's already done. I'll say this: he's no procrastinator. Here's what he's done. He's reversed Sloat and accepted Frémont's 'battalion' as regularly enrolled United States troops, and made Frémont a major and Gillespie a captain."

"That's bad!" cried Andy, startled. "That'll make trouble with the Californians, I'm afraid. It'll be a job to hold them."

"He's not waiting for that. He's going to start things himself. Frémont's 'battalion' are to go to San Diego at once. Stockton goes to San Pedro with his forces. They are to march overland toward each other, 'subduing' the country as they go."

"But," protested Andy aghast, "I thought you told me——"

"That in case of war," Larkin caught him up, "the ports were to be occupied peaceably and no further move made. I did."

"Then are you sure——"

"The orders are published. And more than that. Read this." He thrust a paper into Andy's hands.

"What is it!"

"A general proclamation. Stockton's. Conciliation," said Larkin bitterly.

Andy perused the document in his slow and methodical fashion. One paragraph he read twice. In it Stockton announced that he "could not confine operations to the quiet and undisturbed possession of the defenseless ports of Monterey and San Francisco, but would immediately march against the boastful and abusive chiefs who had not only violated every principle of national hospitality and good faith toward Captain Frémont and his surveying party, but who unless driven out would, with the aid of the hostile Indians, keep this beautiful country in a constant state of revolution and blood."

"He's swallowed whole everything that fellow told him," said Andy.

"Because he wanted to," supplemented Larkin. "They're of a feather, those two. Read on."

Andy obeyed. He learned of imagined "scenes of blood and murder"; of the oppressions of "Castro the usurper" who had not only done all these other things, but had deliberately impoverished his own people. When Andy had finished all this, he refolded the paper and returned it to Larkin, who put it in his pocket.

"Trouble," commented Andy. "Too bad. I'll say this: he's got Castro tied for *pronunciamientos*."

"And useless!" exploded Larkin. "There's absolutely no occasion for fighting and bloodshed. It gains nothing. Perhaps," he said, but without conviction, "there'll be no resistance. He must command over a thousand well-armed and disciplined men; not to speak of Frémont's lot."

"Hopeless," agreed Andy. "But they'll fight. If it was only the ship's men—but they been slapped in the face by this Frémont. And they got to show Mexico that even if she robs them and fails to help them, they're not cowards, like her," he added out of his profound knowledge of his people.

"I suppose so," agreed Larkin gloomily. His eyes blazed.

"That a couple of crazy, self-centred fools," he said violently, "should have the power—just two irresponsible small boys—strutting blind with their own ambitions—— It makes a man feel so helpless, so—— There's no *sense* to it!"

Andy laughed gently and laid his hand on the other's arm.

"Steady, *amigo*," said he. "Steady! We've done our best. It's all a man can do."

"I suppose so," sighed Larkin, "but it's kind of tough to be licked by this sort of thing. What fate sent this Frémont here just at this time? Any other man than Sloat —any other than Stockton! Just at this time!"

"It's always tough to be licked," agreed Andy. "But I see now that John Marsh is a pretty *sabe hombre*."

"Marsh? What's he got to do with this?"

"Just something he said. I laughed at him, for it looked

like everything was fixed to prove him wrong. But he was right; dead right."

"What was it he said?" asked Larkin.

"You can't fight foofaraw," quoted Andy.

"What are you going to do?" asked Andy presently.

"I am an American," replied Larkin stoutly, "and so I shall remain, with all the loyalty that is in me. I go south with the *Congress* to do what I can in conciliation—to try to pick up a few of the pieces," he concluded. His shoulders drooped; for a moment he seemed to give way to profound discouragement. Then he raised his head. "But that's not what I'm here for. You. You've got to get out. And right now, without a moment's delay. It's known to Frémont what you were trying to do. He'll have it in for you."

"Yes," Andy nodded thoughtfully, "I've got to get out. We'll have to try. I don't know whether we'll make it, but we must try."

"Of course you can make it—you, an old mountain man."

"They's good scouts with Frémont," submitted Andy. "They's Carson and Lajeunesse; yes, and a passel more."

It developed that he was thinking, not of himself, but of the others; was envisaging the impossibility, even with a good start, of conducting so large a party safely from any determined pursuit. It was only with the greatest difficulty that Carmel and Larkin together were able to convince him at last that she and Amata could safely be left with the Riveras in Monterey.

"I will pledge myself to their safety," said Larkin earnestly. "Neither Frémont nor Stockton will war against women. And it's the only chance. What good are you to them in irons?"

"I don't trust them," said Andy uneasily. But he yielded, more to the common sense of the situation than to the pleadings of Carmel and his friend. It was characteristic that once he had accepted the necessity, he dismissed the matter from his mind. He was entirely confident.

"Give me an hour's start—a half-hour," he answered Larkin's anxious question, "and I'll g'arantee ary man, Kit Carson or ary other, will never ketch us."

"What will you do? Join the Californians?" asked Larkin.

"Ah, no, no!" cried Carmel passionately. "You mus' not fight!"

He patted her hand in reassurance.

"Fighting's useless," he said briefly. "Djo and I know a good hideout."

Yes, Djo must go with him. Andy was firm on that point.

ANDY and Djo sat side by side on the wide flat rock looking down on Folded Hills.

"We could just as well go down there and live in our own house," said Andy. "Nobody's going to take the trouble to bother us so far away."

"This is more fun," said Djo.

"Just as well take no chances, I suppose—for a while," conceded Andy. "Yes, it is fun," he added after a little. "Remember, when you were playing Wildman, how you used to put out a stone on this rock every day for a signal you were all right?"

Djo gurgled happily.

"Well, we ain't going to play Wildman," stated Andy with decision. "Soon as it comes dark I'll slip down and get hold of Panchito. He can sneak us up what we need."

"Let me," urged Djo.

"Think you can get to Panchito without getting caught at it?" teased Andy. "No; I was only fooling. I know you can."

"I could do it now, in broad daylight," boasted Djo. "I did it in the *milpa*, when I was playing Wildman."

"Mebbe," said Andy dryly. "But I reckon we'll wait for dark. Besides," he added, "I want you should bring Panchito up here. I want to talk to him. I want to send a message to your uncle Ramón."

They hugged their knees, the man and the boy, in companionable silence; and half drowsed in the warm sun. They were comfortably tired. It had been simple enough. They had slipped out of Monterey separately, on foot, to meet again where one of Larkin's men awaited them with horses. Thence they had struck south, and then east, through the tangle of mountains that constitute the Sur. It was slow business. Not only was this a circuitous way to go, but it lay through rough, wild, and uninhabited country. They must save their horses, for they would not be able to get fresh ones. There was no regular route; and the whole terrain was strange to Andy. He grumbled a little to Djo over the needless trouble, for he had no thought that he was now of sufficient importance for any determined pursuit; but he had promised Carmel and Larkin. And, secretly, he was enjoying it. This was like old times, this nosing out a way through rugged country by the dips and angles, the hogs'-backs and *puerto-suelos*. They had some food, provided by Larkin; but on the evening of the second day Andy permitted Djo to shoot a deer.

"We'll want meat in our hideout," said he. "But mind you pick you a little one. We can't lug much weight. Get you a little fat young barren doe: that's the best. Look out and be sure she's barren. You know how to tell the differ?"

"By the neck," said Djo. He was proud and happy at being entrusted with the Boone gun.

The sun was hot on the flat rock. Andy's thoughts floated lazily across his lassitude. He surveyed them curiously from an inner detachment.

Queer how things come out, thought Andy. There've been times, seemed like, when I've felt I was moving with something big, and that I had something to do with it. I suppose Benton put that notion in my head. No, corrected Andy, it was my grandmother first of all. It was she started me out. He pondered this, with a faintly tolerant inner smile at the seriousness with which at times he had taken his youthful exaltations when, in occasional rare moments, he had seemed to see himself as part of a greater destiny.

That was when I happened to be following along with

things, reflected Andy. When he had turned aside, they had moved on without him. A man don't amount to much; he ain't got much to do with it, thought Andy. He did not much care. He surveyed with detached tranquillity the eager purposes of his past, and how on each, at the moment of its climax, had been laid a hand of negation. He regarded himself with a certain humor. To him at this moment it seemed mildly amusing that he had ever harbored, even secretly and uncertainly and dimly, the notion that he was to play a part in the movements of fate. Here he was, atop a rock, looking down on Folded Hills, while things moved on just as though he had never existed. What was he? Or Larkin? Or his grandmother, or Benton or Frémont, for that matter—any of them?

So far his mind drifted idly. Through the very relaxation of its idleness, he began to see, not the details of men's doings, but the finalities of accomplishment. And he perceived that the vision—of the old pioneer woman in the Pennsylvania farmhouse; of the statesman pacing his study in the frontier fur town; yes, of himself carrying the Boone rifle gallantly and blindly into the unknown—had been in reality fulfilled. "One people, one flag, a mighty civilization that shall extend from sea to sea." Queer how these words had haunted him through all these years! Well, it had happened. The trail had led straight, after all, and here he, Andy Burnett, had been privileged to stand at its end.

Andy's long frame tightened, and he held his breath lest he break the moment. For now it was vouchsafed him to perceive the great gods moving high and serene to an end that is inexorably foreordained, so that there could be no possible circumstance but what made to that end; and also the lesser gods that stand near enough to human frailties to amuse themselves with them. Malicious, capricious little gods that delight in frustrations, in mischiefs, in injustices, able through the weaknesses of men to guide events for their purposes, exultant in the illusion that thus they command destiny.

Andy threw back his head. For this moment he seemed to himself poised in a great power. He had risen above the lesser gods, was greater than they. For, looking down on them thus, from above, he saw that they, even they, were moving perforce blindly and unconsciously to serve the constructive purposes which they opposed.

He looked at Djo, and a new certainty came to him. This, he thought, is my son. I have bred him here, in this land of my adoption, to which I have been led. This is not the end of accomplishment. Great things are here to be done. He is of me. What I have brought here, that will he carry on. Better than I will he carry them on; for he is of me, but he is also of this land. Only I could have bred him; only I could have given him what I had to bring. I am again on the trail.

His thoughts were once more with himself as he had been—when he was only a little older than Djo—and the old woman watching after him as, with the long rifle on his shoulder, he had faced the setting sun; and the lift in his mind and the hope in his heart. That was long, long ago, and so many years between. No, it was yesterday; for here was he, and there was he, and the two were the same. So it came to Andy that, after all, one does not live in time, but in accomplishment. He looked again at Djo, staring steadily across the sun-soaked valley, lost in dreams—of what?

And Andy was filled with a strange contentment; and he thought comfortably of his broad acres, and of Ramón, and of his many friends, and of Carmel, and of her words, which he now repeated aloud. Djo looked toward him surprised.

"The grass still grows at Folded Hills," said Andy.

THE END